Nathen and Authia are frantic to save their son. He's injured, and Nathen's and Authia's gifts are useless in their desperate attempt to find him. They also discover that a spirit from their past is hindering any hope they have of finding their son. Against all odds, Nathen and Authia have the daunting task of finding their son before it's too late. However, the search for their son is compromised by forces from not only their world but also from the Land of the Ancestors.

Legacy of the Lion People Part 2
Copyright © 2024 Christine Frances
ISBN: 978-1-4874-4155-5
Cover art by Angela Waters

Published by eXtasy Books Inc

Look for us online at:
www.eXtasybooks.com

Legacy of the Lion People
Part 2
Lord of His People 5

By

Christine Frances

DEDICATION

As always, I dedicate not only this book but my entire series to my sister, Pat. She's been with me from the beginning, and she's proven to be a valued sounding board. Her insight and the questions she asked after every reading enabled me to become an even better writer.

I also want to thank my husband, Ed. He has supported me and encouraged me even when I would disappear into my writing room for hours on end.

And then there's Laura, my editor. I cannot thank her enough for her patience, her input, and her guidance. Throughout these five books, she has transformed me into a writer who's worthy of a place in any bookstore.

CHAPTER ONE

Africa, Congo Region, 1710

L ord Adeeowale surveyed the destruction that lay before him. The majority of the tribe's huts were ablaze. The smoke that bellowed from the huts was so thick that it made his village appear as though the darkest evil had swallowed it whole. The terrifying truth of Lord Adeeowale's assessment weighed heavy on his shoulders. His responsibility was to protect his people, and he was failing. Too many of his people lay motionless on the ground. The blood that once nurtured their bodies now carpeted the dirt they lay on. The Ancestors had released the Destroyer on Lord Adeeowale's people, and he had no idea why. It was at war with the entire tribe and was too close to achieving its objective.

The Destroyer had left the village, but Lord Adeeowale knew he would return. The Destroyer wasn't finished, and the Ancestors wouldn't retrieve him until every last tribe member marked for death perished. Lord Adeeowale stood next to the Gathering Hut as he scanned the tree line for any sign of the Destroyer. Lord Adeeowale was a formable man, and even before he became Lord, no tribesman would dare challenge him. Now, with his anger coursing through his veins, it made him appear even more intimidating. His animal skin loincloth, which covered him from his waist to just above his knees, was drenched in the blood of his fallen warriors. His face and body were also covered in a mixture of their blood, as well as his own. The blood from the wound on his

1

right shoulder trickled down his arm, pooling in the hand that gripped his dagger.

Lord Adeeowale took no notice of his injuries. He had an obligation that he took very seriously. He was the Lord of the Jelani people, and his responsibility was to protect his people. Most of his warriors were severely injured or dead. The children, women, and priestesses had taken refuge in the Gathering Hut. The tribe's wounded warriors and those few who could still fight were also in the Gathering Hut. Lord Adeeowale made it clear to the warriors that they were to remain in the hut and protect those who could not defend themselves. He, and he alone, would face the Destroyer.

The silence that engulfed the village was ominous. It was the calm before the storm. The Destroyer was infamous for leaving the area so that the village inhabitants were left with a false sense of security. However, that was not the worst that he would do. Lord Adeeowale knew the history of the Destroyer. It was something the Council of Five had created. According to the laws written by the Ancestors centuries in the past, the Ancestors themselves could not harm a Lord or Priestess. However, they could enlist someone or something else to inflict punishment and, if required, death. Because of this law, the Ancestors agreed that they needed something to keep the Lords and Priestesses in line.

The Council of Five had given birth to the Destroyer, who was neither alive nor dead. If the Ancestors were displeased with a Lord or Priestess's behavior, all that was required was an audience with the Council. The Council would then give the Ancestor a sealed clay pot which contained the Destroyer's essence. After that, all that was required was for the Ancestor to return to their Realm and unleash the Destroyer. The Destroyer would walk unseen among the tribesmen until it found an appropriate host to contain his essence. Then he would meld his essence with the host. By doing so, he destroyed everything that made the host who he was, including his soul. The host that he had chosen for this battle was Lord Adeeowale's closest friend and bravest warrior. Lord Adeeowale closed his eyes and slowly shook his head from side to side.

I am so sorry, Adofo, but the only way to rid our village of the Destroyer is to kill him. And by killing him, I kill what is left of you. I take solace in knowing that only your shell exists. But by destroying your shell, I destroy any chance of making you whole. Adofo, please forgive me for what I must do.

The Destroyer stood at the edge of the clearing, concealed behind a giant kapok tree. From his vantage point, he could see Lord Adeeowale. His lips curled upwards, creating a sinister smile. He had chosen this vessel because he knew Lord Adeeowale could not kill his best friend — or at least he would hesitate long enough to give the Destroyer the advantage. The Destroyer had taken liberties and killed far more tribesmen than he had been instructed to. Lord Adeeowale and the warrior Imani were the only ones marked for death. However, brutely murdering any member of the tribe gave the Destroyer so much pleasure. He had particularly enjoyed watching his victims suffer in pain before he would deliver the killing blow. Now, it was time to finish what he had started. The only question that remained was who he would kill first.

The Destroyer walked into the clearing and smiled as he approached Lord Adeeowale. He had secured his dagger at his side with straps from his animal skin loin cloth. The Destroyer took a few more steps and then stopped. He wanted to play with his victims. He wanted his victims to cry in pain as they pleaded for their lives. But Lord Adeeowale wouldn't give him the satisfaction. He just stood and glared at the Destroyer, daring him to come one step closer.

"So, my Lord, are you ready to confess your sins and take

your punishment as it has been decreed?"

"I know nothing of what you speak. I have not committed a sin, nor have I shamed my lineage." Lord Adeeowale watched as the Destroyer took a few more steps toward him. He stopped about ten feet away. From that distance, Lord Adeeowale could easily see the gashes on the Destroyer's torso and arms. None appeared life-threatening, and only a small amount of blood trickled from these wounds. Lord Adeeowale focused on the Destroyers' emerald eyes, but all he saw was darkness. The shell might have resembled his friend — however, his friend no longer occupied his body.

"You are cunning, choosing Adofo as your vessel. But do not believe for one moment that his resemblance will stop me from killing you."

"Do you think the Council of Five is wrong? Do you think the Council made a mistake in sending me here?"

Lord Adeeowale was confused by the Destroyer's comment. Why would the Council of Five have anything to do with releasing the Destroyer on his village? They had merely created it. It was the Ancestors who watched over the village that had the power to release the Destroyer.

"The Council? The Ancestors are the ones that summon you. Not the Council." Lord Adeeowale watched as the Destroyer's expression went from sinister to that of someone caught in a lie. However, it only lasted a second, and then the Destroyer smiled as he took another step toward Lord Adeeowale.

"Do not pretend that you know anything of the Council of Five or the Ancestors that ruled the tribe during the tribe's creation. You, and all those that ruled before you, have followed the laws set forth by these Ancestors. Besides, it does not matter who sent me, only that I am here!"

"Why are you here?"

"Where you not listening? I am here to punish you for your betrayal. For your blatant disregard and disrespect for our laws!"

Lord Adeeowale sensed that the Destroyer was becoming angry. Apparently he didn't appreciate being questioned. Lord Adeeowale gripped the dagger he held in his right hand and stepped closer. "Tell me what I have done to warrant the wrath of whoever sent you."

The Destroyer snickered and took another step closer. "You know what you did. So shall we stop this game you are playing? Take your punishment as a true Lord would do. I promise that if you willingly give yourself to me, I will allow everyone hiding in the Gathering Hut to live."

Lord Adeeowale stared at the Destroyer only to have his friend stare back. If Lord Adeeowale wanted to win this battle, he needed to focus on the Destroyer, not his friend. "If I agree, will you tell me why you are here before you kill me?"

The Destroyer smiled as he nodded his head in agreement. "I will show you."

Lord Adeeowale observed the Destroyer as he walked back to the edge of the clearing. He grabbed someone from behind a kapok tree and dragged him by the bindings that kept his hands secured. The body was limp, and Lord Adeeowale prayed that the person was unconscious and not dead. The Destroyer kept the body behind him as he dragged it through the dirt. Because of this, Lord Adeeowale couldn't determine who he or she was. When the Destroyer was ten feet away, he let go of the bindings but remained in front of the body. Lord Adeeowale could feel the anger building inside of him. He wanted to charge the Destroyer and save whoever was lying on the ground. But common sense prevailed, and Lord Adeeowale knew that if he allowed his anger to guide him, then he sentenced all his people to death. "Is your prisoner alive?"

"Of course she is."

"She?"

Lord Adeeowale watched as the Destroyer grabbed the bindings that held her hands in place. Then he threw her body to the ground only a few feet away from Lord Adeeowale. The body was face down and was that of a woman. By her dress, he knew she was a warrior, and he knew exactly who she was. That knowledge caused Lord Adeeowale's eyes to widen, and he felt as if he would be sick to his stomach. He dropped to his knees beside her and placed his dagger on the ground. He then gently turned her onto her back, and his worst fear became a reality. The warrior was Imani, the woman he had secretly loved for as long as he could remember. She had been badly beaten. Her face was covered in bruises, and her arms and legs were covered in injuries that were obviously inflicted by a dagger.

He glanced up at the Destroyer, who was laughing at him. "Why? Why do this to her?"

The Destroyer frowned as he shook his head. "You are a Lord. She is only a warrior. Did you actually believe that your love for her, and her love for you, would go unnoticed?"

"Yes, we both love each other. But that is all it is. We have not taken it further. I am married to a High Priestess. I have not dishonored the Ancestors or my wife. So I ask again. Why are you here?"

"Do you love your wife?"

"Of course I do." Lord Adeeowale picked up his dagger and stood between Imani and the Destroyer. "I am tired of your games. I will end this once and for all!" Lord Adeeowale started to raise his dagger, only to be interrupted by two of his warriors.

"My Lord, you will not face this fight alone. We will help you end this once and for all."

The voices came from either side of Lord Adeeowale.

When he looked over, he discovered that his warriors, Ekon and Massai, had joined him. Lord Adeeowale returned his focus to the Destroyer. "You want me, then I dare you to come and get me."

The Destroyer laughed. "I want you and her." He pointed to Imani's body. "Her death is close, as is the death of the two warriors that stand next to you. You, my Lord, I will keep you alive long enough to watch your beloved Imani die in excruciating pain."

Lord Adeeowale pointed his blood-drenched dagger at the Destroyer. "This ends now! I will watch you suffer, and I will be the one that inflicts the final blow onto you."

Lord Adeeowale and his two warriors charged the Destroyer. The Destroyer was gifted with the strength of ten men and the cunning of a great warrior. It wasn't going to be easy to kill him. Ekon reached the Destroyer first. He plunged at the Destroyer with his machete but only managed to graze the Destroyer's arm. The Destroyer grabbed Ekon's arm and threw him at the other two as if the warrior was a rag doll. Ekon caught both men across their chests and knocked them to the ground.

As they struggled to get up, the Destroyer retrieved Ekon's machete that had been dropped on the ground and skillfully threw it at Lord Adeeowale. Lord Adeeowale grabbed the dagger that had been knocked out of his hand. But before he could stand, Massai threw his body over him, knocking Lord Adeeowale back onto the ground. Lord Adeeowale pushed at Massai's body and called out his name but received no response. He managed to push Massai's body off to the side only to discover a machete buried deep in his back.

"Well, that is a shame. It is a waste of a good warrior."

Lord Adeeowale looked up to find the Destroyer standing over him. "You promised if I engaged you, you would not kill my people."

The Destroyer smiled as he shrugged his shoulders. "That may be true. But they chose to challenge me. When they joined you, they sealed their own fate." The Destroyer straddled Massai's body, placed his foot on Massai's back, and retrieved the machete. He held the machete in front of himself as he watched the blood that once sustained Massai's body trickle down the blade and drip on the dead warrior's body.

Lord Adeeowale decided to take advantage while the Destroyer was preoccupied with the weapon. Slowly, he started to stand, and as he did, he reached for his dagger. He glanced away for only a second, but it was enough. Lord Adeeowale felt the pain radiate through his body as the Destroyer's foot connected with his chest. Lord Adeeowale flew through the air for at least ten feet until his body crashed against the ground. He landed on his stomach with such force that his face smashed against the ground.

He knew his nose was broken, and he had difficulty focusing. Even when the Destroyer grabbed a handful of his hair and smashed his head into the ground, Lord Adeeowale couldn't relate to what was happening. Again, the Destroyer smashed his head into the ground. He could hear the Destroyer laughing, but it sounded miles away. The Destroyer was speaking to him, but he couldn't understand what he was saying.

Lord Adeeowale knew that he had to focus to stay alive. He had to save his people and to save Imani. He had to get up and fight. Lord Adeeowale focused on the Destroyer's voice. What was he saying? It was a name. Whose name?

Lord Adeeowale tried to take a deep breath, but the pain was excruciating. However, the pain brought clarity to his mind, so he took another breath and then another. The pain that gripped his body was crippling, but it cleared his mind, and he could concentrate on his surroundings.

He lifted his head ever so slightly and located where the

Destroyer was. The Destroyer had his back to him and appeared to be talking to someone on the ground. Lord Adeeowale knew that some of his ribs were broken, and he doubted he would be able to stand his ground against the Destroyer. However, if he could surprise him, maybe he would stand a chance.

Lord Adeeowale slowly lifted his head and searched for his weapon. It was too far for him to reach without drawing attention to himself. Ekon's weapon lay close to his own, so neither was of any use. Lord Adeeowale laid his head back on the ground. He had no chance without a weapon, but even without one, there was no way he would go down without a fight. As he slowly sat up, he noticed Massai's weapon was within reach. The Destroyer must have laid it on the ground while pounding Lord Adeeowale's head into the dirt. Even though it hurt, Lord Adeeowale smiled. He had a chance. It was a slim one, but a chance all the same. If he was smart, he might get the upper hand.

Lord Adeeowale slowly stood, trying to be as quiet as he could.

The Destroyer still had his back to him. He was focused on the person lying on the ground.

Lord Adeeowale felt the anger well up inside of him as he realized that it was Imani the Destroyer was focused on. Lord Adeeowale slowly placed the machete in the sheath located on his belt. Then, he repositioned the sheath from his hip to his back. "Get away from her! Hurt her, and I promise I will kill you!"

The Destroyer turned to face Lord Adeeowale. He appeared amused by Lord Adeeowale's threat. "I have already hurt her. Do you not see? She is broken, and she lies on the ground motionless as if she were dead."

Lord Adeeowale took a step closer. "Move away from her. She is only a warrior, not a priestess. Your fight is with me, not her."

The Destroyer snickered. "You are not in a position to tell me who my fight is with. I will decide who I kill and who I allow to live. I will kill you, but not until you watch me chop your lover into little pieces."

The Destroyer started to slowly walk toward Lord Adee-owale. "We shall see how strong she is. We shall see how many pieces I can remove from her body before she succumbs to the pain."

The Destroyer stood so close to Lord Adeeowale that he could feel his breath against his face. Lord Adeeowale squared his shoulders and took one step back. As he did, he discreetly placed his right hand on the machete's handle. "Then you should kill me now. As long as I draw a breath, if you place one hand on her, you will be the one cut into little pieces."

The Destroyer smiled as he reached for the machete he thought was secured to his belt. His eyes went wide, and he appeared both angry and frightened. The Destroyer took one step back and quickly searched the ground.

"Did you lose something?"

The Destroyer looked upon Lord Adeeowale with so much hatred and anger that his face morphed into that of a demon.

"I do not require a weapon to kill you!"

Before the Destroyer took a step, Lord Adeeowale pulled the machete from his belt. Without hesitation, he sliced the Destroyer's face from the right side of his chin to the left side of his temple. The severed flesh splayed open, almost splitting the Destroyer's face in half. However, the injury didn't kill him. Lord Adeeowale watched in shock as the Destroyer placed his hands over his face in what appeared to be a desperate attempt to hold the severed parts together.

"This is not over! You will pay!" the Destroyer turned and disappeared into the jungle, leaving no trace of himself to track.

Lord Adeeowale survived his injuries, as did Imani. For the remainder of his life, Lord Adeeowale always watched for any sign that the Destroyer had returned. As the years went by, that fateful day became nothing more than a blurred memory. Lord Adeeowale became complacent, and the Destroyer was no more than an empty threat. From age thirty, he lived as the Lord of the Lion People and was respected by all who lived within his village. However, hidden deep within his subconscious was a memory that tried to break free. A memory that would reveal the lengths the Destroyer would go to in his strategy for revenge.

CHAPTER TWO

Land of the Ancestors 2010

Serena wore her animal skin halter top and skirt that fell to just above her knees. Her bright red hair fell to her waist in gentle waves. She found Imani kneeling on the very edge of the Land of the Ancestors. Imani's gaze was fixated on the darkness surrounding the Realm, and it appeared as if she were in a trance. Serena walked over to Imani and then turned her attention to Lord Adeeowale. His concern for Imani was not only evident but justified. He sat as close to Imani as he dared to. His loincloth rode high on his thighs, but he seemed to take no notice. His bare chest revealed his every breath, and though Serena wouldn't admit to it, she could see the tears forming in the corner of his eyes. Lord Adeeowale's connection to Imani was more than just friendship. But that, again, was something Serena wouldn't admit to recognizing.

For Serena to understand what was happening to Imani, she had to join her mind with Imani's. Serena knelt behind Imani, closed her eyes, and tenderly placed her hands on either side of Imani's head. Then she stared into the abyss that encompassed the Land of the Ancestors. However, it wasn't the darkness that she saw. Serena had connected with Imani, and now Serena witnessed what Imani was observing.

Imani's mind had joined with the mind of the High Priestess Tamara. Serena was horrified by what she discovered. Dava, the son of Lord Zareb and High Priestess Tamara, was dying, and there was nothing they could do to save him. Lord

Chike had told Serena that she had to get Joshawa to willingly go to the Valley of the Lion People. Serena believed that Lord Chike wanted Joshawa to reign as Lord of the Lion People, and he also wanted to have Dava banished from the tribe. Serena slowly removed her hands and glanced over to Lord Adeeowale. With tears forming in her eyes, she shared her discovery. "I know what Lord Chike's purpose is. He has made Dava very sick, and soon, all that will be left of the child will be his body."

"For what purpose?"

Serena stood and walked over to the edge. Carefully, she glanced down into the darkness. "Dava will be a vessel. A vessel that will be a host to Joshawa's consciousness." Serena turned and faced Lord Adeeowale. "I finally understand the extent of Lord Chike's purpose for me. Joshawa cannot pass between realms unless he is a spirit. However, if he possesses a priestess's essence, he can travel to wherever Lord Chike wishes him to be. He plans to use my essence."

"If you deplete your essence, what becomes of you?"

Serena's expression turned to that of disillusion. "He has promised that I will leave this Realm and join my family in the Land of the Spirits. However, I doubt that will happen. I know too much. He will destroy me, or worse, condemn me to the Realm of the Dead."

British Columbia, Jenkin's Homestead, 2010

Nathen stood at the edge of the clearing, focused on the Jenkins homestead. The evergreens and redwoods that encircled the homestead grew tall, and the scent of moss and evergreen permeated the forest. After years of neglect, the forest was doing its best to take over the open yard and the two cabins. Moss and vines had grown on the sides of the small buildings and reached high onto the roofs.

Nathen crossed his arms over his chest, which accentuated his large biceps. His jeans clung to his thighs, which were often referred to as tree trunks. The wind mischievously played with his shoulder-length wavy red hair. The morning air was chilly. However, Nathen paid no attention to what was transpiring around him. His only chance to save his son had disappeared. The GPS he so desperately needed hung on a lanyard around Dameon's neck, and he'd done nothing as he watched Dameon and Jax walk away down the mountain.

His mind was consumed with what Adrian had said to him. He really wasn't the person Adrian described. Nathen wouldn't kill to serve his own agenda. However, to save his son, could he become the beast that had ruled his life so many years ago?

There was a time when he thought it would be the right thing to do if he gave himself to the beast that tormented him. But then he discovered the cavern that was located high above Burwood. And that cavern had allowed him to be at peace. The whispers reverberating in the cavern sounded like angels singing to him, and the sweet music calmed the beast. It never lasted last long, and Nathen found himself climbing the treacherous face of Mount Serenity every day. Then he met Authia, and her love calmed the beast and eventually banished it so that it would no longer torment Nathen.

Nathen closed his eyes and drew a deep breath. Then, without taking his focus off the cabin, he spoke to Adrian and Billy. "They're gone. We no longer need to whisper." Nathen turned to face Adrian. "Take Billy back home. Have Edward talk to him. I'm sure that this ordeal has been a strain on him mentally."

"Okay, but do I take him home before or after he checks out his old cabin?"

Nathen whirled around to find Billy walking toward the

larger cabin as if he didn't have a care in the world. Billy had been raised by his brother in that cabin. His brother, Dext, was cruel to Billy. Billy was mentally challenged, which could have been the reason for the vicious beatings he received from Dext. Judging from Billy's torso, the beatings occurred frequently. The most shocking revelation was that some very barbaric tools were used. Tools that only had one purpose, which was to inflict as much pain as possible. Even more troubling was that Billy was a large man with great strength. Mentally, he was a child trapped in a man's body and unaware of his strength. But even then, one would think he would have eventually defended himself against his brother.

Billy hadn't seen his home since his brother died twenty years ago. And he made it quite clear that he never wanted to see it again.

Nathen didn't hesitate—he ran up to Billy and blocked his path to the cabin.

"What are you doing, Billy?"

Billy appeared puzzled, as if he didn't understand the question. "Going to cabin."

"I can see that. But why are you going to the cabin?"

Billy smiled at Nathen. "Need supplies to save Amelia." Billy rolled his eyes at Nathen. "So silly."

Nathen was shocked at Billy's response and could do nothing but watch as he continued to head toward the cabin.

Adrian leaned against a redwood tree while he watched the interaction between Nathen and Billy. Adrian slowly shook his head from side to side in disgust. Billy was nothing special, so why would he always get special treatment? Okay, he was mentally disabled. Big deal. Adrian had always considered himself not only the best-looking guy in Burwood but pretty much the best at everything. However, he never received the special treatment that Billy was afforded. Billy was just a pain in everyone's ass, whether they wanted to admit it or not. At twenty years old, Adrian was a little over six feet tall, muscular, with blue eyes and blond hair. The boys and some of the men looked up to Adrian. Some of the adults were even intimidated by him. As far as girls went, he could have just about any girl he wanted. Unfortunately, the girl he wanted was in love with Joshawa.

Adrian had no desire to follow Billy into the cabin. Trying to figure that guy out was a full-time job on a good day. What was going on now was way out in left field of a good day. It was bad enough that Adrian would have to deal with him on the trip back to Burwood. As far as Adrian was concerned, Nathen could deal with him now. Adrian watched as Nathen followed Billy into the cabin.

All his life, Adrian had been told that Nathen was a freak, someone who only looked out for himself and wouldn't think twice about killing you if it suited him. Adrian was beginning to doubt the stories he'd been told. But to play it safe, he would remain cautious when it came to Nathen.

Once Nathen entered the cabin, Adrian walked about ten feet into the yard and then just stood there, taking everything in. The cabins were obviously old, but surprisingly, they were in decent shape. Curiosity got the better of Adrian, so he walked to the back of the smaller cabin and continued on to the larger one. There were no windows in either. He thought of what it would be like to sit in there in the winter for hours on end with no sunlight. Hell, it would be bad enough in the summer. Adrian shook his head as he thought of Billy being stuck in one of these cabins, being beaten by his brother, and he found himself feeling sorry for Billy. *No wonder you're batshit crazy.*

Joshawa rested his back against Amy's pet grizzly, a bear she called Alex. He watched Amy throw the carcasses from their breakfast into the fire pit. Amy was a contradiction in terms, and Joshawa was having difficulty figuring her out. Her blonde hair fell to her waist, and the ends were jagged as if she'd cut them with a knife. She had a slight build, and her facial features were best described as delicate. Sometimes she would come across as a sweet innocent girl, naive to the world outside of her cave. But she was also a girl who could fend for herself and knew enough about the human body and medicines to keep him alive. There was more to this girl than what she portrayed.

Amy had placed the tin plates from their breakfast in one of the empty buckets and then turned to face Joshawa. At that moment, she gazed upon him with the persona of a little girl. "Is it okay if I check your wound?"

"Of course. You're the doctor." Joshawa smiled as he thought of this young, naive girl holding a doctor's degree. However, she had managed to save his life and tend to his injuries. So, a doctor's degree wasn't totally out of the realm of possibilities.

Amy knelt behind him and started to delicately unwrap the bandage from around his head. She was always careful not to hurt him. Joshawa wondered how anyone who spent most of their life without human contact could be so compassionate.

Joshawa gazed down at his hands, and he didn't need a mirror to know that he resembled his father. People whispered behind his back all his life or told him outright that he was a freak. But Amy saw him for who he was. His features didn't scare her or confuse her.

Joshawa closed his eyes and envisioned another girl who treated him as a person. Tears started to roll down his cheeks. *I promise you, Becca, if I survive this, I will tell you how much I love you.* Joshawa opened his eyes and scanned the cave. *Mother, father, why haven't you found me? Why are you not melding with me? Is it because I'm not meant to survive this?*

17

Amy had finished unwrapping the wound. She stood and went to put the wrappings in the pot over the fire. "You're not going to die."

Joshawa couldn't believe what she'd said. "You mean my wound is not that serious."

"No." Amy turned to face Joshawa. "You will survive. I won't let you die."

"Can you hear or see my thoughts?"

Amy chuckled. "No, silly. Alex told me."

Joshawa glanced at the enormous grizzly that Amy called Alex. "Alex told you?"

Amy didn't have to answer. Joshawa watched in disbelief as Alex nodded his head.

Serena, Lord Adeeowale, and Imani returned to their campsite in silence. Imani walked over to the fire pit and added a couple of logs to the dying fire. She then sat on the ground, her hands folded in her lap, and watched as the fire came alive. Serena and Lord Adeeowale joined Imani and decided to sit across from each other around the fire pit. Serena stared into the fire, oblivious to the flames that danced in among the logs.

Her mind was occupied as it tried to sort out right from wrong and the consequences if she chose incorrectly. Serena knew that her companions were patiently waiting for her explanation. She was also very aware of what was at stake if she revealed everything she knew. Serena closed her eyes and gently shook her head from side to side. She was such a fool to think that what Lord Chike offered her would ever come to pass. Serena had sealed her fate when she chose to tell Lord Adeeowale her concern about who Lord Chike might be. There was no turning back, and once again, she had become the protector of those she hated so long ago.

CHAPTER THREE

Land of the Spirits

Lord Chike had been given an errand to do as if he were a lowly tribesman. He despised Lord Adeeowale for even mentioning that he should go to the Land of the Spirits. As if Lord Adeeowale really cared how many Ancestors should be allowed in the Land of the Ancestors. And to think Lord Adeeowale expected him to seek knowledge through the Council of Five. Lord Chike snickered. "You have a lot to learn, Lord Adeeowale, and it will be my pleasure to teach you."

Even though Lord Chike was annoyed with Lord Adeeowale, this errand had given him the excuse he needed to venture to the Land of the Spirits. Lord Chike stood by the Gateway and carefully scrutinized the village. The tribe members of the Jelani Tribe, upon their death, were afforded the luxury of living in the Land of the Spirits. Their acceptance was based on whether or not they had lived as decreed on the sacred scrolls that had been written when the Jelani Tribe was born. In Lord Chike's opinion, the Land of the Spirits should be barren, and the Realm of the Dead would be home to these offenders.

Lord Chike had to be careful that no one noticed him, because the Council of Five was the last place he wanted to be. Lord Chike didn't exactly blend in with the tribesmen. He knew he was an imposing man, standing over six feet tall, and he weighed over two hundred and fifty pounds. Lord Chike grinned as he watched the tribesmen go about their duties.

You will be judged, and you will know your place.

Lord Chike quickly made his way past the village without being seen. Twenty minutes later, he arrived at the waterfall that cascaded into a large lake. He stood at the edge of the jungle and scanned the open area to ensure he was alone. The site before him was breathtakingly beautiful, with pristine waters and the vibrant colors of the jungle that bordered the lake and the falls. Tribe members and children were playing in the water at the far end of the lake, opposite the falls. Lord Chike could hear the children's giggles and laughter from the adults, and the sounds of joy angered him. In his opinion, a great majority of the spirits that lived here didn't deserve that privilege. But that would all change, and when his plan was executed, there would no longer be laughter, only the sounds of retribution.

Billy cautiously walked up to the cabin door, pulled down on the rope, then carefully pushed the door open. Even though he was confident that the evil no longer resided in the cabin, he would still be cautious. When he entered the room, a smile graced his lips, for what he smelled was not foul or rotting flesh. It was the smoke from the fireplace entwined with the aroma of bacon. Billy glanced around the room, ignoring the gear and clothing the hunters had left behind. Billy's mind was in a different place, and as far as Billy was concerned, only he and his brother occupied this cabin. Billy carefully scanned the cabin, and as he did, he felt overjoyed because there were no signs of cruelty or fear. The only evidence that he and his brother lived here were the jackets on the wall and the steamer trunks on the floor under the jackets.

Billy knew what he had to do to save Amelia. He removed the oversized jacket he was wearing. Billy then carefully folded it over the back of one of the kitchen chairs. Earlier,

he'd stuffed the pockets with food and water. Billy gently patted the coat pockets to confirm that the food and water were
still there. Satisfied that they were, he walked over to the two
steamer trunks. Billy quietly stood by the trunks as he scrutinized both. He knew he had to be brave. He had to save Amelia, so he placed his hands between the trunks and pulled
them away from each other. He grabbed the rope handle on
the side of one of the trunks and pulled it away from the wall.
Billy abruptly stopped as he let go of the handle.

A memory from long ago filled his mind with fear. He
wasn't allowed to move the trunks or take anything from
them. He knew that Dext would be mad, and he would punish Billy. As quickly as the fear came to him, it left. Billy
smiled as he rolled his eyes. "Billy silly. Dext not here. Dext is
dead." Billy grabbed the handle and dragged the steamer
trunk to the kitchen table.

He opened the hinged lid and rested it against the table.
The trunk was full of clothing that had been locked up for
over twenty years. The pungent odor of mothballs used to
keep the mice and insects away filled his nostrils. But even
more potent than the mothballs was her scent. He closed his
eyes and took a deep breath of the sweet perfume. His mind
filled with images of the woman who had been so kind to him.
He spoke to her as if she were standing next to him, "Billy
keep promise. Billy save Amelia." He opened his eyes and
started to pull clothing out of the trunk.

Nathen quietly stood in the cabin's doorway as he watched
Billy drag an old steamer trunk over to the kitchen table. Billy
made no indication that he was aware of Nathen's presence.
To Nathen, Billy seemed to be miles away, as if he was all
alone in his own little world. He spoke of a promise to save
Amelia, and then he started to rummage through the trunk.

Nathen approached him, stood next to the trunk, and watched as Billy carefully placed a pair of worn, tanned bib overalls on the lid of the trunk. He then retrieved oversized t-shirts and placed them on the kitchen table.

"Can I help you, Billy?"

Billy looked up at Nathen, and his expression was sincere. "Billy not need help." Billy glanced away from Nathen and slowly scanned the room. Then, with determined strides, he walked over to the second trunk. Billy opened the lid with his left hand and held it against the wall. Then, with his right hand, he carefully rummaged through the contents.

Billy pulled out a large backpack and placed it on the floor. Then he took his time as he carefully rearranged the clothes he'd disturbed. Nathen watched as Billy patted the top layer of clothing with the palm of his hand, then gently lowered the lid. He grabbed the backpack, and when he turned to face Nathen, he appeared surprised, as if he'd been caught doing something wrong. Billy glanced down at the backpack, then back up to Nathen. "Dext not know. Trunk is good."

"What will Dext not know?"

Billy returned to the table and placed the backpack on the floor beside his trunk. He answered Nathen while he continued to pull clothing out of his trunk. "Not know backpack is gone."

Nathen was desperate to figure out what was going on with Billy. What was so important with the clothing? Nathen picked up the oversized bib overalls and noticed a label on the inside of the back panel. Written in black marker were the initials A.W.J. "Billy, were these Amelia's?"

Billy glanced up to Nathen, nodded his head, indicating they were, then returned his focus to the trunk.

Nathen placed the overalls on the lid and walked over to the kitchen table. All the t-shirts and sweaters on the table had the same initials. "Were all these Amelia's?"

Billy placed the bib overalls on the table next to the rest of the clothing. He closed the lid to the trunk and then turned his attention to Nathen. "Yes. Amelia's."

"Was Amelia family to you?"

Billy snickered. "Yes. Nathen silly."

Nathen was surprised by Billy's affirmation. As far as Nathen knew, it was only Billy and his brother that occupied the cabin. Nathen would have loved asking Billy questions about Amelia, but he thought better of it. Billy was in his own little world, and he was happy. There was no way Nathen would do anything to disrupt Billy and that happiness.

Billy unzipped the backpack and held the opening against the table. With his right hand, he started stuffing the backpack with all the clothing. Nathen watched in awe as Billy knelt on the floor with the backpack in front of him. Billy was determined to get all the clothing into the bag. When he succeeded, the smile on Billy's face was like that of a child who was proud of what he'd just accomplished.

Nathen knelt on his haunches and rested his right hand on Billy's left shoulder. "Good job, Billy. Not exactly sure what you're doing, but I'm confident you'll let me know when the time is right." Nathen stood and helped Billy to his feet. "Do you need anything else?"

"No, Billy good. We fix things, then go."

"Fix things?"

Billy placed the backpack by the door, put the trunk back where he found it, made sure the two trunks were close together, and then used his right foot to erase all the drag marks left by the trunk. "Fixed. We go now." He put the overcoat back on, grabbed the backpack, slung it over his left shoulder, and headed into the yard.

Nathen stood in the middle of the cabin, dumbfounded by what had just occurred. Billy had been acting strange ever since they'd left earlier this morning. Nothing he'd said or done made any sense. This cabin was in every one of Billy's nightmares. Just getting him to show Nathen where the cabin was had Billy hyperventilating. What had changed to make Billy so at ease now? Nathen took inventory of where he stood in his plan to rescue his son. He didn't have the GPS, and there was no guarantee when Jax and Dameon would return. When they did return, what were the chances that Nathen would retrieve the GPS without incident?

Nathen hoped Authia would have more success in her endeavor. She planned to use Becca as a conduit to reach out to Joshawa. Authia was sure that Joshawa had imprinted on Becca, and doing so would allow Authia to see what Joshawa saw.

Authia's melding abilities were second to none. However, Joshawa had to be alive and conscious for the meld to work. Nathen quickly scanned the cabin to ensure there were no signs of them being there. He watched Billy through the open door. "What do you have in store for us, Billy? I guess time will tell."

Adrian would have loved to check out the cabins but decided not to. Nathen had told him to stay put, and the last thing Adrian wanted to do was to piss him off. Adrian returned to the open yard, and as he passed the smaller cabin, his foot hit something that was lying on the ground. Adrian looked down and was surprised to discover what appeared to be the leg bone of a deer. He knelt down on his haunches and picked the bone up with his right hand. The bone was picked clean, and if Adrian had to guess, it had been lying around for a long time. He scanned the yard's perimeter, and that's when he noticed a slight opening in the bush not far from the smaller cabin.

Adrian stood and headed toward the opening without

giving it a second thought. When he reached the edge of the yard, he stopped dead in his tracks and stared at what lay before him. It was a graveyard of bones thrown haphazardly in an open pit. Adrian guessed that the pit was about six feet across. He walked around it, scrutinizing the bones and feeling relieved that, as far as he could tell, they all appeared to be animal bones.

Adrian knelt on the ground at the edge of the pit. He placed the bone he was carrying next to him, and then he started sifting through the bones. Adrian wasn't looking for anything in particular. He was only curious as to how deep the pit was. He'd already cleared dozens of bones when he found something unusual buried beneath them.

Carefully, he cleared away some of the smaller bones, and that was when he discovered the skeletal remains of a human hand. Adrian's heart started beating wildly in his chest. He glanced up, and from his vantage point, he could see the doorway to the large cabin. He couldn't see Nathen or Billy, so he assumed they were still in the cabin. Adrian glanced down at the skeleton hand, then back up at the cabin. He considered calling out to Nathen, but something deep inside told him to keep digging.

He had uncovered the person's arm, shoulder, and part of the torso when Billy tackled him onto the ground. Adrian found himself on his back, staring up at Billy, who'd straddled him and was now sitting on Adrian's stomach. Billy's right hand was clenched into a fist and raised up, ready to deliver a serious punch. But that wasn't what scared Adrian. The anger etched on Billy's face frightened him beyond measure.

"What the hell, Billy? Get off of me!"

"She's mine!"

The last thing Adrian remembered was Billy's fist as it connected full force with his face.

CHAPTER FOUR

Authia sat back in her chair, absolutely giddy with excitement. The meld had worked, and now she could see through Joshawa's eyes. Not only did she know that he was alive, but she also knew how to find him. She closed her eyes and sought out Nathen.

Nathen, I have great news!

I could use some right now.

You're on the right track. Find the bear, and you'll find Joshawa.

Are you certain?

Yes! I was able to reach Joshawa with Serena's help. I saw the bear through Joshawa's eyes. You'll need the GPS.

Believe me, I know. I'm sending Billy and Adrian back to you. Adrian can explain everything when he sees you. You'll need to take Billy to see Edward as soon as possible.

Why? What happened? Is Billy okay?

Physically, Billy's fine. Mentally, I don't even know where to begin. One moment, he's scared to death about going anywhere near the cabin. Next thing you know, he's inside rummaging through an old steamer trunk, saying he has to save someone named Amelia.

Wow, this whole ordeal has really messed with him. I'll have Hansen take Billy to Burwood as soon as he arrives.

Thank you, my Love. I'll wait for Dameon to return and then see if he'll help us.

You have a plan?

No, not really. From here on in, I'm going by my gut, and my gut says Dameon's the answer.

Okay, but please be careful.

I will. I'll let you know as soon as I have the GPS. I love you.

26

Love you, too.

Joshawa could feel the damp rag as Amy carefully cleaned his wound, and even though Joshawa still suffered from headaches, the pain associated with the injury was gone.

"Is my wound healed? I don't feel any pain."

"Almost. I don't have to bandage it anymore."

"Thank you, Amy. I really appreciate all you've done for me." Joshawa observed Amy as she submerged the soiled bandages in the pot of hot water that hung over the fire pit. He wondered if he should pursue her claim that Alex talked to her. Curiosity won out, and he ventured down that path.

"Amy. What did you mean when you said Alex speaks to you?"

Amy was pushing the rags under the water with a stick. She stopped and slowly turned to face Joshawa, her face puzzled. Then she smiled at Joshawa. "You're so silly. Alex can't talk."

"But you knew what I was thinking, and you said Alex told you."

Amy shrugged her shoulders. "I don't know what you're thinking." Amy turned around and continued her endeavor to clean the rags.

Joshawa didn't know what to think. Was he losing his mind? One thing was clear, and that was that he was on his own. He had to figure out a way to get home himself. He glanced at Amy and decided that maybe now would be a good time to remind her about his ribs.

Earlier this morning, she'd been reluctant to help him. It was as if she didn't want him to leave. Joshawa closed his eyes and took a shallow breath. If she didn't help him bind his ribs, he'll be in this cave indefinitely. Joshawa opened his eyes and glanced over at Alex. Even if she did help him, he would still have to deal with Alex.

"Would you have some more material that we can use to bind my ribs?"

It was almost as if she was ignoring him. Amy completely avoided the question and instead went to attend to his leg. Amy knelt on the ground facing his leg, and with her left hand, she gently applied pressure, starting at his knee and working her way down to his ankle.

Amy didn't even look up at him when she asked, "Does it hurt?"

There was some pain when she applied pressure, but Joshawa decided that, for now, he would keep that information to himself. "Not really. You did a good job. I'll be walking before you know it."

Amy glanced over at Joshawa, and the sadness that was so clearly expressed in her eyes and on her face struck Joshawa to his very core. "What's wrong?"

Amy quickly glanced down at Joshawa's leg and didn't attempt to look back in his direction. "I'm happy you're feeling better."

"I sense a *but*."

Amy repositioned herself so she could sit on the ground and face Joshawa. Her eyes were focused on a large pebble she'd picked up from the ground, and she was now moving it from one hand to the other. Joshawa couldn't tell if she was sad, frightened, or scared to say whatever was on her mind.

Amy glanced up at Joshawa, and with her right hand, she tucked the long strands of her blonde hair that had fallen across her face behind her ear. "As long as I can remember, it's only been me and Alex."

"How long have you been alone?"

"Not sure." Amy crooked her head slightly, and she appeared to be trying to remember something from her past. She returned her focus to Joshawa and shrugged her shoulders. "It's been a long time."

"Do you know how old you are?"

Amy looked as if she was searching her mind for an answer, but she shrugged her shoulders instead. "No. Do you?"

"Yes. I'm nineteen."

Amy returned her focus to the pebble and was quiet for several minutes. Then she glanced up, and Joshawa knew that the girl who sat in front of him was both frightened and sad. Her voice was soft, almost timid, when she asked, "You want to leave?"

Joshawa wasn't sure how to answer her. It was obvious that she wasn't looking forward to being alone again. How ironic, he thought. All he ever wanted to do was to run away to Grot. To run away from the people who loved him. All he wanted was to be alone. Joshawa wanted to be away from his family, but Amy had no choice. She was always alone, and she probably wouldn't know any better if he hadn't come along.

"Yes, I want to go home. You know, Amy, you could come with me."

Amy appeared as if she'd seen a ghost. Her eyes went wide, her hands trembled, and she shook her head from side to side. "No! It's not safe out there. The cave is safe."

Alex lifted his head and started growling. It was as if he knew Amy was upset. Joshawa felt such compassion for her that he ignored Alex's warning and held his arms out to her. "Come here."

Amy was hesitant, but Joshawa continued to hold his arms out. "Please."

Amy moved close enough so that Joshawa could gently wrap his arms around her and hold her tenderly against him. She rested her head on his chest, and to Joshawa, it felt as if he were cradling a small child. Joshawa could feel the anger building deep within him. Whoever had left her here wasn't expecting her to live. Joshawa couldn't care less about the reason—she didn't deserve this. Maybe falling out of a tree was fate, and it was meant to happen. Amy was his savior, and now he could be hers. "Amy, I promise that you and Alex can come with me when I'm well enough to leave the cave." He cupped her chin with his fingers and lifted her face so she could see him. "Trust me. With Alex and me protecting you, I promise that no one will be able to hurt you."

Nathen had just left the cabin when he witnessed Billy throw his backpack on the ground. Billy screamed *no*, then tackled Adrian to the ground. Nathen ran to Billy, grabbed his coat collar, and tried to pull him off Adrian. Usually, it wouldn't have been an issue, but Billy was incredibly strong and far beyond angry. His anger fueled his strength, and even when Nathen pleaded for Billy to stop, his voice fell on deaf ears.

Nathen had to be more aggressive, so he straddled Adrian directly behind Billy. Then Nathen maneuvered his right arm around Billy's neck while Billy continued to pummel Adrian's face. Using his left arm, Nathen grabbed his right wrist, which locked the neck hold in place. It still took some effort, but Nathen finally pulled Billy off Adrian. Nathen kept a firm grip on Billy's neck while he backed up. Nathen wanted to put some distance between Billy and Adrian. But no matter the distance, Billy was still screaming about someone being his, and he continued to punch and kick even though he couldn't reach the recipient of his anger.

Nathen glanced over to Adrian, who lay motionless on the ground and was most likely unconscious. His face was smeared in blood, as were Billy's hands. After several minutes, Billy started to calm down, and Nathen finally got his attention. He relaxed his hold on Billy. However, he didn't want to release him until he was sure Billy would cooperate.

"Billy, can you tell me why you're angry at Adrian?"

"She's mine! He no touch her!" Billy screamed at Nathen while he tried to free himself from Nathen's grip.

It was evident to Nathen that Billy was still a threat to Adrian and had no intentions of calming down. Somehow, Nathen had to reach out and find the child within Billy. Nathen had never witnessed this side of Billy and knew there would be no appeasing him in his current state of mind. However, the child could be reasoned with, and the child would listen to him.

"Billy, it's Nathen. I want you to calm down."

"Let go! Now!"

"I'll let go as soon as you calm down."

"Adrian, bad!"

Nathen figured that if he had any chance of calming Billy, he would have to take Adrian out of the equation. His first thought was to get Billy to the open yard. However, judging by Billy's irrational behavior, seeing the cabin might make the situation even more tenuous. Nathen decided to take him deeper into the woods, so he slightly tightened his grip around Billy's neck and started to back away from Adrian. At first, Billy fought him by dragging his feet, kicking, and screaming as if he were a spoiled child.

As soon as Adrian and the cabin were out of sight, Billy started to calm down. Nathen could feel Billy's body relax as he became more docile. Nathen decided to take a chance and slowly removed his arms from around Billy's neck. Free from Nathen's grip, Billy turned to face him. When their eyes met, Nathen didn't see a face full of anger but rather the image of a scared and confused child. Nathen wrapped his arms around Billy, drew him close, and didn't say a word while Billy cried like a child who'd lost something very special to him.

Amy felt content and safe in Joshawa's arms. However, she had no understanding as to why she felt that way. A few minutes later, she opened her eyes only to find Alex staring at her. Amy knew that look only too well. He was concerned for her. To appease Alex, she smiled at him, which was all that was needed to alleviate Alex's apprehension. He laid his head back on the ground, which allowed Amy to focus on her own thoughts and feelings.

She attempted to focus deep within herself as she listened to Joshawa's heart beating in a rhythm that soothed her. However, her thoughts and feelings were anything but soothing. They bombarded her mind, confusing her and leaving her feeling conflicted. She didn't want Joshawa to go for reasons she didn't understand. She knew she couldn't force him to stay, because something about that scenario felt wrong. Could she leave the safety of the cave? Could Alex and Joshawa protect her from the evil that lived deep in the forest? Leaving the cave went against everything she was told not to do. She was told that cabins were not safe, but Joshawa lived in one.

Amy was so frustrated as she tried to sort through her memories, not knowing which were real and which had been distorted with time. She spent her entire life in fear. Fear of being hurt, fear of the evil that lived in the cabin and in the forest. However, she never knew exactly who or what should be feared. Should she fear Joshawa? Would he be angry with her if she did something wrong? The word promise echoed in Amy's mind. It was a word she'd heard over and over. A word that, to her, had a negative connotation.

Amy remained perfectly still as she listened to Joshawa's heartbeat, felt his warmth against her face, and when he spoke, his words were not of anger. To her, his words were soft and comforting. Amy sat up, wiped the tears from her face, and made her decision. "You can't protect me this way." Amy pointed to Joshawa's chest and leg. "So we have to fix you."

"Isn't that what you've been doing?"

Amy rolled her eyes at Joshawa. "No. I healed you. Now I have to fix you. You're so silly."

Amy stood up and headed to the back of the cave. She returned carrying one of the sheets she'd used to make the tent for Joshawa. She dropped the sheet in Joshawa's lap and smiled at him. "I'm going to get water so I can clean the plates. You can rip the sheet up so we can bind you."

Amy stood while staring at Joshawa. She'd been watching him since she brought him to the cave, and now Amy felt she could trust him. She knew she had to save him, and maybe, in turn, he could protect her from the evil that resided outside her cave. Perhaps he could even save her. Amy turned, grabbed the two buckets, and headed to the river.

CHAPTER FIVE

Serena stared out into the jungle without seeing its beauty. All Serena saw was Lord Chike, and all she felt was the mental and physical pain he'd inflicted on her. Serena returned her focus to Lord Adeeowale and Imani. She held her head up high, squared her shoulders, and then decided that she was prepared to do what was right, even if it cost her a lifetime in the Realm of Despair.

"Do either of you sense Lord Chike is near?"

Imani and Lord Adeeowale looked at each other, then returned their focus to Serena. They both closed their eyes for only a few seconds, and when they opened them, they didn't seem concerned.

Lord Adeeowale addressed Serena. "And you, Serena, do you sense Lord Chike?"

"No, my Lord. I do not. In which case, I think we should speak openly. That would free our minds to keep watch on the Gateway."

"I agree. I believe you have something to tell the both of us?"

Serena smiled sarcastically. "That would be a grave understatement."

Imani moved over to sit closer to Serena. She placed her hand on Serena's knee and looked upon her with great empathy "When you were with me, I sensed great turmoil within you. You are not pleased with the task that has been bestowed on you."

"No, I am not. But I still accepted it for no other reason than to benefit myself."

Imani gazed upon Serena with compassion and tenderness. "That may have been true in the beginning. It is not true now. You are not the priestess that lived so long ago. You are not the Priestess that cursed our Lord and his child, Lord Nathen. Is that not true?"

"Of course, it's true."

Lord Adeeowale interjected, "Serena, do not blame yourself for Lord Chike's actions. The minute you knew that he was being deceitful as to who he was, you came to us. When you realized that what he asked of you was cloaked in conspiracy, you came to us to warn us. Is that not true?"

Serena thought for a minute as she tried to remember the exact moment she became prepared to betray Lord Chike. "I am not as innocent as you make me out to be. I did what Lord Chike commanded me to do. I started poisoning Joshawa's mind against his parents and against the woman he loves."

Lord Adeeowale smiled at Serena. "That may be true. But now you sit with us. You have joined us to fight against Lord Chike. You have made a choice that only protects everyone around you, not yourself. A choice that, as you see it, could send you back to the Realm of Despair."

Serena nervously laughed. "As I see it? If Lord Chike wins, then there is no doubt. I will be going back. And when I return to that horrid place, I intend to take Lord Chike with me."

Imani gave Serena's knee a slight squeeze. "Now this is the Serena I have heard so much about." Imani stood, brushing the dirt from her skirt. "I take my leave and will secretly watch the Gateway for Lord Chike. I leave the two of you to devise a plan to expose him."

Before Imani could leave, Serena interrupted her. "There is one more thing. Imani, I sensed that Lord Chike is very angry with you."

Imani and Lord Adeeowale exchanged glances, and then

Imani spoke up. "If I had to guess, it could be because I was only a warrior when I died. The Ancestors chose to empower me with the gifts that a Priestess would possess. Not all the gifts, just those I needed to watch over our tribe."

Serena smiled at Imani. "You died protecting your Lord. Of course, the Ancestors would reward you."

"Many warriors have died protecting their Lord. I was the only one afforded this gift in all the centuries of our tribe's history."

Imani turned and headed into the jungle, leaving Serena with only one question. *What was so special about Imani that she was singled out to receive these gifts?*

Adrian opened his eyes and discovered that he was lying on the ground. His head was pounding as if someone was continually hitting it with a mallet. His first thought was to look for Billy, so as he slowly sat up, he scanned his surroundings. Billy was nowhere in sight. However, Adrian could still hear him screaming out in anger. A few minutes later, the screaming stopped, and at that point, Adrian realized that Nathen was also nowhere to be seen.

The pounding in Adrian's head made him want to throw up, and his face felt as if he'd been beaten with a baseball bat. Adrian used his right hand to wipe his face and discovered blood oozing from his nose and mouth. Adrian's forearms were also sore, and when he checked his jacket, he could see the bloody outline of Billy's fists smeared all over the inside arms of his jacket. Adrian recalled that when Billy started his attack, Adrian raised his arms to shield his face as best as possible. There was no telling how much damage Billy would have caused if he hadn't been able to ward off some of the blows.

Adrian slowly stood up, and as he did, he could feel the

dizziness encompassing his body. It took a couple of minutes, but finally, Adrian could stand without fear of falling. He was about to head to the cabin to inspect his injuries when he heard something approaching him from behind. Adrian turned, pulled his *Ruger* from his gun belt, and aimed it toward the woods.

Nathen held Billy in his arms and continued to soothe him until Billy stopped crying. Surprisingly, it didn't take much time. Billy went from out-of-control anger to crying, then became eerily quiet. When Billy glanced up at Nathen, it was as if nothing had happened. Nathen stood back from Billy so that he could see his surroundings and know that he was safe.

Billy slowly looked around, then returned his gaze to Nathen. "Why is Billy here?"

Nathen wasn't sure how he should respond. Billy's eyes were red from crying, and his cheeks were wet from his tears, yet he seemed completely unaware. If Nathen told him the truth, how would Billy react? If he lied to Billy, how would he react when they returned to the grave site? Nathen decided that honesty was the best approach and took a couple of steps closer to Billy in case he broke out in another fit of anger.

"Do you remember leaving the cabin with your backpack?"

Billy rolled his eyes at Nathen. "Yes, Billy remember. Not Billy's. Dext's backpack. You're silly."

"Okay. Do you remember the place where all the bones are?"

Billy glanced down to the ground and then returned his focus to Nathen. "Yes. Backpack there. Billy must get backpack."

Billy went to leave, but Nathen quickly blocked his path. "One more question, Billy. Do you remember what happened to Adrian?"

Billy stared at Nathen with a blank expression. It wasn't as if he were trying to remember an event. It was more like his mind was miles away. "Billy, do you understand the question?"

Billy's expression immediately changed, and now he was smiling at Nathen. "Billy fix her."

Billy tried to move around Nathen, but he stood his ground. Billy glanced up at Nathen, obviously confused by Nathen's actions. "Billy fix her. Must go to grave."

"Okay, Billy, but what about Adrian?"

Once again, Billy smiled at Nathen as if he didn't have a care in the world. "Billy like Adrian. Adrian is Billy's friend."

At that moment, Nathen wished that Authia was with him. Her gift would allow her to get inside Billy's head and hopefully discover what triggered Billy to become so violent. But that wasn't an option, so Nathen would have to keep an eye on Billy and protect Adrian if Billy snapped again. Nathen glanced over his shoulder in the direction of the grave, and then he returned his focus to Billy. "Okay, Billy, we're going back to the grave, but I need you to do something for me."

Billy excitedly nodded his head. "Billy help. Billy like Nathen."

"Thank you, Billy. I want you to follow me back to where the bones are, but before we get there, I want you to wait until I tell you it's safe."

"Billy wait. Cabin not safe. Grave is safe. Billy fix her."

Nathen had no idea what was going on in Billy's head. But at least now he knew Billy had a violent side, and Nathen would do his best to keep it from surfacing again.

Amy returned with the fresh water and placed the buckets by the fire pit. Joshawa had torn half the sheet into long strips and laid them across his thighs. Amy went over to Joshawa, knelt on her knees facing him, and began to help him take his shirt off. "We should bind most of your ribs, even ones that aren't broken."

"Why all of them?"

Amy placed his shirt next to her and glanced over at him. "Because silly, we have to bind past the broken ones. Do you not know how to fix people?"

Joshawa smiled at Amy. "Apparently not."

Amy rolled her eyes at Joshawa, picked up one of the strips, and placed it across his chest just below his armpits. "Raise your arms."

Joshawa held his arms up, and Amy began to bind his ribs. She tucked the end of the first strip into the fold of the cloth, then continued with the second strip. After four strips, Amy had Joshawa's ribs bound. She sat back as she scrutinized her work and was very happy with the results. She placed the palm of her hand on Joshawa's chest. "Take a breath." She could feel his ribs as they worked in unison while Joshawa took a shallow breath. She glanced up at Joshawa, eager to ask, "Did it hurt?"

Joshawa took a shallow breath and was pleasantly surprised that the pain was manageable. Of course, the true test would be when he tried to move. "Actually, it's not bad."

Joshawa moved his upper body slightly forward and back with very little pain. "Wow! You did a great job." He glanced over to Amy and could tell that his comment pleased her. Joshawa had now realized that his parents wouldn't be the ones to save him. It was Amy. She was the answer. He just needed to convince her.

"I owe you so much, Amy. I would be dead if it weren't for you. I promise you, help me get better so I can go home, and

I'll take you with me. You'll never be alone again. You'll never have to live in fear again. I promise you, Amy."

Amy had heard that word before but couldn't recall what it meant. "What do you mean by promise?"

"It means I will do whatever it takes to bring you with me, protect you. That I won't leave you behind."

The words he spoke echoed in her mind. Then, another voice deep within her subconscious was telling her no. The cave was safe. "I've heard that word before. It's not a good word."

Joshawa silently observed Amy. Her expression was a combination of sadness and anger, though Joshawa couldn't be sure which emotion was dominant. Joshawa was puzzled by Amy's reaction and unsure if he should pursue the conversation. If he continued down this path, the outcome could sway her away from helping him, so he decided to drop the subject.

Amy took advantage of the silence and decided to curl up with Alex. She sat on the cave floor close to Alex's head and pressed her back against his body. *Alex, you are my protector* Amy brought her knees up to her chest, wrapped her arms around her legs, and laid her head on Alex. She closed her eyes and listened to the voice that resonated in her mind.

He is not the one to save you.

CHAPTER SIX

Nathen headed back to the grave site, with Billy following close behind. Within a few minutes, he could see Adrian standing beside the grave. Nathen was relieved, but unfortunately, the sense of peace knowing that Adrian hadn't suffered serious injuries was short-lived. Adrian had his *Ruger* out and was pointing it in their direction. Nathen immediately turned around, causing Billy to walk right into him. Nathen reached out and grabbed Billy's arm to keep him from falling.

"Sorry, Billy."

"Billy not hurt." Billy stood staring at Nathen. "We go now?"

"No. This is where I want you to wait. Just sit on the ground and remain quiet. When I call for you, then you can come."

Billy's face brightened up. "We play a game?"

"Yes, Billy. We play a game."

Billy sat cross-legged on the ground, his hands resting on his knees, his demeanor happy and carefree. "Billy play. Billy like games." Billy looked up at Nathen and placed his right index finger across his lips. "Shhh. We play a game."

Nathen whispered, "That's right, Billy. Come when I call you."

Nathen left Billy and started heading in Adrian's direction. When he decided he was close enough for Adrian to hear him, he called, "It's me, Adrian. Holster your gun."

"Is that idiot with you? Cause if he is, I'm not holstering

41

my gun."

Nathen walked up to Adrian, stopping only five feet away from him. Adrian's face was a mess of bruises and blood. "I'm so sorry, Adrian. Billy's in the forest, about ten feet from us. He's waiting for me to call him. And he's not an idiot."

Adrian kept his *Ruger* pointed at Nathen. "Are you kidding me! Can't you see what he did to me?"

Nathen took a step closer to Adrian. "Yes, I can. But Billy didn't mean it. Adrian, Billy grew up in horrific conditions. I can't even begin to imagine the atrocities he had to suffer at the hands of his brother. Billy has buried many of those memories deep inside his head. So deep that Billy's forgotten that they ever happened. Billy has forgotten, but his mind hasn't, and sometimes a smell, a sound" — Nathen glanced over to the bones scattered on the ground — "or, in Billy's case, a pile of bones, can awaken those memories."

Nathen returned his focus to Adrian, who was still pointing his gun at him. Nathen stepped closer to Adrian, then reached over and placed his right hand over the gun barrel. "All that is required with Billy is patience. He considers you his friend. Under normal circumstances, Billy wouldn't hurt a soul."

Nathen focused on Adrian's bruised and bloodied face. His right eye was swollen, and the bruising on his face was already turning purple. Nathen slowly removed his hand from the barrel of Adrian's gun. Nathen stood for what seemed to be several minutes. Then, finally, Adrian lowered his gun until it pointed at the ground.

Adrian glanced into the forest behind Nathen. "Did you know he would snap if you brought him here?"

Nathen struggled with the answer to Adrian's question. He'd known that when Billy saw his old home, there was a chance that he would have an adverse reaction. It could have scared him or caused him to withdraw inside of himself.

However, it had never crossed Nathen's mind that Billy would become violent. "In all honesty, Adrian, no. I never thought that his old homestead would cause Billy to exhibit such a violent outburst." Nathen hesitated for a moment as he glanced over to the cabin and then back to the grave. "Actually, the cabins and the yard never really affected Billy. It was only when he saw you touching the grave."

Adrian holstered his gun as he glanced over to the grave. "He kept shouting, *she's mine*. Do you think he knows who the bones belong to?"

"Yes, I do." Nathen glanced back to the cabin and then re-focused on the grave. "Billy keeps saying that he has to save Amelia."

"So, do you think that these bones belong to Amelia?"

Nathen slowly shook his head. "I have no idea. Something happened in that cabin, and I'm almost afraid to discover the truth."

Jax and Dameon headed down the mountain, making their way toward their *Suburban*. They'd hidden the vehicle in the bush far enough away from the road that it wouldn't easily be seen. Neither Jax nor Dameon wanted any unwarranted attention during any of their hunts. They'd had the vehicle painted forest green so it would be easier to camouflage. They also had camouflage netting that covered the entire *Suburban*, making it almost impossible to see from the road. Their camouflage clothing and skull caps blended well with the forest. Jax and Dameon carried their side arms and left the rifles and compound bows back at the cabin.

When it came to Dameon, Jax's patience was almost exhausted. But he knew how to keep his mouth shut. He needed Dameon, at least for the time being. Jax and Dameon had been best friends, practically brothers, ever since they met at the age of six.

Hunting had always been their passion, and for many years, they hunted legally and for food. However, it had been a long time since that was the case. Now they hunted for money, and this hunt was for a bear worth upwards of two hundred thousand dollars. But that wasn't what excited Jax. The bear was tagged and was basically money in the bank. It was the creature described in the journal that Jax wanted.

It was pure luck that Jax had come across the homestead in the middle of nowhere. But his prize wasn't finding the homestead. It was the journal he'd found hidden under the bunk beds. It spoke in detail of a creature that roamed the forest. Jax wanted to find the creature, not to kill it or display it. He wanted to take it to the smaller cabin and torture it. Jax smiled at the thought of carving the creature open while it was still alive. Unfortunately, the idea of what he would do to the creature had to be put aside for now. Jax's primary focus had to be on Dameon.

Jax and Dameon arrived at their vehicle, and within twenty minutes, they were on the road heading toward town. Dameon drove, which allowed Jax to pretend he was sleeping in the passenger seat. He needed time to think, which he wouldn't have been able to do with Dameon jabbering the entire drive in to town. Jax knew that, according to Dameon, after they crated their bear, Dameon wanted to retire. That was something Jax couldn't let happen. He needed Dameon to help crate the bear, but more importantly, he needed Dameon for his cartographer abilities. Jax needed a map of the area to find and capture the creature. After that, Dameon was nothing more than a loose end.

Jax knew Dameon would never mention anything about their illegal activities. However, he didn't know or trust that Dameon would keep his mouth shut about the journal and the creature. If Dameon did become a threat, Jax could overpower him. Dameon was just shy of six feet tall and weighed one hundred and eighty pounds of pure muscle. Jax had the advantage of being taller at six feet two inches and weighed an additional thirty pounds. He was confident that he could take Dameon down with little difficulty. However, that wasn't how Jax wanted to end their relationship. Jax was optimistic that the creature existed, and if he let Dameon read the journal, he would agree. But that wasn't an option, because if Dameon read the journal, he would figure out what Jax was planning, which wouldn't go well for either of them. At that moment, Jax decided that once the bear was crated, and after he convinced Dameon to map the area out, Dameon would have to die.

Lord Chike quietly walked along the jungle's edge until he reached the falls. The jungle bordered the falls on either side, which made it easy for him to enter his secret place without being seen. His secret place was hidden by the falls just as the entrance to the Valley of the Lion People was. He scanned the area one last time, then slipped in behind the waterfall. His bare feet easily maneuvered the slippery rocks, and he could feel the cool mist from the falls as it sprayed delicately against his skin. Halfway through the width of the falls, there was a gap in the solid rock wall. A gap that could only be seen by those who knew it was there. The five-foot high and four-foot-wide gap carved out of the rock was the entrance to his world, the world he controlled, a world filled with darkness and despair.

Authia opened her eyes to find everyone staring at her, except for Becca, who was still under the effects of the sedation. Becca's mother, Tammy, was the first to speak, "I'm assuming from that ear-to-ear grin that you found Joshawa."

"Sort of. Joshawa showed me the bear that the hunters were tracking. He's in a cave with Joshawa."

Tammy looked at Authia in complete astonishment. "And that's a good thing?"

"I'm not sensing that Joshawa or Serena is afraid of the bear. I believe that they're telling me that the bear is the only way to find Joshawa. Nathen's at the Jenkin's cabin waiting for Dameon to return." Authia shifted her attention to Edward, Burwood's resident physician, who was monitoring Becca's heart rate. "Edward, Adrian is returning with Billy, and Nathen asked if you would check on Billy."

Edward glanced over to Authia, obviously concerned by Nathen's request. "Is Billy okay? Does he require medical attention?"

"I don't believe that he's hurt. At least not physically. But maybe seeing his old home has brought back some bad memories. Nathen asked if you could speak with him and that Adrian would fill us in on what happened when he returned. They're on their way to our cabin now."

Edward turned away from Becca and headed for his office. "Tammy, you watch Becca. I'm going with Authia."

Authia stood up and followed Edward to his office. When Edward reached for his jacket, Authia gently placed her hand on his arm. "You can't walk that distance. You know that."

Edward let go of his jacket and turned to face Authia. "I have to. Billy needs me."

"Yes, he does. But it can wait until tomorrow. It'll be late by the time they reach our cabin. If Billy's okay, I'll have Adrian bring him to you first thing in the morning. If it turns out that he needs immediate attention, I'll have Adrian bring him straight to Burwood." Authia hugged Edward, and when she stepped back, she could see the tears forming in the corner of Edward's eyes. She took his hands in hers and lovingly smiled at him. "I know you love him, and you want to be there for him. But you won't be any good to him if you're exhausted by the time you arrive at my cabin."

Edward closed his eyes, and when he opened them, tears ran freely down his cheeks. "What use am I if I can't attend to my patients?"

"Don't even go there. You attend to all the people that live here, twenty-four-seven. Why don't you find my dad and go to the main lodge? As soon as Billy arrives, I'll radio you. I'll make sure that Billy's taken care of. Just remember, it's probably going to take a while before you hear from me."

Edward let go of Authia's hands and then wiped the tears from his face. "I'm sorry. Old age has made me more emotional than I should be."

Authia giggled. "You're just as emotional now as you were when I first met you. It's one of the many traits that I love about you." Authia kissed Edward on his cheek, then placed the palm of her hand over the cheek that she kissed. "I'm heading out. I promise to radio you as soon as Billy arrives." Authia grabbed her jacket off the back of the chair. As she headed for the main gate, she realized that for the first time since Joshawa went missing, she felt confident that Nathen would find their son and that he would be alive and well.

Lord Chike disappeared behind the rock wall. He followed the darkened path, and even with all the twists and turns, he did not falter. He had traveled this path since the dawn of time in his mission to imprison those he felt were unworthy of the right to exist in the Land of the Spirits. In the Land of the Ancestors or in the Land of the Spirits, the trail he walked would be evident. However, in the Realm of Despair, there was no sunlight, moonlight, or stars to see by. The path was a mere shadow that appeared suspended in midair, surrounded only by darkness.

When Lord Chike reached the end of the path, he turned and smiled to himself as he surveyed his domain. Through his eyes, he found beauty in the world he'd created to punish the unworthy. Beauty in the design and beauty in the darkness that encased his prisoners. In his Realm, there was no lush vegetation, no pristine waters, and no sound of laughter or happiness. Only the cries of his prisoners as madness slowly ate away at their minds over decades of solitude. Their cries were sweet music to his ears, and he often closed his eyes as he listened to their pitiful wails resounding against the cavernous walls — walls that only he could see, a path only he could walk on, a Realm where he was Lord.

CHAPTER SEVEN

Joshawa observed Amy as she curled up next to Alex. Then Alex maneuvered himself as if he were a human cradling a child. The bond they shared was unlike any bond that Joshawa had ever witnessed before. Joshawa knew he needed her help if he wanted to go home. Unfortunately, time was foreign to Joshawa in the confines of Amy's cave. He was unaware of the time of day or how many days he'd been in the cave. What he did know was that it was getting colder, and he didn't want to spend the winter in Amy's home. He had to find a way to become mobile and get Amy willing to help.

"Amy, are you sleeping?"

Amy glanced over at Joshawa and shook her head, indicating she wasn't.

"I want to try to move, but I could use your help."

Amy's demeanor changed, and she became the happy child who wanted nothing more than to help him. Joshawa thought that if he could figure out what affected Amy's mood swings, then maybe he could keep her happy and more willing to help.

Joshawa heard Alex make a soft growl. He glanced over to Alex and opened his mind to him.

You can understand what I'm thinking. Joshawa didn't receive a response from Alex, so he tried a different approach.

Amy is my ticket out of here. And I'm going to do whatever is needed to get her to help me. You can't stop me.

Alex got up and positioned himself between Amy and Joshawa. *I knew you could hear me!* Joshawa smiled at Alex.

Don't worry, Alex, I would never hurt Amy. Alex stared at Joshawa for several minutes, then went to stand next to Amy.

Amy started to walk over to Joshawa, only to have Alex block her way. He was looking at Joshawa and didn't appear to want to move. "What are you doing? Move."

Alex didn't budge. He just continued to stare at Joshawa.

Amy was getting frustrated and went to walk around Alex. But he moved with her and wouldn't let her pass. "You're making me mad. What's wrong with you?" Amy glanced over to Joshawa and then back to Alex. "Are you mad at Joshawa?" As if to answer her, Alex moved away and returned to his spot at the mouth of the cave. Amy slightly shook her head and mumbled, "Silly bear."

Joshawa observed the interaction between Amy and Alex. He'd give anything to understand how they communicated. But that wasn't a priority, at least not now. Joshawa's focus was to get mobile. He turned his attention from Alex to Amy, who was straddling his legs. She held her hands out to him.

"Take my hands and try to move."

Joshawa did as he was instructed and held onto her hands. He was lying on the ground, knowing this wouldn't be fun. Joshawa's challenge would be to sit up straight without Alex's help. He took a shallow breath, and with Amy's help, he slowly sat up straight. At first, when Amy started to lift him off the ground, the pain was excruciating. It felt as if a dagger had plunged into his chest over and over again. Joshawa tried not to show the pain, so he glanced over in Alex's direction. Amy couldn't see his pain, but Alex could. Alex had lifted his head up and looked directly at Joshawa. Joshawa could have sworn that Alex was mocking him.

The pain had diminished the minute he'd stopped moving and was sitting upright. Joshawa breathed a sigh of relief, for this was the first step toward him being able to go home. He glanced at the cave wall and then focused his attention on Amy. "That was easy. How about we try to move me to the wall?"

Amy had stepped back and had let go of Joshawa's hands. She didn't appear too enthusiastic about the idea.

"That's a long way. Alex can hold you up."

"I know he can, and I appreciate that, but if I'm going to get better, I have to start moving on my own. You can help me, or I'll get there myself. Either way, I'm going over there."

"You're being stupid." Amy moved so that she was standing between Joshawa and the cave wall. "You need to rest."

"Look, Amy, I'm rested enough. Now I need to fix myself, just like you said. I have to start moving on my own."

Amy glanced over to the wall and then back to Joshawa. He was sitting parallel to the wall. "How are you going to get there?"

Joshawa smiled at Amy. "I can get there, but I would appreciate it if you would stay close to me in case I need your help."

Amy shrugged her shoulders and moved aside. She looked at Joshawa as if she didn't care. "Fine, move all you want."

Joshawa placed his hands, palms down, on the ground. Carefully, he tried to lift his buttocks off the ground. He succeeded with little pain, but only because his arms did most of the work. He lowered his buttocks back onto the ground and glanced at the wall. To get there, he would have to twist his body so that his back would be facing the wall. Then, it would only be a matter of moving backward.

Joshawa lifted his buttocks a couple of inches off the ground, then tried to shift his body and legs to the right. The pain shot from his broken leg right through his entire body as if an arrow had sliced its way to his very core. He lowered himself as he closed his eyes and waited for the pain to subside. When he opened them, Amy was sitting on the ground at his feet. She looked at him with so much compassion, as if she felt his pain.

"Your leg is not healed. You shouldn't move it." Amy sat quietly for a moment and stared at Joshawa. She glanced down at Joshawa's leg and returned her focus to him. "I can move your legs. Will that help?"

"Yes, Amy, it will. I need my back to be facing the cave wall."

Amy knelt on the ground, ready to help Joshawa. She glanced over at Alex, who was no longer at the mouth of the cave. He'd moved and was now lying directly behind Joshawa.

"You're in the way. I don't need you to help Joshawa anymore. He's going to use the cave wall."

Alex did as she requested and returned to his usual spot.

Amy looked up at Joshawa, and at that moment, he suddenly realized that every time she spoke to Alex, she had a childlike innocence about her. Even her voice and her facial expressions were childlike. However, when she spoke to him, she bounced between a little girl and the child who seemed older than she appeared.

Joshawa was brought back to the present when he heard Amy call out his name. She was staring at him with her face scrunched up as if she were trying to understand something.

Joshawa thought she'd asked him something. "I'm sorry. What did you say?"

"Why do you look like that?"

"Like what?"

"You're looking at me funny."

Joshawa softly chuckled as he smiled at Amy. "Sorry. It's just that . . ." Joshawa hesitated because he wasn't sure how to put what he was thinking into words.

"What?"

"You're amazing. Amy, you saved my life. You've taken care of me. You've lived in this cave for most of your life with no human contact. Yet you act as if you know what it's like to be loved and to be cared for."

Amy had reached for Joshawa's ankles but hesitated just inches away. She sat back down and looked at Joshawa, trying to understand what he was saying. "Human contact?"

"It just means contact with people. I'm saying that you haven't had another person like yourself or me in your life."

Amy thought for a moment and slowly nodded her head. "I sometimes dream about being with others. But I never see who they are. You're wrong about love. Alex loves me, and he takes care of me, and I love him."

"You're right, Amy, and I was wrong. You do know about love and caring."

Amy didn't respond. Instead, she took hold of Joshawa's ankles and carefully moved his legs to where he wanted them. Amy sat quietly while Joshawa slowly moved backward toward the cave wall. Her thoughts were not on Joshawa. They were miles away to a time she barely remembered — to the time when she was left at the cave and was told not to leave. She tried to remember the evil that lived outside of the cave. But there was no memory, only fear. The only memory that was as clear as the day she heard it was the memory of a word. Just one word. She was left alone with the promise that they would return. Amy closed her eyes, and the word promise repeated itself over and over in her mind. They promised that they would come back, but they never did.

Lord Chike would have preferred to spend hours listening to his prisoners, but he had a purpose. He had a plan that needed to be executed. It was a plan to rid the Lion People of their traitors and give birth to a new breed of tribe members. An untainted breed that would honor him as their Lord for eternity.

He turned and gazed upon the threshold that opened to a place he considered home. A place that had witnessed his birth and would soon witness his most profound victory. Lord Chike crossed the threshold and entered a room that was full of color and rich adornments. The light from the torches shone brightly in this room. However, the light could not penetrate the darkness on the other side of the threshold. The room appeared as if it had been meticulously carved out of marble running rich with colors that resembled the rainforest.

The marble walls glistened and were adorned with tapestries and golden artifacts that had been awarded to him from different lifetimes of the Lion People. Each tapestry spoke of a specific battle between him and the ruling Lord. They depicted images of how he destroyed the reigning Lord and those who protected the Lord, leaving the village in ruin. However, what the tapestries didn't reveal were all the innocent tribe members, women, and children who died in Lord Chike's quest for a pure and devoted bloodline.

Lord Chike walked over to the only furniture that occupied his personal chamber. It was a table and chair built out of the wood from the kapok trees that flourished in his valley. The table was four feet wide and six feet long. The chair had a high back that was inscribed with beautiful carvings, as well as two armrests. There were several scrolls on the table. Each scroll contained the names of all the residents condemned to the Realm of Despair. Soon, he would start a new scroll, and the thought of whose names he would add to the scroll thrilled him beyond description.

Joshawa sat on the cave floor, his back against the wall, his legs stretched out in front of him. At that moment, he realized how alone he really was. Amy had gone for water and food, and as he always did, Alex had followed her. That didn't matter because even with her company, Joshawa still felt alone. But wasn't that what he wanted? To be alone in his private place where he could feel sorry for himself. Joshawa shook his head and thought about what a fool he was. He had a family that loved and cared for him, and he had Becca. It was at that moment that Joshawa made a vow to himself. If he ever found his way home, he would throw caution to the wind and tell Becca how much he loved her.

Joshawa stared beyond the cave's opening and wondered how much time had passed since Amy had brought him here. Time was lost to him mainly because he didn't know how long he'd drifted in and out of consciousness. He'd asked Amy, but she didn't relate to time as he did. For Amy, the changing of the seasons and the behavior of the animals was all she needed to know. The last coherent memory he had was of Alex charging his tree. Afterward, everything was a blur. His memories seemed to meld together, and no matter how hard he tried, he couldn't separate them or put them into chronological order.

Joshawa sighed as he closed his eyes and rested his head against the cold stone wall of the cave. Joshawa tried to recall everything his mother had told him about her vision. She saw him on the ground inside a cave, she heard him crying out in pain, and she saw someone else. So if she could see this cave in her vision, why couldn't she see it now? Why couldn't she hear his pleas? Why couldn't his father not feel how scared he was? For what seemed to be the one-hundredth time, Joshawa reached out to both his parents, hoping that one of them would respond.

Mother, father, I beg you to find me. Help me! Reach out to me so that I know you're searching for me. Why can't you hear me?

Frustration, anger, and fear amassed deep within him. Like a volcano, his emotions exploded and surged throughout his body as if he'd been struck by lightning.

Please hear me! Please find me!

At that moment, Joshawa's mind was consumed by a brilliant blue light. *I hear you.*

Joshawa's eyes shot open only to discover that the entire cave was filled with a blue light that shimmered as if it contained thousands of stars.

Mother?

Calm yourself.

Joshawa's breathing became more rapid as he searched the cave for the source of the voice.

The voice is from within you. Stay focused, my young Lord. Concentrate, and they will find you.

Joshawa closed his eyes and allowed everything he was to be consumed by the blue light.

I hear you. Please find me. I'm in a cave to the north. Help me!

Your father is coming!

The blue light dissipated from Joshawa's mind, and when he opened his eyes, the only light he saw was from the sunlight that brightened the cave entrance. Joshawa focused on the entrance of the cave. He'd heard something, and he'd definitely seen something. Joshawa wanted to believe what he heard was true. However, Serena had been playing with his mind, so could he trust what he heard? Could he trust what he saw? Joshawa gazed about the cave. It was at that moment that he realized that it was a game. A game Serena was playing with his mind. It was a game with no rules and no instructions. A game he couldn't possibly win.

CHAPTER EIGHT

Nathen called out to Billy, and as he did, Adrian moved closer to Nathen. Billy walked into the small area that surrounded the grave. Nathen was cautious as he observed Billy check out his surroundings.

Then Billy turned to Nathen, his eyes wide in excitement, and he was smiling as a child would. "Billy win?"

"Yes, Billy, you won."

Nathen watched as Billy clapped and chanted, "Billy won," over and over.

Adrian moved even closer to Nathen and whispered, "Is he safe?"

Nathen kept his focus on Billy. "Yes, I believe he is."

Once again, Adrian whispered to Nathen, "What the hell, Nathen! You believe he is? I was hoping for something a little more substantial than you believe he is."

Nathen turned to face Adrian. Mixed in with the bruises, a swollen eye, and blood, Nathen could easily see the fear that encompassed Adrian. "Just follow his lead and don't interrupt him. He'll be fine."

Adrian turned to face Billy, and as he did, he placed his hand on the butt of his gun.

"I saw that, Adrian. Take your hand off your gun, or I'll take it from you."

Nathen didn't wait for a response. He turned to face Billy. "Is everything good, Billy?"

Billy nodded his head, excitement evident. "Billy good. Billy fix." Billy glanced over to Adrian, and his expression slowly changed to confusion. He started to walk toward Adrian, but Nathen stepped in his path.

"Billy, is everything okay?"

"Adrian hurt. My friend hurt."

"Yes, Adrian is hurt, but he'll be fine."

Adrian mumbled loud enough for Nathen to hear. "Like hell, I will."

Nathen ignored Adrian and focused on Billy. "So, you want to fix her?"

Billy turned to face the grave. "Yes, Billy fix."

Billy knelt by the pit and started to put the skeleton remains of the woman back together. Billy was talking to the bones as if he were speaking to the person the bones had belonged to. He held up the jawbone and placed it with the skull. "You have pretty smile. Billy like your smile." Billy then picked up the alma bone and placed it where the humerus should be. He stared at it briefly, then quickly picked it up. Billy appeared frightened as he held the bone close to his chest.

He scanned the area around him and smiled as he returned to the skeleton. "Dext not here. Billy not get hurt." Billy quickly placed the ulna bone where it should be and continued with this task.

Nathen could think of at least a dozen questions that he would have loved to ask Billy, but now wasn't a good time. There was no telling what would set Billy off again and no guarantee that Nathen would be able to calm him a second time. Nathen glanced over to where Adrian was standing and motioned for Adrian to follow him. They walked together into the open space of the yard where he could speak to Adrian in private but still be able to keep an eye on Billy.

"Leave him while he puts his skeleton together. When he's done, take him back to my home."

Adrian glanced over his shoulder at Billy, then returned his focus to Nathen. "What if he goes bat-shit crazy again and decides to attack me?"

"Have you ever seen him become that angry before?"

Adrian hesitated for just a moment, then shrugged his shoulders. "I guess not."

"He hasn't. If you take him away from these cabins and the gravesite, he should be his contented, happy self."

Adrian raised an eyebrow. "Should be?"

"This place has triggered old memories that Billy buried long ago. These memories have surfaced, causing Billy to react the way he did. Take him away from this place, and you remove the triggers. He'll become Billy, who's a child and happy with life."

Adrian glanced over to Billy and then back to Nathen. "It's against my better judgment, but I'm going to trust you on this."

"Thank you, Adrian. I know that's not easy for you."

"So, what are you going to do?"

"Wait for Dameon to return and see if I can get him to help me."

"Seriously? That's your plan? You're gonna knock on the cabin door and ask for help?"

Nathen smiled at Adrian. "Not exactly. I plan to be a little more discreet. I'm going to say goodbye to Billy, then I'll find a place to wait until Dameon returns."

"Okay. When I get back to your cabin, is there any message for Authia?"

"No, but thank you. I'll be speaking to her long before you get back. Adrian, it'll be dark before you get to my home. You're more than welcome to spend the night and head out to Burwood in the morning."

"Seriously? I don't get you, Nathen. You should hate my father and me. But yet, here you are, offering your home to me."

"And I sincerely hope you take me up on the offer." Nathen smiled at Adrian and then walked over to Billy. Billy's back was to Nathen, so he gently touched Billy's shoulder, hoping not to startle him. Billy looked up at Nathen and appeared very happy with himself.

"See. Billy fix her."

"Good for you, Billy. You did an excellent job. I'm going to wait here for the men to come back. I want you to go to my cabin with Adrian."

Billy looked at Nathen as if he didn't understand what was being said. "You stay here?"

"Yes, Billy. I'm going to stay here."

Billy's demeanor went from carefree to frightened. "Not safe." Billy gently shook his head from side to side. "Not safe at cabin."

"I'm going to be fine. Remember, Dext is dead. He can't hurt us anymore."

Billy smiled at Nathen. "Dext dead."

"Billy, I want you to stick close to Adrian and listen to what he tells you."

Billy nodded to indicate that he understood, then returned his focus to the grave. Like a child with a secret, he carefully glanced over to Nathen and Adrian. They weren't watching him, so he returned his focus to the grave. Billy kissed his fingertips and then placed them tenderly on the grave. "You safe now. Billy love you. Billy save Amelia."

Billy stood and brushed the dirt from his pants. He grabbed his backpack and carefully pulled his arms through the straps. Once his backpack was secured, he glanced back up at Nathen. "Billy ready." Billy glanced down at the grave he'd just fixed. "She safe. Now Billy save Amelia."

Nathen was completely confused by what Billy was saying. There was more to Billy, his brother, and their homestead. More than Nathen believed he would ever discover.

When Billy headed into the forest, Nathen motioned to Adrian. "Stay close to him. Don't let him out of your sight for a single moment."

Adrian nodded his head in agreement and then ran after Billy.

Serena gazed at Lord Adeeowale from across the fire pit. "Your faith in me is most reassuring. However, when this is done, I fear the Council will not be so compassionate."

Lord Adeeowale rested his hands on his knees and looked upon Serena with sincerity and compassion. "The Council will judge us as they see fit. Us, Serena, not only you. We are all conspirators in this endeavor to discover the truth. With that in mind, what knowledge can you offer us?"

Serena was empowered by Lord Adeeowale's words, for he had witnessed the wrath of the Council, and even with that knowledge, he was prepared to stand by her side.

"You honor me with your trust. If memory serves me correctly, the scrolls that speak of our past are in the Land of the Spirits."

"That is correct. They are kept with the Council."

"Oh, that is disappointing. I had hoped the scrolls were available for us to read without the knowledge of the Council."

Lord Adeeowale's expression was that of confusion. "Why would we need the scrolls?"

"As you know, I believe that Lord Chike is a vessel for the Destroyer. I was hoping that the scrolls would confirm my suspicions."

The tone in Lord Adeeowale's voice told Serena that he was not pleased with her revelation. "This is a serious accusation, Serena. Imani and I have discussed this matter since you told us of your suspicions. We agree that Lord Chike is not behaving as a true Ancestor should. However, other than his use of forbidden words, what other evidence do you have to support such a harsh accusation?"

"As a wisp, I flew here to see if I could learn more about Lord Chike. I planned to become one with his mind and to do so without his knowledge."

"And did you?"

"Unfortunately, no. However, I did discover that Lord Chike is not one spirit but two. I cannot access him without the other sensing my presence. The second spirit that resides within him consists of hatred and anger and is driven by revenge. It is the purest personification of evil I have ever encountered, including my mother."

Lord Adeeowale was obviously taken aback by Serena's observation. "Are you certain of this?"

Serena gave Lord Adeeowale a look that implied frustration and annoyance. "You doubt my gifts? I know what I saw, and I know what I felt. Lord Chike is hiding a monster within him. I have never had to face the Destroyer, so I know little about him. I thought that if we could read the scrolls, we might gain insight on how to deal with not only the Destroyer but also his vessel."

Lord Adeeowale sat quietly, offering no facial expression as to what he was thinking. He was focused on something beyond Serena's understanding. She was about to meld with him when he turned to face her. Lord Adeeowale's facial expression had morphed into that of sadness and fear.

"The scrolls are available to me if the Council permits. However, they are not needed. A long time ago, I had the misfortune of meeting the Destroyer in battle."

Serena couldn't believe what was being revealed to her. She had never known anyone who had personally fought with the Destroyer because, to her knowledge, no one ever survived. "I do not understand. You are a Lord and an Ancestor. You are revered among our people. What possible reason could there be for the Council to send the Destroyer to you?"

"I have no answer. I recall that after the battle, I had asked the Council that very question. But, as far as I know, I received no reply. The next day, all memory of my encounter with the Destroyer was washed away. And it was not just my memory. The entire village continued life as if nothing happened."

"No disrespect, my Lord, but if you have no memory of the encounter, then how is it that you know you fought him?"

"That is a fair question, and I wish I had a logical response. All I can say is that rooted deep within me is a fragment of a memory. That fragment tells me I battled the Destroyer. At that time, I had nothing to validate my memory of the battle, so I dismissed it. If I had not, my people might have thought my mind was compromised. I would not have remained Lord for very long."

Serena listened to what Lord Adeeowale had to say, and suddenly, everything became clear. She figured out how she could expose Lord Chike. "When Lord Chike first brought me here, he made it very clear that I was not to leave my post. He was evasive in his answers to my questions concerning you and Imani. He inferred that I would meet you when my obligation was completed."

Serena chuckled as she glanced at Lord Adeeowale. "He was not very pleased when you showed up in my little piece of the Realm."

"No, he was not. But what has that got to do with discovering who he is?"

"He brought me here partly because of my familiarity with Lord Nathen and his family. But mostly, he was interested in my special talents. However, I did get the impression that I was chosen out of necessity and that he would have preferred if someone else did his bidding."

"Continue."

"You remember you had an encounter with the Destroyer, but you have no memory of the actual event, correct?"

"Yes."

"Do you have memories leading up to and after the encounter?"

"Yes, very fond and vivid memories." Lord Adeeowale hesitated, then he smiled at Serena. "You think my memories of the encounter have been erased."

"No, I do not believe that your memories have been erased. Otherwise, you would have no memories of the past, not even a fragment. I believe that the memories of the battle were suppressed, and Lord Chike did not want us to meet because I am possibly the only priestess who would be able to unlock those memories."

Chapter Nine

L ord Chike sat at his table and started to unroll the new parchment. He was elated at the prospect of adding Lord Adeeowale and Imani's names to the list of spirits imprisoned in the Realm he controlled.

A voice that was weak from years of captivity spoke in defiance of Lord Chike. "You are a fool if you think you will be adding his name to your scroll."

Lord Chike stopped unrolling the parchment and glanced in the direction the voice came from. "My prisoner speaks."

Lord Chike carefully rolled the parchment up, then casually walked over to the back of the room. This area was quite different from the main area. It was cold, damp, and shadowed in darkness. The only light that penetrated this far into the room emanated from the main area. Chained to the back wall was a tribe member who, in his day, was a great warrior and fierce protector of the Lord who ruled during his time. Exhausted from years of captivity, the prisoner sat on the cold marble floor. His knees were drawn to his chest, his head rested against the marble wall, and his long red hair was severely matted. His loincloth that once covered his thighs now barely covered his manhood.

His body was thin from malnutrition, and his complexion was pale from years of captivity in a room that bore no sunlight. He wore a metal collar around his neck that was so wide it encased his neck from his jawbone to the trapezius muscle located at the base of his neck. When he was first shackled with the collar, it had pressed uncomfortably against his jawbone. However, after a century of wearing the collar, it was now an inch below his jawline. The collar's weight had caused severe indents in the trapeze muscles to the point that whenever he moved his shoulders, it would cause him excruciating pain.

The collar was attached to the wall with a ten-foot chain that weighed over twenty pounds. The prisoner's wrists and ankles also bore the burden of metal cuffs that wore his skin raw. The cuffs on his wrists were attached to each other with a one-foot chain, as were the cuffs on his ankles. To further impede his movements, each ankle cuff was independently secured to the wall with chains weighing over twenty pounds.

Lord Chike smirked at his prisoner. "As if you are in a position to stop me."

"I might not be, but he is so much more than a Lord. He is a powerful warrior. You will lose."

"Not only will I win, but he will willingly take his place in the Realm of Despair. Once he discovers that you are my prisoner and he recognizes the infinite power I possess, he will relinquish his position."

Lord Chike relished his authority over his prisoner and considered him his most prized tapestry. He walked over to his table and picked up a dagger that boasted a twelve-inch blade that had been horned on either side, making it twice as deadly. The blade's handle had been fashioned out of ivory and was precisely carved to fit his hand. With the dagger in his right hand, he pointed at his prisoner.

"Let's see if we can find you in any of these tapestries."

"You know you will. I'm the warrior whose blade is at your neck."

Lord Chike mocked his prisoner. "Really? I do not recall that tapestry." Lord Chike gazed about the room, randomly pointing to the tapestries with his dagger. "I have gazed upon these magnificent renderings of my dominance over the Lion People since the dawn of time. I do not recall the tapestry you refer to."

Lord Chike walked over to one of the walls, and using his dagger, he pointed to half a dozen tapestries. "I believe these represent your time period. Shall we take a closer look?"

Lord Chike didn't wait for a response. Instead, he gazed upon each tapestry, recounting the battle each one depicted as if they took place only yesterday. When he came to the last one, he studied it more intently. At the story's beginning, a tall and proud warrior stood shoulder to shoulder with his Lord. The warrior's weapon was a lance, and he was ready to strike at the Destroyer that stood before him. At the end of the story, the warrior was on the ground, the ornate ivory handle of a dagger protruding from his belly. Lord Chike pressed the tip of his dagger against the drawing of the wounded warrior. He gazed back over his shoulder at his prisoner.

"Perhaps this is you? But then, how could it be?" Lord Chike returned his focus to the tapestry. "This warrior's body reveals no scars, no prior injuries, and according to the parchment, he died."

"The parchment lies!"

Lord Chike walked over to his prisoner, stopping just short of the prisoner's reach. "You, on the other hand, are weak, and your body is disfigured with the scars you bear. Not to mention that you are very much alive."

The prisoner awkwardly stood up, which to Lord Chike was a laughable attempt at showing his resolve. However, when the prisoner stood before him, his body erect and his feet planted firmly, Lord Chike was taken aback. A distant memory flashed before his eyes, and for a fleeting moment, Lord Chike felt vulnerable.

He dismissed the memory and smiled at his prisoner. "You have something to say?"

"I stand before you, a reflection of what you are. The scar you bear is proof that, at one time, you were almost bested. The scars I bear will one day be yours, and I will gladly give my life to see you destroyed."

Lord Chike was not impressed by his prisoner's revelation. "In this cavern, you will live for an eternity, hidden from those who could be your salvation."

Lord Chike took his dagger and pierced his abdomen until only half of his blade was exposed. He did not feel the pain inflicted by the blade of his dagger. However, his prisoner did. Lord Chike laughed while his prisoner screamed in agony and then dropped to his knees. Lord Chike knelt next to him, their eyes met, and then Lord Chike deliberately ran the blade upward to his rib cage. His wound didn't bleed, and when he pulled the dagger out of his body, the incision healed as quickly as it was made.

The same could not be said for his prisoner as blood oozed from the wound that tore open from his belly to his rib cage. The prisoner's eyes went wide, and then he crumbled to the ground. Lord Chike stood and glared down at his prisoner, who lay in a pool of his own blood. "You are mine to do with as I please, as you have been since the battle foretold in the tapestry. You will suffer my injuries and suffer my pain so that I live on, and there is nothing you can do to stop me."

Serena had opened a Pandora's box when she revealed she could unlock Lord Adeeowale's memories. There were times when some memories should not be awakened. Sometimes, memories could destroy all that is good within a person. But in Lord Adeeowale's case, she was confident that his memories might help their endeavor to stop the Destroyer.

Imani had returned from her vigil of watching Lord Chike. Without hesitating, she took her place on the ground next to

Lord Adeeowale. Imani gazed upon her Lord with so much tenderness. Then she focused her attention on Serena. "Lord Chike is beyond my ability to sense him. He has traveled deep into the Land of the Spirits. It will be some time before he returns."

Serena was puzzled by Imani's report. "Lord Adeeowale, did you not send him to the Council?"

"I did. The Council resides in the Gathering Hut. That is where he should be."

"Well, whatever he is doing, he has allowed us some time to discuss your lack of memory."

Imani placed her hand on Lord Adeeowale's knee. She glanced over to Serena and then back to Lord Adeeowale. "You are having difficulty with your memories? You have not mentioned that to me."

Lord Adeeowale covered Imani's hand with his own. "I just realized it myself. We were talking about Lord Chike possibly being the Destroyer."

Serena was quick to interject. "My Lord, he is the Destroyer. Of that, I am certain."

"Serena, you will have to provide proof of your accusation."

"I intend to. My Lord, do you wish for me to try and unlock your memories?"

"Yes. I am certain that at some time in my life, I have dealt with the Destroyer. We need to discover what that encounter was."

"A word of warning, my Lord. You may not like what I unlock."

"Serena, I may be a spirit, but I am also an Ancestor. I have a duty to my people, to the Jelani Tribe. I will risk my well-being to save my people."

"Very good, my Lord. I can unlock the memories and see them for myself. But there is no promise that I can permanently release these memories. It will depend on the skill of the person that sealed them in the first place."

"Then let us proceed before Lord Chike returns."

Imani stood and placed her hand on Lord Adeeowale's shoulder. She looked at him with the sweetest smile. "Do you require me to be here?"

Serena glanced at Lord Adeeowale and then over to Imani. The smile they both shared made it obvious to Serena that there was a connection between them. She was about to question them but thought better of it. She had already opened one Pandora's box. There was no rational reason for opening another.

Serena smiled at Imani. "No, I do not believe so. Actually, what I plan to do could take some time. Maybe you should return to the Gateway and continue your watch for Lord Chike."

"I will be glad to."

Serena observed Lord Adeeowale as he watched Imani disappear into the jungle. Serena cleared her throat, which brought Lord Adeeowale's attention back to her.

"Are you ready, my Lord?"

"Yes." Lord Adeeowale squared his shoulders, placed his hands on his knees, and parted his lips to allow Serena access to his mind, his very core.

Serena transformed into a wisp and flew past Lord Adeeowale's parted lips. She immediately sought out the chamber of his mind that contained his memories. The memories she saw revealed a compassionate and trustworthy man who was also a strong and dedicated leader. He governed the Lion People as he was taught to do. When his son Massai turned thirty, Lord Adeeowale proudly passed the title of Lord onto his son.

So why would the Council send the Destroyer to kill a Lord who was pure and worthy of his title? Serena searched every memory of Lord Adeeowale's life while he held the title of

Lord and found every memory intact. Not one memory was hidden from his view. Serena was not one to give up, so she returned to the beginning and probed even deeper into his memories. When she approached the memory of when he learned that he would be a father, she noticed that his memories had a strange appearance. They appeared to shimmer as if they were distorted. It was as if his memories were layered one memory on top of the other, but that made no sense. How could someone have more than one memory of the same event?

Serena returned to the surface of his memories to understand what she was seeing. She chose a memory and experienced that memory as she had done before. On the surface, the memory was clear and vivid, leaving no doubt that it was factual. Once again, Serena dove deeper into his memories, and as before, the memory became distorted. She continued to travel through his memories until his death, and every memory had the same distortion.

Serena knew what she had to do, but as she was about to examine the complexity of the distorted memories, she heard Imani's voice. Lord Chike had entered the Gateway and was on his way back. Serena had to think fast, so she linked all the memories affected by the distortion and then reached out to Lord Adeeowale.

See the memories that have become as one.

Lord Adeeowale replied, *See the memories.*

My Lord, you must concentrate on only the memories that have become as one. You must see past the distortion.

See past the distortion.

Yes, my Lord. See past the distortion. See the memories. Peel back the layers. Find the original memories and relive those memories as if they happened yesterday.

Serena had run out of time, so she left Lord Adeeowale and returned to her little piece of the Realm. She had just settled at the edge when Lord Chike emerged from the jungle. Serena stood, clasped her hands in front of her, and bowed her head to her Lord.

"My Lord, you honor me with your presence."

When Serena met Lord Chike's gaze, it sent shivers down her spine. On the outside, he appeared annoyed, even frustrated with her. However, the spirit that dwelled within him was angered and consumed with hatred. Serena knew that she didn't have much time before Lord Chike became the monster that lived within him. When that monster surfaced, Lord Nathen's family would cease to exist.

CHAPTER TEN

Adrian had caught up with Billy but kept his distance and walked several feet behind him. He didn't trust Billy's state of mind, and even though Nathen said Billy would be okay, Adrian wasn't convinced. He didn't trust that Billy wouldn't erupt in a fit of rage again. So Adrian ensured that if Billy snapped, he would be able to protect himself. His gun was no longer in its holster, and the safety was off. Adrian's right arm was at his side with the gun held firmly in his hand. His finger was on the trigger, and he was fully prepared to use it on Billy.

There was no conversation between the two, and Adrian was okay with that. Billy's limited vocabulary frustrated the hell out of Adrian, and all he wanted was to get Billy to Nathen's cabin and end his part in this insane search for Joshawa. Adrian was so focused on what Billy might do that he didn't notice that Billy had been slowly diverting them in a northerly direction. They had hiked for almost an hour when Adrian finally noticed that the sun was no longer in front of them.

Adrian holstered his gun mostly because he had to get closer to Billy, and the last thing he wanted was an accident. Adrian didn't want to be in a situation where he could be on the wrong end of the gun's barrel. Frustrated more with himself than Billy, Adrian called out to get Billy to stop. But Billy kept walking as if he were in a world all of his own.

"Billy, stop!" Adrian finally got in front of Billy so he would have no choice but to stop. "Billy, what the hell? You're going the wrong way." Adrian slowly maneuvered his right hand and placed it on the butt of his gun. He kept his guard up as he observed Billy waiting for any sign that he may be aggressive.

Billy slowly glanced around until his focus was back on Adrian. He was happy and smiled at Adrian as he tried to walk around him. "No, Billy go this way. This right way."

Once again, Adrian stepped in front of Billy. "No, Billy. Nathen's cabin is that way." Adrian pointed to the West of them.

"Billy not go to cabin. Billy save Amelia."

"Who the hell is Amelia?"

Billy stared at Adrian as if he was unsure of how to answer the question. Then he lowered his head so that he would be looking at the ground and not Adrian. Gently, Billy shook his head from side to side as if something was very wrong. When Billy glanced up, he looked like he had lost something very dear to him. He was sad, his eyes filled with tears, and when he answered Adrian, his voice stammered as if he couldn't get the words out.

"Billy must save her. Billy promised." Billy broke down and started to cry.

Adrian had to calm Billy, but other than letting him go north, he had no clue how to manage an insanely strong child who was impossible to reason with. At that moment, Adrian wished Nathen was with them, but since he wasn't, Adrian didn't have many options. Adrian faced Billy and placed his right hand on Billy's shoulder.

"Billy, everything's gonna be okay. So you have to save Amelia?"

Billy glanced up at Adrian and started nodding his head. "Billy save Amelia."

"Who's Amelia?"

Billy stopped crying and cautiously eyed Adrian. "Amelia

secret."

"Secret from who?"

"Everyone. We leave now."

Adrian glanced up the mountain and then back to Billy. "How far is Amelia?"

"Not far. Be there by dark."

"By dark? It'll be cold on the mountain. How are we gonna stay warm?"

Billy rolled his eyes at Adrian. "In the cave, silly. We go now."

Billy was happy again as he continued to climb up the mountain. However, all Adrian could think of was the conversation he overheard about Joshawa and the fact that he might be in a cave. What were the odds that Joshawa was in the same cave that Billy was leading him to?

Becca and her parents had arrived at her aunt's cabin just before the sun disappeared on the horizon. They spent a little extra time in Burwood to give Becca the time she needed to recuperate from the propofol she was given earlier. Becca had decided to curl up on her aunt's love seat with a blanket over her lap and a roaring fire in the fireplace. She'd complained about being chilled, so her mother had prepared her a mug of hot chocolate. When Tammy passed the mug to Becca, she wrapped her hands around it and rested it on her knees.

The scent of chocolate was enticing, and the heat that emanated from the mug warmed Becca's hands. She watched the flames playfully dance among the logs and welcomed the warmth radiating from the fireplace. However, her thoughts were not on the mug of hot chocolate or the splendor of the fire. They were fixated on Joshawa and the fact that he could be sharing a cave with a bear that could easily rip him apart.

Her aunt Authia told her that she didn't sense any danger.

But Becca still felt ill at ease to the point that she felt like she could vomit. Becca was so nervous for Joshawa that she had to use two hands to steady the mug of hot chocolate. She would give anything to have Joshawa beside her, safe and happy, knowing she loved him.

Becca glanced out the window, but not because she wanted to see the beauty of the forest. Her only objective was to see the majestic trees that surrounded the cabins. She wanted to observe the last rays of the sun as they disappeared from view. When that magical time happened, it allowed the darkness to penetrate all it touched with its icy grip.

Joshawa had been gone for three days, and Becca had no way of knowing if he had a fire to keep him warm at night or water to keep him alive. Authia was confident that Joshawa was alive and that Serena was watching over him. But that didn't relieve Becca's anxiety for Joshawa. Since she was not allowed to look for him, she decided to stay on Authia's couch and wait for Authia to hear from Nathen. No matter the outcome, she wasn't budging until she could hold Joshawa in her arms.

Nathen watched as Adrian disappeared into the forest. When he was sure they were both out of sight, Nathen walked over to the grave to get a closer look. He examined many of the bones in the grave. To his relief, the woman Billy had reburied appeared to be the only human bones. Nathen sat on his haunches and stared at the bones used to conceal the woman. As far as Nathen could remember, Billy never mentioned that he had a mother or a sister or that any woman was a part of his and his brother's life. There was also Amelia, a woman Billy repeatedly said he had to save.

Nathen sighed as he stood and brushed the dirt off his pants. Did anyone have the right to resurrect Billy's memories to satisfy their own curiosity? Because, in the end, it would only be to satisfy Nathen's curiosity. If Billy lived with the mentality of a child and was happy and carefree, then there was no reason to find out who these women were.

Nathen had to put Billy aside and focus on his plan to get the GPS. He headed in the direction of the open yard, and at the same time, he reached out to Authia.

How is the love of my life doing?

Much better now that I know Joshawa's alive. Is everything okay with you? Has Dameon returned?

Yes, I'm fine, and no, Dameon hasn't returned. But I expect both of them to return before it gets dark.

I hope that Dameon will help us. I know that Joshawa is alive, but I'm still worried that you won't find him in time. Becca has planted herself on our couch and refuses to budge until Joshawa comes home.

Nathen smiled as he recalled Joshawa and Becca on the dance floor at the banquet. *She really does love him.*

Yes, she does, and she intends to tell him the second he gets back home.

I know I asked you to get Edward to speak to Billy, but maybe Adrian should talk to Edward first.

What's going on, Nathen? What happened to Billy?

Billy's fine. Trust me. Adrian will fill you in, and I'll let you know more when I have a chance to speak to Dameon.

I'm not happy with you being so secretive about what's going on. But I trust you, so please keep in contact with me. I don't know if I could keep it together if I thought something had happened to you, as well.

Don't worry, my love. I promise to stay in contact with you, and I'll be careful.

Nathen ended the meld and went toward the cabin to find a place where he could conceal himself until Dameon and Jax returned.

Billy held onto the backpack's front straps for no reason other than to reassure himself that the backpack would remain in place. He followed a path that he'd traveled many times before. It was an overgrown path that hadn't been disturbed in years. But as far as Billy was concerned, it had only been a couple of months since he walked it. The memory of that last time he was here was as vivid as it was on the day it had happened.

The day progressed, and the sun slowly descended behind the mountains that rose high in the sky. Billy stopped and scanned the mountain range until he saw his landmark. It was a carving in the rock created by the hand of nature. It resembled the image of an eagle with its wings spread out, its head slightly lowered, and its claws ready to snatch its prey. The carving was three stories high and could only be seen if you were standing in the right spot at the right time of day.

Billy couldn't contain his excitement as he proudly pointed to the eagle. "See, we close. We safe."

Billy turned, but when he saw who was behind him, all the joy that had built up inside him had vanished. He slowly lowered his arm, and as he did, he quickly checked the area for his brother. Dex was nowhere in sight, and instead of the woman he loved, a strange man was standing behind him. "You not her."

"What are you talking about, Billy?"

Billy didn't understand what was transpiring right in front of him. He recognized the voice but not the face. Billy was confused and scared, and his mind exploded with voices screaming at him in unison.

Billy closed his eyes as he raised his hands to cover his ears. "Go away! Billy no, like you!" Billy dropped to his knees and began to shake his head violently, hoping that the voices would stop. He felt someone touch his arm, and he heard a man's voice that was soothing and calm. Something deep inside of Billy told him to listen and to trust the man who stood in front of him.

CHAPTER ELEVEN

Adrian followed Billy north through the dense forest in their endeavor to find a cave that, apparently, was very special to Billy. They'd been quietly walking for about an hour when Billy started to talk to himself. He was mumbling, so Adrian couldn't make out what he was saying and was in no hurry to ask. However, he wasn't taking any chances, so he unfastened the strap that held his gun in its holster. Nathen trusted that Billy would be fine if he was removed from his old homestead, and Nathen was probably right. Unfortunately, Billy was leading them to some place from his past, and Adrian had no idea how he would react when they arrived.

There was no path to follow, and to keep up with Billy, Adrian was forced to maneuver around giant redwoods, evergreens, and trees that had either been uprooted during violent storms or had fallen because their time had come.

Adrian was about to ask Billy how much further it was to the cave when Billy abruptly stopped in his tracks. He was giddy with excitement as he pointed to the mountain range that stood high above them. But when Billy turned and saw Adrian, his mood changed, and Billy was no longer excited. At first, he appeared startled, but then fear took over, and Billy covered his ears and started screaming for something to go away.

Adrian didn't know how to react to Billy, but that wasn't his primary concern. He didn't even know which Billy he'd be reacting to. Adrian watched Billy fall to his knees, screaming as if he were in excruciating pain. Adrian snapped the strap for his gun back in place and knelt by Billy. Gently, he placed his right hand on Billy's left arm.

"Billy, it's Adrian. I need you to calm down a little."

Billy kept his hands over his ears and eyes closed. However, he stopped screaming and shaking. Adrian took that as a good sign and moved over so that he would be facing Billy. Adrian was rendered speechless when he gazed upon Billy's face. It was the face of a child that was terrified beyond anyone's imagination. When Billy opened his eyes, Adrian's heart sank, for those were the eyes of a child pleading for help. Adrian placed his hands over Billy's, and with compassion that he never thought he was capable of, he reached out to Billy.

"Why are you scared, Billy?"

"The voices angry. Billy no like."

Adrian knew there was no sense in asking who the voices belonged to. He had to find a more indirect method of calming Billy.

"Well, Billy, tell them to go away. Tell them that your friend Adrian will be angry with them if they continue to bother you."

Billy stared at Adrian as if he were deciding if he could trust him. But he still didn't remove his hands from his ears.

"Adrian help Billy?"

"Yes, of course I will. Tell the voices to go away."

Billy slowly removed his hands, and as he did, he smiled. "Voices gone. Adrian fix voices."

"That's good, Billy." Adrian stood and offered his hand to Billy. "Let's get to your cave before it gets dark."

Billy was happy again, as if nothing had happened. He pointed at the rocks that were in the shape of an eagle. "See, Adrian. Cave is there. Save Amelia. We protect Amelia."

Adrian gazed up at the eagle and was mesmerized by its

beauty. He could see a shadow at the tip of the lower wing. However, if he moved slightly in any direction, the shadow disappeared.

"Wow, Billy! That's incredible."

"We go now. We save Amelia."

"Billy, can I ask you a question?" Billy nodded his head in agreement. "Who or what are we saving Amelia from?"

Billy seemed surprised by the question. "We protect Amelia. We save Amelia. You silly."

"Okay, then, who or what are you protecting Amelia from?"

Billy's expression was dire, and as he leaned closer to Adrian, he scanned the forest as if he expected someone to be listening. Billy leaned closer to Adrian and whispered, "My brother."

Nathen scrutinized his surroundings as he tried to find the best hiding place that would allow him an unencumbered view of the main cabin. He also needed to be close enough to get Dameon's attention without alerting Jax. There were many places where he could conceal himself, but few allowed him the proximity he required. As he navigated the yard, he determined from the sheer number of footprints that Jax and Dameon went either to the back of the cabin or the outhouse.

Nathen followed the footprints behind the cabin and discovered a path leading away from the cabin. At the end of the path was a small open area. To his right, he found several metal drums and to his left was a hand pump obviously used for water. Nathen was going to help himself to the water, but as he approached, he hesitated. The area around the pump was dry, and it wasn't warm enough for the water to evaporate. Nathen knew either Jax or Dameon would become suspicious if he drew water and they discovered the fresh water on the ground.

The forest that surrounded the open area was dense and could easily conceal him. It would also allow him to be close enough to Dameon to get his attention. However, he couldn't see the cabin from where he stood, and there was no guarantee that either Dameon or Jax would need to come back here anytime soon. Nathen had to ensure that at least one of them would have to replenish their water supply, and he had to devise a plan in case that person was Jax.

Amy returned to the cave with a bucket full of fresh water and a bucket that contained two skinned rabbits. She placed the buckets by the fire pit, filled a mug with water, and walked over to Joshawa.

"You must be thirsty. I'm sorry it took so long." Amy passed Joshawa the mug and watched as he gulped down the water.

Joshawa passed the empty mug back to Amy. "Where's your sidekick?"

Amy frowned at Joshawa. "What's a sidekick?"

"A sidekick is someone who's always with you. In your case, I mean Alex."

"That's a silly word. Sidekick. I don't know where Alex is."

Amy returned to the fire pit and started to build a fire to cook the rabbits on. Usually, Alex would take off, and she would think nothing of it, but today was different. Alex was different. He had been behaving oddly, as if he sensed that danger was near. They'd been halfway to the cave when Alex suddenly stopped, sniffed the air, and bolted through the forest. Amy tried to follow him, but he was too fast, and Amy was scared to be alone in the forest.

"So, what's for dinner?"

Amy realized that Joshawa was talking to her, although

she didn't hear what he said. She glanced up at the entrance to the cave, hoping to see that Alex had returned. But Amy saw nothing, and she was afraid for reasons she didn't quite understand. Not so much for herself, but she was afraid for Alex.

Joshawa was speaking again, so Amy focused on him. "I'm sorry. What did you say?"

"I asked what was for dinner."

Amy proudly held up the two skinned rabbits. "They're rabbits."

"I can see that. There's a lot of meat for the two of us. Is some of that for Alex? Is he joining us for supper?"

Amy placed the rabbits back into the pot and once again glanced over to the entrance to the cave. Amy decided to go to the edge of the forest one last time. As she stood in the small clearing, sadness overcame her. The sun was setting, and soon, it would be dark.

Where are you, Alex? Please don't leave me alone. She turned to face Joshawa. "I hope he does."

Nathen had decided that his best opportunity to confront Dameon undetected would be to conceal himself close to the water pump. However, he still needed to be able to see when Dameon and Jax came home, and he had to make sure that they had no choice but to go to the water pump. Nathen returned to the cabin and cautiously made his way over to the door.

He figured he had two or three hours before they returned, but that didn't mean he could be reckless. Nathen opened the door but remained in the doorway as he took stock of Billy's old home. Since there were no windows, the sunlight could only reach what was directly in front of the door. The rest of the cabin was in darkness.

Nathen's eyesight was designed to see what was hidden in the shadows. It was a gift bestowed upon all the members of the Jelani Tribe.

He closely scrutinized the room and was satisfied that any evidence that he and Billy had been there was cleared away. Nathen felt a little more confident as he entered the cabin and made his way toward the back wall where the sink was. He assumed that there would be some sort of vessel for the water, and it would be close to the sink. As he made his way to the back of the cabin, he accidentally bumped into the kitchen table, and to his surprise, he could hear the sound of metal on metal. The table was bare and made of wood, so the clanging sound had to come from something else. Nathen checked the floor to see if he'd knocked something over, but nothing on the floor indicated he had. However, judging from the marks on the floor, it was apparent that he'd moved the table out of place. As he carefully moved the table back to its original position, he heard the clanging sound again. Nathen was curious as to what was causing the sound and was seriously thinking about checking it out. However, the simple fact was that he had to put his plan into action, leaving no time to satisfy his curiosity.

Nathen's assumption proved correct when he found a bucket filled with water on the floor next to the sink. A quick glance around the room assured him that the bucket was the only container they had for water. Nathen took hold of the bucket's handle and was extremely careful not to spill on the floor as he headed outside. Nathen dumped the water in the bush behind the outhouse. Then he dried the outside of the bucket with his sleeve. He then returned the bucket to where he'd found it. Once he felt secure that everything was in place, he left the cabin, taking one last look as he closed the cabin door.

Nathen went behind the cabin, and from the entrance to

the path that led to the water pump, he could see the tree line that Dameon and Jax had taken when they left. There was no reason to believe they would return from any other direction, so Nathen chose that spot to wait for their return. Now, all that was left was to select a place to hide that was close to the water pump. Nathen wanted to find a spot before the men returned so he wouldn't be panicked if they decided to head in his direction as soon as they returned.

Nathen returned to the water pump and selected a giant redwood that was located right behind it. The tree's position would allow him to be behind the person pumping the water. Satisfied with his plan, he started to head back toward the cabin when a flash of metal caught his attention. He could see something nailed to one of the redwoods, and when he approached the tree to check it out, he could feel the anger building inside of him. A set of metal shackles that were rusted with age were nailed to the tree, and attached to the shackles was a four-foot length of rusted chain. Nathen held one of the rusted shackles in the palm of his hand, but it wasn't the shackle that occupied his mind. All he could think of were Billy's scars on his wrists and ankles.

Angrily, he threw the shackle against the tree, and when it collided with the other shackle, it made a clanging noise. Nathen's eyes widened in shock, and without giving it any thought, he took off for the cabin. Once inside, Nathen knelt on one knee and examined underneath the kitchen table, and to his horror, he found a pair of shackles.

Flashes of what Billy must have gone through filled Nathen's mind. From his position on the floor, Nathen had a clear view of the bunk beds. Something under the lower bunk caught Nathen's attention, and as far as he could tell, it was a large briefcase. Did he have time to check it out? Or, the better question was, could he afford not to check it out? The briefcase could contain anything, and its contents could have nothing to do with Joshawa. Nathen's mind was reeling with suspicion. *So why keep it under the bed? If there was nothing to hide, why not keep it where it was easily accessible?*

Nathen threw caution to the wind and went over to the bunk beds. He knelt on the floor and made a mental note of exactly how the case was situated. Carefully, he pulled it out until it was clear. Nathen glanced over his shoulder at the door and realized that the sunlight was fading, which meant that Jax and Dameon would be home soon. Nathen focused on the case and wondered if he should open it. Once again, he glanced at the door, and Nathen realized it was now or never. He opened the case and discovered what appeared to be a mini surveillance apparatus.

Nathen was perplexed as to why they would need surveillance equipment. Did they actually have cameras on the bear? As Nathen studied the blank screen and the multitude of buttons, he realized that if they had cameras on the bear, maybe they'd caught Joshawa on camera, as well. The thought of Joshawa on camera both thrilled Nathen and, at the same time, caused him to panic. Jax was looking for his Bigfoot. If he'd seen Joshawa on one of the cameras, it would've given him the excuse that he needed to hunt Joshawa down. The cabin started to darken, indicating to Nathen that he was out of time. He closed the case and put it back exactly where he found it, and then he went to hide by the entrance to the path and wait for Dameon.

Dameon and Jax had just finished camouflaging their truck. They loaded the last of their supplies in the portable basket stretcher. They'd constructed the stretcher to transport their supplies to remote locations. Dameon had designed the stretcher and was quite proud of the finished product. It was eighty-four inches long, twenty-four inches wide, and could carry all the supplies they would ever need.

The frame was made of hollow steel rods, and the netting that held their supplies was a water-resistant canvas. Dameon had added nylon web strapping to keep everything in place. The entire stretcher could be broken down so they could carry it strapped to the side of their backpacks. They'd chosen to paint the steel a matt black and construct the netting out of a dark brown canvas so it wouldn't be easily spotted. There were handles at either end of the stretcher. Dameon had also fashioned harnesses at either end for heavier loads. The harnesses could be strapped to their bodies to help distribute the weight. Because of the rugged terrain, they used the handles to carry their supplies to the cabin.

By the time they reached the cabin, the sun had already begun its descent into the horizon, basking the cabins in an eerie glow. Dameon had taken the lead for the hike up the mountain, and for the entire time, Dameon had the uneasy feeling that something was up with Jax. Dameon had tried to start a conversation, but Jax would only respond with one-word answers. After several attempts, Dameon had given up and decided that whatever was eating away at Jax was Jax's problem. Dameon was done trying to pacify him and his mood swings.

Dameon gently placed the end of the stretcher on the ground, opened the door, and then helped Jax carry the stretcher into the cabin. Dameon removed his backpack and placed it on the floor beside the bunk beds. He glanced over to Jax, who was unpacking the stretcher.

"Do you want me to do that? It's your turn to cook dinner."

Jax stood and actually smiled at Dameon. "And after I bought you that steak lunch."

"Oh, so you're talking to me now." Even though Dameon's statement was dripping with sarcasm, he tried to make it sound carefree—and given Jax's reaction, he'd succeeded.

Jax grabbed the last box of supplies and walked over to the

kitchen table. He placed the box on the table and then glanced over to Dameon. "Talking to you is a full-time job. Sometimes I just like the quiet."

"Okay, I'll give you that one. How about you start the fire, and I'll cook. But you'll have to get more wood from the woodpile."

"Yes, boss."

"And since you're going anyway, bring in enough wood for tomorrow morning, as well."

Jax left the cabin, giving the impression that he was in a better mood, but it was anyone's guess how long that would last.

CHAPTER TWELVE

Serena continued to stand before Lord Chike, her hands clasped in front of her as she waited for him to address her. But Lord Chike didn't speak—he just stared at her as if he were purposely trying to intimidate her. Serena decided to take the upper hand and start the conversation herself.

"Is there something I can do for you, my Lord?"

Lord Chike didn't respond. Instead, he stepped around her and walked over to the edge of the Realm. Serena turned to face him but remained where she stood. She observed the Lord and was astonished to discover that he didn't seem interested in what Joshawa was doing. He just gazed out into the darkness, and even though Serena couldn't see his face, she could sense that he was calm, almost at peace.

Without turning to face Serena, Lord Chike finally spoke, "Is the darkness not a wondrous sight?"

"No disrespect, my Lord, but I find it cold and unsettling. There's no beauty in the darkness."

Lord Chike turned to face Serena. "Beauty is in the eye of the beholder. And where you see the cold and unsettling, I see the warmth and peace that total darkness offers those who are willing to embrace its beauty."

His words sent shivers down Serena's back, and if she was correct, Lord Chike was describing the Realm of Despair. "Is there anything else, my Lord?"

"Yes. Have Lord Joshawa ready for his host in two days."

"Two days, my Lord? I thought you had given me a week to prepare him." Serena was alarmed by his request, and judging by Lord Chike's reaction, her dismay did not go unnoticed.

"Is there a problem, Serena?"

"Of course not, my Lord. However, he grows stronger with each passing day that he is allowed to heal. The extra time would ensure his ability to take over his host."

Lord Chike walked up to Serena until his face was mere inches from hers. "You have two days. If he is not ready for his host by then, your punishment will be severe."

Lord Chike's tone was harsh, and Serena knew he would carry out his threat. "He will be ready, my Lord."

Lord Adeeowale sat cross-legged on the ground in front of the fire pit. The flames contained within the pit mischievously played with the charred logs. However, their spirited dance was unnoticed by Lord Adeeowale, for his mind was focused on Serena's voice. He rested his hands on his knees, closed his eyes, and then blocked the voices of the jungle so that his mind would be at peace. He was aware that Serena had left his body, but her words remained, and they repeated themselves over and over.

See the memories that have become as one. See past the distortion. Peel back the layers. Find the original memories and relive those memories as if they happened yesterday.

Lord Adeeowale searched his mind for the memories that Serena spoke of. He wasn't sure what she meant about seeing the memories that had become as one. She also spoke of memories that were distorted. He went back in time to a memory when he was given the honor of being Lord of the Lion People. He continued to search his memories, and as the years passed, not one memory seemed out of place. As far as he could tell, none of his memories appeared to be distorted in any way.

He watched the birth of his son, and he continued to watch

as his son turned into a man and became the new Lord of the Lion People. He continued to search his memories, but as he observed other memories, something about his son's ceremony didn't feel right. He went back to that memory and studied it very carefully. The entire village was at the ceremony celebrating their new Lord. Lord Adeeowale watched the memory repeatedly but couldn't figure out what he was missing. Then, he heard Imani's voice announcing that Lord Chike was close. Suddenly, Lord Adeeowale knew what he was looking for. He knew what he had missed. Lord Adeeowale replayed the memory of his son's ceremony, and as he did, he scanned every face. He was sure that Imani was present for his son's ceremony. However, in this memory, she was nowhere in sight. Lord Adeeowale opened his eyes and stared deep into the fire. He would wait for Imani's return and see what she recalled from that day.

Lord Adeeowale reached out to Serena. *I might have discovered something, and if I'm right, I require your unique talents to help uncover the deception.*

It will be my honor, my Lord. Lord Chike has just left, and I would guess he is heading in your direction.

Thank you, Serena. We will continue this conversation very soon.

Yes, my Lord.

Lord Adeeowale took a deep breath and slowly released it. If Lord Chike could erase the fact that Imani was present at the ceremony, then Lord Adeeowale had no way of knowing which memories were real and which had been tampered with.

Dameon had unpacked all the supplies, folded the stretcher, and placed it on one of the large trunks. Jax had already brought in one load of firewood and started the fire, which surprised Dameon. Jax was being helpful, which hadn't been his nature ever since they arrived at the homestead. Dameon knelt in front of the fire and placed the cast iron pot onto the metal frame. When the pot was secured, Dameon leaned back and continued to stare at the flames.

Dameon's thoughts were on Jax, and he had a gut feeling that he needed to start watching his back. It was apparent that Jax wanted to bag their bear at the heaviest weight possible, even if it meant that they could be stranded if the weather didn't cooperate. He also made it quite clear that he wasn't leaving the mountain until he bagged his Bigfoot. As far as Dameon was concerned, the bear was ready to crate, and he had no desire to hunt down whatever was in the journal. Jax needed his help to crate the bear, but other than that, there was no reason for Dameon to stick around. The problem that he was dealing with was that Jax wasn't the same man who'd started this hunt. Dameon feared that Jax's obsession with his Bigfoot was escalating, and the more obsessed Jax was over the creature, the more dangerous he would become.

The sound of Jax pushing the door open startled Dameon, and he quickly stood up and walked over to the kitchen counter. Dameon chuckled to himself as he chose the ingredients for the chili he was making. Obviously, Jax couldn't hear his thoughts. However, if he started to appear skittish around Jax as he just had, then Jax's paranoia would kick in. Dameon grabbed the can opener, and as he opened a can of beans, he imagined Jax in his current state of mind with a healthy dose of paranoia on top of it. Dameon wanted to believe that Jax would never hurt him, but his gut was telling him that Jax was dangerous and their future together wouldn't work well for Dameon.

Jax dropped the armful of wood on the floor and then went to join Dameon.

"Looks like we're having chili. Good choice."

"Of course it is. Why don't you clean up and help me

prepare the ingredients?" Dameon selected a knife to use for chopping vegetables and glanced over to Jax. "It'll save time."

Jax looked at Dameon with what could only be described as contempt. "I don't think so. I got the wood, you're cooking dinner, which was the arrangement. Besides, I have something to do that's more important than babysitting you."

Dameon stood motionless as he stared at Jax. Jax's comment stunned Dameon to the point that he was rendered speechless. He could only watch as Jax glanced down to the floor and back up to him.

"Where's the water?"

Dameon glanced down at the bucket to discover it was empty. Anger toward Jax started to build up in Dameon. "How the hell should I know? I filled it this morning."

"Obviously, you forgot. Fill it. I'm going to check out my cameras."

"First of all, I'm not your servant. And you can bloody well fill the bucket yourself." Dameon slammed the knife down on the counter and then turned to face Jax. "And I don't give a shit about your cameras or your creature. You want dinner, cook it yourself."

Dameon went to step around Jax, but Jax wouldn't move. At first, Jax glared at Dameon, and Dameon was sure Jax was going to hit him. But as they stared at each other, Jax appeared to be calming down. He smiled at Dameon, then, with an open hand, he playfully slapped the side of Dameon's left arm.

"That was fun! I'm going to set up my equipment while you get some more water. Then we can both cook dinner." Jax didn't wait for a response. He just turned around and went to retrieve his surveillance case. Dameon observed Jax as he placed the case on the kitchen table and went about doing his thing. Dameon didn't say a word, but deep down, he was wondering what the hell had just happened. It was as if Jax had two personalities and was bouncing between the two of them. Dameon decided that from here on in, he'd have to be on his guard and watch Jax like a hawk. He also had to be ready to leave at a moment's notice in case Jax went full-out ballistic. Dameon grabbed the handle to the bucket and headed outside.

Joshawa had finished the dinner Amy prepared for him, and as she burned the carcasses, he silently watched her. She'd been unusually quiet during dinner, and he couldn't help but notice that she kept watching the entrance to the cave. Alex hadn't returned, and Joshawa was sure that Amy was worried about him. During dinner, Joshawa had attempted to start a conversation with her in the hope that he could cheer her up. But sadly, each attempt failed, so he decided to leave her alone for a while and then try again.

Joshawa glanced around the cave for no other reason than sheer boredom. He knew every crook and cranny in the cave and could find his way blindfolded if he had to. One of his daily rituals was that after every meal, he would try to move his leg. But each time, the pain would consume him, and even though he didn't want to admit it, deep down, he knew that he wouldn't be walking out of the cave anytime soon.

Joshawa returned his focus to Amy, who was sitting on the ground, watching the entrance to the cave. Joshawa's heart went out to her, and he wished more than anything that he could help her. He wanted her to have what he had. To live her life feeling loved, to have an actual home, and to have people in her life who cared about her. How ironic that everything he wanted Amy to have was what he'd spent the better part of his life resenting.

Joshawa rested his head against the cave wall and closed his eyes. An image of Becca filled his mind. She was smiling at him, and her blonde hair was cascading over her shoulders. Her beautiful blue eyes revealed how much she cared for him. *Becca, I wish you could hear me. I love you with all my heart and soul. I love you, Becca!* Joshawa wasn't expecting a response. He'd only wanted to say the words, even if they were just in his head. Joshawa was about to focus on Amy when an image of his father filled his mind. His father was smiling, and even if Joshawa couldn't hear his father, Joshawa was sure that the words he was speaking were *I love you, son.* Once again, he reached out.

I know you're coming, Father. I'm so sorry for everything. Save me, Father, so I can make amends.

Joshawa's tears filled his eyes, and he silently began to sob.

Serena observed Lord Chike as he disappeared into the jungle. The problem was, he wasn't heading in the direction of Lord Adeeowale's camp. Sadness and fear washed over Serena as if it were a tidal wave. She questioned herself, wondering if she would be strong enough to protect Joshawa.

Serena walked over to the edge of the Realm and observed Joshawa and Amy. The knowledge she had implanted in Amy's mind had saved Joshawa's life, and for that, she was ever so grateful. Now, she had the daunting task of delaying Lord Chike long enough so that she could possibly discover who and what he was. The key to unlocking Lord Chike's treachery was buried in Lord Adeeowale's memories. They needed to discover what the connection was between Lord Adeeowale and the Destroyer. Serena walked over to the edge of the jungle. She closed her eyes and reached out to Imani.

Have you returned, Imani?

Yes. I am with Lord Adeeowale.

What about Lord Chike?

No, he is not here.

I will see if I can find him. If he should return . . .

I will let you know immediately. Be careful, Serena.

Serena immediately transformed into a wisp and headed into the jungle. She had flown to the Gateway, and as she approached, she felt an essence that didn't belong to any spirit that resided in the Realm. Serena landed on a nearby branch and focused on the Gateway. She was trying to understand where this essence was coming from. There was only one way that Serena would be able to recognize the essence, and that would be if it were her own.

Serena left the branch and started to fly in the direction where the essence was most potent. She came across a small clearing at the edge of the Realm, close to where the Gateway was. Kneeling at the edge was a spirit facing out into the emptiness that surrounded the Realm. Serena moved as close as she dared, then hid behind the root of the kapok tree. The spirit was completely encased inside an orb which emitted an unusual iridescent glow. The glow appeared to be alive as it glimmered and moved around the spirit.

Serena felt as though she had an intimate connection to the spirit but couldn't understand why. She tried to meld with the spirit, but the meld failed as if the orb was empty. Serena was so confused. She could see the spirit, but, according to her meld, the spirit didn't exist. Serena was so focused on the spirit that she didn't realize Lord Chike was there until he came up behind the spirit.

Lord Chike stood directly behind the spirit and was raising his hands toward it when he suddenly stopped. Slowly, he turned his head until he was looking in Serena's direction. Serena didn't move, and she prayed that in the sunlight, he wouldn't see the bluish glow that she emitted. Lord Chike paused for only a second, then returned his focus to the spirit that knelt before him. He placed his hands on either side of the spirit's head, and then the glow that surrounded the spirit enveloped him, as well. When the glow reached out to Lord Chike, Serena's mind exploded with visions and sounds.

These visions and sounds frightened her because she had no idea where they were coming from.

Serena was attempting to block the visions and sounds when, above all the noise, she could hear a single voice. The voice was familiar to her, but it was too faint for her to actually know whose voice it was. Lord Chike had blocked Serena's view of the spirit, so she carefully moved to a tree that was at the edge of the Realm. She now had a side view of the spirit, which was not enough to identify it. The voices and sounds in Serena's head started to diminish as if they were traveling away from her. When they were gone entirely, she heard the voice again, only this time she heard Lord Chike's voice as well.

Yes, my Lord. I will do your bidding

See the child that is false.

Yes, my Lord.

Prepare the child for the true Lord.

Yes, my Lord.

Use my strength to reach out to the child.

Yes, my Lord.

Do as I say, and I will reward you. Do as I say, and I will release you from the Realm of Despair.

Yes, my Lord. Shall we start?

Yes, Casandra.

Serena gasped, for she knew that name, and now she knew what spell possessed the young Dava.

Nathen watched Dameon and Jax as they carried their supplies into the cabin. Shortly afterward, Jax came out and retrieved some firewood. When Jax went back into the cabin, Nathen headed down the path to the hiding place at the water pump. He stood behind the tree, hoping and praying that Dameon would be the one to fetch the water. If not, Nathen would have to spend a long, cold night with nothing to keep him warm. He would also need to devise a new plan that might have to include Jax.

It wasn't long before he heard footsteps heading down the path. Nathen moved over slightly so he could see who was approaching, and when he discovered it was Dameon, Nathen felt like a heavy weight had been lifted off his back. Nathen watched as Dameon placed the bucket on the ground underneath the waterspout. Then, when he reached for the pump, Nathen came out behind him.

"Don't move, Dameon, and don't turn around."

Dameon stood still but kept his hand on the pump. "Who are you, and how do you know my name?"

"I'm a father who needs your help. How I know your name is not important."

"Help with what?"

"Help to find my son."

"And how am I supposed to do that?"

"Your partner, Jax, is looking for Bigfoot."

"How do you know that?"

"I also know that you don't share his passion for killing." Nathen could feel the tension building in Dameon. "I'm not here to hurt you or Jax. I need your help to find my son. Your help, not Jax's."

"What makes you think that Jax won't help you?"

"Because I'm the one he's hunting. I'm his Bigfoot."

CHAPTER THIRTEEN

Billy was on a mission that he'd embarked on over twenty years ago. But to Billy, time was fractured, and to him, only days had passed since he'd last been on this trail. He could no longer see the eagle or the entrance to the cave, which meant he was close. The great redwoods and ever-greens of the forest hid the cave from view. They protected Amelia, and they kept her safe.

The sun had begun its descent behind the mountains, and soon, they would be in darkness. But Billy wasn't afraid because he knew he would be at the cave before the sun disappeared and before the animals that hunted at night left their dens. Billy glanced over his shoulder to Adrian.

"Come! Close now!" Billy was so excited at the prospect of seeing Amelia that he couldn't contain his happiness. Like a child in a candy store, he giggled when he spoke, and nothing could erase the smile he wore. "Hurry! Dark soon."

"Billy, I hope you know where you're going."

Billy glanced back and rolled his eyes at Adrian. "Billy knows. Silly Adrian." Billy turned around and picked up the pace as he maneuvered around the trees and underbrush with Adrian close behind him. Billy stopped to get his bearings when Adrian grabbed his arm.

Billy was confused, and he tried to pull his arm back, but Adrian wouldn't let go. Softly, Adrian whispered to him, "Billy, stay perfectly still."

"Billy want to go."

"Shhh! Keep your voice down."

Again, Billy tried to leave, but Adrian pulled him back and turned him so that Billy would be facing him.

Adrian continued to whisper when he spoke to Billy. "I'm not trying to hurt you. There's a bear just ahead of us. You have to be still and quiet."

Billy searched the trees but couldn't find the bear. He looked over at Adrian and whispered, "Billy, no see bear. Billy go now."

Billy tried to leave, but Adrian grabbed the strap to his backpack with his left hand and pulled Billy within inches of his face. Then, with his right hand, he cupped Billy's chin and made him look to his left. Billy saw the bear, and his first thought was how beautiful she was. He watched as the bear emerged from behind an evergreen and stopped not ten feet away from them.

Billy used both his hands to free himself from Adrian's grip. He turned to face the bear, and the joy of reuniting with his bear warmed Billy's heart. "Hi. Billy happy. Billy find you."

Adrian couldn't believe what he was witnessing. It was as if Billy had no fear of the bear. "What are you doing, Billy? That's a grizzly and a freaking big one. He's gonna rip us apart."

"No, she not hurt us."

Adrian's heart was racing, and he was beyond scared. Yet Billy seemed to be perfectly calm. Adrian had no idea what was going on in Billy's head. All Adrian knew was that he had to try to protect him. When Billy tried to get closer to the bear, Adrian grabbed his backpack and pulled Billy back so the two could stand side by side. With his left hand, he held on to Billy's backpack, and with his right hand, he drew his *Ruger* out of its holster. Adrian held the gun down at his side and took a small step back, bringing Billy with him.

Adrian focused on the bear as he spoke to Billy. "Billy, this is not one of your forest friends that you talk to and play with. He's not a rabbit or a squirrel. He's a friggin grizzly, and he's not your friend."

Again, he took a small step back, dragging Billy with him. "We're not going to make any unnecessary noise or moves. He doesn't appear to be threatened by us, so I'm hoping that we can just slowly back away."

Again, Adrian took a small step back, only this time Billy stepped back with him. "Good Billy. If he charges, I'll try to distract him, and if I do, I want you to get the hell out of here as fast as you can. I only have my gun, so if I shoot him, all I'll accomplish is to piss him off. If I can't distract him, I want you to drop to the ground and curl up like a ball. Put your hands at the back of your neck."

Before Adrian could finish his sentence, Billy reached over and grabbed his gun. Adrian watched in disbelief as Billy threw the gun away. "God damn it, Billy! Are you crazy?"

Billy gave Adrian a sour look, then turned and headed toward the bear. Adrian's heart sank. He didn't know what to do. "Billy, please. He'll kill you."

Billy glanced back at Adrian. "Bear not kill Billy. Bear is friend. Bear is a she. Adrian silly. "

Adrian couldn't move. Every muscle in his body just froze. He watched in horror as Billy slowly walked up to the bear. It was then that Adrian noticed that the bear wasn't making any threatening gestures. He just stood there and allowed Billy to approach him.

Billy walked toward the bear without a care in the world. When he was about two feet away, he stopped and smiled at the bear.

"You know Billy. Billy your friend." The bear remained motionless, his dark eyes staring at Billy. "Billy save Amelia. Billy protect Amelia. You help Billy." The bear approached Billy and pushed his snout into Billy's hand. Billy was beyond happy, and as he dropped to his knees, he placed his arms around the bear's neck and buried his face in its fur. Tears started running down Billy's cheeks. "You know me. Billy save you. Billy love you." Billy leaned back and placed his hands on either side of the bear's face. "We go now. We save Amelia." Billy stood up, wiped the tears from his face, and then called to Adrian. "We go now. We follow her."

Dameon's eyes almost popped out of his head as if he'd just witnessed a ghost hovering before him. His mind was racing as he attempted to process the fact that Jax's Bigfoot actually existed. Then, the reality of the situation hit Dameon as if someone had punched him in the stomach. Jax's Bigfoot was a man, not an animal, and Dameon had a moral obligation to protect him. He knew what Jax would do to this person, and none of it sat right with Dameon.

"Can I turn around? I already know what you look like."

"I was told that there was a drawing of me."

"That's right. Look, we don't have much time before Jax starts wondering what I'm up to. I'm gonna start pumping the water for the bucket. If you want my help, then stand in front of the pump so I can hear you and see you."

Dameon only had to wait for a couple of seconds before the man came out of hiding. Dameon was astounded by the man who stood before him. He'd been sure that Jax was wrong and that the drawing was the imagination of a man who spent too much time alone in the woods. But here he was, in the flesh. A living, breathing Bigfoot. He had many questions to ask, but they would have to wait. Dameon started pumping the water, focusing on the bucket and not the man.

"You know my name. What's yours?"

"It's Nathen."

"What do you want with me?"

"I need your GPS to find my son."

Dameon stopped pumping and glanced up at Nathen. "The GPS? How is that gonna help you?"

"It's a long story that I'll explain tomorrow, and as you pointed out, we don't have much time. There's only one question you need to answer. Will you help me find my son and not involve your friend?"

Dameon finished pumping the water and then grabbed the handle of the bucket. "Actually, that's two questions, and the answer is yes to both. I have to go before Jax decides to come looking for me. Meet me behind the smaller cabin tomorrow morning at six. I'll bring the GPS, and then you can tell me how my GPS and I can help you."

"My wife tells me that I can trust you, so I will. Tomorrow at six. I'll be there."

Dameon quickly glanced over to the path to make sure Jax wasn't approaching. When he turned to speak with Nathen, he was gone. Dameon scanned the area, but he could see no signs of Nathen. He couldn't believe what had just transpired. A conversation with an actual Bigfoot. Dameon gently shook his head. This person was a man, not an animal or a creature. He started down the path to the cabin, knowing that by helping Nathen, his friendship with Jax would be coming to an end.

Nathen disappeared into the forest but only went as far as the small cabin. From there, he could see the bigger cabin, which enabled him to keep an eye on Dameon and Jax. His first thought was to climb one of the larger trees and wait there.

Unfortunately, he had nothing to secure himself to the tree if he fell asleep. Nathen glanced up at the massive redwoods that surrounded him. He realized that if he fell from any one of these trees, he would probably incur injuries similar to the injuries Joshawa had suffered. Instead, he found a spot underneath a redwood where he could be reasonably comfortable for the night. Nathen sat on the ground at the tree's base, rested his back against the tree trunk, and then reached out to Authia.

How are you, my love?

I'm doing as well as can be expected. How about you? How's your plan going? Do you have the GPS?

Nathen smiled as he chuckled. *Serena was right. You are full of questions. I'm doing well. As far as my plan goes, I was able to speak with Dameon. He's gonna help us and keep Jax out of the loop. I'm meeting him and the GPS here at six in the morning.*

So you're not coming home?

No, I'm staying here. I don't want to put any distance between myself and the GPS.

Is it cold? Are you gonna be all right?

Nathen gazed up at the darkened sky and took in the beauty that shimmered above him. *I'm gonna be fine, my love. Do you know what I'm doing right now?* Nathen wasn't seeking an answer — his comment was more of a statement. *I'm looking up at the sky. And now that the sun has set, the sky is dark and ominous. But no matter how dark the sky becomes, thousands upon thousands of stars will eliminate the darkness. They come to us every night, and they help us find our way in the dark. They are the beacons that give us the courage to face the unknown.*

Nathen closed his eyes and envisioned his son. *Joshawa is in a dark place, but I will find him. I'll be his star and light up the darkness.*

You're gonna make me cry. I love you so much.

I love you, too. How's Billy?

I don't know. They're not back yet.

Nathen's heart felt like it had sunk to the pit of his stomach. He leaned away from the tree and sought out the grave site. From his vantage point, he could see the clearing. For a second, he thought that maybe Billy had come back, but there was no one there.

They should have been back before nightfall.

Well, you know Billy. He's on his own time schedule. I'm sure he had to talk to every animal he saw. Adrian knows the woods, and if he had to, he'd find shelter for the night. I'm sure they're okay. And I promise to let you know the minute they get here.

You're right, my Love. I have nothing to worry about. Get some sleep, and I'll talk to you in the morning.

Nathen turned his attention to the larger cabin. He had every right to be worried. Authia hadn't witnessed what happened between Billy and Adrian. Nathen leaned back against the tree, closed his eyes, and prayed that Billy and Adrian were safe.

CHAPTER FOURTEEN

A drian searched for his revolver while Billy hugged his bear. Adrian could hear Billy repeatedly telling the bear how much he loved him. The connection Billy had with the forest animals was always disturbing. However, what Adrian was witnessing now bordered on psychotic.

Ten minutes later, Adrian located his gun and placed it in his holster.

Adrian was becoming a little concerned about locating Billy's cave before dark. The last rays of sunlight were slowly sinking into the horizon, and from what Adrian could tell, there wasn't a cave anywhere close by. The shadow Billy had pointed out earlier was either just a shadow or the cave was a lot further away than it appeared. None of his concerns mattered because Adrian had already passed the point of no return. All he could do now was follow Billy, who was following the bear, and hope that some sort of shelter would present itself. As they trekked through the woods, Billy kept turning around to look at Adrian. Billy wouldn't say anything—he would only grin from ear-to-ear and nod his head in excitement.

The darkness of the night was starting to work its way through the forest, leaving a chill in the air that felt cool on Adrian's skin. If someone had told him that he would be following Billy and his friend the bear blindly into the forest and doing so in the dark, he would've told them that they were crazy. But here he was, doing just that. Adrian picked up the pace and caught up with Billy.

"This cave of yours, is it showing up anytime soon?"

Billy turned to face Adrian and smiled while he nodded his head. "Yes, soon."

"How soon? You do realize that in about five minutes, we're gonna be in pitch darkness."

"Billy know. We good."

"I'm glad you know, but I don't suppose you can give me an idea? Are we minutes away, hours away?"

Billy didn't turn to face Adrian this time. He just focused on the bear. "Bear fast. We be there soon."

"Fast, my ass. He's the slowest grizzly I've ever seen."

Either Billy didn't hear Adrian's comment, or he chose to ignore him. A few minutes later, Adrian could hear wolves howling in the distance. He was about to point that out to Billy when they emerged from the forest onto a very narrow but well-traveled path.

"Finally! So, does this path take us to the cave? The howling we just heard tells me there's a den of wolves nearby. We really need to get to the cave."

Adrian glanced over to Billy, who was looking down at the path and slowly shaking his head. Billy was no longer smiling . . . he was scared.

"Not good. Path not good."

"What's wrong, Billy? Is this not the right path, or are you scared of the wolves?"

Billy pointed to the path that headed deeper into the forest. "Cave this way. Wolves not hurt us. Path not good. Amelia not safe."

Adrian was about to question Billy, but the bear started making its way down the path with Billy right behind him. They'd only taken a dozen steps when the path veered slightly to the north. Adrian couldn't believe his own eyes. Straight ahead of them was a cave, and from where he stood, the cave was lit up like a beacon.

Serena flew back to the Ancestor's camp as fast as she could. When she arrived, she flew over to the fire pit and took her human form. Lord Adeeowale and Imani were sitting side by side and appeared pleased to see Serena. However, Serena was scared and confused, and those emotions were so strong they hung over the Ancestors like a heavy veil. Lord Adeeowale and Imani's expressions went from happiness to that of concern.

Serena sat on the ground across from Lord Adeeowale and Imani. "Do either of you know of Priestess Casandra? At one time, she was a High Priestess."

Lord Adeeowale was the first to respond. "Yes, we both know of her. Why do you ask?"

"Is there any reason why her spirit would have been condemned to the Realm of Despair?" Serena could tell that both Ancestors were very confused.

Lord Adeeowale quickly checked the camp and then turned to Serena. "Is it safe to speak out loud?"

"Yes, my Lord. I am certain of it."

"Priestess Casandra's spirit was taken to the Land of the Spirits. I know that to be true."

"So she was not judged on her past indiscretions?"

"Her actions while she was High Priestess would have condemned her to the Realm of Despair. However, when Lord Nathen took his rightful place, he forgave her. From that day and to the time of her death, she remained loyal to her Lord."

Imani interjected, "Why do you ask about Priestess Casandra? Did you find Lord Chike?"

"Yes, I did. While I was a wisp, I discovered a small clearing at the edge of our Realm, very close to the Gateway. There was a spirit kneeling on the outer edge, and surrounding the spirit was some sort of orb. I have never seen such an orb before. It completely encased the spirit and kept moving around her as if it were alive."

Imani continued the conversation. "And you believe that this spirit is Priestess Cassandra?"

"I know it is. You both are aware that when my spirit was sent to help Lord Nathen against my mother, Priestess Cassandra was my vessel."

Lord Adeeowale slightly nodded his head in agreement. "Yes, we are aware."

"I recognized the essence contained within the spirit because a portion of it was mine. I told you that Lord Chike had cursed Dava. I was wrong. It was Priestess Cassandra who placed the curse. However, I believe she has been threatened to do so just as I was."

It was obvious that Serena's discovery concerned Imani. However, Lord Adeeowale seemed to be miles away. Imani glanced over to Lord Adeeowale, then returned her focus to Serena.

"Were you able to speak with her?"

"No, I could not penetrate the orb. But somehow, I was able to hear what was being said. Lord Chike came up behind her and placed his hands on either side of her head. The second his hands touched Casandra, the orb grew and encased both of them. He told her that she would return to the Realm of Despair if she did not do what he asked of her. And she agreed."

Serena focused on Lord Adeeowale. His eyes stared straight at her, but they appeared as though they saw nothing at all. "My Lord, are you all right?"

Lord Adeeowale glanced down at the ground and then back up at Serena. "This orb that you speak of. I believe that I have seen it before, but I cannot recall as to when or where I saw it."

"Perhaps it is one of your missing memories. You

mentioned that there was a memory that you needed my help with. What did you discover?"

Lord Adeeowale looked at Imani. "Do you recall the ceremony when my son became Lord?"

Imani smiled lovingly at Lord Adeeowale. She placed her hand over his and gave his hand a gentle squeeze. "Yes, of course I do. It was a wondrous event."

Lord Adeeowale turned to Serena. "My memory of the event did not include Imani."

"Do you have any memories of Imani after the ceremony?"

Lord Adeeowale paused for a moment, then gently shook his head. "No, I have no memory of her after the ceremony."

Imani glanced over to Serena and then back to Lord Adeeowale. The expression on Imani's face was that of a person who had lost someone very dear to her. "You have no memory of me at all? Not even the memory of my death?"

Lord Adeeowale cupped Imani's chin and tenderly smiled at her. "Of course I do. You died protecting your Lord. You died protecting me."

Serena watched as Imani's expression changed to that of sorrow. Imani took Lord Adeeowale's hand in hers and slowly shook her head. "Yes, I died saving my Lord. But you were not that Lord. I died protecting Lord Manson, your son."

Dameon entered the cabin carrying the bucket of water. He glanced over at Jax, who was preoccupied with watching the recordings from the cameras. Dameon walked over to the kitchen counter and placed the bucket of water on the floor. Then he picked up a knife and started cutting up the vegetables. He was debating whether he should remind Jax that he'd offered to help make dinner. Dameon glanced over his shoulder at Jax. He didn't appear to have noticed how much time Dameon took to get water, so Dameon decided to let sleeping dogs lie and cook the dinner himself.

While they ate their dinner, Jax never took his eyes off the recordings and didn't engage in conversation. When they were finished, Dameon stood up and started to gather the plates.

"Don't worry, I'll do the dishes." Dameon didn't hide the fact that his comment was dripping with sarcasm.

"Thanks. I have a lot to go through."

Dameon rolled his eyes at Jax and piled the dishes on the counter. There was some chili left in the cast iron pot, and as Dameon scooped it out onto a plate, his thoughts were on Nathen. Dameon went to his bunk and grabbed the blanket that was under his sleeping bag. He folded it up and draped it over his arm. At the same time, he kept watch on Jax, who didn't seem to notice anything Dameon was doing. Dameon piled all the dirty dishes into the cast iron pot and then carefully placed the plate for Nathen on top. He grabbed the lantern located next to the bunk beds and headed for the door.

"I'm heading to the pump to clean the dishes."

Jax didn't reply, so Dameon dialed it up a bit. "Hey, earth to Jax."

Jax pushed a button on the console and looked over at Dameon. "I heard you the first time. Do you want me to hold your hand?"

Dameon frowned at Jax. "Unbelievable." Dameon left the cabin and headed toward the pump.

Amy continued her vigil at the entrance of the cave. She was sitting on the ground with her legs drawn close to her body and with her arms wrapped around her legs. Amy stared into the darkness that had engulfed the forest, and still, Alex hadn't returned. Her black sweater was not sufficient to keep her warm, and the cool night air sent shivers up and down her tiny body. Amy paid no attention to her own discomfort because all she could think about was Alex. He had never been away from the cave for this long, and Amy was terrified that he might be hurt. Alex was always there to protect her, and now he may need her help, but she had no idea how to find him.

Amy wiped the tears off her cheeks with her right hand, which was a fruitless endeavor because no matter how many times she wiped her face, the tears kept coming. The night belonged to the wolves, and it wasn't until they started to howl that Amy realized how late it was. She glanced over her shoulder and discovered that the fire had gone out. Joshawa was rubbing his arms in an obvious attempt to keep warm. The survival instinct kicked in, and Amy rushed to the back of the cave to collect more firewood. She dropped it next to the pit and then returned to the back of the cave. This time, Amy retrieved a couple of the blankets she'd used to make Joshawa's tent. She went over to Joshawa and handed him the blankets.

"I'm sorry. I didn't see that the fire had gone out."

"That's okay, Amy. It's all good, and thank you for the blankets."

Amy started to sob as she tried to speak, "No, it's not. The wolves will come if there's no fire. I know better." Again, she wiped her face with the back of her right hand.

"Amy, it's okay. The wolves aren't here now. You have plenty of time to start a fire."

Amy glanced over to the cave's entrance and then looked back at Joshawa. "I'm afraid for Alex."

"I know. I'm worried, too. But Alex is smart, and I'm sure he's okay. One thing is for certain, he would want you to keep yourself safe."

Amy nodded her head in agreement. "Yes, he would." She walked over to the fire pit and, within minutes, had a fire going. Then she started another fire close to Joshawa so he could keep warm. Amy surveyed the cave, and with the two fires ablaze, the entire cave was lit up. She sat by Joshawa's fire and smiled. "No wolves will come here. Alex will be happy."

Dameon had left the cabin and headed for the water pump. He was sure Nathen was watching, and he hoped he would come out of hiding. Dameon placed the pot of dirty dishes underneath the waterspout. He took out Nathen's plate and placed it on the ground. Dameon was about to start filling the pot with water when he heard Nathen's voice coming from behind him.

"Are you alone?"

"Yes. You can come out."

Dameon started pumping the water into the pot, hoping that the mundane gesture would keep Nathen at ease. Dameon smiled when Nathen came out of the woods and stood beside the pump. Dameon knew then that Nathen trusted him.

"I want to thank you for helping me. My son has been missing for days, and I have no idea where I should start looking."

Dameon stopped pumping water into the pot. He picked up the plate that was lying on the ground and handed it to Nathen. Then he reached into the pot and retrieved a fork. He wiped the tines of the fork against his pants, then handed it to Nathen.

"I thought you might be hungry. I also brought you a blanket. It's not much, but it should help keep you warm."

Nathen was overwhelmed by Dameon's generosity and his compassion. "Thank you. I appreciate your help. However, I do have one more question for you. You haven't asked me what's in it for you."

"I capture animals for money. I won't lie about that, but you're not an animal, and I have an obligation to protect you and your son. Especially if he looks like you."

"An obligation?"

"Jax has a journal with a lot of information on you and what its author wanted to do to you. Judging from the smaller cabin, it wouldn't be pleasant. Jax also has cameras set up at your home to monitor your yard."

Fear enveloped Nathen, though not for himself, but for his family. "Cameras!"

"Yes. And I'm not very proud of this, but I helped him set them up. Are there any others that resemble you and your son?"

"No, just the two of us. When did you set the cameras up?"

"Right after we met your family. Look, Nathen, I can promise you that your family isn't in any danger. I know your wife said you can trust me, and she's right. Jax has changed. He isn't the same person I started hunting with when we were kids. He's going down a path that I can't, I won't, follow. I made a deal with Jax that if we caught you, we would decide at that time if you were a man or an animal."

"Does the picture of me resemble what I look like?"

"It's close. I'd say some of your facial features were exaggerated."

Nathen was stunned, and he didn't know what to say. Jax and Dameon had seen a picture of him and decided to hunt him down as if he were an animal. "Wouldn't you say that I resemble a man and not an animal?"

"To be honest, yes, you do resemble a man. But you have to agree, and no offense, you also resemble what we consider a Bigfoot would look like."

There had been a time when Nathen considered himself

more animal than man. That was a long time ago. However, to hear Dameon decide if he were a man or animal brought all the pain from the past to the surface. "So, what did you and Jax agree on?"

"If you were an animal, then Jax could do whatever he wanted. Which, in itself, is pretty disturbing. However, if you were a man, then Jax would have to go through me to get you."

"You would risk your life and your friendship with Jax for me and for my son?"

"No, not for you. I would do it for Jax. Look, he may be an asshole, but I grew up with him. I'd like to hope there's some part of the original Jax still locked away inside of him. If there is, I'll be able to reason with him. If not, then there won't be a friendship to save, and it won't be just your life I'll be protecting."

CHAPTER FIFTEEN

Jax had been sitting at the kitchen table for hours reviewing the recordings from the four cameras. He watched the people he'd met at the cabin leave the area and return hours later. Unfortunately, there was no sign of his Bigfoot. He turned the screens off, sat back in his chair, and folded his arms across his chest. Jax sat for several minutes staring at the blank screens while he calculated what his next move would be. He was optimistic that Bigfoot existed, and he had no doubt that Dameon was up to something.

When Dameon returned with the dishes, he'd announced that he was going to bed and getting up early to check on their bear. Jax had acted as though he didn't care, and Dameon didn't seem alarmed by his lack of interest. Jax glanced over to the bunk beds where Dameon was asleep and then back at his surveillance equipment. Jax stood and moved to the chair so that it was facing the bunk beds. Then, he moved the equipment so that the screens were facing him. That way, if Dameon woke up, he wouldn't see what Jax was working on.

Jax pulled his chair closer to the table and moved the case a little further away from him. Then he removed the keyboard from the case and started typing in codes that only he knew, and as he did, one of the screens lit up and started displaying time stamps.

Dameon might have thought that Jax was too preoccupied to care about what he was doing, and he'd have been right. Jax's priorities were the recordings from the cameras. However, there was something else that Jax was very interested in, and that was how much time Dameon had taken to fetch water. As he read the timestamps, he smiled and whispered to himself. "So, my friend. You took a long time to fetch water. I wonder what you're up to?"

Jax was fixated on his Bigfoot, and he was sure Dameon knew more than he was saying. Jax switched off the screen and placed the keyboard back in its case. He'd come to terms with the possibility that when this was all over, he would have to kill Dameon. Now, as far as he was concerned, he had proof that Dameon was up to something. Jax had allowed his Bigfoot to take over all rational thought. He'd allowed his paranoia to rule all his decisions. His thirst for the perfect kill overruled his friendship, and now Dameon was nothing more than an obstacle.

Jax stood and was about to close the case when he had an idea on how to keep tabs on Dameon. Jax was confident that Dameon wouldn't want, or for that matter ask for, his company to check on the bear. Jax lifted the keyboard from the case and removed the black felt-lined base, which revealed a secret compartment. Dameon had no idea that this compartment existed, and now Jax felt vindicated that he'd installed it without Dameon's knowledge.

Jax removed a small device, which was about the size of a cell phone, and placed it on the table. Then he removed a tracking chip that was no bigger than his fingernail on his pinky. He placed the chip on the felt liner, turned on the device, and scanned the chip. The small screen on the device lit up, and as Jax moved the device, the screen revealed where the chip was located in relation to the device. It had a range of one mile, which would suffice for Jax's plan.

The problem was, where to hide it? Jax had to think of something Dameon would definitely take with him. He also had to find someplace to hide the chip where Dameon wouldn't notice. Jax glanced at the GPS case that Dameon had placed beside his backpack. Of course, he would take the GPS to track the bear. Jax quietly walked over to the bunkbeds, took the GPS case, and then placed it on the kitchen table. With his back to the bunk beds, he opened the case and removed the GPS. Jax turned it over and removed the battery cover and the battery. Carefully, he placed the chip so that the battery would conceal it. Then he put the battery back in place and put the cover over the battery. Jax put the GPS back in its case and then placed the case exactly where he'd found it.

Jax closed the surveillance case and put it back under his bunk. He was excited beyond measure at the prospect of following his friend without his knowledge. Maybe Dameon was up to something, or perhaps he wasn't. All that mattered was that Jax believed he was. A wicked smile crossed his lips, for he was excited at the knowledge that tomorrow would be his first time hunting a human.

Adrian had to admit that he was surprised they'd located the cave. He was also relieved that they'd found shelter for the night. Adrian quickened his pace, and when he was just a few feet from the bear, the bear took off. Adrian watched as the bear ran toward the cave, and he didn't stop until he reached the entrance.

Adrian frowned as he called out to the bear. "So now you hurry."

Adrian was about to make another snide comment when he heard a scream originating from inside the cave. Before he could draw his gun, a young girl ran out of the cave and threw her arms around the bear's neck. Adrian just stood there, completely stunned by what he just witnessed. He removed his gun from its holster but kept it at his side while he cautiously approached the cave.

Billy had reached the cave first, and when he did, he looked at the young girl and then turned to face Adrian.

"Not Amelia." He turned to face the girl. "Where is Amelia? Who are you? Billy not know you."

Adrian could tell that Billy was devastated. His face and his eyes revealed how much emotional pain he was in. Adrian started to approach Billy to find out what was going on when a familiar voice called out.

"Billy, what are you doing here? Is my father with you?" Billy turned to look inside the cave, then a big smile crossed his lips.

He ran inside the cave, shouting with glee. "Joshawa! Billy find Joshawa!"

Adrian stood still with his mouth gaped open, totally confused by what was happening right before him. The girl Billy was looking for wasn't here, but by the sounds of it, Joshawa was. And how was it that both Billy and the girl could hug a grizzly?

Adrian walked over to the cave, keeping a wide berth between him and the bear. When he looked inside, Adrian couldn't believe what he found. Joshawa was sitting on the ground only twenty feet away from him. There was a small fire next to him, and Billy was sitting on the ground next to the fire. He was rocking back and forth, staring at the ground, and as he continued to rock, he muttered what sounded like the exact three or four words over and over.

Adrian then focused on Joshawa. "Your dad said you'd be in a cave. Looks like he was right." Adrian took pleasure in Joshawa's stunned appearance.

"Adrian? What the hell are you doing here, and where's my father?"

Adrian walked over to Joshawa and quickly took stock of his injuries. He didn't appear to be at death's door, so Adrian decided to ask his own questions. "Okay, we'll come back to that. The main question is, who's that girl, and why is the bear not tearing us apart?"

"Bear's name is Alex, and he won't hurt you unless you try to hurt Amy."

Adrian showed Joshawa his *Ruger*. "Do I need this?" Adrian glanced over his shoulder at the bear, then returned his focus to Joshawa. "Not that it would help."

"It wouldn't, so put it away."

Adrian holstered his gun and looked back at Joshawa. "So you're telling me that this little girl has a bear . . . actually, let me take that back . . . she has a grizzly for a pet, and she named him Alex?"

"Pretty much. Now, how about my question?"

"Mind if I sit?"

Joshawa motioned to a place by the fire. "Don't get me wrong. I'm grateful that someone's finally found me. But if I were to make a list of all the people in the entire world who would come to rescue me, you would be at the very bottom of that list. Actually, I take that back. You wouldn't even be on the list. So, Adrian, why are you here?"

Serena, Lord Adeeowale, and Imani sat by the fire in silence. Serena closed her eyes and tried to make sense of all the information she had received. She knew that Imani had died saving a Lord. Both Imani and Lord Adeeowale remembered the same fact. However, the issue was that they disagreed as to which Lord was saved. Lord Adeeowale's memories were compromised, and there was no way to know how long it would take to reach his true memories.

Serena opened her eyes and focused on Imani. "Imani, do you recall the events leading up to the battle and the battle itself?"

"I can only speak of the events leading up to the battle. I died before the battle began."

"Can you tell us what happened? I need to know every detail, no matter how small."

Imani glanced over to Lord Adeeowale and then back to Serena. Serena could sense that Imani was upset. However, she didn't know if it was because she had to relive her death or because many of Lord Adeeowale's memories didn't include her. Serena folded her hands in her lap and patiently waited for Imani to begin.

Imani stared out into the jungle and imagined herself when she was alive and living among her people. "The tribe was at peace as it had been for as long as I can remember. Massai was Lord." Imani turned to look at Lord Adeeowale. "And you were his protector." She immediately regretted revealing that fact because she knew he would be ashamed. It was his responsibility to protect Massai, even if he had to forfeit his life to do so. Unfortunately, it was not his life that was given. Imani looked over to Serena and continued recounting that day's events. "The entire tribe was in the Gathering Hut, and Lord Massai was revealing to us that the entrance to our world was being protected. He was standing on the platform with Lord Adeeowale on his right side and two other warriors standing close to Lord Massai. I stood on the ground, close to the platform, looking up at..." Imani hesitated as she glanced over to Lord Adeeowale. She felt shame and sadness for what she was about to admit. The shame prevented her from making eye contact with Lord Adeeowale, and the sadness was evident in the tone of her voice.

"My eyes were on Lord Adeeowale when they should have been on Lord Massai. It was not my place."

Lord Adeeowale smiled as he took her hands into his. He lifted her hands to his lips and tenderly kissed her fingers. "And I am certain that my eyes would have been on you when they should have been on my son."

The show of affection would normally please Imani, but all she heard was the fact that Lord Adeeowale had no memory of her. His words overshadowed any happiness she felt by his actions.

Imani placed her hands in her lap as she tried to hold back her tears. She wouldn't look directly at Lord Adeeowale because she knew she would have no control over her emotions if she did. "It is regrettable that you do not remember that day."

Imani could feel Lord Adeeowale's hand on her arm. "I remember the many times I stood on the platform next to my son. However, I do not recall an attempt on his life." Lord Adeeowale became quiet, and it appeared as if he were trying to remember something. "I am sorry, Imani, but my memories after my son's birth do not include you."

Imani felt as though someone had just ripped her heart out of her body. She posed her question to Serena. "Is this Lord Chike's doing?"

"I believe so. For whatever reason, Lord Chike does not want Lord Adeeowale to remember the true events of that day or any day after. And he has gone to great extents to make that happen. Please continue."

Imani took a deep breath and then slowly let it out. She straightened her back and then continued her story. "I remember there was a discussion, but I was not listening. I was watching the warrior that stood behind Lord Massai. The warrior's body had started to spasm. It would not have been obvious if you were not paying attention. But I was looking at Lord Adeeowale, and from where I stood, I could clearly see the warrior."

The fear she had felt that day washed over her like a tidal wave. She could hear the shouts and feel the panic rise inside her until she almost choked on it. Lord Adeeowale placed his right arm around her shoulders, and with his left hand, he cupped her chin and gently turned her face.

"You have nothing to fear. I am here with you, and I will not allow anything or anyone to hurt you." He leaned in and tenderly kissed her. Then he smiled at her, and in that smile, she found her courage.

Imani closed her eyes and focused on the warrior. "The spasms became more evident but only lasted for a few seconds, and then they stopped. The warrior turned and looked directly at me with eyes that were as black as night." Imani opened her eyes and focused on Serena. "He smiled at me, but it was not a smile of tenderness. He appeared to be mocking me as if he were daring me to stop him. It was then that I saw the machete in his hand. He no longer watched me. He had turned his attention to Lord Massai. I have never seen so much hatred or so much anger as I did that day. I remember shouting and looking at Lord Adeeowale. Then I remember jumping onto the platform and feeling the pain as the machete sliced through my body." Imani knew there was something else that happened just before she died. She played the scene repeatedly in her mind, but whatever she had witnessed was now lost in her memories.

Chapter Sixteen

A uthia sat curled up in her favorite chair with a patchwork quilt wrapped around her. She stared at the fire that playfully danced in amongst the logs in the fireplace. Authia had left the light that hung over the kitchen table on but turned the remainder of the lights off. The cabin had a feeling of serenity and calm. Usually, Authia loved the ambiance, but tonight, she was frightened, and all the ambiance in the world wouldn't calm her.

Billy and Adrian still hadn't returned, and although she'd told Nathen not to worry, Authia was frightened for the two boys. Nathen was at the Jenkins homestead alone and in the cold. Authia knew that Nathen could take care of himself in most situations. But if Billy and Adrian didn't find shelter for the night, then they would be exposed to the cold. However, that wasn't what worried Authia. Being cold was one thing, but what Authia feared the most was that they would be easy prey to the wolves that roamed at night. Authia's thoughts then turned to Joshawa, and she prayed that he would survive long enough for Nathen to find him and bring him home.

"Aunty?"

Authia glanced over to the loveseat to find Becca awake. She was still under her blanket, and her head rested on her pillow. Her long blonde hair had fallen over her left shoulder, and the light given off by the fire made her hair shimmer as if it were made of gold.

"You should be asleep, Becca."

"You should be asleep, too, Aunty. Why are you still

awake?"

Authia sighed as she turned her focus on the fire. "I'm worried, and I guess I'm hoping that Billy and Adrian will walk through our door and complain that they're hungry." Authia didn't know if she should cry or laugh. All her emotions were entangled with each other, and Authia had no idea how to separate them.

"You shouldn't worry about them. Adrian knows the woods, and he knows how to make a shelter if they need one. And he can trap. Knowing Adrian, he won't try to find his way home in the dark. He'll wait till daylight."

Authia glanced at Becca and smiled. "You know a lot about Adrian."

Becca returned the smile. "Adrian may be an ass, especially toward Joshawa. But he respects the forest, and he wouldn't put Billy in danger."

"If you have faith in Adrian, then so will I. Why are you awake?"

"I had a dream, and it woke me up."

"A nightmare?"

Becca moved so she could lie on her side facing the fireplace. She brought her arms close to her chest and placed her hands by her face, palms together. She then placed her cheek on her hands and stared into the fire. "No. I dreamed of Joshawa. I dreamed that he was in a cave, and I was with him. We were sitting with our backs against the wall of the cave, and there was a fire keeping us warm. I dreamed that he told me that he loved me."

Authia was fighting to keep the tears from flowing down her cheeks. "That's a good dream."

"Yes, it is. Good night, Auntie." Becca closed her eyes, and for the next hour, Authia watched her as she slept.

Amy was so excited that Alex had returned. When she saw him, she squealed with delight and ran up to him, throwing her arms around his neck. "I was so worried about you. I thought you were hurt." Amy pulled away from Alex, knelt in front of him, then placed her hands on either side of his snout. She looked directly into his eyes and frowned at him. "Where did you go? You scared me. Don't do that again."

Amy was so focused on Alex that she didn't hear the man approaching her until he was standing right next to her. Amy let go of Alex and slowly stood, not taking her eyes off the man. He was talking fast and not making any sense. He wanted to know where Amelia was, and then he ran past her, shouting Joshawa's name. Amy instinctively moved so Alex's head was between her and the man. Then another man came, and even though he wouldn't take his eyes off her, he still steered away from her, and he too seemed surprised to find Joshawa.

Amy leaned close to Alex's ear and whispered so no one else could hear her. "Who are these men? They're in our home. Why are you not protecting our home?"

Alex gently rubbed his head against Amy, and then he ambled into the cave toward Joshawa. When the second man noticed Alex was approaching him, he jumped to his feet and backed away. However, the first man smiled at Alex, and when Alex reached him, the man showed no fear.

Alex allowed the man to stroke the top of his head. Amy was so confused, and she was scared. She scanned the cave to find everyone looking at her. Amy didn't know what to do. There were too many people in her home, and she wanted them all to go away.

Serena was in awe of Imani's rendition of the day she forfeited her life for that of her Lord. It was one thing to know what happened, but to hear the actual events as they unfolded, moment by moment, was empowering. Imani deserved the honor of being an Ancestor and so much more.

"I hope that reliving that day did not overwhelm you."

"I am fine and welcome any questions you may have."

Serena smiled at Imani like a mother would smile at her child. "I think we can all agree that what you witnessed was the Destroyer taking possession of the warrior." Both Imani and Lord Adeeowale nodded their head in agreement. "The question is why?"

Serena directed her attention to Imani. "Are you sure that Lord Manas ruled in a manner that would please our Ancestors?"

"Yes. He ruled our tribe as any other great Lord has done in the past."

Serena went over the events of that fateful day and dissected every moment. The tribe was in the Gathering Hut. Lord Manas was explaining how the entrance to our world was being protected. Serena stopped and thought of what she had just said. The entrance was being protected? Serena knew there was a village of people, outsiders, living on the other side of the falls. These outsiders were the only ones she knew of who were protecting the entrance to their valley. So the question was, who was Lord Manas referring to?

"Imani, why did Lord Manas feel the need to tell the tribe that the entrance to our world was being protected?"

Imani appeared puzzled by Serena's question. "I do not understand. Any decision that affects the entire tribe must be accepted by the entire tribe. It is our way, it is our law, and it has been since the birth of the Jelani Tribe."

"I am aware of that. Let me ask you this. How was the entrance being protected?"

"There was a tribe of outsiders that lived on the other side of the falls. They swore an oath to protect and conceal the entrance to our world."

"Yes, I know of them. They have been protecting the entrance long before Lord Manas."

Serena noticed that both Lord Adeeowale and Imani appeared confused. Lord Adeeowale looked at Imani, who only shrugged her shoulders. Lord Adeeowale then turned his attention to Serena.

"We are unaware of any outsiders protecting our valley before Lord Manas."

Serena was perplexed by Lord Adeeowale's admission. "How can you not? They have been there forever."

Imani interrupted. "If Lord Chike has altered Lord Adeeowale's memories, is it not possible that he has buried them so deep that to Lord Adeeowale, the outsiders never existed before that day?"

"Of course, it is possible. However, I do not understand why you, Imani, were unaware of the outsiders." Serena was quiet as she tried to make sense of what Imani had revealed to her. It was one thing for Lord Adeeowale to have no memory of the outsiders. But how was it that Imani did not?

"Was the entire tribe unaware of the outsiders?"

Imani nodded her head, "Yes. No one knew of the outsiders until that day. Lord Manus had just learned of their existence."

Lord Chike stood behind Cassandra. His eyes were closed, and his hands were on either side of her head. To further his plan, he used himself as a conduit so Casandra could access the false Lord. Through him, she could inflict the false Lord with a dark spell that only a few priestesses knew. Soon, the false Lord would die, and his body would become a vessel for the true Lord of the Lion People. Lord Chike opened his eyes and gazed out into the emptiness that surrounded the Land of the Ancestors. His scarred lip curled upward, forming a hideous grin. His plan to purge the Jelani Tribe of its traders was only days away. Lord Joshawa would occupy the body of the false Lord, and in turn, Lord Chike would control Lord Joshawa. The outsiders that lived among the tribe would die, and then the Jelani Tribe would once more be pure.

Lord Chike glanced down at Cassandra. *You are doing well, Priestess Cassandra. In two days, the vessel will be ready for the spirit of Lord Joshawa, and once Lord Joshawa is in his rightful place, you will be rewarded.*

You'll return me to the Land of the Spirits?

Yes.

And I will be free of the orb and the pain?

Is that not what I promised?

Yes, my Lord, it is. Please forgive me.

Lord Chike removed his hands, and as he walked away, the orb shrank until it completely encased Cassandra. Then the orb floated out into the emptiness that surrounded the Realm until it, too, was lost to the darkness.

CHAPTER SEVENTEEN

Joshawa's heart went out to Amy as she stood trembling at the entrance to the cave. She appeared so frightened that Joshawa was fearful if anyone made a wrong move, she would turn and run into the darkness. He wanted to go to her and hold her in his arms. Prove to her that there was nothing to be afraid of.

"Amy, please don't be afraid. These are my friends. They won't hurt you."

Amy didn't say a word. She only stood there, her eyes darting between him and Adrian.

"Amy, can you come to me? Come and sit beside me." Joshawa smiled at her as he patted the ground beside him. It was then that he realized that Alex wasn't at her side. Amy was obviously scared, yet Alex didn't go to her. He remained lying on the ground, and for whatever reason, he seemed to be at ease with Billy touching him. Joshawa glanced over to Billy, who had stopped his rocking and chanting. Now he was grinning at Alex as he continued to run his hand from the top of Alex's head down his neck. Joshawa's mind was swimming in a pool of questions, but they would have to wait. His priority was Amy. He had to find some way to get through to her and ease her fears.

"Amy, I know you're scared. I am, too. You don't have to come close to my friends if you don't want to. My friend who's standing by your fire . . . his name is Adrian. He won't hurt you." Joshawa observed Amy as she glanced at Adrian and then back to him. "Adrian is afraid of Alex, but I know he'll come closer to Alex if that makes you feel safer."

Adrian's eyes widened, and his right hand automatically went for his gun. The tone of his voice was wrapped in fear and surprise. "I will? You're not serious?"

Joshawa was perplexed that Adrian was posing a question rather than his usual snide remarks. He glanced over to Adrian and hoped that Adrian would hear the desperation in his voice. "Yes, you will, and I'm serious. Alex won't hurt you. Please come over here so that Amy feels safe."

Joshawa returned his focus to Amy. "I need you, Amy. You still need to fix me. If you don't want to come near my friends, then please, go stand by your fire. You're not safe standing where you are. You're too close to the forest, too close to the wolves."

Amy took a few steps into the cave, stopped, and glanced over in Alex's direction. "What did you do to Alex? I need him to protect me."

"I didn't do anything, Amy. And neither did my friends." Joshawa hesitated, then looked over to Billy. "Billy, do you know Alex?"

Billy rolled his eyes at Joshawa as he continued to stroke Alex. "Yes. Billy know Mona. Billy loves Mona. Joshawa silly."

"Mona? The bear's name is Alex."

Billy giggled at Joshawa. "No. She is Mona. Mona safe. Mona protect Amelia."

Joshawa glanced at Alex and then back to Billy. "Who are you talking about?"

Billy looked up at Joshawa, and what Joshawa saw was not only confidence but also defiance. "Mona. Billy protect Mona. Make her safe. Billy protect Amelia. Mona protect Amelia." In a split second, Billy's expression went from confidence to that of a child. "Billy happy to see Mona. Mona thinks Joshawa silly, too."

Amy stood halfway between the entrance to the cave and her fire. She was so scared, more than she'd ever been. However, her fear wasn't because of Joshawa's friends. She was afraid because not only did Alex not come to her, but Amy could no longer hear Alex. His voice was gone from her head. Did he not love her anymore? Amy felt sick to her stomach, and even though she tried, she couldn't hold back her tears. Her legs no longer supported her tiny frame, and she dropped to her knees.

Amy covered her face with her hands and started to cry uncontrollably. She lowered her head as if she wanted to look at the ground, but that wasn't the case. Amy continued to cry hysterically, her body shuddering with every gasp. Her long hair spilled over her shoulders, effectively concealing her face. Amy couldn't control her crying to the point that even Joshawa's pleas were oblivious to her. Then, one word pierced her subconscious and kept repeating itself until she slowly looked up at the one called Billy. He was speaking to Joshawa, and he was the one repeating the word *protect* over and over. Amy remained on her knees and closed her eyes. She listened to the voice, and for some reason, the voice was familiar to her. It made her feel at peace, just as Alex's voice did. She opened her eyes to find Billy kneeling in front of her. Her first thought was to run, but deep inside, something told her to trust Billy.

"Hi. Me Billy. You know Billy? Mona say you know Billy."

"I don't know you. Who's Mona?"

Billy sat on the ground, crossing his legs in front of him. He smiled at Amy and motioned to the ground. "Sit."

Amy did as she was told and sat in front of Billy. He looked at her in such a way that he seemed to be studying her. He tilted his head slightly to one side and then frowned. He glanced over his shoulder at Alex and gently shook his head. "No, Billy, not see." He returned his focus to Amy. "Mona say Billy has to look harder."

Amy was so confused. She was trying to understand, but nothing made sense to her. "What are you looking for?"

Billy giggled. "Billy look for girl."

"What girl are you looking for?"

Again, Billy giggled. "Billy look for Amelia. You silly."

Amy was going from confused to frustrated. She folded her arms across her chest and frowned at Billy. "Is this a guessing game? I don't like guessing games."

Billy's face lit up. He pointed at Amy as he looked over his shoulder at Alex. "Billy know this face." He looked back at Amy. "Amelia doesn't like games. Amelia scared of games."

Amy slowly unfolded her arms and stared at Billy. Something about him was so familiar, but she couldn't figure out exactly what it was. She was so focused on Billy that she didn't notice Alex standing beside her. He gently nudged her, then lay beside her, resting his head close to her legs. Amy smiled at Alex as she stroked his head.

"You still love me."

"Billy love Mona. Billy love Amelia."

Amy looked over to Billy. When their gazes met, Amy couldn't help but feel love for Billy. He placed his right hand on the side of her face. "Hi, Amelia. Billy save you. Billy protect you. Billy love Amelia."

Serena returned to her section of the Realm with more questions than she had answers. She made her way to her usual place so that when Lord Chike checked on her, he would find her where she belonged. Serena sat at the edge of the Realm but didn't check on Joshawa. Her mind was consumed with Lord Chike. Something had gone horribly wrong for the

Destroyer on the day of Imani's death. It was so wrong that he felt it necessary to alter not only the memories of Lord Adeeowale but also the memories of the entire tribe. According to the legends, the Destroyer was a punishment unleashed on the tribe when the reigning Lord was unworthy of his station. The Destroyer would take possession of a warrior, then proceed to kill any tribe member whose name appeared on the parchment provided by the Council. Serena had always believed that the Council of Five were the only ones who could unleash such a demon — that was, until she met Lord Chike. Now, she doubted not only the history of her people but also the purpose behind the Council of Five.

Adrian stood next to Joshawa, observing the interaction between Amy, Billy, and Alex. He was in a state of complete bewilderment, mostly because he couldn't believe what he was witnessing with his own eyes. "What's going on, Joshawa? Is this some sort of joke?"

Joshawa also watched the trio and didn't look back at Adrian when he responded. "I don't think so. These last few days have been weird, to say the least."

Adrian looked down at Joshawa and tried to understand these new emotions that enveloped him. Adrian had always hated Nathen and Joshawa, and his only emotion for them was contempt. If he was asked why, he would've answered without hesitation. But now his understanding of both Nathen and Joshawa was being challenged. The contempt he'd felt for them was no longer the ruling emotion.

Adrian was torn between his loyalty to his father and what he was experiencing firsthand. After listening to Joshawa speak with Amy, the man he'd envisioned Joshawa to be was not even close to the man who sat before him. Joshawa and Nathen had shown Adrian they were loving and caring individuals. But most importantly, they were protective of not only the people they loved but also of anyone they encountered.

Adrian sat next to Joshawa, and without taking his eyes off Billy, he started building a rapport with Joshawa. "So, I wouldn't make the list?"

Joshawa turned to face Adrian. From Joshawa's expression, Adrian figured that Joshawa had finally noticed the bruising and swelling on his face. "What the hell happened to you?"

"Billy did."

Joshawa gave Adrian a *you're full of shit* look. "Right. Billy, our resident giant who wouldn't hurt a mouse, did this to you?"

Adrian smiled at Joshawa. "Like you said, the last couple of days have been weird. Can we get back to the part about me not even being on your search party list?"

"Sure. You hate me. Why would you want to help find me?"

It was apparent that Joshawa was keeping his guard up, and Adrian didn't blame him in the least. "Actually, I didn't. My job was to get Billy safely home once he led us to his old homestead."

Joshawa appeared shocked. "You took Billy to his old homestead?"

Adrian watched Joshawa as he glanced over at Billy. Billy seemed quite content where he was and took no notice of either of them. Joshawa then turned his focus onto Adrian, and there was no mistaking how upset Joshawa was. "That was dangerous. How did he take it?"

Adrian used his right hand to circle his face. "Not great."

"I still can't believe Billy did that to you. What idiot told you to take him there?"

Adrian laughed. "Long story that I really don't understand

myself. But it was your father that asked Billy to show him where he used to live."

"My father's here?"

"Not exactly. We had no idea where you were other than being in a cave with your rather large friend over there. Your dad knew that a couple of hunters had tagged the bear and were following it. Your dad's hoping to get his hands on their GPS and, by doing so, to find you."

"So, where's my father?"

"At the Jenkins homestead waiting for one of the hunters. Your mother believes he'll help us."

"Why would he need the GPS? You found this place."

"Actually, Billy found this place. I started taking him back to your cabin, and he just took off. Kept saying that he had to save Amelia. Then, when the bear came into the picture, there was no stopping Billy. So, just how badly are you hurt?"

Amy must have heard Adrian because she came over, sat next to Joshawa, and started to explain his injuries. "He fell out of a tree. It was a bad fall, and he was badly hurt. He had a bad gash on the back of his head that caused a concussion. He had a dislocated elbow, three broken ribs, and his leg is broken."

Adrian was shocked at the laundry list of injuries. "How did you survive?"

Joshawa took Amy's hand in his and smiled at her. "I don't know how she did it, but Amy saved my life. She knows a lot about healing." Joshawa returned his focus to Adrian. "How long have I been here?"

"As far as I know, it's been three days."

"Only three days? I thought it was a lot longer. I can't walk, so I'll need help to get off the mountain. How far away is my father?"

"Not sure. It'll depend on how soon he gets that GPS. In the meantime, we should just stay here and wait."

"Couldn't you find our way home?"

"To be honest, no. I really didn't pay attention to where Billy was leading me. I was more concerned about him going ballistic again. Our best bet is to wait here for your father. I have no doubt that he'll find us."

Adrian glanced over to the entrance of the cave. According to his dad's story, he had put all his faith in Nathen that fateful day. In the end, Nathen hadn't kept his promise, and his mom died because of it. Now, here he was, waiting for Nathen to save him.

Adrian stared out into the darkness that had consumed the forest. *Don't let us down, Nathen. Don't be the monster my dad believes you are.*

Serena glanced down to check on Joshawa and was elated to discover he had company. However, as she searched the cave, she realized Lord Nathen was not among them. Serena closed her eyes and listened in on the conversation. She learned that Joshawa was safe, and Lord Nathen wasn't far behind. Her problem now was that she only had two days to discover the truth about Lord Chike. If she failed, Lord Chike would try to claim Joshawa, and Serena wasn't confident she could protect Joshawa against the Destroyer.

Serena was about to leave when something from the cave caught her attention. Once again, she gazed down and found Joshawa and the one he called Adrian sitting together. Amy was with her bear and a strange man she called Billy. There was something about those three and the connection they shared. Serena was deciding if she should get a closer look when the bear looked up at her.

I know you, and I know what you face. Go and protect your people, and I will protect mine.

Serena was in shock, and for the first time in her life, she had no idea how to process what she had just experienced.

The bear spoke to her . . . he melded with her. Serena watched the trio, and at that moment, she realized that the bear was also communicating with Billy and Amy. Serena sat back as she searched through her memories for an explanation of how this bear could meld with her. She couldn't find any situation where an animal was given the gift afforded only to the Ancestors and priestesses. Serena peered down over the edge of the Realm and tried to meld with the bear.

How is it that you have the ability to meld with me?

Once again, the bear lifted his head and looked up at Serena. *It was a gift. A gift bestowed unto me and Billy.*

A gift? Who gave you this gift?

I have no idea who the benefactor was.

Can Billy hear us?

Not exactly. Billy can only hear me and Amy when I allow him to listen. You must go now. You must protect your people.

Who are you?

Amy calls me Alex.

That is the name of the bear, not your name. I believe that you are using the bear as a vessel. How did you become the bear?

In a manner similar to how Amy knew how to heal Joshawa.

CHAPTER EIGHTEEN

Nathen had kept watch all night to ensure no one left the cabin. He was confident that Dameon would help him. However, he didn't trust Jax. Nathen wasn't prepared to take the chance the Jax wouldn't slip out in the middle of the night with the GPS. The sun was just beginning to creep over the horizon, and if Dameon was true to his word, he should be exiting the cabin at any time. Nathen folded his blanket and placed it on the ground behind the smaller cabin. Then, he stood behind a redwood tree at the edge of the yard and waited.

Dameon had been awake since four in the morning but remained in bed so he wouldn't cause Jax to be suspicious. It was sad that their friendship had come to this. Jax questioned every move he made, and Dameon knew it was for no other reason than the fact that Jax no longer trusted him. Jax was so wrapped up in his Bigfoot and his desire to torture and maim that he'd become paranoid. So much so that Dameon had no doubt that Jax wouldn't think twice about taking him out of the equation. A quick glance at his watch told him it was a quarter to six, which meant it was safe to prepare for his day.

Dameon jumped down from his bunk and pulled on his jeans and a black t-shirt. He was starting a fire when Jax woke up. Jax pulled on his jeans and a dark blue hoodie, then headed toward the kitchen counter.

"Morning, Jax. I should have this fire roaring in a couple of minutes. Do you want to get the coffee pot ready?"

"Not a problem. You still planning to check on our bear this morning?"

Dameon stood and wiped his hands on his jeans. "Yes. What are your plans for the day?" Dameon was hoping that Jax wouldn't offer to join him. He tried to act nonchalant as he accepted the coffee percolator from Jax and hooked it on the stand over the fire.

"Not sure. Are you planning to actually find the bear or just confirm where he is?"

Dameon walked over to the door and started to put his boots on. He didn't look up at Jax when he replied. "We know where he is by the GPS. I just want to make sure he's healthy and that he's still putting weight on." Dameon grabbed his jacket, and as he put it on, he glanced over to Jax. "It was your idea to have eyes on him as much as possible. I'm heading to the ladies' room. Are you cooking breakfast?"

Jax leaned against the kitchen counter and folded his arms across his chest. To Dameon, it appeared that Jax was deciding if he should accept his explanation. But in the time it took for Dameon to prop the door open, Jax was already heading over to the fire with the frypan.

"Sure, I'll cook. I was thinking that I might head out with you. Not much else to do here."

Dameon's heart sank, but he managed to compose himself, and hopefully, his reaction appeared normal to Jax. "Hanging with me and our bear instead of hunting your Bigfoot? Wow, I feel honored." Dameon chuckled as he headed out the door. But as soon as he was out of sight, he stopped and took a deep breath. He felt as if he was going to be sick. And it was at that moment when he realized just how scared he was of Jax.

Amy had spent the night curled up with Alex. He kept her

warm and safe from the bitter cold and the wolves. When she woke the following morning, she found Adrian sitting on the ground next to the large fire pit. He'd started a fire and was holding his hands close to the flames in an obvious attempt to warm himself. Amy cautiously scanned the cave and found Joshawa still sleeping. However, Billy was nowhere in sight. Amy stood and went to give Alex a good morning hug, only to find Billy curled up behind Alex's head. Billy was still asleep, and he had his arm lying across Alex's neck.

"Good morning, Amy."

Amy turned to face Adrian. She knew Joshawa said he was a good person, but Amy still had reservations. "Good morning."

"I hope you don't mind, but I used some wood that I found in the back of the cave for the fire."

Amy remained standing next to Alex, where she felt safe. "That's what it's for. But we have to replace it, or it won't last the winter." Amy didn't understand the puzzled look Adrian gave her. "Did I say something wrong?"

"No, not at all. It's just that you won't have to stay here for the winter. You can come with us to Burwood."

"Joshawa said the same thing. But this is my home, and I won't leave Alex." Again, Adrian looked at her as if she said something stupid. Amy rolled her eyes at him. "I'll get wood for Joshawa's fire, then I'll get food for us to eat."

Adrian stood and then approached Amy, which made her feel very uncomfortable. She watched him come closer, and as he did, she realized she wasn't scared of him. What she felt was more like being cautious than fear. Amy glanced behind her and discovered that not only was Alex awake, but he was paying attention to her interaction with Adrian.

Amy heard Alex's voice, and the soothing tone calmed her. *It's okay, Amy. You can trust him. Let him help you.*

"Are you sure?"

Yes. Amy, you're going to be safe with these people. Billy tells me they are kind and they will take care of you.

Amy turned back to face Adrian. He seemed kind enough, but she still had a gut feeling that something wasn't right. "Alex told me to trust you, so I will." Amy took a step closer to Adrian. "But if you try to hurt me or Joshawa, Alex will hurt you."

Adrian smiled at Amy, though she was sure he was also apprehensive. "Message received and understood."

Adrian stepped to one side of Amy and looked directly at Alex. "I won't hurt anyone here. I just want to help." Adrian returned his focus to Amy. "Do you want me to get breakfast while you start a fire for Joshawa?"

Amy giggled. "Alex says you're funny." She then took a more serious stance on his offer to catch breakfast. "Do you know how to catch animals?"

"Yes. I hunt all the time."

Amy scowled at Adrian. "The animals are my friends, and I only take what I need to survive."

Adrian smiled at Amy, and for reasons she didn't understand, she started feeling safe with him. "Neither do I. What would you like me to catch for us to eat?"

"Fish would be best, but the water is really cold. You can catch rabbits, but only enough to feed us. Make sure that you tell the animals you meet that you're a friend. That will make them happy."

Adrian smiled at Amy. "Okay, I'll be sure to tell them." Adrian started walking toward the cave entrance but stopped and turned to face Amy. "So, you talk to the animals?"

"Yes. All the time."

"Do they talk back?"

Amy rolled her eyes. "Of course not silly. Animals can't talk."

Adrian chuckled as he shook his head. "My friend Billy talks to animals, too. He also thinks I'm silly. You two must be related." Adrian laughed as he headed out into the woods.

Lord Chike joined his fellow Ancestors shortly after his encounter with Priestess Casandra. He sat at the fire pit across from Lord Adeeowale and Imani. Together, they welcomed the new day as its brightness consumed the darkness of the night. Lord Chike observed his companions and noticed they didn't appear concerned or curious that he had been away since the previous day. Now that a new day had begun, Lord Chike felt confident that tomorrow, the false Lord would be dead, and Lord Joshawa would take his place. He was so lost in his thoughts that he didn't hear Lord Adeeowale call his name. It was only when Lord Adeeowale slightly raised his voice that Lord Chike acknowledged him.

"My apologies, Lord Adeeowale. It seems that my mind was wandering."

Imani smiled at Lord Chike. "Where did it wander? I trust somewhere pleasant."

Lord Chike tried to appear courteous with Imani even though he disapproved of her appointment and the gift bestowed upon her. "Yes, somewhere very pleasant. How are the people of the Jelani Tribe doing?"

Lord Adeeowale closed his eyes and sighed. When he opened them, it was obvious to Lord Chike that Lord Adeeowale was troubled. "Our people are sad. Lord Zareb's son has been stricken with an illness that could very well take his life. The priestesses have no knowledge of what this illness is. Nor do they know how to cure him."

Lord Chike tried to appear shocked and saddened by the news. It was a façade that he manifested with ease. "That is most unfortunate. How is it that our High Priestess cannot cure him?"

Imani also appeared troubled and even a little disillusioned. "The priestesses have gone over every parchment and every scroll, but they cannot find an answer to Dava's illness."

It was hard for Lord Chike not to smile, and it was even more challenging to contain his laughter. As he listened to Imani, he discovered an opportunity to explain Dava's illness and possibly convince both Ancestors that Lord Joshawa was the answer to the tribe's existence. "Are you saying that there is no reference to an illness similar to what Dava is facing?"

Imani nodded. "Yes, that is true."

Lord Chike tried to appear as if he were deep in thought, and after a few minutes passed, he started to weave his web of deception. "If there has been no record of his illness plaguing our tribe in its long history, maybe we should be examining the circumstances that surrounded him before he took ill."

Both Lord Adeeowale and Imani appeared puzzled by his comment, which pleased Lord Chike. "What I am trying to say is that maybe we need to look at what is different in Dava's life that has not been present in our history."

Lord Adeeowale's expression was that of distrust and concern. Lord Chike knew he had to be careful and make sure that he divulged just enough information to cause his companions to be curious. He wanted to avoid his companions becoming cautious and untrusting of him.

Lord Chike continued to embellish his lie. "I have been an Ancestor from the dawn of time. I have watched our tribe grow. I have watched them falter, and I have watched the Destroyer as it nearly wiped the tribe from existence on more than one occasion. However, what I have not witnessed is an outsider chosen to be Lord of our people. Maybe that has something to do with Dava's illness." Lord Chike stood and then used his hands to brush the dirt from his loincloth. "Of course, I am only speculating. I must take my leave and join Priestess Serena."

As Lord Chike turned to leave, Lord Adeeowale called out to him. Lord Chike slowly turned to face Lord Adeeowale.

"Lord Chike, are you saying Dava is ill because his father is an outsider?"

"I am only stating that as far as I am aware, no other Lord has been sired by an outsider."

Lord Adeeowale stood and walked over to Lord Chike until he was only a few feet away from him. "Lord Nathen had an outsider for a mother, as did his son, Joshawa. Neither of them has suffered the illness that Dava is consumed with."

It took every ounce of willpower that Lord Chike possessed to keep him from berating Lord Adeeowale. Instead, he shrugged his shoulders and was about to turn around but changed his mind. "That is true, and this illness is baffling. But is it not written in our scrolls that a true Lord of our people must come from the lineage of a true Lord? As far as I know, the scrolls make no mention of who the mother has to be."

Lord Chike watched Lord Adeeowale and could tell he was carefully considering what he had been told.

"Lord Chike, I almost forgot. What did the Council reveal to you concerning the number of Ancestors that occupy this Realm?"

Lord Adeeowale was not the only one who forgot about his mission. Lord Chike was furious with himself because one mistake could undo everything that he had worked so hard to accomplish. "Yes. Unfortunately, the Council was unavailable, so I could not seek an audience with them. I must take my leave. I will visit with Priestess Serena, and then afterward, I will go to the Land of the Spirits and seek another audience with the Council. Hopefully, they will be available and offer some insight on what is ailing Dava." Lord Chike didn't wait for a response. He turned and headed into the jungle.

CHAPTER NINETEEN

Jax knelt by the fire and started to cook breakfast for himself and Dameon. He'd placed the frypan at the edge of the fire so that the bacon and eggs wouldn't burn. As Jax flipped the eggs over, he reviewed his options for dealing with Dameon. He had no intention of accompanying him. Jax only wanted to watch Dameon's reaction to his offer. He smiled as he recalled Dameon's expression because it vindicated his suspicions. Dameon was hiding something, and Jax was sure it had to do with his Bigfoot, though he had to admit that Dameon did a pretty good job concealing his true intentions. Again, Jax smiled, because he knew he was the master of deceit and Dameon was blind to Jax's betrayal. Jax would know when Dameon was lying, and the more he thought of it, the more he convinced himself that Dameon had turned on him.

The coffee and bacon had filled the cabin with enticing odors. However, Jax was oblivious. His mind was focused on calculating how much time to give Dameon before he started to follow him. Jax would take his *Ruger*, the *Pax* rifle, the crossbow, and the *Barrett* rifle. The crossbow would be helpful if Jax was put in a situation where he needed to make a clean and quiet kill. Jax had no intention of using the crossbow on his Bigfoot or the bear. They were each worth a lot of money to him, so if he happened upon them, he would use the *Pax* rifle and tranquilize them. The crossbow would also be helpful in case Dameon decided to become righteous and stand between him and his prey. If that was the case, Jax would choose the crossbow to take Dameon out of the equation. He would rather not be weighed down taking the *Barrett* with him, but it would be useful if Jax found himself backed into a corner.

Dameon headed toward the outhouse, and just before he reached it, he quickly checked over his shoulder to see if Jax was watching him. He wasn't, and judging from the aroma coming from the cabin, Jax was busy cooking breakfast. Dameon shook his head at the thought that he was becoming as paranoid as Jax. Dameon checked the entrance to the cabin one more time, then headed toward the smaller cabin. When he walked to the back, he found Nathen exactly where he'd left him. He was leaning against a large redwood with his arms crossed over his chest.

"Good morning, Nathen. How are you doing?"

Nathen walked over to Dameon and extended his hand, which Dameon readily accepted. "Not bad. I'll be doing much better when I find my son."

Dameon couldn't even begin to know or understand what Nathen was experiencing. What he did know was that he had to help him at all costs. "Jax is making breakfast. He said he wanted to come with me and check out our bear, but I think he was just trying to appease me. I doubt he'll give up his hunt for you, especially if it's just for the sake of accompanying me."

"Irony at its best. So, when do we leave?"

"I'll have breakfast with Jax and try to save you some as long as he doesn't notice."

"Don't jeopardize our plan for my sake. Right now, my only concern is my son."

"Okay." Dameon glanced over to the larger cabin and then returned his attention to Nathen. "I shouldn't be more than thirty minutes. I want you to head out in this direction."

Dameon held his arm out and pointed in a northerly direction. "Do you have a compass?"

"No. I didn't think to bring one."

Dameon reached into his pants pocket and retrieved a small compass. To look at it, you would think it was a pocket watch. Dameon handed it over to Nathen. "I want you to head in a straight line north of here. Don't deviate, or else I may not find you. Keep going for about twenty minutes and then wait for me there. That way, if Jax decides to come out into the yard, he won't see you."

"I can't tell you enough how much I appreciate what you're doing for me."

"In all honesty, I'm doing this more for Jax than I am for you. He's dangerously close to losing his humanity. If he finds you and your son, then he'll become something that I can't allow to live. It'll come down to one of us killing the other, and I don't plan to be on the business end of his *Ruger.*"

Dameon left Nathen, trusting that he would follow his directions. As he entered the cabin, Dameon's entire body shivered in fear as if he'd crossed over into the depths of hell. He stood still for only a second, removed his coat, placed it on the floor, and then walked over to the table. Dameon sat at the table and watched Jax as he transferred the eggs from the frypan onto two tin plates. Dameon's mind was racing, and he struggled to restrain himself from hog-tying and gagging Jax. The only problem with that scenario was that it wouldn't solve anything other than infuriating Jax and making him even more determined to catch his Bigfoot.

Authia sat on her porch swing, slowly rocking it back and forth with her right foot. She was still wearing her white flannel PJ pants, a long-sleeve flannel top, and moccasin slippers. Her left knee was tucked against her chest, and her arms were folded around it. Her chin rested on her knee, and as she rocked back and forth, she gazed into the forest.

The sun hadn't graced the morning sky with its presence yet, so to keep warm, Authia had chosen to wear one of Nathen's sweaters. It was so huge on her small frame that she could easily wrap it around herself and the leg that she was holding close to her. She could have used a blanket to keep warm, but she'd chosen Nathen's sweater instead. She could smell his scent that lingered on the sweater. It filled her mind and her heart with images of him, and to Authia, it felt as though he had his arms around her, holding her, keeping her safe.

She closed her eyes and imagined Nathen rescuing their son. He had Joshawa cradled in his arms as he carried him off the mountain. When she finally opened her eyes, the reality of the situation was all around her. Nathen hadn't yet found Joshawa, and she'd been told to stay at the cabin, which made her feel pretty much useless.

The sun was just starting to rise and light up the morning sky. Authia wondered how Nathen was after spending the night outside in the cold with nothing to keep him warm.

As if Nathen knew she was thinking of him, he reached out to her. *Good morning, my love. How did you sleep?*

I was just thinking of you. How was your night? I hope you weren't too cold.

I spent most of the night watching the cabin. You haven't answered me, how did you sleep?

Authia closed her eyes and recalled her sleepless night staring into the fire. *I got about as much sleep as you did.*

That's not good, my love. One of us has to stay strong.

I agree, and I'll get some sleep, but not until Joshawa is safe in your arms.

Well, then, I better find him soon. Did Adrian and Billy show up?

No, not yet, but I believe that Billy is safe with Adrian.

I hope so. Dameon's having breakfast with Jax, and hopefully, he'll convince Jax not to accompany him. I'm actually heading north right now. I'll meet up with Dameon in about half an hour.

Be safe, sweetheart. You're going to find him today. I know you will.

I hope so. Go get some sleep or coffee and get out of the cold. I can sense you're shivering.

Authia smiled as she stood up and headed for the cabin door. *I'm going in now. Please let me know how things are going. You know I'll go crazy if I don't hear from you.*

I will. I love you, and I'll find our son.

I love you, too, and I have complete faith in you. You're going to find Joshawa, and he'll be alive.

Serena sat at the edge of the Realm and observed the interaction between Adrian and Amy. They were both learning to trust outside of their comfort zone. This was important, because their ability to trust would be tested. For Joshawa to survive, they all had to trust one another. Serena wanted to check on Nathen, as he, too, played an integral part in her plan. But as she stood up, Lord Chike came out of the jungle. Serena's first reaction was fear. If Lord Chike decided to check on Joshawa, he would discover that Serena had deceived him. She had to think quickly, so she decided that her best chance of preventing Lord Chike from checking on Joshawa was to put distance between the two.

Serena walked over to Lord Chike, and to show respect, she bowed her head. When she raised her head, she smiled. "My Lord, how are you on this beautiful morning?"

Lord Chike appeared perplexed by her sincerity. "You believe that this is a beautiful morning?"

"Yes, I do."

"You surprise me, Priestess Serena. I thought that taking Joshawa's essence displeased you."

"It does not make me happy. However, as of tomorrow, I will be free, and my obligation to you will be met."

"I take my earlier assessment back. You are exactly as I thought you would be. You are egotistical to the point of being a narcissist. You will always only care about yourself. You exist to punish those who you feel have wronged you."

"Is that not why you chose me?"

"No. It was your gift. Your penchant for putting yourself first was a drawback." Lord Chike started the walk around Serena. "Shall we take a look and see how our new Lord is doing?"

Lord Chike maneuvered his way past Serena and was heading toward the edge of the Realm. She needed to think fast and find a way to anger him so that he would concentrate on her, not Joshawa.

"My Lord, there is one thing that has puzzled me."

Lord Chike stopped and turned to face Serena. "I do not care what puzzles you." Lord Chike hesitated for just a second. "However, you have accomplished what was asked of you, so I will indulge you. What puzzles you, Serena?"

Serena was pleased that she had his attention, and to show respect, she folded her hands in front of her. "You often speak of making the tribe pure again. What I do not understand is that your plan is to kill the son of the current Lord and then replace him with the son of the previous Lord. Neither are pure in their lineage, so how does that make the tribe pure again?"

Lord Chike approached her, and she knew she was in trouble by the anger evident in his facial expression. Serena braced herself for the reprisal that she was sure to come.

Lord Chike stood less than an arm's length away from Serena. He placed his right hand tight against her neck. "You think that I am a fool? That I do not know the ways and practices of our people?"

Serena could barely breathe and couldn't utter one word. All she could do was gently move her head from side to side to indicate that her answer was no. Her action didn't appease Lord Chike. He strengthened his grip on her neck and raised her until she was several inches off the ground. Serena wanted to grab his arm and try to pull it away. However, she knew that any effort on her part would only anger him more. To survive and protect Lord Joshawa, she had to keep her arms down at her side and endure his wrath.

Lord Chike was so angry that he spat at Serena as he spoke. "You are no better than the outsiders that call themselves tribesmen of the Jelani Tribe! You are no better than the Lord and High Priestess that allowed such depravity as the joining of an outsider with our people!" Lord Chike threw Serena to the ground and stood over her, glaring at her as if he were daring her to speak. "You think you know so much, Priestess Serena. It does not matter which bitch the Lord impregnates. The line is pure if the child is a descendant of a Lord!"

Serena lay on the ground, fearful that if she tried to move, Lord Chike would inflict more pain upon her. She tried to speak, but her voice was hoarse and barely audible. So, instead of using her voice, she melded with him. *Why do you hate the outsiders so much?"*

Lord Chike's expression frightened Serena because, at that moment, she could only see hatred and cruelty. Those two emotions were so pronounced that Serena believed they ruled his mind. These emotions were the puppeteer, and he was the puppet.

"I hate them because they are filth. I hate them because they are the reason I was conceived. I hate them because it is my responsibility to hate them. my responsibility to see to their destruction, and you, Priestess Serena, will never see the Land of the Spirits. Once Lord Joshawa is safely transferred to his host, I will personally escort you to the Realm of Despair." Lord Chike violently kicked Serena in her abdomen and then made his way into the jungle.

Lord Adeeowale remained at the fire with Imani. Lord Chike had to be stopped, but it wouldn't be as easy as going to the Council of Five. If he was the vessel for the Destroyer, then there would be only two ways to stop him. They would have to either convince the Council of who he was and then pray they were not the ones who released him. Or, they would have to find Lord Chike's original essence and destroy it. Both avenues seemed highly unlikely. Lord Adeeowale was about to suggest that Imani and he go to the Council when Serena's voice seeped into both their minds. Her voice was weak and sounded as if she was in distress.

Please come find me. I am in need of your assistance.

Lord Adeeowale replied, *Where are you?*

Where Lord Chike has placed me.

Lord Adeeowale offered his hand to Imani and helped her to her feet. *We are coming. Are you safe for the moment?*

There was a pause, and Lord Adeeowale could feel Serena slipping away. *Serena! Serena, can you hear me?*

A voice that sounded a lifetime away answered. *Yes. Barely.* There was another pause, and then Lord Adeeowale could no longer sense Serena.

CHAPTER TWENTY

Dameon sat at the table as Jax poured coffee into the two tin mugs. Then Jax placed the coffee pot on the table and sat across from Dameon. Jax was smiling at him, but as far as Dameon was concerned, it wasn't because he was happy. It was more like he was taunting him. It was as if Jax knew Dameon was up to something and was waiting for him to slip up.

Dameon picked up his mug and took a sip of his coffee. "Thanks for breakfast." Dameon placed the mug back on the table and started dipping his toast into his eggs.

"You're welcome. So, how long are you planning to follow our bear?" Jax used his fingers to pick up a piece of bacon and then proceeded to place the entire piece into his mouth.

"I was thinking about coming back just before sunset."

"Really? You honestly believe that our bear will be that hard to track?"

Dameon was lapping up the last of his egg with his toast. He took a large bite and used the fact that it was taking a while to chew to think of a response. When he was finished, he gulped down the last of his coffee and placed the mug on the tin plate. "Tracking him will be easy. I was going to see if I could use the GPS's memory to find his den."

"Well, we know that it's north of here."

"Yes, but there's a lot of acreage north of here. It could be anywhere. If I can find the den, we can use those coordinates to give to the chopper. It's the one place that we're guaranteed that our bear will return to on a regular basis."

"You have a point. Are you sure it's gonna take you all day?"

"Probably. If I find something that could be his den, then I want to stake it out and make sure he's the one who claimed it and not another grizzly."

Dameon was having difficulty interpreting Jax's mannerisms and facial expressions. He appeared to be on board with everything Dameon had said, but something in Dameon's gut told him Jax was playing a game. Jax's games were not for the lighthearted. He played his games as if they were real life, and he had no boundaries, nor did he suffer any consequences. He actually enjoyed inflicting mental or physical pain on his opponent. Dameon sat back in his chair and rested his arms on the table. It was do-or-die time, and Dameon knew he would have to be convincing.

"It'll be a long day. You don't have to come with me." Dameon smiled at Jax. "Besides, I'm a big boy. I can take care of myself."

Jax stood and smirked at Dameon as he gathered the dishes from the table. He took the dishes, walked over to the kitchen counter, and placed them in the bucket for washing. He turned, leaned against the counter, and folded his arms across his chest. "You couldn't find your way out of a paper bag."

Jax seemed to be in good spirits and didn't display any paranoid actions. "Says you. But seriously, Jax. I know how important it is for you to track down your Bigfoot. I'd have no problems if you wanted to stay and work on locating him."

Dameon carefully observed Jax as he continued to lean against the counter. His facial expression was nondescript, so Dameon couldn't tell which direction Jax was taking. Finally, Jax laughed as he stood away from the counter.

"You're right. I don't want to waste a day on our bear when I could be tracking down the creature." Jax headed toward the door and grabbed his jacket. "I'm heading for the outhouse.

Have fun, but you're doing dishes when you get back."

"Fair enough." Dameon watched Jax as he made his way to the outhouse. That was easier than he'd thought it would be. Maybe even a little too easy. Dameon slowly shook his head. "You're getting as bad as Jax. Stop being paranoid!"

Dameon quickly holstered his gun and packed his backpack with food and water for the day. Then he placed the GPS in his backpack and walked over to the rifles. He debated whether or not he should take one, and if so, which one. Dameon reached for the *Pax*, then hesitated. His gut was telling him to take the *Barrett*, which meant anything he shot at, he was shooting to kill. Dameon strapped the *Barrett* to his backpack, added the extra ammunition, and then headed out to meet up with Nathen.

Joshawa was leaning against the cave wall, observing the comradery between Amy and Adrian. What he witnessed was incredibly amazing, and he couldn't help but smile. The two were conversing about each other's lives while they cooked the rabbit and fish that Adrian had caught. But it wasn't their laughter or the fact that they were obviously captivated by each other's stories that astounded Joshawa. He was witnessing a completely different side of Adrian, and he couldn't help but think that maybe, all these years, he'd misjudged him.

The Adrian he'd grown up with wouldn't help anyone unless it benefited him. There was nothing beneficial for Adrian here, and since his arrival, he hadn't uttered one disparaging word against Joshawa or his father.

Joshawa glanced over to the entrance of the cave to check on Billy. He was sitting in front of Alex, and it appeared as though Billy was conversing with Alex. Billy would giggle and tenderly stroke Alex's snout. Billy kept referring to Alex as Mona, and if they corrected him, he would stand his ground and insist that the bear's name was Mona. What Joshawa wouldn't give to spend a few minutes inside Billy's head.

Joshawa rested his head against the stone wall and closed his eyes. He could feel the warmth from the fire that was next to him. He could smell the aroma of the fish and rabbit as it cooked over the open fire. He could hear the laughter, and he could sense that everyone felt safe not only in their surroundings but also with each other. He was enjoying the serenity when he felt something gently kick the bottom of his right foot. Joshawa opened his eyes to find Adrian standing in front of him with two plates of food.

"Rise and shine." Adrian passed Joshawa his plate, then sat beside him, crossing his legs in front of him. "How do you feel?"

"Good. Actually, it's excellent. I can't believe that I'm finally going to leave this place and go home." As the words left his lips, Joshawa realized what he'd said and how badly those words would hurt Amy. He quickly scanned the cave and found Amy sitting with Billy and Alex. Thankfully, she had her back to him and hadn't heard his comment.

"That was close. I really have to learn to watch what I say."

Adrian took a bite of the rabbit meat and then glanced over to the entrance of the cave. "What are you talking about?"

Joshawa continued to watch Amy as he answered Adrian. "It's Amy. She's been living in this cave for God knows how long. Then I came along, and finally, she has a companion." Joshawa turned to face Adrian. "She doesn't want me to leave."

"So what's the issue? She can come with us."

"I've already told her that, but she's scared. Whatever happened when she was left here frightened her beyond description. She believes that some sort of evil lives outside of this cave. If she leaves the cave, then the evil will find her."

"That doesn't make sense. Amy leaves the cave to get water and food."

"I know, but she usually doesn't leave the cave without Alex. And when she does leave without Alex, she keeps to the areas that she's familiar with, and she never leaves the cave at night. Living all these years alone with your only companion being a bear has to mess with your brain."

"I agree. Speaking of the brain, how is it that she speaks so well? You'd think if she was isolated in this cave since she was a child that her speech would be minimal at best."

Joshawa glanced back to Amy to find her smiling as she listened to a story that Billy was regaling. "When I first met her, she spoke more like a child, but she still had an extensive vocabulary. In the time I've been here, I've noticed a change in her speech. It's as if she's a supercomputer learning on the fly."

"Well, no matter what, she has to come with us. We can't leave her here."

"I know." Joshawa returned his focus to Adrian. "Do you have any idea how long it will take for my dad to get here?"

"It took Billy and I the better part of a day to find this place, though I'm pretty sure Billy knew precisely where he was going. I guess it's all depending on whether or not your dad gets his hands on the GPS."

"And if he does?"

Adrian smiled at Joshawa. "Well, then, he should be here before nightfall."

Lord Adeeowale and Imani rushed through the jungle in an attempt to reach Serena as quickly as possible. However, even in their desperation to help Serena, they also had to be cautious in order to avoid Lord Chike. When they reached Serena's portion of the Realm, they found her sitting on the ground with both of her hands covering her neck. Judging from her facial expression, she was in a lot of pain. Lord Adeeowale hastened to her side and knelt in front of her. He tenderly moved her hands aside so he could see the damage Lord Chike had inflicted. Lord Adeeowale was shocked at the amount of bruising, but what sickened him the most was the imprint of a hand on her throat. The attack had happened only moments ago, yet the bruising was already evident in shades of black and purple. Lord Adeeowale was saddened by the brutality of the attack. However, when he looked into Serena's eyes, he didn't see fear or pain. What he saw was determination and strength.

Imani knelt next to Serena and tenderly placed her right hand on the side of Serena's neck. "Lord Chike did this to you?"

Serena's voice was hoarse, and watching her as she tried to speak, you could tell she was having difficulty. "Yes, and it is not the first time."

Anger was building deep within Lord Adeeowale, and if Lord Chike had been present, he probably would have killed him. Even if it meant spending an eternity in the Realm of Darkness, he would have at least tried. Lord Adeeowale had a decision to make. He could keep playing Lord Chike's game to its end. Unfortunately, he had no way of knowing how or when the game would end. His other option was to confront Lord Chike now and hopefully take control of the game. If he did choose the latter, he could possibly bring an end to Lord Chike's conspiracy against the Jelani Tribe. He looked at Serena and Imani and knew that the two women that sat before him were strong and they were also ready to defend the Jelani Tribe.

Lord Adeeowale stared at Serena's injuries. "In order for Lord Chike to inflict pain and injury upon you, Serena, then you were correct in your theory that he is not one but two spirits. Judging by the severity of your injuries, we must proceed with caution until we know exactly what we are dealing with."

My Lord, it is very difficult to speak.

Before Serena could finish her sentence, Lord Adeeowale injected. *Of course. Serena, save your voice, and we will communicate within our minds. Do you know when and how Lord Chike wishes to execute his plan?*

Lord Chike is planning to take Joshawa's spirit tomorrow. He will then place Joshawa's spirit into Dava. At that time, Dava will be nothing more than a vessel for Joshawa.

Imani interjected. *Do you mean that Dava will cease to exist?*

Yes, and that is when Lord Chike becomes even more dangerous. He plans to control Joshawa and have him do his bidding. We need to stop him, and we need to do it now.

Lord Adeeowale knew what had to be done. For whatever reason, he knew it had to be him. He had to be the one that would challenge Lord Chike. *Is Joshawa safe?*

Yes, he is safe and well. His friends are with him, and Lord Nathen should reach him before nightfall. If Lord Chike tries to take Joshawa when his parents are present, he will soon discover just how strong Lord Nathen is. He will also learn that he has greatly underestimated Mistress Authia. I do not wish that day to come, but if it does, it will give me great pleasure to watch Lord Chike being destroyed.

Lord Adeeowale extended his hand to help Serena to her feet. *We have to make sure that Lord Chike never has the opportunity to try to take Joshawa's spirit.*

Lord Adeeowale took Imani's hands in his and gently brought Imani to her feet. He placed her hands on his chest and gazed into her beautiful eyes. "I need you to stay here. And watch over both Serena and Joshawa."

"What are you saying? Do you plan to face Lord Chike alone?"

Lord Adeeowale gave Imani's hands a gentle squeeze.

"No, I will go to the Land of the Spirits and seek an audience with the Council of Five."

"And what if they will not help you? Do you plan to face Lord Chike on your own?"

"My dear, sweet Imani. I will do whatever is required of me to stop Lord Chike. I need you to stay with Serena. Help her protect Joshawa in case I fail."

Serena observed the interaction between Imani and Lord Adeeowale. He might have lost a good portion of his memories of his time with Imani, but there was no question about how much he loved her.

Serena didn't want to intrude on a tender display of love, but sadly, she needed to gain Lord Adeeowale's attention.

You must be cautious, my Lord. As you know, you are facing not one spirit but two, and one is definitely the Destroyer.

I will be careful. The last time he and I spoke, Lord Chike inferred that he might go to the Land of the Spirits. If he is there, I will find him. I promise both of you that this will be Lord Chike's last day to walk among us. His spirit will know the agony of spending an eternity in the Realm of Despair.

Lord Adeeowale stepped closer to Imani and wrapped his arms around her, bringing her close to his body. Imani, in turn, wrapped her arms around him. As Serena watched their tender embrace, it became abundantly clear what her hatred and the need for retribution cost her. For 200 years, she was focused on destroying Lord Nathen. Because of her obsession, she never knew what it was to love or be loved.

Lord Adeeowale gently pulled Imani away from him and gazed upon her face. "I may not have all my memories, but what I am certain of is that I love you, and I believe that I have always loved you." Lord Adeeowale leaned in and kissed Imani. He then took her hands in his and smiled at her in such a way that Serena couldn't help but feel moved by the tenderness that he showed for Imani.

Again, Serena didn't want to intrude, but time was not their friend. They needed to act now. *I apologize for the interruption, but we are short on time.*

Lord Adeeowale brought Imani's hands to his lips and affectionately kissed them. He then let go and directed his attention to both women. "Yes, you are right, Serena. I will go to the Land of the Spirits and see if I can find Lord Chike there or at least see the Council of Five. Serena, you said Lord Chike was using Cassandra to kill Dava."

Yes. He is the conduit to the tribe, and through him, Casandra has cast a spell on Dava.

"Is there any way to stop him from using Cassandra?"

We would have to gain control of her. Currently, she floats in the darkness, completely entombed in a transparent globe. If I knew that Lord Chike was otherwise occupied, then maybe between Imani and myself, we could find a way.

"Then that is what you will do. Serena, do you believe that Cassandra will help us?"

I cannot say for certain, but we have no choice. We must convince Casandra to help because she is the only one who can reverse the spell. Serena paused as she recalled the time when Lord Nathen forgave Cassandra and allowed her the opportunity to redeem herself. Serena smiled as a plan to persuade Cassandra formulated in her mind. *Actually, there is one person who could convince Cassandra if she proves to be uncooperative.*

Lord Adeeowale's blank expression revealed to Serena that he had no idea of whom she was referring to. *Cassandra owes her life to Lord Nathen. He spared her life when he had every right to take it. She vowed to spend the life he had given her, showing her gratitude. If we tell her Lord Nathen's son is in danger, she will help us.* Serena glanced over her shoulder at the edge of the Realm, then returned her focus on Lord Adeeowale. *I must go and watch over Joshawa to make sure his father finds him.*

Lord Adeeowale nodded his head in agreement. "Yes.

Joshawa must be protected, as well as Dava. You said that Lord Nathen will find Joshawa by nightfall."

Yes. That is what I believe.

"Good. Then take care of Cassandra first, then return to watch over our young Lord. I will let you know how things are transpiring in the Land of the Spirits." Lord Adeeowale kissed Imani on her cheek and then turned to leave.

Serena and Imani watched as he headed toward the jungle. Then suddenly, Serena thought of the bear. She reached out to Lord Adeeowale before he had a chance to disappear into the jungle.

My Lord, I have a question. The bear that is in the cave with Joshawa can meld. It has spoken to me. Have you ever seen or heard of an animal possessing this gift?

Lord Adeeowale stopped and turned to face Serena. He glanced over to Imani and then back to Serena. "This bear, is it a grizzly?"

Yes.

"And this bear, it lives in a cave with a young woman?"

Serena was taken by surprise at Lord Adeeowale's knowledge of the bear. *Yes. So you are aware of this bear?*

"I am aware that this bear exists, but Imani can explain her bear far better than I can."

Serena's eyes went wide. She turned to face Imani, and in a voice that was horse and barely auditable, she spoke to Imani. "Your bear?"

Chapter Twenty-One

Nathen spent twenty minutes navigating the dense forest. The area was thick with underbrush, redwoods, and evergreens, and the morning dew enhanced the sweet smell of the forest. Usually, Nathen would stop to appreciate the beauty that surrounded him. But this outing was far from normal, and Nathen had only one objective, which was to find his son.

Nathen finally reached the area where Dameon wanted him to wait. He scanned his surroundings to see if he could easily conceal himself in case Jax had decided to join Dameon. Nathen glanced up to check out a large redwood and confirmed that he could easily climb it. However, he'd be trapped if Jax accompanied Dameon and somehow discovered him. According to Dameon, that wouldn't work out too well for Nathen. About ten feet away was an evergreen with lower branches that were thick with needles and pinecones. The underbrush had grown very close to the evergreen, making it an ideal place for him to hide. Nathen scanned the area once more, then crawled underneath so that he would be facing south. Hopefully, he would be able to see anyone entering the area from the direction he came.

As soon as he was settled, Nathen reached out to Authia.

Has there been any sign of Adrian or Billy?

No, nothing yet. Do you have the GPS?

In a way. Dameon is bringing the GPS to me. Problem is, we don't know if he'll be alone.

What are you talking about?

Jax might be with him.

That's not good. What I saw through Dameon is that he's unsure of Jax. Jax is a loose cannon, and he's fixated on his Bigfoot. Which means he's fixated on you.

I know. Dameon spoke of the irony that he was with Jax's Bigfoot.

Nathen couldn't help but smile as he recalled his conversation with Dameon. Unfortunately, the smile was short-lived when Authia interrupted his thoughts.

This isn't funny. Jax is a serious threat to you and Joshawa.

I'm sorry, my love. I am *taking this very seriously. I'm well-hidden and have a full view of anyone approaching this area.*

What happens if Jax sees you?

If he does see me, then I'll deal with that situation when it arises. To be honest, I'm more worried about Adrian and Billy. They should've been home by now. They should've been home long ago.

You let me worry about them. Hansen and I will check it out. You need to focus on Joshawa and nothing else.

I will. I'll let you know what's happening as soon as I know.

Thank you, sweetheart. Stay safe.

I will. I love you.

Authia had said something, but Nathen didn't hear her. He was focused on the sound of someone making their way through the forest. He pulled one of the branches from the evergreen further down to ensure he was completely concealed. The sound was getting closer, and Nathen held his breath as he prayed that it would only be Dameon making his way through the trees.

Jax hid behind the outhouse and watched as Dameon left the yard, heading north. When he was sure Dameon was far enough away, Jax returned to the cabin to get ready to follow him. That didn't take long, because Jax had already packed his backpack the night before and hidden his quiver filled with arrows under his bed. He retrieved the crossbow and arrows and placed them with his backpack on the kitchen table. Jax then retrieved the *Pax* rifle and laid it on the table, as well. He double-checked his backpack to make sure he had ample ammunition, then loaded the *Pax* rifle with the most potent dose of tranquilizer he had on hand. His *Ruger* was on his hip, loaded and ready to use. He retrieved the device he needed to track Dameon from an outside pocket on the backpack and placed it on the table.

Within minutes, he was dressed, wearing his hiking boots and a winter jacket in case the pursuit continued into the night. Both his pants and jacket were camouflaged with colors that you would find in the forest. He pulled on his toque, put his backpack on, and then picked up the device off the table. Jax glanced back at the *Barrett* and gently shook his head. No matter how cumbersome the rifle would be, he needed it. Jax placed the device back onto the table and then retrieved the Barrett rifle. That was when he noticed that the second *Barrett* was missing.

Jax slowly shook his head from side to side. "So, my friend, are you preparing yourself for a fight?" Jax grabbed the rifle and then took it over to the kitchen table. "If it's a fight you want, then I'll give you one." Jax strapped the two rifles and crossbow to his backpack. Then he packed the ammunition, along with food and water, inside his backpack.

Jax stood at the table, running every imaginable scenario through his mind. There was one event he hadn't thought of, and he was ill-prepared if that event played out. Jax's gaze fell on the stretcher. If he found himself in a position where he had to tranquilize his Bigfoot, he wouldn't be able to bring them back to the cabin on his own. The stretcher would add extra weight to his already laden-down backpack. But Jax knew if it came down to it, the stretcher would be invaluable.

Jax quickly added the stretcher to his backpack. Then he picked up the tracking device off the table and held it in his left hand, and as he pressed the button to turn it on, he could feel the excitement building within himself. The device lit up, and the chip Jax had hidden in the GPS case was doing its job. Jax smiled as he gently shook his head. "I got you!" Jax left the cabin feeling more exhilarated than he ever had before.

Lord Adeeowale made his way through the dense jungle, heading toward the doorway that separated the Land of the Ancestors from the Land of the Spirits. He stopped just at the edge of the jungle and cautiously scanned the area for Lord Chike. Feeling confident that Lord Chike was not close by, he approached the doorway. Before him was a toxic wall of fog that barred anyone from crossing the Gateway without permission.

Lord Adeeowale quickly checked his surroundings and then called out to the Gatekeeper. "Gatekeeper, I request safe passage to the Land of the Spirits."

Lord Adeeowale watched as a large figure moved toward him through the fog. When the Gatekeeper reached the edge of the fog, Lord Adeeowale greeted him with a smile. "You look well, Gatekeeper."

The Gatekeeper was at least two feet taller than Lord Adeeowale. He had a body of pure muscle that accentuated his massive shoulders, thighs that resembled a tree trunk, and a stomach that was ripped with muscle.

"Thank you, my Lord." The Gatekeeper bowed his head with respect. "What can I do for you?"

"I only seek passage to the Land of the Spirits."

The Gatekeeper once again bowed his head, then stood to one side as he extended his spear outwards. He maneuvered the fog to one side until the pathway was clear to pass. Lord Adeeowale stepped onto the lush green grass that lay before him, then turned to face the Gatekeeper. "Gatekeeper, walk with me, please."

The Gatekeeper appeared as if he didn't understand the request. "You wish me to join you, my Lord?"

"Yes. Is that not possible?"

The Gatekeeper smiled at Lord Adeeowale. "Well, yes, it is possible, my Lord. This is the first time that I have been asked to accompany a Lord."

"That is unfortunate. I want you to walk with me because I have questions that you may know the answers to."

"You seek my guidance?"

"Yes. You are the Gatekeeper and have been for a very long time. I am sure that there is much I can learn from you." Lord Adeeowale smiled at the Gatekeeper and then started down the path with the Gatekeeper next to him.

"Has anyone sought passage from you other than the Ancestors?"

"No, my Lord. The only ones who have requested passage are you and Lord Chike and no one else."

"Are you certain?"

"Well, Lord Chike did bring a Priestess with him. I cannot recall how long ago."

"No problem, my friend. Are you referring to Priestess Serena?"

"Well, she was the first Priestess he brought with him."

Lord Adeeowale stopped and looked directly at the Gatekeeper. "How many priestesses has he crossed over with?"

"Only two, my Lord. Priestess Serena and Priestess Casandra."

"When was that?"

"I am sorry, my Lord, I have no measure of time in the Gateway, but I can tell you that he brought Priestess Casandra over shortly after he brought Priestess Serena."

"You do not need to apologize. Your information is most helpful."

The two continued down the path, and just as they reached the end, Lord Adeeowale once again stopped and addressed the Gatekeeper. "Do you know if anyone has requested an audience with the Council?"

"As far as I know, there has been no one. It has been a very long time since anyone has entered the Gathering Hut to seek an audience with the Council."

Lord Adeeowale was shocked by the Gatekeeper's revelation. "Are you certain?"

"Yes, my Lord. I am to remain here, on this side of the Gateway, until someone requests passage." The Gatekeeper pointed in the direction of the Gathering Hut. "From the Gateway, I can watch over the Council. No one has entered the Gathering Hut of their own free will for a very long time."

"What did you mean by their own free will?"

"I have seen Lord Chike bring spirits to the Council, but he brings them so that the Council can judge them and sentence them."

"Do you know where Lord Chike is now?"

"He crossed over earlier today. He still remains in the Land of the Spirits."

"Would you do me a favor?"

The Gatekeeper bowed his head. "It would be my honor."

"If Lord Chike requests passage back to the Land of the Ancestors, it would be beneficial if you let me know. I would also request that you do not inform Lord Chike of my request or that I am in the Land of the Spirits."

The Gatekeeper appeared uncomfortable with Lord Adeeowale's request. "My Lord, I know that the Ancestors are aware of my melding ability. But I have been warned that if I ever used my ability, it would mean a lifetime in the Realm of Despair."

"Which Ancestor threatened you?"

"It is of no consequence. He left the Valley of the Lion

People a very long time ago. Now he resides in the Realm of Despair."

"If this Lord is dead, what stops you from using your ability."

The Gatekeeper looked upon Lord Adeeowale as if he didn't understand the question. "I gave my word. The word of a warrior cannot be broken."

"I understand, but besides Lord Chike, I am the oldest Ancestor. That being said, I can release you from your promise. However, if you prefer to honor your promise, I will not be offended."

The Gatekeeper was quiet for several minutes. He finally glanced over to Lord Adeeowale. He stood tall and proud. "I would be honored to help you, so, yes, I am ready to be released from my promise."

Lord Adeeowale approached the Gatekeeper. "Gatekeeper, you have honored your promise for many centuries. Today, I release you from your promise."

"Thank you, my Lord. I give you my promise that no one will know that I am helping you. But I should tell you that Lord Chike said that his reason for requesting safe passage was seeking an audience with the Council. I stood at this very spot and watched him. He did not enter the Gathering Hut."

"Where did he go?"

The Gatekeeper pointed to the path on the outskirts of the village.

Dameon headed north to meet up with Nathen. He focused on the forest and his destination, but he was mostly on autopilot. His mind was consumed with thoughts of Jax, and none of them were pleasant. Best case scenario, he would meet up with Nathen, find his son, and be back at the cabin before dark. But as he trekked through the forest, he realized that any path he took would lead to Jax, and none would appease him enough to stop looking for his Bigfoot. As long as Jax was alive, Nathen and his family were in danger. The only way to guarantee that Nathen and his family could live in peace would be to kill Jax.

Dameon stopped and stared out into the forest. He didn't see the beauty that was all around him. Dameon's mind was consumed with Jax and possible scenarios where he didn't have to kill him. Dameon knew that he couldn't kill Jax, or anyone else for that matter. However, Dameon also knew that he could not, in good faith, turn a blind eye when he was aware of what Jax was planning. If Jax remained alive, then Nathen and his family were condemned to death, and that was something Dameon couldn't condone.

Serena was shocked when she heard Lord Adeeowale refer to the grizzly from the cave as Imani's bear. Serena stared at Imani, waiting for an explanation. Still, instead, Imani appeared as if it were normal for a bear to have the ability to meld. The only reaction Serena received from Imani was a smile. Then she turned and headed in the direction of the jungle.

Serena immediately melded with her. *Where are you going?*

Imani turned to face Serena only to appear puzzled by the question. "Are we not supposed to find Cassandra?"

Yes. Are you going to tell me about the bear?

Imani glanced down at the ground and then looked back up at Serena. Imani's carefree expression was now that of a guilty person who felt no shame for their actions. Serena remained quiet to give Imani a moment to think about her answer seriously. A few minutes later, Imani squared her shoulders and joined her hands in front of her.

"Priestess Serena, I apologize for my actions today. However, I do not apologize for my decision and actions where the bear is concerned. The Council granted me the honor of becoming not only a priestess but also an Ancestor. It would be disrespectful to speak of the incident surrounding the bear."

Obviously, Lord Adeeowale knows about what you did.

"Yes, he helped me. If the Council discovers what we have done, the ramifications would be horrific."

Serena could tell that Imani was scared, and she had cause, for Serena knew firsthand the cruelty of the Council. That being said, Serena knew that the bear was important. If she was going to protect Joshawa, she needed to know what the bear was capable of. Serena smiled at Imani and held out her right hand for Imani to take. *Do you want to see your bear?*

Imani's eyes widened, and she felt like she couldn't breathe. She had hoped that her bear would live a long life so it could carry out the responsibility that she had imposed on it. Imani had believed that after that fateful day, she would never see her bear again. Reluctantly, Imani took Serena's hand and then followed her to the edge of the Realm. They stood there side by side, looking at the vast emptiness that surrounded the Realm.

After a few minutes, Serena let go of Imani's hand and pointed down toward the cave. *He is right there. Go ahead and look.*

Imani slowly gazed over the edge of the Realm and down into the cave. She saw her bear lying on the ground next to Amelia. The bear seemed to be aware of Imani's presence because he lifted his head and gazed up at her. At that moment, Imani's mind came alive with the bear's voice. *You have returned. Is it time now? Must I leave my child?*

All the emotions Imani felt so long ago came flooding back, and she moved away from the edge and started to cry.

Serena walked up to Imani and gave her a hug. *I am so sorry. I did not plan for this encounter to be so upsetting to you.*

Imani stood back from Serena and used her hands to wipe her tears away. "You have not upset me. These are mostly tears of joy." Imani walked back to the edge of the Realm and once again looked down at her bear.

I have returned, but not to take your child. I am here to protect not only your child but you, as well. She has grown so much.

Yes, she has. And I am so grateful to you for allowing me to protect her. To watch her grow. For allowing me the ability to speak with her. Can you see my sweet Billy is also here?

Yes, I see him. You must be overjoyed.

Imani, what did you mean that you had to protect us. Are we still in danger? Is Dext nearby?

Dext is dead, so you have nothing to worry about. Just be cautious and look after our little girl. I have to leave, but I will return. I promise. We will speak again, Mona.

Chapter Twenty-Two

Nathen held his breath as he watched to see who was coming toward him. When Dameon came into view, and Nathen could see that he was alone, he closed his eyes and whispered, *thank you*.

"Nathen, are you here? Jax isn't with me."

Nathen moved the branches that were in his way and crawled out of his hiding place. As he stood, he brushed the dirt off his clothes, and then he approached Dameon. "Are you sure? Is there any chance that he would change his mind and follow you?"

"No chance. Jax is staying behind to work on finding his Bigfoot." Dameon had a canteen of water that was slung over his right shoulder. He took it off and offered it to Nathen, who gladly accepted it. Dameon chuckled and gently shook his head. "Talk about irony. Jax is looking for his Bigfoot, and here you are, standing right in front of me."

Nathen was about to drink from the canteen when he noticed the rifle that Dameon was carrying. "Are we expecting a problem?"

"What do you mean?"

"That rifle? It's a fifty caliber, right?"

"Yes. We're following a grizzly that weighs almost a thousand pounds. Anything less would just piss him off."

Dameon placed his backpack on the ground then glanced over to Nathen. "Don't drink too much. There's no water source close to the direction we have to take, and finding your son may take us the better part of the day."

Nathen screwed the cap back on and offered the canteen back to Dameon. "I can't begin to tell you how much I appreciate you helping me, especially when it could cause a rift between you and Jax."

Dameon knelt on the ground in front of his backpack and retrieved the GPS. He looked up at Nathen, and his facial expression revealed sadness and defeat. "If there's a rift between Jax and me, trust me, it started long before you came into the picture. If you're guilty of anything, it would be because you opened my eyes so I can see the person Jax is becoming."

Dameon laid the GPS on the ground and then removed a food storage bag from his backpack. "Here, take this. You can eat it on the move."

Nathen accepted the food and watched as Dameon slung the backpack onto his back. Dameon then picked up the GPS, and when he turned it on, Nathen could see the green screen light up. Nathen moved closer to Dameon so he could better see the GPS's screen. It revealed a red and yellow dot, each contained within its own circle. There was also a blue line running through the entire screen.

"What am I looking at?"

"It's simple. The circles give you an idea of how far away the animal is, in this case, our bear. The red dot in the center of the screen represents us. The yellow dot represents our bear. The blue represents a water source, in this case, a river."

"I can see what you mean by the water not being close." Nathen pointed at the yellow dot. "So, is this where the bear is now?"

"Yes. However, our best bet is to check the GPS's memory and see where the bear has spent most of his time. That should tell us where his den is, and most likely your son."

The phrase *most likely* hit Nathen so hard it was as if someone had punched him in the stomach. His son didn't have time for *most likely*. Anger and fear built up in Nathen so quickly that he felt like he was going to explode. He took a step closer to Dameon so that they stood almost toe to toe. "What do you mean by most likely? I told you my son is in a cave with your bear. How difficult is that to find?"

Dameon's heart skipped a beat as he looked at Nathen in disbelief. Before this little outburst, he'd found Nathen to be logical and reasonable, but standing in front of him was a man not in control of himself. Dameon now wondered if Nathen was more beast than man. Dameon didn't move a muscle. He focused on Nathen and hoped that the fear he felt wasn't evident.

"What the hell, Nathen? Should I be regretting my choice to help you?" Dameon remained focused on Nathen and watched as every muscle on Nathen's body started to relax. Nathen no longer seemed to be the confident man who'd waited for Dameon by the water pump. Now, he appeared desperate, but not in a way that Dameon felt he should be leery of him. This was a man who was grief-stricken because his son was missing.

"I'm sorry, Dameon. I shouldn't have yelled at you. And please, you don't have to fear me. It's just that my son has been missing for four days and I have no way of finding him without your help. And to make matters worse, he's been hurt, and I don't believe I have much more time to find him."

"I get it, Nathen. I don't have children, so I can't even begin to understand what you're going through. All I ask is that you save your anger for someone else." Dameon smiled at Nathen. "You're damn scary when you're mad, and I would hate to be on the receiving end of that anger."

Nathen smiled as well. "And you never will. I promise."

Ever since Dameon met Nathen, he knew he could trust

Nathen, and he wasn't about to stop. Dameon held out his GPS so Nathen could see it. Then he started pressing buttons to tell the GP S What to do. "Watch the screen. It's gonna call up everywhere the bear has been in the last two weeks."

The two watched the screen as yellow dots started appearing all over the upper part of the screen. There were so many yellow dots that there was no way to distinguish where the bear was. Dameon had to scale down the search area. He typed in a code so the screen would now show a topographical view of the area and would only reveal the yellow dots from the last week. Again, the yellow dots appeared on the screen, but this time, they were in three distinct places.

"Okay, Nathen, I think we have something." Dameon pointed to the screen. "These dots by the water source, we can ignore them. He goes there to eat and drink. That leaves two different areas." Again, Dameon pointed to the gathering of dots. "As you can see, these dots are more in the forest, and he probably goes there for food." Dameon turned to Nathen and smiled. "These dots are higher up where the bear could possibly have a den. There's a water source close by, and there's still enough forest for our bear to forage for food. But the best part is that both these areas are close together, so we can check out each site without losing much time. We know where our bear is, so let's go find your son."

Lord Adeeowale left the Gateway and headed toward the path that the Gatekeeper pointed out to him. It led him behind the village and through the jungle all the way to the lake. He remained at the edge of the jungle as he observed the men, women, and children playing in the water. Lord Chike was nowhere in sight, which didn't surprise Lord Adeeowale. Lord Chike had always thought of himself to be better than the common tribe members, and he would never associate himself with them for any reason whatsoever.

Lord Adeeowale continued to scan the area, hoping to find some sign of where Lord Chike could be or at least a sign that he had actually been here. He was about to give up when he felt a tug on his loin cloth. Lord Adeeowale looked down to find a small child, no more than four years old, smiling at him. Lord Adeeowale knelt in front of the child and returned his smile.

"And who might you be?"

The child continued to smile at Lord Adeeowale, showing no fear as most children do at that age. "My name is Joshawa."

"That is a strong and powerful name. I am most honored to meet you. Do you play here often?"

"Yes. I like it here."

"I do not blame you. Do you know who I am?"

The child giggled as he nodded his head, indicating that he did.

"Do you see many Lords by the lake?"

The child immediately went quiet, and it was obvious to Lord Adeeowale that the child knew something. "What is wrong?"

"He said I would be in trouble."

"Who said such a lie?"

The child appeared puzzled and frightened. Lord Adeeowale knew that he was terrified of revealing what he heard or saw. "You do not have to tell me his name."

The child's eyes lit up. "Really! You will not be angry with me?"

"How could anyone be angry with you? You are such a brave boy. You do not have to tell me the Lord's name, but I do have to find him. Could you show me where he went?"

The child nodded his head as he grabbed Lord Adeeowale's finger. "Come, I show you."

Lord Adeeowale followed the child along the edge of the

jungle to the base of the falls. The child pointed to the rocks and looked up at Lord Adeeowale.

"He disappeared here."

"Through the rock?"

The child scrunched his face as he slowly shook his head. "Of course not. He went behind the falls. Can I go now?"

"Of course. And how about we keep this our little secret."

The child nodded his head, then ran back to where the tribe members were gathered.

Serena and Imani walked through the jungle in silence. Serena wasn't sure how to approach Imani on the subject of the bear, so she decided to wait until Lord Adeeowale was present. In the meantime, she had to figure out a way to reach out to Cassandra. It wasn't long before they arrived at the clearing where Serena had seen Cassandra and Lord Chike. Serena walked over to the edge and peered into the depths of the darkness, hoping to see the orb that imprisoned Cassandra. If only it was as easy as calling her name.

Imani joined Serena and also gazed out into the darkness. "Do you have a plan on how to reach out to Cassandra?"

Serena carefully cleared her throat and tried to speak. She was amazed by how much the pain had subsided. "It appears that I can speak again, so we do not need to meld. To answer your question, unfortunately, is no. Do you?"

Imani turned to face Serena. "Did you not say that she would answer to Lord Nathen?"

"Yes, but he is not here."

Imani grinned at Serena. "I am aware that Lord Nathen is not here. Can we not meld with him?"

"Of course, but we would have to meld with him from my area of the Realm, and from there, Cassandra cannot hear him."

"I agree. If you were the only one to meld with Lord Nathen, the connection would be weak. However, what if we became the conduit for Lord Nathen to reach Cassandra? Would that not work?"

"In theory, it could. However, we would still have the issue of being on the wrong side of the Realm. I could reach out to Mistress Authia. She is a strong melder, but I fear that even with her, we still would not have the strength needed to act as a conduit. We would require four strong melders, and we only have three."

"What about Joshawa? Is he not a melder as well?"

"Yes, but Lord Chike had me block his parents from being able to meld with him, so he is of no use to us."

"That is sad. I wonder if he believes that his parents do not care enough to find him? Can you not reverse the block?"

"Yes. But that would take time, and time is not our friend right now." Serena was quiet while she envisioned Imani's plan. "Your plan could work. However, we do not know how strong the bond is between Cassandra and Lord Chike. There is a chance that he may be able to hear us."

"Is that not worth the risk?"

"Of course it is. But then, even with the two of us and Mistress Authia, I doubt that we are strong enough for Lord Nathen to reach Cassandra. We must wait until Lord Adeeowale returns."

Imani appeared perplexed by Serena's comment. "Why would we have to wait?"

Serena was beginning to lose patience with Imani. They needed four strong melders, and they only had three. What part of that did she not understand? Serena decided not to show her impatience, and instead, she would play nice and calmly question Imani.

"Did I not just say that it would take four of us to create a conduit strong enough for Lord Nathen to be heard?"

"Yes. I do not understand the issue."
"The issue is that there are only three of us."
"You have forgotten about Mona."
"Mona?"
Imani smiled at Serena. "My bear."

Chapter Twenty-Three

Jax took his time preparing to leave so that Dameon would have a thirty-minute head start. He didn't want to get too close and risk revealing himself to Dameon. Dameon was an excellent tracker, and he also had an uncanny way of knowing when he was being followed. That was the reason Jax had chosen this particular tracking device. It would allow Jax to keep far enough away so that, hopefully, Dameon would never be the wiser.

Jax had put the tracking device onto a lanyard and placed it around his neck. The lanyard was long enough so that Jax could easily hold and read the device in his left hand, leaving his dominant hand free to grab his *Ruger*. If he found himself in a situation to use the *Pax*, he could drop the device without losing it, grab the strap to the *Pax* that was over his right shoulder, and within seconds, be ready to shoot.

He cautiously made his way through the forest, doing his best not to make any unnecessary noise. However, Mother Nature had chosen not to cooperate, which resulted in the forest floor being littered with dead branches. Also, the leaves that had once filled the canopy of the forest were now lying on the ground, shriveled and dry. The sounds of the branches cracking and the leaves crunching under Jax's feet would've alarmed any creature that was within earshot. However, according to his device, Dameon was at least half a mile away, nowhere near close enough for Dameon to hear anything. At least not for now. But as Jax closed the gap between him and Dameon, he would have to be a lot more cautious.

As Jax trekked through the forest, his path became more unyielding, with redwoods and evergreens growing larger and closer together. He found signs that Dameon had traveled in the same direction, primarily due to the fact that not many humans had traveled this far north. There was also the fact that Dameon's shoe print was irrefutable. Jax had also found remnants of a shoe print other than Dameon's. But all he could decipher from the print was that it belonged to a human. Jax walked another ten minutes when he came across a more precise outline of the mysterious shoe print. He knelt down on one knee and delicately brushed away a few leaves. Then he ran his fingers carefully along the outline of the shoe print. It was only a partial print, which didn't appear to be from a hiking boot, at least not one Jax readily recognized. What he did know was that the shoe print was human, and, judging from the size, it was most likely made by a male.

Twenty minutes later, he came across a small clearing that wasn't as dense as the forest he'd just walked through. Jax stood at the edge of the small clearing and examined the ground. Multiple shoe prints covered almost the entire area. He walked to a spot where it was evident that Dameon had spent some time. He knelt down and carefully ran his fingers along the edge of the shoe print. The prints were definitely Dameon's. However, about a foot away was another set of shoe prints. Jax remained kneeling as he examined the ground more carefully, and his reward was that he was able to follow the second set of prints to a large evergreen.

Jax stood and walked over to the evergreen, paying strict attention to the mysterious shoe prints. He followed the prints as they led him behind the evergreen, and then they just disappeared. Jax retraced his steps and found another set of the mystery prints that led away from the evergreen and toward Dameon's prints. Jax turned to face the evergreen and pulled back a couple of the evergreen's lower branches so he could examine the ground underneath the tree. What he discovered was the imprint of a very large person who had lain on the ground. Jax was giddy with excitement because he knew who it was that lay on that spot. His smile was ominous as he turned from the evergreen and checked the device.

"So, my friend, you did come to meet my Bigfoot." Jax stared into the forest in the direction his device told him to go. "I hope you'll see reason when I catch up with you. I would sure hate to end our friendship with your death."

Lord Adeeowale stood before the massive wall of rock, which yielded no sign of a passageway. He glanced over to the waterfall that was so tall it seemed to originate from the heavens. He had never considered that the falls concealed a secret pathway, at least not in the Land of the Spirits. There was one in Africa that led to the Valley of the Lion People, but here, there was no need for one. With the exception of the hidden pathway, the Land of the Spirits was precisely the same as the Valley of the Lion People. The only difference was that the inhabitants of the Land of the Spirits were, in fact, spirits. So why would there be a need for a secret passageway? And, if there is one, where would it lead to? There was nothing beyond the Land of the Spirits or the Land of the Ancestors except for the emptiness that was consumed by darkness.

Lord Adeeowale walked over to the rock wall and followed it until it disappeared behind the falls. He focused on the ground that was at the edge of the falls, and through the heavy mist, he found a path made of stones. The stone path hugged the rock wall and continued behind the falls as far as Lord Adeeowale could see. As he stared at the stones, he ran different scenarios through his mind as to where this path would lead him. After several minutes, he realized that what was at the end of the path was of no consequence. Lord Chike had taken this path, so no matter where it led, Lord Adeeow-ale would also follow it.

Lord Adeeowale disappeared behind the falls as he followed the stones that created the pathway. He had to be careful because the rocks were slippery and he could easily lose his balance. As he cautiously stepped from one stone to another, he could feel the cool mist from the falls as it sprayed delicately against his skin. There was something familiar about being on this path. Lord Adeeowale stopped and closed his eyes as he tried to make sense of what he was feeling. It was as if he had been here before. However, he couldn't remember when, or for that matter, why he would have ventured to these falls. Lord Adeeowale dismissed the vague memory and concentrated on the path, searching for any indication of an entrance in the wall of rock. He finally reached the end of the path only to find a solid wall of rock.

Lord Adeeowale turned around and stared at the rock wall that ran the length of the pathway. He had missed something—he was sure of it. He started back down the path, but as he did, he ran his right hand along the wall. He was halfway down the path when his mind became distracted, and the same sensations he had experienced earlier returned. He decided to ignore the memory and took two more steps. But when he took the third step, the wall disappeared from behind his hand. Lord Adeeowale lost his balance and started to fall toward the wall. He instinctively leaned back, and at the same time, he tried to keep his feet planted on the slime-covered stone. After a few seconds of slowly wavering back and forth, he regained his balance.

Lord Adeeowale turned to face the rock wall and discovered a significant gap. If his hand hadn't been there, he would have walked past it for a second time. The opening was at least five feet high and four feet wide and had been meticulously carved out of the rock. Lord Adeeowale stared at the gap in disbelief. How did he miss it?

It was then that he recalled that he had been distracted by the same memory when he passed by this spot the first time. Lord Adeeowale believed the gap, or doorway, was cloaked in a spell that would distract anyone who ventured too close. The distraction would produce a memory so that anyone who ventured behind the falls would miss the entrance altogether. He tried to look past the doorway, but all he could see was darkness. It was a darkness that was so black it blended into the rock. So many questions were running through his mind, and in the end, he knew if he wanted answers, he would have to take a leap of faith. Lord Adeeowale took a deep breath and then stepped into the darkness.

Nathen followed Dameon deeper into the forest as they headed toward the location that was closest to them. Nathen was overwhelmed by the beauty of the forest. Even after the redwoods had shed all their leaves, the forest was still magnificent. The redwoods and evergreens that made up the forest that surrounded his home had their own beauty. But there was something about this part of the forest that was different. Nathen didn't know if it was because this area was so pristine or if it was because the forest was so much thicker. Whatever the reason, if this was where Joshawa's special place was, Nathen now understood why.

Nathen had been following Dameon for well over an hour. With the forest being so thick and the fact that there was no path to follow, they were forced to walk single file. Nathen felt bad that Dameon was getting the brunt of having to deal with branches that were low enough to cause injury to their face. They also had to deal with climbing over trees that had fallen over their path, which made their trek arduous and time-consuming.

This was Nathen's burden, not Dameon's. But even so, Nathen never heard one word of complaint from Dameon. Nathen and Dameon had kept communication down to the minimum, mainly because it was difficult to understand what was being said without actually stopping, which was a luxury they didn't have.

Nathen glanced up at the sky and realized that the sun was directly above them, which meant that the day was halfway over. Nathen was about to question Dameon when Dameon stopped short. He turned to face Nathen and placed a single finger over his lips. Nathen stepped closer to Dameon and whispered to him.

"Are we close to the first site?"

Dameon also kept his voice at a whisper. "We're very close." Dameon pointed off to the left. "Our bear isn't there, but that doesn't mean other bears aren't close." Dameon quietly knelt on the ground, turned off the GPS, and placed it inside the backpack. Then he unstrapped the rifle and handed it to Nathen. As Dameon stood, he put the backpack on and took the *Glock* out of his holster.

"You take my *Glock*, and I'll take the rifle."

Nathen was holding the rifle in his right hand as he stared at the gun. The realization that he might have to shoot something or someone didn't sit right with him. He glanced up at Dameon and slowly shook his head.

"I can take care of myself. I don't need a gun."

"I have no doubt that you can take care of yourself. But we don't know what we're up against. And I would feel a lot safer if you had a gun to back me up."

Nathen took a deep breath as memories of Authia lying on the ground with blood seeping from her wound flooded his mind. Dext's gun had almost taken Authia's life, and Nathen had never been able to shake those images from his mind.

"I'm not comfortable using a gun."

Dameon continued to hold his gun for Nathen to take. "It's easy. Just aim and then pull the trigger."

Nathen passed the rifle to Dameon and took the gun. "It's not that I don't know how to use one. I just don't particularly like them. What exactly do you think we're walking into?"

"Probably nothing, but it doesn't hurt to be prepared. Keep quiet and follow me."

Joshawa had spent the morning staring at the entrance to the cave, waiting for his father to appear. He barely took notice of what was transpiring around him. It wasn't until Amy sat facing him and offered him something to eat that Joshawa snapped out of his trance. He accepted the plate she was offering him and placed it on his lap. When he glanced up, he discovered that Amy hadn't moved. She remained sitting cross-legged on the ground and stared at him, her face scrunched up as if she were trying to understand something.

"So, what's on your mind?" Joshawa smiled at Amy, hoping to get a smile out of her, but she just continued to stare.

"Alex tells me that I have to leave the cave with you."

"That's a good thing, isn't it?"

"This cave has been my home forever. All the time that I have lived here, Alex always told me not to leave the cave. Now your friends are here, and now I'm told to leave."

"I know, Amy, it's been a strange couple of days. But I want you to know that you're welcome to come with us. You'll be safe with us."

Amy glanced down at the ground and picked up a small pebble. She tossed it from hand to hand and didn't look up. Joshawa had seen her do this before, and he interpreted the action to mean that she was confused and scared. "Is that all that's bothering you?"

Amy lifted her head slightly but still continued to play with the pebble. However, she was no longer focused on what she was doing. Joshawa followed her gaze and discovered she was watching Alex and Billy. Amy sighed, then returned her focus to the pebble. "I love Alex, but he's different now."

"How is he different?"

"He loves Billy, and the voice I hear has changed."

"You can hear Alex? He actually speaks to you?"

"Yes, I hear his voice in my mind all the time. But it's changed." Amy glanced up at Joshawa. "I can't explain. His voice is softer. And this new voice, I know I've heard it before."

Joshawa knew Alex could meld, but what surprised him was that Amy could hear him, as well. "Does Alex still love you?"

"Alex is now Mona, and she loves me. Billy loves me, too, but I don't understand why."

Joshawa thought of all the years Billy and his brother lived secluded in the forest. Then, as he thought of Billy, the questions started. How did Billy know how to find the cave? How did he know Amy was here? Why would he keep that a secret?

"Have you met Billy before?"

Amy shook her head. "No, but I do feel safe with him. His voice and his smile are kind."

"Do you know who Amelia is?"

Amy rolled her eyes at Joshawa, and suddenly, she became the little girl he had first met. "You silly. That's my name." Amy glanced over to Billy and Mona. "They saved me from the evil." She glanced back at Joshawa, and now she no longer appeared confused or scared. The smile she gave Joshawa reassured him that she was content. "This is their home. Billy saved me. Billy brought me here."

CHAPTER TWENTY-FOUR

Serena and Imani returned to Serena's section of the Realm. Their first order of business was to meld with Lord Nathen and explain what it was that they needed from him. Serena knew that persuading Lord Nathen wasn't going to be easy. She was probably the last person he would trust, and she had no time to convince him otherwise. If he agreed, then they would join their minds with Mistress Authia and Mona. Serena had reservations about Mona, primarily due to the fact that Imani hadn't volunteered any additional information that would put Serena's mind at ease. Serena needed to be patient, which wasn't one of her stronger attributes. However, once Dava was saved, she would confront Imani and Lord Adeeowale.

Serena stood at the edge of the Realm, closed her eyes, and sought out Lord Nathen. When she located him, she was highly pleased with his progress in finding Joshawa. He was getting close, and before nightfall, he would be with his son. Serena reached out to Lord Nathen, knowing full well that it wouldn't be a pleasant conversation.

My Lord, I am in need of your help to save a life.

Nathen's voice flooded her mind, and it wasn't difficult to tell he wasn't pleased. *Serena! Whose life? My son's?*

Your son is safe from harm, but you must find him before night-fall.

That is my intention. Do you know where Joshawa is?

Yes. As do you. I am sorry, my Lord, but we have no time. Rick's son, Dava, is dying, and we need to help save him.

He's dying? What happened?

I'm truly sorry, my Lord, but we have no time for questions. We need you to reach out to Cassandra and ask her to reverse the spell she has cast on Dava.

If you want my help, then we're gonna make time for questions. I don't know what you're up to, Serena, but if I find that you have anything to do with my son's injuries . . .

My Lord, we have no time for this. You must trust me. I gave my life so that Mistress Authia could live. Now, I'm putting my entire existence in jeopardy so that Joshawa and Dava will live. I am risking everything, and all I ask of you is to trust me.

Nathen was standing in a small area where shrubs had been flattened and trees had been scarred with claw marks. It was evident that the shrubs in the area were laden with berries, and according to Dameon, more than one bear feasted here. There were no signs of any bears nearby, so they didn't need to be cautious. Nathen observed Dameon as he placed his backpack on the ground and retrieved the GPS. Dameon was about to show Nathen something on the GPS when Nathen's mind came alive with Serena's words. Anger built up inside him, and he couldn't believe what Serena was asking of him. At one time, he had trusted her, but that was almost two decades ago. Now, with everything that had transpired around Joshawa, trust was not something he was willing to do.

Trust you? Why would I trust you, Serena? You have been poisoning my son's mind to the point where he wants nothing to do with me or our family.

I understand. However, I had no choice. Your son lives because of me. You will discover that when you find him. I need you to trust me, to help me right now, or else it will be too late.

Nathen didn't know what to do. There was too much at stake, and one wrong choice could result in his son's death. *What do you need of me?*

Cassandra is a captive of an Ancestor, and he is using her to kill Dava. We must get through to her. However, she is entombed inside an orb, and reaching her will be difficult. I believe if we use four strong melders as a conduit, then maybe you can get through to her and convince her to reverse the spell.

Why would an Ancestor try to kill their own?

My Lord, I could spend the better part of the day explaining everything that has happened in the last week. We have no time for that. Joshawa has no time for your questions. You must reach him before nightfall or risk losing him. I promise you, my Lord, that I will explain everything later. I just need you to trust me now.

Nathen was so conflicted. Part of him wanted to help, and the other part wanted nothing to do with Serena. Nathen sighed and was about to meld with Serena when Authia's voice filled his mind.

Sweetheart, you must trust Serena. It is the only way to save Joshawa. His injuries are not his only enemy, and we must do what we can to save him.

Are you sure?

Yes. Trust Serena and those who help her. You must help her reach out to Cassandra.

Authia's voice was gone and was replaced with Serena's. *Will you help?*

Yes, but only because Authia trusts you.

Thank you, my Lord.

What do you need of me?

Once you have found Joshawa and you know he is safe, I need you to reach out to me. At that time, you will use us to reach out to Cassandra. You must tell her to stop what she is doing. Tell her that she is safe. If she mentions Lord Chike, tell her that he has been dealt with. Tell her to use us to reach Dava and reverse the spell. This must be done by the end of this day, or all is lost.

What Serena asked was more than trust. It was blind faith. But if Authia trusted Serena, then so will he. *I'll contact you as soon as I find Joshawa. But I warn you, Serena, if anything happens*

to my son, I'll become a spirit and make your life a living hell.
I understand, my Lord. Go now. Find Joshawa.

Imani stood by while Serena convinced Lord Nathen to help them. When Serena completed her task, she opened her eyes and faced Imani. "Lord Nathen will help us."

"I see now how you achieved your reputation. You were correct in asking me to reach out to Mistress Authia. It is astonishing to witness how strong her abilities are. She could see beyond my words, and she knew she could trust me. I would very much like to meet her one day."

"Depending on how successful Lord Adeeowale and we are, you may get your wish. Did you speak with Mona?"

Imani grinned and nodded her head. "Yes, and she will help us."

Lord Adeeowale stepped into the darkness, and he was immediately taken by surprise when he didn't fall into the emptiness that surrounded him. He appeared to be standing on something, though in the darkness, he couldn't make out what it was. He turned and reached out to confirm where the doorway was, but all he could find was solid rock. The doorway had vanished, leaving him alone in a place where there was no sunlight, moonlight, or stars to see by.

Lord Adeeowale was known for his bravery and his strength. But here in the darkness, any bravery or strength he had was being drained from his body. He scanned his surroundings in the hope of locating a source of light, but none could be found. There had to be some explanation for this place, and there had to be some way to navigate in the darkness. Lord Adeeowale glanced down at what he was standing on. It was possible that it was a path, but the pathway was as dark as its surroundings, which made it nearly invisible to the naked eye.

Lord Adeeowale tentatively placed his right foot in front of him to determine if a path actually existed. His foot found solid ground, so he took one step forward. Carefully, he knelt down and leaned forward, using his hands to determine the width of the path. It was no wider than he was, a discovery which caused Lord Adeeowale great concern. Then he used his hands to feel underneath the path and was surprised when he discovered nothing. The path seemed to be suspended in the darkness with nothing to support it. Lord Adeeowale stood and wondered what he'd got himself into. He couldn't go back, and remaining where he was would get him nowhere. His only option was to go forward. He placed his right foot in front of him and again found solid ground. Lord Adeeowale took a deep breath and slowly released it. He had no way of knowing how far this path would take him and could only imagine what he was going to find at the end of it.

"I must admit, you have impressed me."

Lord Adeeowale was startled by the voice resonating in the darkness. "Where am I, Lord Chike?"

"Welcome to my home in the Realm where I am the ruling Lord."

Lord Adeeowale scanned the emptiness as he tried to locate where Lord Chike's voice was coming from. "You are no Lord. You rule nothing except emptiness."

"Are you sure? Listen to my subjects. They call out to me."

Lord Adeeowale was assaulted by the cries and moaning of what seemed to be hundreds of voices. "These are your people? What place is this that holds such misery?"

"You are in the Realm of Despair where I am Lord. This is your home now, Lord Adeeowale, and you will pay for your treachery."

Dameon retrieved the GPS from the backpack and turned it on to calculate their next heading. "It's not far now, Nathen. Maybe three or four more hours of hiking." Dameon turned to show Nathen the GPS, only to find him staring off into the forest, his face blank of expression. "Nathen, are you okay?" Dameon placed the GPS on the ground next to his backpack and walked over to Nathen. He placed his hand on Nathen's shoulder and gently gave him a nudge. "Hey, Nathen, are you with me? What are you looking at?" Dameon followed Nathen's gaze into the forest but saw nothing. He took a step back and was actually concerned not only for Nathen but also for himself. He had no idea where Nathen's head was or what he was going to be like when he came out of this trance.

At that moment, Dameon thought of the gun he'd given Nathen and was having serious doubts about the decision to insist he carry a weapon. Nathen had placed the gun in the back of his waistband, and Dameon thought that this would be a good opportunity to take it back. He stood off to one side facing Nathen so he could keep an eye on him as he reached for the gun. Slowly, he maneuvered his left hand toward Nathen's waistband, but before he could grasp the gun, Nathen grabbed his right arm and twisted Dameon so that he was standing in front of him.

"What the hell, Nathen? You're hurting me." Dameon tried to read Nathen's expression to figure out how much trouble he was in. But Nathen didn't appear angry, and if Dameon had to guess, Nathen was more surprised than anything else. Nathen let go of Dameon's arm, and immediately, Dameon picked up his rifle and aimed it at Nathen.

"What are you doing, Dameon?"

"Protecting myself. What the hell just happened?"

Nathen felt for the gun in his waistband and discovered it was still there. He then focused his attention on Dameon. "What makes you think you need to protect yourself from me?"

"Are you kidding me? First you go into some sort of trance, and then you try to rip my arm off."

Nathen realized that in order to speak with Serena and Authia, he would've been deep-rooted in the meld. With that knowledge, he could understand why Dameon would think he was in a trance. "I can explain what happened, though you may not believe it."

"Why don't you try me?"

"I will, but we have to keep going. We need to reach the cave before nightfall." Nathen retrieved the gun from his waistband and then offered it to Dameon. "I don't blame you if you don't trust me with the gun. Take it."

Dameon lowered his rifle and took the gun off Nathen. He placed it back in its holster, grabbed his backpack, and threw it at Nathen. "From now on, I'm following you. I'll tell you where to go, but keep in mind that I'm going to have my rifle pointed at your back the entire time. You make one move I don't like, and I will shoot you."

"I promise it won't come to that."

Dameon picked up the GPS off the ground and took a quick look at it. "Start walking straight ahead. You have three hours to convince me why I shouldn't hand you over to Jax."

CHAPTER TWENTY-FIVE

Lord Adeeowale tried to shut out the cries of the spirits that were imprisoned in the Realm of Despair. He had always wondered if the Realm actually existed. Lord Adeeowale had heard about the spirits that were condemned to this place and how they suffered atrocities beyond imagination. He always believed that after the spirits received their punishment, they were then released to the darkness that surrounded the Land of the Spirits. But here he was, unable to see anything, and listening to thousands of anguished cries.

The Realm of Despair did exist, and as the wails of the prisoners echoed around him, Lord Adeeowale wondered if he had made a mistake that could cost him his existence. He held his hand in front of his face, and even though he knew it was there, he couldn't see it. The darkness swallowed him, and he knew if he spent any amount of time in this horrid place, he would surely go mad.

Somehow, Lord Chike had found his way in the darkness, and if Lord Adeeowale was going to survive, he was going to have to be smarter than his opponent. Lord Adeeowale sat cross-legged on the narrow path, then grabbed the edges to secure himself. If Lord Chike had any intentions of causing him to fall into the void, well, then he was going to have to work for it. "Lord Chike, you have me at a disadvantage. Apparently, you can see in this bleak darkness that has swallowed the entirety of this Realm. However, I cannot."

Lord Chike chuckled. "You believe that you are so superior, so much better than me. Look around, Lord Adeeowale.

I am the one who is superior, and you are nothing."

"That is easy for you to claim while I sit here in the darkness."

"My claim is valid no matter where you are, and soon, I will reign over all our people."

Silence surrounded Lord Adeeowale, which was a reprieve from the horrific cries of the Realm's inhabitants. However, the inability to sense the simplest of directions, such as what was up from what was down or what lurked in the darkness, made him uneasy. If he was going to get the upper hand, he would have to keep his eyes closed and not allow the darkness to consume him. Lord Adeeowale also knew that, most importantly, he needed to keep Lord Chike talking.

"You claim to be better than myself, yet you hide in the darkness. If you are truly superior, then show yourself." Lord Adeeowale waited for a response, but none came. "You are nothing more than a coward hiding in his hole. The outsider that rules our people is far more superior than you will ever be."

"You know nothing! I am not afraid of you. You cannot harm me. You cannot kill me. But I can control you, and if it pleases me, I can destroy you."

"Then prove it. If you're not afraid of me, show yourself." The path before Lord Adeeowale lit up, and at its end was a doorway bathed in a bright light.

Adrian stood outside the cave entrance with his jacket zipped up and his hands shoved into the pockets. The cool mountain air caused Adrian to shiver, and as he scanned the forest, he could see that some of the plant life still bore the signs from the early morning frost. These were all signs of an early winter, which could prove problematic if Nathen didn't arrive. Adrian scanned the forest again and listened for any signs of

Nathen. At the very latest, he should be there before nightfall. However, that all depended on whether or not he had obtained the GPS.

Adrian gazed up at the sky, and by the positioning of the sun, he figured that Nathen was only two or three hours away. If Nathen didn't arrive, then Adrian was going to have to come up with another plan to get Joshawa home. He turned to face inside the cave and watched Amy and Joshawa interacting. Then there was Billy and his bear, who he called Mona. There was something really odd about Billy and his devotion to the bear. Adrian smirked to himself because the words *odd* and *Billy* were regular companions.

Adrian's gaze fell on Joshawa, and he figured that there was no time like the present to figure out a Plan B. Adrian walked over to Joshawa and stood at Joshawa's feet. Joshawa was wrapped in an old, worn blanket, and there was a small fire close to him so he could benefit from the heat. On the other side of the fire was Amy. She was sitting on the ground cross-legged, and her focus was directed at Adrian. Joshawa glanced up at Adrian, as though he was waiting for Adrian to say something. Before Adrian could start the conversation, Joshawa beat him to it.

"What's up, Adrian?"

"Your dad should be here in the next few hours, but I think we should have a Plan B worked out just in case he doesn't make it."

"Why wouldn't my father make it here?"

"He's counting on one of the hunters, Dameon, to help him. There's no guarantee that he will. If I'd known that Billy knew of this place, your dad would have been here yesterday."

"Could you and Billy go there now and find out if my father needs help?"

"I thought of that. Problem is, if he's already on his way,

we could miss him. He's gonna be following the bear's route, which may be completely different from Billy's route. If we do get to the homestead and your dad's not there, we'd have no idea of where he was. We have no way of communicating with anyone." Adrian thought of what he just said. He'd forgotten that Joshawa and his family could communicate through their minds. "I'm an idiot. You can communicate with your parents. You call it melding, right?"

Joshawa slowly shook his head, and the anguish he felt was etched on his face. "Normally, yes, but ever since I've been here, I haven't been able to connect to them. And I'm guessing that my father can't sense my emotions either. Otherwise, he would've been here days ago."

Adrian appeared surprised at Joshawa's revelation. "So your family can also sense each other's emotions?"

"No, just my father and me. And you're right. If we can't communicate, then there's no sense in Billy and you going to look for my father."

"Maybe not today, but if they're not here by tomorrow morning, then we're gonna have to find our own way off the mountain. How are your injuries?"

"My head is doing pretty good, and my elbow feels fine. However, my ribs and my leg are a different story. I was thinking of straddling Alex and riding him off the mountain."

Adrian's face lit up. "That's perfect." Adrian glanced over at Amy. "What do you think, Amy? Will Alex let Joshawa ride on his back?"

Amy glanced over at Billy and Mona. "It's Mona now. I don't know. Maybe you should ask her."

Joshawa looked at Amy, who was still focused on Billy and Mona. "So we're calling your bear Mona now?"

Amy maintained her focus on Billy and Mona. "That's her

name."

Joshawa reached over and cupped Amy's chin with his fingers and gently turned her head so that she looked directly at him. "You do know that the bear is a male?" Amy nodded her head, which indicated that she did. "Okay, we need to figure out what's going on. But first, how about you and I speak to Mona? See if she'll help."

Amy shrugged her shoulders. "I guess we can ask."

When Amy went to stand, Joshawa put his hand on her knee. "Stay here."

Amy scrunched her face at Joshawa and was extremely sarcastic in her comment. "Are we gonna yell at her?"

Amy's comment caused Joshawa to chuckle. "No, we're not going to yell at her. Can you ask her to speak directly to me the same way she speaks to you?"

At that very second, Joshawa could feel Mona's presence within his mind. "You understand what we're saying?"

Yes, I do.

Can Amy and Billy hear us?

Only if I allow it. This conversation is just between you and me. I will help you off this mountain. It's the least I can do. You have been so kind to my Amelia.

How is it that you can meld? Animals shouldn't be able to meld.

If animals are not allowed to meld, then what does that make me?

I have no idea. Care to enlighten me?

This body belongs to a grizzly, but his mind belongs to me.

That doesn't explain anything. Actually, all it does is create more questions.

I'll tell you what I know, but you can't tell Amelia. She's not ready yet.

What do you mean she's not ready yet?

She's not ready to relive the past. Mona went silent, and Joshawa waited till she was ready to continue.

Our past, that of Billy, Amelia, and myself, is not something we care to dwell on. I'm happy that Billy has been able to bury all that went on in that horrid cabin. And, as I said, Amelia is not ready.

Okay, that's fair. So, let's go back to the original question. How is it that you can meld?

I was given a great gift many years ago. The plan was for Amelia and me to hide in this cave until it was safe. On the day we were to leave, I was severely beaten by a man who was cruel and deranged. He was the personification of pure evil. Billy carried me to the edge of the forest. He sat on the ground and held me in his arms. He cried so much I could feel his tears on my face. That's when a grizzly cub came up to Billy. It was incredible to witness. The cub came up to us and lay down in front of Billy. That's when I heard her. She was in my mind, speaking so softly. I don't know who she was or how she did it, but she took my mind, my very soul, and placed it inside the bear. I became one with the bear, and my human body went limp in Billy's arms.

So you're saying that a human mind is able to exist inside an animal?

Obviously.

Who are you, and what is your relationship to Amy?

I guess it's safe to say now. The evil has been dead for many years. My name is Monique. But Billy has always called me Mona. Amy is Amelia, and she's my daughter.

Nathen followed Dameon's instructions to the letter as they made their way deeper into the forest. They hadn't uttered one word since they left the berry patch. Nathen knew he was in trouble and had no idea how he was going to explain himself to Dameon. However, whatever explanation he was going to use, it would have to wait until they arrived at the cave. It was already mid-afternoon, which meant they only had a couple of hours until sunset, and according to Serena, by then, it might be too late.

Half an hour later, Nathen and Dameon came across a narrow path that was obviously used quite often. Nathen stopped and waited for Dameon to join him. When Dameon stepped out into the path, he was still carrying his rifle, only now it was pointed at the ground and not at Nathen.

Nathen waited while Dameon checked the GPS, and when Dameon glanced up, Nathen decided to start the conversation. "So which way?"

Dameon looked up and down the path, then rechecked the GPS. Nathen watched him closely, hoping to get a feeling of what his mood was. Dameon glanced over to Nathen, and for a split second, it looked like Dameon was about to show Nathen the GPS. But instead, he hesitated, then turned the GPS off. Without taking his eyes off Nathen, he placed the GPS on a large boulder that was nestled in between several smaller boulders at the outer edge of the path. Dameon took a step forward, which placed himself between Nathen and the GPS.

"Maybe now would be a good time to explain to me what happened back there."

"I will as soon as we get to the cave. Once I know Joshawa is safe, I'll tell you everything."

"The problem with that scenario, Nathen, is that I don't know what's waiting for me at the cave. I also don't trust that you won't zone out again. We're not going anywhere near the cave until I'm certain that I'm gonna be safe at the cave with you and your son." Dameon raised his rifle at waist level and pointed the barrel at Nathen. "I'm waiting."

CHAPTER TWENTY-SIX

L ord Adeeowale followed the lighted path, and with all the twists and turns, he was glad he hadn't gone any further in the dark. When he reached the doorway, he stood on the threshold, completely astonished by the lavish adornments inside the room. Cautiously, he walked inside and scanned the room, looking for Lord Chike, but he was nowhere to be seen.

Lord Adeeowale stood in the middle of the room with his mouth gaping open and his eyes widened in disbelief. The Lion People lived a simple life. They had no use for gold or silver or precious gems. But in this room, Lord Chike surrounded himself with luxuries grander than Lord Adeeowale could ever dream of.

The room appeared as if it had been carved out of marble that ran rich with colors similar to the rainforest in Africa. The marble walls glistened, and they were adorned with tapestries that were meticulous in their detail. Lord Adeeowale walked over to the first tapestry. He examined it carefully and realized that it spoke of a battle between the Destroyer and the ruling Lord.

Each tapestry depicted images of how the Destroyer defeated the reigning Lord, as well as those that protected the Lord. From what Lord Adeeowale could tell, each time the Destroyer was called upon, a tapestry was created to commemorate the battle. The brutal slaying of the Lords and those who fought for them sickened Lord Adeeowale.

"What do you think of my tapestries? They are beautiful.

Do you not agree?"

Lord Adeeowale turned and found Lord Chike sitting behind a wooden table. On the table were several rolled-up scrolls, as well as one that laid flat. The scroll that laid flat was positioned directly in front of Lord Chike. From where Lord Adeeowale stood, he could see that the scroll was blank.

"I would not describe anything you have here as beautiful. Since when do our Lords have to surround themselves with adornments such as these?"

Lord Chike placed his elbows on the table, joined his hands together, and rested them on top of the rolled-out scroll. "As a Lord, do you not believe that we are entitled to such adornments, as you put it?"

"Our entitlements are offered to us by the Council of Five. Are you saying that the Council gifted you these atrocities?"

Lord Chike stood and walked around the table. The first thing that Lord Adeeowale noticed was that he wore a belt tied to his waist, and strapped to his left hip was a long, curved machete.

Lord Chike gently shook his head as he grinned at Lord Adeeowale. "There is so much that you do not know. Let me ask you a question. Who is the Destroyer?"

Lord Adeeowale knew that Lord Chike was playing with him. Unfortunately, Lord Adeeowale was not privy to the rules of this game. "Why ask a question that you already know the answer to?"

"Are you afraid to answer the question?"

Lord Adeeowale scanned each tapestry, and in every tapestry, the Destroyer took on a different appearance. So why ask the question when the answer was sitting right in front of him? "The Destroyer is not a person. It's an entity that is released by the Council and takes possession of a warrior's body."

"You have not answered the question. Who is the

Destroyer?"

Lord Adeeowale remembered what Serena had told him about Lord Chike and that he was two entities. Lord Adeeowale smiled at Lord Chike. "Okay, I'll play. You are the vessel for the Destroyer. The Destroyer lives within you."

"Very good. Next question. Who is the Council of Five?"

Again, Lord Adeeowale scanned the tapestries and the room itself. He returned his focus to Lord Chike. "Do you not mean who are the Council of Five?"

"You tell me."

"Lord Chike, I am not here to play games with you. I'm here to find out what your intentions are. If you truly are the Destroyer, then what are you doing here? Why did the Council release you?"

Lord Chike shook his head as he walked to the back of the table, only this time he didn't sit down. "You displease me, Lord Adeeowale. Serena would know the answers. She is clever, way too much for her own good. That is why when I am done with her, she will join you here, in the Realm of Despair. And you need not lament about your Imani. She will also join you."

"You are delusional. You have no say as to who resides in this prison."

"My Lord, you are the one who is delusional. You have seen the tapestries, yet you do not question them. You have spent time with me, yet you do not recognize me. You gave me this scar, yet you do not remember doing so."

Lord Adeeowale was shocked by Lord Chike's words. He searched the tapestries, and then he focused on Lord Chike's face, but nothing sparked a memory. "I do not understand. I have no memory . . ." Lord Adeeowale's voice trailed off as he remembered what Serena had said. His memories were buried deep within him, and a false one was put in its place. He closed his eyes and gently shook his head. "It was you."

Lord Adeeowale opened his eyes, and staring back at him was his likeness that had been woven into the fabric of the tapestry. If anger was a color, it would be the color of his eyes, which were as black as the Realm of Despair. "You are correct. Serena is smart. She figured it out. You took my memories from me and gave me false ones."

Lord Chike smiled as he slowly clapped his hands. "Well done, Lord Adeeowale." Lord Chike placed his hands, palms down, on the table and leaned forward. "Would you like your memories back?"

Lord Adeeowale walked over to the table, and with both hands, he grabbed the edges of Lord Chike's vest. He pulled Lord Chike toward him until his face was mere inches away. "Give me back what you stole from me, and I will let the Council deal with you. Refuse to do so, then I will be the one who confines you in the Realm of Despair."

Nathen walked over to another grouping of boulders that was at the edge of the path. He sat on one of them, which put him ten feet away from Dameon. Dameon remained standing and kept his rifle pointed at Nathen. Nathen had no idea how much further the cave was. All he knew was that he had no time to explain to Dameon how the melding of minds worked. Nathen was facing the path that continued up the mountain. Judging from the last time he looked at the GPS, Nathen assumed that the path leading away from the mountain would lead him to a water source. If Nathen were to guess, he would say the logical path to follow was the one that headed further up the mountain.

Nathen stood and approached Dameon until he was only three feet away. "What happened to me can't be explained in a couple of minutes. Yes, I was zoned out, but I wasn't dangerous."

"Come on, Nathen, you have to do better than that."

"I don't have time. Think about it, Dameon. I could have taken your GPS at any time. If I'm so dangerous, then why didn't I hurt you and Jax when I was hiding at the old Jenkins homestead? Do you think I like spending my nights in the cold?" Nathen could tell that he was getting through to Dameon, so he continued. "All I want is to find my son, and I will do whatever it takes to accomplish that. I like you, Dameon, and I know you're a good person, as am I. But if I have to, I will tie you up and drag you until we find the cave."

Nathen observed Dameon as he shook his head and rolled his eyes. "Right, Nathen, you're going to tie me up. You may be strong, but do you honestly think you can make that three-foot gap between us before I fire my rifle?"

Nathen quickly took a couple of steps, grabbed the rifle, and pulled it out of Dameon's hands. By the look on Dameon's face, he was shocked, and his hand remained extended as if he were still holding the rifle.

Dameon lowered his arm and placed his right hand on the butt of his gun. "Now what, Nathen?"

Nathen used the rifle to point to the path. "We continue up the path. I assume the cave would be higher up in the mountain."

Dameon couldn't believe how fast Nathen could disarm him. Then the realization that Nathen could have disarmed him at any time hit him hard. His entire body felt clammy, and for the first time since he was a child, he was undeniably scared for his life. There was one other fact that Dameon was trying to come to terms with. Nathen could have hurt or even killed him. God knew he'd had plenty of opportunities. So, why didn't he? "What are you going to do with me?"

Nathen appeared puzzled by the question. "What do you

mean?"

"You have what you need to find your son and protect yourself. Though I'm thinking that you don't need firepower to accomplish that."

"Dameon, I need you to help me. I'm not going to hurt you. I trust you to find my son." Nathen handed the rifle back to Dameon. "We don't have much time. Can we leave now?"

Dameon took the rifle as he stared into Nathen's eyes. What he saw were the eyes of someone in great emotional pain. Not the eyes of someone that was planning to kill him. And Dameon would know what those eyes look like after years of living with Jax. The fear that consumed Dameon's body was dissipating. His instincts were shouting loud and clear that he could trust Nathen. "Okay, we can leave. But you'll still have to explain yourself when we get there."

"I promise."

Jax had kept his distance from Dameon for most of the morning, but as the sun started to make its way closer to the horizon, Jax began closing the distance between them.

In the fall, when the forest shed its leaves, it allowed sounds to echo within the forest. It was a disadvantage to Jax because he had to be extremely quiet as he closed the gap. However, it also meant that he didn't have to get too close to hear what they were saying.

It was mid-afternoon when Jax was positioned close enough to listen in on their conversation. He could make out that there were two people. But unfortunately, he couldn't get close enough to Dameon's friend to make out any physical details. By the conversation, Jax knew that Dameon was with his Bigfoot, and the thought of capturing Bigfoot sent shivers of delight up and down Jax's spine. However, when he heard about Bigfoot's son, Jax couldn't contain his excitement. He closed the distance even more, which put him dangerously close to Dameon. He gambled that Dameon wouldn't figure out that he was being followed.

From what Jax could get out of the conversation, time was an issue. They were heading for a cave where they figured Bigfoot's son would be. Jax's plan was to take them as soon as they got close enough to tranquilize Bigfoot. However, when he heard about the son, he decided to follow them all the way to the cave. With two Bigfoots in his possession, he could sell one and then spend his time with the other.

Serena and Imani remained at the edge of the Realm so they could see when Lord Nathen arrived at the cave. They sat cross-legged as they stared out into the darkness. Serena gazed down upon the bear and observed the interaction between the bear and the man they called Billy. Her curiosity was churning her insides into knots. She needed to know what had happened between Imani and the bear.

Serena continued to watch the bear, as well as Billy. She glanced over to Imani. "So what part does Billy play in the transformation of your bear?"

"Billy loves the bear."

"That is not what I asked." Serena moved so that she could directly face Imani. "I need to know about your bear. We are staking a lot on the fact that your bear can meld as well as we do. I have to know everything because if we make one mistake, then Dava dies, and Lord Chike wins."

Imani moved to one side so that she, too, could face Serena. Imani closed her eyes, and when she opened them, Serena could see the tears forming in the corner of her eyes. "Serena, you helped Lord Joshawa. He was dying, and you intervened."

"Yes, I did. That was the only way to save him. How do

you know that? Not even Lord Chike is aware of what I did."

"Mona knows. I will tell you, but please do not think badly of me. I am not sorry for what I did, and I will accept my punishment. But you have to know that Lord Adeeowale had nothing to do with this."

"I have no intention of reporting you or Lord Adeeowale to the Council. But I do need clarification about Lord Adeeowale's evolvement with the bear. You say he has nothing to do with it, and if that is true, then how does he know it happened?"

"I would rather not speak of that."

"All right then, let's speak about how your bear became Mona." Serena could feel Imani's anguish. She could see the turmoil that Imani felt just by looking into her eyes. Serena placed her hands on Imani's knees.

"I will not judge you." Serena chuckled as she smiled. "If you knew half of the things that I have done in my lifetime, then you would know that I am in no position to judge anyone. And what we discuss here will never go any further."

Imani wiped the tears from her face, then folded her hands in her lap. "I was here in the Land of the Ancestors watching our people with Lord Adeeowale." Imani glanced around, taking in her surroundings. "I came upon this place quite by accident. The clearing was much smaller than it is now. I was curious about what I would see from here, so I came to the edge and looked down. I saw outsiders living in a beautiful forest, and then I saw him."

"Who did you see?"

"Lord Nathen, but he was only a child. I was so taken aback that I ran to Lord Adeeowale to tell him what I saw. He already knew of Lord Nathen's existence. There was a curse on Lord Nathen, and I was told not to interfere."

"Yes, I know of that curse because I was the one who placed it on him."

Imani gasped, and her eyes went wide. Serena's emotions of guilt and shame slammed against her heart as if they were tidal waves.

"As I said, I'm not one to judge."

"Why?"

"It's a long story and one that should be kept for another time, but please continue with yours and start with why your bear can meld and who is Mona?"

CHAPTER TWENTY-SEVEN

Authia sat at the kitchen table with Hansen and Tammy. They were on their third pot of coffee while trying to figure out how to find Billy and Adrian. Authia sighed while she stared at her cup of coffee. "They could be anywhere." Then Authia gazed over to where Becca was sleeping. "According to Becca, we shouldn't worry."

Tammy interjected, "How can we not worry? This is the second day they've been gone. And what's with Adrian's father? You'd think he'd be at your doorstep banging on the door, looking for his son."

Hansen took a long sip of his coffee, placed the mug on the table, and wrapped his hands around the mug. "Fact is, Adrian's father wouldn't come here even if his life depended on it."

There was no denying that Tammy was angered by what Hanson had said. "You've got to be kidding! Your telling me that his decades-long hatred for Nathen would prevent him from asking for help to find his son?"

Hansen shrugged his shoulders. "He definitely has a hate-on for Nathen, and it's obvious he's not thinking straight. Adrian's father could easily just come to Tammy's and my cabin. He doesn't even have to see Nathen. Hatred can really mess with your brain. But getting back to Billy and Adrian, Billy survived for years in the woods. Adrian is an awesome hunter, and he knows the woods. At least the woods around Burwood and here."

Authia wasn't convinced. "My gut says they're not where

they should be. When I connected with Serena and we were putting a plan together to save Joshawa, she never mentioned Billy or Adrian." Authia hesitated for a moment. "Actually, when I was in the meld with Serena, Imani, and Nathen, I also sensed that a bear was present. I shouldn't have been able to. It's just an animal."

At that moment, Becca woke up and headed to the kitchen. She helped herself to a mug from the kitchen cupboard and then poured herself a coffee. Becca turned around and leaned against the counter, holding the mug in front of her. "There's no need to worry. They're all together, and they're expecting Uncle Nathen before dark."

Everyone looked at Becca as if she'd grown horns.

Authia was the first to speak up. "How do you know that, Becca?"

"It was in my dream. I felt Joshawa's presence, and through his eyes, I saw Adrian, Billy, and a girl they call Amy. Oh yes, the bear was there, as well."

"And they're all in a cave?"

"Of course, Aunty. Where else would they be?" Becca walked away from the kitchen and went to curl up on the loveseat. Before she sat down, she glanced over to Authia. "I'm not sure why, but I think you should stop melding with Uncle Nathen."

"Why? That's my only connection to what's going on with him and Joshawa."

Becca shrugged her shoulders. "I don't know, but deep down, I feel that Uncle Nathen needs to focus on reaching the cave. He'll meld with you when he gets there." Becca sat down on the loveseat and started to drink her coffee as if everything she shared was normal.

Imani was scared to tell the truth. What she had done was

wrong in the eyes of the Council. However, she had never regretted it, and still, to this day, she harbored no regrets. If the Council decided to seek punishment, then Imani would welcome it. "I would come often to watch the young Lord. I felt so sorry for him. He was lost, a prisoner in his own body. One day, I ventured further down the Realm, and I came across a cabin where two men lived. One of them was Billy, and the other was his brother, Dext. The brother was so cruel, not only to Billy but also to the animals that he would capture. What I witnessed was so horrific that I decided never to come back to this part of the Realm."

"But you did. What made you go back?"

"Billy. Lord Adeeowale said that I could not interfere. I could not help him, but he was being beaten every day. Somehow, I had to help. I could not sit back and ignore what was happening. It had been a very long time since I was in that area of the Realm, and I have regretted that decision every day. When I arrived and looked down on the cabin, what I witnessed made me ill. The brother had a woman with him who was badly beaten and shackled. Serena, there was also a child, a young girl they called Amelia. It was then that I realized how long I had been gone."

"How long had it been?"

"From what I understand, Dext had kidnapped the woman, and when he brought her to the cabin, she had no child. I will never forgive myself for waiting so long to get back."

Serena took Imani's hands in hers and gave them a gentle squeeze. "Time here in the Realm is much different from their time. You must know that."

"I do, but that knowledge does not lessen my guilt. I went to Lord Adeeowale, and again, he could not help me. I am a warrior, not a priestess. I did not possess the knowledge I needed to save Billy and Mona. Lord Adeeowale accompanied me to see for himself. When we arrived, Billy had taken the child to a cave, and he was coming back for Mona. Before Billy returned, his brother discovered their plan to escape, and he beat Mona without mercy. Billy came upon them, and for the first time, probably in his entire life, Billy attacked his brother. Serena, you would not believe how this timid, gentle man became so angry that in one punch, his brother fell to the ground unconscious.

"I watched as he carried Mona's body to the edge of the clearing. He sat cross-legged on the ground and held her in his lap, close to his body." Imani remembered that day as if it just occurred. She relived the pain and the anguish she felt for Billy. Imani wiped the tears from her face and continued. "And then he started to rock back and forth, crying uncontrollably. I turned to Lord Adeeowale, and from the way he looked at Billy, I knew he also felt Billy's pain. That was when the bear cub came and lay next to Billy.

"The bear had no fear of Billy or the constant crying. It was then that I begged Lord Adeeowale to help, and he did. He took my hands and spoke to someone from the Land of the Spirits. At that moment, I knew what to do. I left the Realm and went to stand next to Billy. I took Mona's mind and her soul and placed them in the bear. I gave her the ability to meld with both her daughter and Billy. She was going to be Amelia's protector until Billy returned to the cave." Imani closed her eyes and drew a deep breath. When she opened her eyes, she saw the tears running down Serena's cheeks. "Have I said something distasteful?"

"No, not at all. The truth is, I knew about Billy and Dext. But I was so focused on Lord Nathen that I did nothing. You are brave, Imani, and you have strength that no one can see. Please continue."

"I spoke to Billy and told him what I did. He buried her, but he did not go back to the cave."

"Why not?"

"Because of his brother. If Billy left, he knew his brother would hunt him down, and he could not take the chance of his brother finding Amelia."

Serena smiled at Imani as she reached out and placed her right hand on Imani's hands. "You saved Amelia. She would not have lived if you had not interfered."

"Yes. But as her mother was shackled in that cabin, I shackled Amelia to the cave. She grew up alone."

"You are missing the obvious. Amelia grew up in a safe environment, and she is healthy because of you. She had her mother to care for her, to protect her."

Serena smiled as Imani said, "Thank you. I still wish I could have done more."

"There was not much more you could have done. Do you know who the father was?"

Imani was perplexed by the question. "Is it not obvious? Billy is Amelia's father."

Lord Adeeowale pushed Lord Chike away from him and then took a couple steps back himself. "Why? Why take my memories?"

Lord Chike smiled at Lord Adeeowale as he walked over and stood in front of a large, black curtain. "Really. You have no idea as to why I would do that?"

"I do not."

Lord Chike gently shook his head. "Tsk, tsk, tsk. And I thought that you were smarter than that. I took your memories so that you would forget."

"Forget what? You took my memories and planted new ones. Why would you do that?"

"Once again, you fail to see what is standing right in front of you."

Lord Adeeowale didn't know if he was referring to himself or the tapestries. He decided to take a shot in the dark. "May I examine your tapestries more closely?"

Lord Chike smiled as he held his hand out toward them. "Please, I welcome you to."

Lord Adeeowale walked over to the first tapestry. It was depicting a time well before his own. At the very top of the tapestry were five figures cloaked in black, which Lord Adeeowale assumed to be the Council of Five. Just below them was a bolt of lightning that struck a man carrying a shield and a machete. He was obviously a warrior, and the Council had chosen him to be the Destroyer's vessel. The remainder of the tapestry depicted a great fight in which the Destroyer conquered all. At the bottom of the tapestry, the warrior that was possessed by the Destroyer stood on top of the bodies of men, women, and children. He had his weapon raised, and his face, though smiling, was pure evil.

Lord Adeeowale went from tapestry to tapestry, and each one told the same story. However, when he was about half-way through, he immediately noticed a difference. He took a step closer so that he could touch the tapestry. The Destroyer was fighting the Lord, and he was losing. The bottom of the tapestry revealed that the Lord won, but there was an emptiness in the Lord. It was as if the Lord was hollow inside. The bottom of every other tapestry revealed the Destroyer's victory. However, on this one, the bottom of the tapestry was blank. Lord Adeeowale ran his fingers over the face of the Lord. Something was terribly wrong. Something deep within him told him that this tapestry was false. Lord Adeeowale turned to face Lord Chike. "Your tapestries speak of your victories, but not this one. Why is that?"

Lord Chike moved over to the center of the curtain. "That is my least favorite. The tapestries give me much pleasure, at least everyone but that one. The tapestries appear after I conquered the reigning Lord. I have no say over what is woven into the fabric or the story it tells."

"Why do I not believe you?"

"Believe what you must. Do you now know who I am?"

Lord Adeeowale didn't answer Lord Chike. He turned and went back to the tapestry, only this time, he closed his eyes and placed the palm of his hand on the fabric. As he ran his hand slowly along the width of the tapestry, a great battle appeared in his mind. But the tapestry wasn't telling him the story. He remembered it. He was there. He was the Lord that had to be destroyed. He felt the machete in his hand, and he felt anger as the tip of the machete ran across the Destroyer's face. Lord Adeeowale turned and faced Lord Chike.

"I remember. I was the one who gave you that scar."

Lord Chike ran his index finger along the scar. "Yes, you did. You proved to me that I am not immortal. You proved to me that I could die."

"Then why did you not honor the tribe and die?"

Lord Chike took a deep breath and slowly released it. "Because I realized at that moment what had to be done so that I could be immortal. Occupying the body of a warrior was not the answer. However, placing my essence in the body of a warrior and having that warrior as my prisoner ensured my immortality."

Lord Chike snickered at Lord Adeeowale. "Do you now remember that fateful day? Do you not remember which warrior I took?"

Lord Adeeowale's mind was confused with true memories crashing into false ones. He was remembering the battle but not the outcome. "No, I do not. Since you took my memories, the least you could do is tell me why you are so desperate for me to remember."

Lord Chike smiled as he grabbed the curtain. "I will do better than that. I will show you which warrior."

Lord Chike pulled the curtain to one side, and chained to the back wall was a man from the tribe. He sat on the ground with his head resting on the wall. He was so thin, and his entire body was covered in scars. Some were healed, and some were gaping wounds that oozed blood and pus. Lord Adeeowale took a step closer and noticed that the prisoner wore a metal collar around his neck. The collar was attached to the wall with a six-foot chain. His wrists and ankles also bore the burden of metal cuffs. Lord Adeeowale was angered beyond description. He glanced over to Lord Chike. "What have you done?"

"I have done what was needed to ensure my survival. Can you guess how?"

Lord Adeeowale thought of all the tapestries and all the injuries that had been inflicted on the Destroyer. However, Lord Chike only bore the injury that Lord Adeeowale inflicted. He then turned his attention to the prisoner. "Are you saying that this man bears your wounds?"

"Yes. That is precisely what I am saying. You see, I am immortal because any wounds that I am inflicted with are passed on to him. He feels the pain. He watches as his body is ripped open, his bones crushed, and he waits in agony for the wounds to heal."

"Are you telling me that the Council approves of this atrocity?" Lord Adeeowale pointed toward the prisoner.

Lord Chike walked over to the prisoner and knelt down so that he would be at eye level. He didn't take his eyes off the prisoner when he replied, "They approved because they had to. But that is a story for another time. Do you recognize this man?" Lord Chike looked up at Lord Adeeowale. "Come closer and take a good look."

Lord Adeeowale approached the prisoner as Lord Chike grabbed a handful of the prisoner's hair and held his head up for Lord Adeeowale to clearly see. The prisoner's eyes locked onto Lord Adeeowale, and instantly, memories started to bombard Lord Adeeowale's mind. He could hear Lord Chike laughing in the background, and in his mind, he could hear the prisoner's voice.

Help me, Father, please end my suffering. Please kill me.

CHAPTER TWENTY-EIGHT

Nathen picked up his pace as the sun became dangerously close to sinking into the horizon. He figured that he had, at the most, three hours to save his son. Nathen paid no attention to Dameon, as if he wasn't even there. His mind was consumed with only one thought, and that was saving his son. Nathen was confident that Joshawa was close, and that fueled his determination. He approached a bend in the path, and as he made his way past it, he immediately stopped short. Nathen couldn't believe what was only a few yards ahead of him.

Dameon walked over to Nathen and stood next to him. "Holy shit, Nathen! We found it!" In front of them was a small clearing and the entrance to a cave. "Okay, Nathen, it may . . ."

Before Dameon could finish his sentence, Nathen ran toward the cave, calling Joshawa's name.

Joshawa was trying to make sense of what Mona had revealed to him. How on earth could she be Amy's mother? And how the hell could she meld with him? Joshawa was about to meld with Mona when he heard his name being shouted from outside the cave. "That's my father. He found me!" Without giving it any thought, Joshawa instinctively tried to stand up. Unfortunately, the pain from his injuries encompassed his entire body, so all he could do was to call out, "Father! I'm here!"

Nathen stopped when he reached the entrance to the cave. He glanced inside and found his son less than ten feet away from him. Nathen ran into the cave, fell to his knees, and tried to hug his son. But when Joshawa grimaced in pain, Nathen let go and leaned back on his haunches. "Are you okay?"

Tears were streaming down Joshawa's face. "I'm fine, Father. I almost gave up all hope of you finding me."

"Your mother and I never stopped searching for you. We love you, son, and the thought of losing you was more than we could bear."

"Didn't you hear my melds or sense my emotions?"

"No. I couldn't sense any of your emotions. And neither your mother nor I could hear your melds. I'm sure Serena is responsible, and I intend to talk to her when this is all over."

Nathen was about to ask Joshawa about his injuries when an unfamiliar voice filled his mind.

Don't waste precious time on conversations. They can wait. Joshawa is fine, but he won't be for long. You must reach out to Serena. But first, let Authia know that you are with Joshawa and he is safe.

Who are you?

Mona.

Nathen was about to ask who Mona was when he felt as if someone was watching him with an intensity so strong that Nathen couldn't ignore it. He glanced slightly to his left and discovered a large grizzly making its way toward him. Nathen couldn't believe that he'd missed seeing the bear when he first entered the cave. Especially one as large as this bear. The grizzly's focus was on Nathen, and when their eyes met, Nathen knew that this bear was no ordinary bear. Nathen didn't divert his attention as he reached out and melded with the bear. *Don't you mean the bear?*

No, I mean exactly what I said.

I agree time is precious, but the meld with Serena can wait until I know what's going on here.

Just be cautious. When the day is done, there will be no turning back, and Joshawa will be lost to you forever.

The voice was gone, and when Nathen glanced over to Joshawa, he could see the fear in his eyes.

"What did she mean father? Is something bad going to happen to me?"

Since Nathen couldn't hug his son, he gently placed his hands on either side of Joshawa's face and smiled at him. "No, Joshawa, you're going to be fine." Nathen sat next to Joshawa, facing the entrance of the cave, and placed his right hand on Joshawa's good leg. "I need to let your mother know that I found you. She'll want to know how badly you were hurt when you fell out of the tree."

"Tell her that I'm fine and that I'm so sorry that I put you both through this." Joshawa paused for a second, then looked at Nathen. "How did you know I fell out of a tree?"

"Your mother, of course. And you have nothing to be sorry about."

Joshawa gently shook his head, indicating that he disagreed with Nathen. "I've treated you so badly."

"You're no different than I was at your age."

Nathen hadn't noticed Amy until she sat down at Joshawa's feet. Nathen turned to face her and found her staring at him. "You look like your son. Does his mother look like you?"

"Father, this is Amy."

"Hi, Amy, pleased to meet you. No. His mother looks like you." He turned back to Joshawa. "Speaking of your mother, I have to let her know you're okay. She'll want to know how badly you're hurt, so what should I tell her?"

Amy spoke up as she pointed to where the injuries occurred. "He had a bad concussion and a gouge to the back of his head. His elbow was dislocated, he has three broken ribs, and his leg is broken."

Nathen was overwhelmed at the list of injuries Joshawa suffered. "How did you survive?"

"It was Amy. She mended me, took care of me, and fed me. I owe my life to her."

To Nathen, Amy didn't come across as someone who possessed any knowledge in the medical field. "And you were able to help him?"

"Yes. I healed him, then I fixed him. He still needs a lot of fixing."

Nathen laughed. "Yes, he does. Thank you, Amy. Thank you for saving Joshawa's life."

Joshawa reached out and took Amy's hand in his. Then he turned his attention to Nathen. "I know that I haven't been a very good son. But the last few days here, with Amy, I now know just how lucky I am."

Nathen smiled at Joshawa. He desperately wanted to pull Joshawa into his arms and hold him. However, with his injuries, such affection wasn't possible. "I'm going to reach out to your mother, and then we'll deal with Serena."

Nathen closed his eyes and then sought out Authia.

My Love, I have found our son, and he's fine.

Authia was so excited it sounded as if she was shouting inside his head. *Oh my god! You found him! What about his injuries?*

Nathen smiled to himself. It was a great relief to him to hear Authia happy again. *They're nothing that Edward and time can't heal. I have to reach out to Serena. If I understand her correctly, then just finding Joshawa isn't enough to save him.*

I know. You reach out to Serena, and I will, too. But it has to be done now.

Nathen opened his eyes and focused his attention on Joshawa.

Joshawa smiled and motioned toward Adrian. "Did you notice my companions?"

To be honest, Nathen didn't see anyone other than his son. He glanced up, and the first person he saw was Adrian. Nathen stood up and wrapped his arms around Adrian.

"I'm so glad to see you." Nathen let go of Adrian and took a step back. "How did you find this place?"

"Actually, it was Billy who led me here." Adrian motioned over to Billy, who was sitting next to Mona. "Remember the Amelia that he had to save?"

"Yes." Nathen glanced over to Amy. "Is that her?"

"Yup. Now, who's your friend?"

Nathen glanced over to Dameon. "Come here, Dameon, and meet my son." Nathen waited for Dameon to come closer before he started the introductions. "This is my son, Joshawa and this is Adrian."

Dameon held his hand out to Joshawa. "I'm glad to finally meet you, Joshawa." Dameon held out his hand to Adrian. "So what is your part in this rescue?"

"Long story to be told later."

Joshawa interjected. "So Dameon, how do you play out in this scenario?"

Dameon glanced over to Mona. "The bear over there is tagged with a microchip. Your dad believed that you were in a cave with a bear. We took a chance that it was my bear."

Joshawa appeared puzzled. "My bear? Why would you tag him?"

"Because he's worth a lot of money to me and my partner."

Lord Adeeowale knelt before the prisoner and placed his hands on either side of his face. Sadness washed over him as he gazed into the prisoner's eyes. These were the eyes of a man who had been tortured without cause, and anything pure and joyful had been drained from his soul. "I am so sorry. I have no memory of you. My son, at least the one I can remember, lives in the Land of the Spirits."

Lord Chike tightened his grip on the prisoner's hair and pulled his face up closer to Lord Adeeowale. "Take a good look, Lord Adeeowale. Does he not trigger even a flicker of memory?"

Lord Adeeowale looked up at Lord Chike, his voice filled with anger. "Release him, now!"

Lord Chike violently let go of his prisoner. "The fact that he cannot breathe life into even a sliver of your memories is proof of just how powerful I am."

Lord Adeeowale scanned the emaciated, scared face of the prisoner. Even with his memories intact, the man who knelt before him was a ghost of his former self.

"I hold no ill will, Father. Your memories of me have been lost since the battle." The prisoner tried to smile. "A battle you won. A battle that almost saw the extinction of the Destroyer."

Lord Chike looked down at his prisoner. "His mind is quite addled. He knows nothing of any battle other than the pain inflicted on him." Lord Chike returned to his table, sat down, and held up one of the rolled-up scrolls. "Do you now understand what these scrolls represent?"

Lord Adeeowale gently laid his son on the floor, stood, and then walked to the center of the room. He scanned every tapestry, then returned to one depicting a battle that the Destroyer almost lost. "Should I understand what they represent?" Lord Adeeowale walked over to the tapestry and ran his fingers over the image of one of the warriors. "Should I understand why you would keep a tapestry that you detest?"

"Detest is a strong word. I do not like the tapestry. However, it did open my eyes, and for that reason, I keep it. Now, do you wish to speak of my tapestries, or do you wish to learn who I am?"

Lord Adeeowale returned to the center of the room. He glanced over to the prisoner and then returned his focus to Lord Chike. "You are the Destroyer. What more is there to learn?"

"And you, my friend, are narrow-minded. You have seen

my tapestries, you have seen the scrolls, I have given you clues, and still, you do not possess the intelligence to know who I am."

Lord Adeeowale recalled everything Lord Chike had said to him since he entered this room. There was one comment he made that interested Lord Adeeowale. "You said *who* is *the Council of Five* instead of *who* are *the Council of Five*. A mistake on your part, or an oversight on mine?"

"Very good, and since I do not make mistakes, then it is safe to say the oversight is on you."

"There are five entities on the platform inside the Gathering Hut. I have seen them myself. What do they have to do with who you are?"

"Are you sure of what you saw?"

"I saw five black robes with hoods sitting on the platform."

Lord Chike sighed. "This game is becoming tiresome, so allow me to speed it up. Have you ever spoken to them or seen past their hoods?"

Flashes of memory bombarded Lord Adeeowale's mind. Memories of spirits that had been taken inside the Gathering Hut, never to be seen again. Memories of two warriors fighting to protect their Lord. Lord Adeeowale glanced back to the prisoner and then returned his focus to Lord Chike. "You call this a game? What is the purpose of this game, and what is my reward if I win?"

Lord Chike laughed. "You will never win. You do not possess the intelligence to decipher a game that has been centuries in the making."

"Then what do you have to lose?"

Lord Chike entwined his fingers, placed his elbows on the table, and then leaned forward. "A challenge. So Lord Adeeowale, what do you want as your prize?"

Lord Adeeowale once again glanced over to the prisoner and then back to Lord Chike. "Release the prisoner. If I lose, then you can shackle him. If I win, then you and I will finish what was started on the tapestry that you detest."

Lord Chike smiled as he gently shook his head from side to side. "You think much of yourself."

"If I am being arrogant, then why do you hesitate?"

Lord Chike stood and walked over to the prisoner. "He is worth much to me. But as you can see, he is spent. His wounds take longer to heal. I will release him from his bonds, but if you lose, you will take his place."

CHAPTER TWENTY-NINE

A my could feel the anger building up inside of her. She stood and approached Dameon, and if looks could kill, Dameon would have been a pile of ash. "What do you mean that she's worth a lot of money?"

Dameon looked at Amy with a puzzled expression. "My friend and I are hunters. We have a client that wants your bear. We tagged it so we could keep an eye on it."

Amy took another step closer to Dameon. "The bear's name is Mona, and she's not a bear. She's my mother! You lay one hand on her, and you'll be sorry." Amy stormed off and went to sit next to Mona.

Dameon watched Amy in disbelief. She sat next to Mona, crossed her arms in front of her chest, and glared at him. It was as if she were daring him to make one wrong move toward her bear. Dameon glanced around at his surroundings. In this cave, there were two men that could easily be mistaken as Bigfoot. A child who claimed that a thousand-pound grizzly was her mother, and then there was the grizzly. A ferocious bear that could easily rip anyone to shreds was lying calmly on the ground, taking no notice of the six people who occupied his cave.

Dameon felt as if he'd fallen down the rabbit hole into a world that made no sense. He glanced over to Amy, who continued to glare at him. Common sense, if such a thing existed in this rabbit hole, was to make amends. It appeared to Dameon that Amy was at the center of this craziness, so he had to calm her down and make sure she no longer considered him a threat.

"Look, Amy. We didn't know the bear belonged to anyone. Of course, we won't take your bear. If you want, I can even remove the tracking device."

Amy relaxed her arms, and she appeared a little calmer. "Will it hurt her?"

"A little, but it will only take a minute." Dameon leaned the *Barrett* against the cave wall next to Joshawa. Then he grabbed his backpack and cautiously approached Mona. Dameon didn't want to make any sudden movements so he slowly placed his backpack on the ground next to Mona's head. He couldn't believe that he was actually standing inches away from a grizzly, and he was surprisingly calm about it. Dameon glanced over to Amy. "May I?"

"Yes. But if you hurt her . . ."

"I know." Dameon smiled at Amy. "And trust me, I'm more afraid of you than your bear." Dameon knelt on his knees and reached into his backpack. He removed a black case, placed it on the ground, and opened it. He chose a scalpel from the various tools contained in the case. He was about to find the spot where he'd placed the microchip, but instead, he felt the need to look at the bear. Dameon glanced down and made eye contact with Mona. "I'm not trying to hurt you. This will sting a bit, but then you'll be invisible to our tracking devices."

Dameon placed his free hand on Mona's neck and separated her fur. He immediately found the small scar that had been left when he'd initially implanted the tracker. He held the scalpel steady and made a tiny incision over the one that already existed. Mona remained calm, and when Dameon replaced the scalpel and retrieved the forceps, he could have sworn that Mona was smiling at him. It only took seconds to remove the tracking device, and Dameon was confident that the tiny incision would quickly heal on its own.

Nathen returned his focus to Joshawa. "How does the bear play in all of this? I don't know of many grizzlies that calmly allow humans into their den."

"The bear, Mona, has been Amy's companion for as long as she can remember. And the best part is that Mona has told me that she's Amy's mother."

Nathen was dumbfounded. "This is who Billy had to protect? And Mona is the bear that caused you to fall out of the tree?"

"Yes."

Nathen glanced around the cave to find all eyes on him, including Mona's. "We'll come back to the part about the bear being Amy's mother. I have a lot of questions, as I'm sure you do as well. But first, I need a place where I can meld with Serena without interruption."

Joshawa pointed to the back of the cave. "There's plenty of room for you at the back of the cave. What's going on, Father?"

"Not too sure myself. Hopefully, I'll know more when I speak to Serena."

"Just so you know. I believe that she's been with me since the accident. I also believe that she's been helping me, protecting me."

"Are you sure? She's been playing with your mind for quite a while now."

"I know, and I can't explain it. Trust her father. I really believe that she wants to help us."

"I hope so, son. For all our sakes."

Nathen made his way to the back of the cave. The two fires from the entrance of the cave couldn't illuminate the back of the cave. Nathen's eyesight allowed him to see what the others couldn't. The cave continued deep inside the mountain, and the further Nathen ventured, the darker his surroundings became. Nathen had passed the area where Amy had kept firewood and the steamer trunks that Nathen assumed were filled with the necessities of life. Nathen glanced over his shoulder to check if he could still see Joshawa. He could, which allowed him some comfort. However, he knew that no one would be able to see him. The darkness of his clothing would blend in with the darkness of the rocks.

Nathen decided that this would be a suitable place to reach out to Serena. He sat cross-legged on the ground, facing the entrance to the cave. He rested the palms of his hands on his knees, closed his eyes, and sought out Serena.

I'm at the cave, Serena, and I've found Joshawa. I'm told by both my wife and my son to trust you. So tell me, what exactly are we doing?

We are saving the life of your son and Dava. And we only have a short time to accomplish this.

Why? What's going on, Serena?

We do not have the privilege of time. I will meld with Imani, Mistress Authia, and Mona. When the bond is made, you must reach out to Casandra. Use us as a conduit. You must convince her to reverse the curse she has placed on Dava. You must convince her that Lord Chike is no longer a threat to her.

Who is Lord Chike?

We do not have time, my Lord. Do as I ask, and the lives of two young Lords will be spared. Open your mind and see the corridor that we are opening for you. Travel past this corridor and find Casandra.

Nathen was fast approaching his breaking point as far as his patience was concerned. There were so many secrets and so many unanswered questions. In the past, Serena had proven her loyalty to Nathen at a significant cost to herself. Should he trust her based on her history? Nathen was about to continue his conversation with Serena when Authia's voice filled his mind.

Sweetheart, I can feel your anguish, and I know your trust in Serena is standing on shaky ground. So, instead of trusting Serena, trust me. We need to do this or Joshawa will be lost to us forever. Serena and I will explain everything later. But for now, I need you to focus. We need you to convince Casandra to reverse the curse. I love you, sweetheart, and I have faith in you.

Authia's voice drifted away, and all Nathen's reservations and doubts drifted away with her. Nathen allowed his mind to empty and focus only on the corridor that Serena spoke of. Within minutes, he could feel their strength, and he could see the corridor. Nathen looked beyond it and found himself in the jungle. He could feel the dampness, and he could smell the sweet fragrances of the jungle. The trees grew tall around him, and the bird's songs echoed throughout the immense canopy of the trees. Then he heard Serena's voice softly whisper to him.

Call out to her. Insist that she come to you. Do not forget that she owes you her life.

Serena was gone, and even though he could feel their strength, Nathen felt very much alone. He took a deep breath of the fragrant air and threw caution to the wind.

Casandra, are you here? Can you hear me? Nathen couldn't hear her voice or feel her presence. *Casandra, it's Lord Nathen. I very much wish to speak with you.* Again, there was no response. Nathen was becoming annoyed. Not at anyone in particular. It was mainly the situation that he found himself in. Again, he tried to reach out to Casandra. *Whatever game you are playing, it stops here! I am still your Lord, and you will respond to me.*

I hear you, my Lord.

Where are you?

I am close. What do you require of me?

Nathen scanned the jungle but could find no sign of Casandra. *To start with, I require you to show yourself.*

I am here. I am where the jungle ceases to exist.

Nathen scanned the jungle once more but still could not see any sign of Casandra. *No games, Casandra. What do you mean?*

I am imprisoned in the darkness. I answer to Lord Chike.

Lord Chike no longer exists. You answer to me.

If that is the case, my Lord, then why do I remain a prisoner in this orb?

Nathen started to pay attention to Casandra's voice. It sounded as if it were coming from behind him. Nathen turned around and reached out to Casandra. *Casandra, I'm sure you know that I don't want to hurt you. I only need to speak to you, and I wish to do that in person.*

I wish that, too, my Lord. But Lord Chike has imprisoned me in an orb that only he can release me from.

Lord Chike is no longer a threat to you. If you help me, then I know at least two priestesses that can extract you from the orb.

Nathen found himself at the edge of the jungle that was surrounded by darkness. Deep inside the abyss, he could see what appeared to be a circle of light. As it drew closer, he realized that the light was the orb Serena spoke of. The orb stopped at the edge of the darkness, and even though Nathen was only a couple of feet from it, he still couldn't see what was inside. The light that encompassed the orb glistened as if it were alive. Nathen reached out to touch the light, but as he did, he received a slight shock. He tried again and received another shock, but this was stronger.

How long have you been imprisoned inside this orb?

There is no time inside the orb. Only pain and solitude. Lord Chike placed me here, and as long as Lord Chike lives, I remain a prisoner.

Casandra, do you have any reason not to trust me?

Never, my Lord.

Then trust me now. Lord Chike will be killed, and you will be freed. In the meantime, I need a favor.

Does my release depend on this favor?

No, it does not. You will be freed even if you don't grant me this favor.

What is the favor, my Lord?

Release Dava from the curse you have placed on him. Allow the child to live.

Jax was getting closer to his Bigfoot and Bigfoot's son. The thrill and excitement that he felt was more tantalizing than when he'd killed the park ranger so many years ago. Jax's mind was consumed with a multitude of scenarios, each one more horrific than the last.

Jax smiled to himself as he played out each and every scenario in his head. He would sell the father simply because he had no idea what the lifespan of a Bigfoot was. But the son, Jax would keep that one. He would stock up on winter supplies so he could spend the entire winter at the homestead. The small cabin was too good to pass up. It would be his killing room, and he would keep Bigfoot's son shackled and alive in that room. Causing someone's death was a thrill all on its own. But to torture a living being to the brink of death, to Jax, that was a pleasure beyond description.

Jax was so preoccupied with his thoughts that he almost fell headfirst onto a narrow footpath. He jumped to his feet and immediately checked his surroundings. Next, he studied the device to discover that Dameon had stayed at the exact same location for some time now. And that location was close enough to alert Dameon if Jax made another stupid mistake. Jax was infuriated with himself. His focus should have been on Bigfoot, not what he planned to do with him.

Jax quietly followed the path further up the mountain until he came across a sharp bend that didn't allow him to see further than where he stood. Jax studied his surroundings and then carefully moved off the path and into the forest that bordered the path. He hid behind an evergreen and checked his device. Dameon was only twenty feet away from where Jax stood. Jax quietly stepped away from the tree and once again scrutinized his surroundings. How had he managed to get this close to Dameon without alerting him?

Jax took a deep breath and slowly released it. If Dameon was with Bigfoot, he might be distracted enough not to notice his surroundings. Jax cautiously crept toward the edge of the path but stayed behind the tree line to avoid detection. He followed the path until it opened up into a clearing, and from his vantage point, he could see the entrance to a cave.

Lord Adeeowale stared into the deep, black emptiness that was Lord Chike's eyes. "Am I allowed to ask questions?"

"Of course not! Do you take me for a fool? I have given you many clues, Lord Adeeowale. Make use of them."

"All right, then we should confirm what the actual question is."

Lord Chike appeared puzzled by the request. "What is there to confirm? It is the same question that I have asked repeatedly since you arrived at my home."

"You have asked me many questions, Lord Chike. You need to be more specific. If I am endangering my own existence should I fail to answer your question, then you must ask your question one more time."

Massai's voice was weak, but when Lord Adeeowale turned to face his son, he was sitting erect, and his facial expression was one of determination. "Since my freedom is also on the line, then I shall help my father to answer your question."

Lord Chike laughed at Massai. "As if you could answer the question, or any question for that matter. You are broken. Your mind is broken. The answer to your freedom has been staring at you for as long as you have been here." Lord Chike walked over to his desk and picked up an old, rusted key. He walked back over to Massai and started to release the metal cuffs and neck collar. He chose to remove the neck collar last, and when it came loose, Lord Chike threw it on the floor. He shook his head as he walked around Massai. "And to think that you were once a great warrior. Now look at you. You can barely hold your head up."

Lord Chike glanced over to Lord Adeeowale and smiled. "Yes, your son can assist you. Not that he will be of any use." Lord Chike violently kicked Massai in the stomach, and before he even faced Lord Adeeowale, he issued him a warning. "I would not, if I were you." Lord Chike turned to face Lord Adeeowale. "Hurting me would only cause more suffering to my prisoner."

Anger burned deep within Lord Adeeowale. He wanted to destroy Lord Chike just as Lord Chike had destroyed so many others.

"You see, that is your problem. You let your emotions rule your decisions." Lord Chike chuckled and then went back to his desk, sat down, and placed his forearms on the table. "Since there are two of you to answer the question, then I will ask two questions. Both must be answered correctly. Do you accept these terms, Lord Adeeowale?"

Lord Adeeowale glanced over to his son. "I have faith in you, my son. Are Lord Chike's new terms agreeable with you?"

Lord Adeeowale watched as his son stood up, proud and tall. Even though Lord Adeeowale could see the pain and suffering that it took for his son to stand, Massai did not utter one word. He didn't reveal any facial expression that would show the level of his discomfort. He stood as a proud warrior, and he glared at Lord Chike as he answered his father's question. "Yes, Father. I stand with you, and together we will defeat our enemy!"

CHAPTER THIRTY

Nathen patiently waited for a response from Casandra. He observed the orb as it hovered only a couple of feet in front of him. It made him feel sick at the thought of Casandra curled up into a ball in order to fit inside an orb that was only, at best, four feet in diameter. How could anyone be that cruel? How could anyone inflict such pain and find pleasure in it? At that moment, Nathen decided that he would save Casandra no matter what it cost.

Nathen moved as close to the orb as he could, and then he reached out with his right hand. He wanted so much to touch the orb, to have some connection with Cassandra. But that would only inflict pain on himself and possibly even Casandra.

Casandra, I give you my word that I will release you from your prison.

I wish I could believe you, my Lord, but hope and faith no longer reside inside this orb or inside my heart. Even though Lord Chike promised to release me once Dava was dead, I do not believe him. I do not trust him. Lord Chike takes immense pleasure in inflicting pain and suffering on anyone he chooses. There is no happy ending for me, and I have come to terms with that revelation. However, it would give me great pleasure to save Dava and ruin Lord Chike's plans.

Then you will help us?

Yes, my Lord. Please inform Serena that I will need her assistance to reach out to young Dava.

Will Lord Chike be aware of what you are doing?

Casandra didn't respond for what felt like several minutes. Nathen finally reached out to her, fearing that Lord Chike already knew of the plan.

Casandra? Are you okay?

Yes, my Lord, I am okay. Lord Chike will be aware, and when he discovers what I am doing, he will cause me unbearable pain. But, since no matter whom I help, whether it be you or Lord Chike, I will suffer beyond imagination. If I am to suffer, then it will be for saving Dava, not killing him. And it will be for you, my Lord.

Jax crept closer to the cave but remained hidden at the edge of the forest. He had to know what he was up against before he revealed himself. Jax managed to get close enough to the cave entrance and still remain hidden. When Jax peered into the cave, he couldn't believe what he discovered. A younger Bigfoot was sitting on the ground with his back against the cave wall. As far as Jax could see, the adult Bigfoot wasn't in the cave. There was also a boy in his late teens and a young girl. But what he couldn't believe was that his grizzly was lying on the ground, and Dameon was kneeling right beside him, removing the chip they used to track the bear. At first, Jax thought that Dameon had tranquilized the bear, but when Dameon was finished, the bear stood and walked over to the entrance of the cave. Jax held his breath as the bear stared right at him, as if the bear knew he was there.

Lord Chike observed Lord Adeeowale and Massai as they stood before him, ready and willing to play the game. Even though Lord Chike showed no emotion outwardly, inside, he was smiling. Lord Adeeowale would soon be his prisoner for life, and his son would spend an eternity in the Realm of Despair.

Lord Chike stood and walked over to his tapestries. He

stopped in front of one of the earlier ones and ran his fingers across the stitching of the Destroyer. He then turned to face Lord Adeeowale. "All my victories are beautifully depicted on these tapestries." Lord Chike motioned to the ones that adorned his walls. "Tell me, Lord Adeeowale, how many tapestries adorn your walls?"

"I do not require adornments for my accomplishments. Now, ask your questions."

Lord Chike walked closer to Lord Adeeowale. "You continue to avoid conversation concerning my tapestries. Why is that?"

"Why would I want to discuss your tapestries when all they depict are the battles where you massacred so many innocent lives?"

Lord Chike was about to answer Lord Adeeowale when he noticed Massai slowly moving toward him. He scoffed at Massai. "You move like an old lady. You will never be whole. You will never see the light of day. It is laughable that you even try."

Lord Adeeowale walked over to his son and stood by his side. "Enough! Ask your questions."

Lord Chike snickered and gently shook his head from side to side. "You are so eager to die. And you shall, both of you." Lord Chike went back to his table and sat down. "Question one, who am I? Question two, who is the Council of Five?"

Serena had been listening to the conversation between Lord Nathen and Casandra. When her presence was requested, she immediately joined with Casandra.

I am here, Casandra. Thank you for helping us.

It is my pleasure and my pain.

I am so sorry. We do not wish to cause you pain.

I have been in pain for so long that it no longer frightens me. Yes, by helping you, the pain Lord Chike will inflict on me will be agonizing. But if we succeed and Lord Chike fails, then it will be worth it.

I cannot believe that the Council allows Lord Chike such leverage. I do not understand?

We know that Lord Chike is the Destroyer, and he is under the control of the Council of Five. Why would they allow this? He is trying to murder a future Lord.

I still do not understand. Lord Chike did not present me to the Council for punishment. He and he alone put me in this orb.

Are you saying that the Destroyer decided your fate?

Yes.

For the first time in a very long time, Serena was frightened. If the Council was not controlling the Destroyer, then who was? *This is not good. First, we must save Dava and Joshawa. Then we need to figure out who is controlling the Destroyer. Are you ready, Casandra?*

Yes. Open the corridor, and I will join with Dava, and I will save his life.

Dameon moved aside and watched Mona as she stood and walked toward the entrance to the cave. Something was off. It nagged at Dameon, but he couldn't put his finger on it. He walked over to Mona and placed his right hand on Mona's head. "You feel it, too. What's out there, Mona? What do you see?"

It all happened so fast. Mona turned and ran into the cave, putting herself between the cave entrance and Amy. Dameon glanced over his shoulder at Mona, and that was when he heard the whistling sound of an arrow. A second later, he felt the pain as the arrowhead penetrated his right shoulder.

Serena shifted the corridor away from Nathen and toward Cassandra. She was about to focus the corridor toward Dava when Mona suddenly left the meld. Just before she left the meld, Serena could feel Mona's fear and her anger as if it were her own. Franticly, Serena reached out to Mona.

Mona, where are you? We need your strength to save Dava.

I'm sorry, Serena, but I'm needed here. I must protect Amy and Billy.

Mona, we need you. We will not be able to save Dava without you.

Serena felt as if they had lost the battle even before it began. Then Casandra reached out to her, stating the obvious.

Serena, if all that you are seeking is the strength of the meld to create the corridor, then you have that strength.

You do not understand, Casandra. We require four strong melders to create the corridor.

And you have them. Or have you forgotten that I am part of this corridor?

Serena sighed as she gently shook her head. *I am so wrapped up in my quest to save Dava and Joshawa that I did not see beyond the obvious. Yes, you are our fourth melder, as well as the only one who can save Dava.*

Not only had Serena missed the fact that she could use Cassandra as the fourth melder, but she also hadn't inquire why Mona had to leave the meld. She reached out to Mona, only this time, there was no fear, just anger. *Mona, what is happening?*

I'm not totally sure, but there is evil just outside of the cave, and it has already struck down Dameon. I'm sorry, but I must remain to protect Amy and the others. You must reach out to Nathen and tell him to stay in the shadows. He will soon learn why.

Nathen opened his eyes and found himself once again in the cave. Before he could focus on what was transpiring inside the cave, Serena's voice came to him.

Be still, my Lord. Mona has asked that you remain in the

shadows.

What about the corridor?

Do not concern yourself with the corridor. Something in the cave has caused Mona to feel the need to protect Amy.

Nathen quickly scanned the cave and discovered that Mona had put herself between Amy and the entrance of the cave. Nathen's eyes went wide as he witnessed Dameon being shot with an arrow. *I've got this, Serena. Take care of Dava and Casandra.*

Yes, my Lord. I feel your anger. Please remain where you are. If you reveal yourself now, then you will lose.

Serena was gone, and Nathen knew it was Jax who had released that arrow. He wanted to run to Joshawa and protect him, but Mona and Serena had told him to stay in the shadows. How could Nathen sit back and not protect his son when he could clearly see the danger? Before Nathen could even try to answer the question, Mona spoke to him.

Nathen, you must stay where you are.

Why? You're protecting Amy. Why can I not protect my son?

By staying in the shadows, you are. Nathen, you are our wild card. The person in the forest doesn't know you're here. Trust me, you will know when to reveal yourself.

Sitting back and doing nothing did not sit well with Nathen. What if he missed that opportune time that Mona referred to? What if he couldn't save Joshawa? According to Mona, Nathen was their wild card. But how could he just sit around and do nothing? Did he have to wait for another arrow to fly through the air and possibly kill Joshawa? Nathen needed his own wild card. He closed his eyes and reached out to Authia.

My love, we have a problem, and I need your help.

What is it, Nathen? Is Joshawa okay?

Yes, he is. I'm watching him right now. If Joshawa had imprinted on Becca, could she find the cave?

She sees what Joshawa sees, but if he wasn't conscious when he arrived at the cave, she might not be able to.

What if I got Joshawa to focus only on Becca? Would that work?

It might. Actually, now that I think about it, Becca did reveal some aspects of Joshawa that she shouldn't have been able to.

What aspects?

She was sitting in the cave with Joshawa, their backs against the cave wall, and he told her he loved her.

That's precisely where Joshawa is sitting. I'll get Joshawa to focus on Becca, and then Becca can tell Hansen where the cave is.

Not so fast. Just because Becca knew where Joshawa was sitting doesn't mean that she could find the cave. I know very little about imprinting, especially when it involves imprinting without the melding ability.

And that could make a difference?

Yes, a rather large one.

Well, we have to try. I need Hansen to find the cave as soon as possible.

Why, Nathen? What's going on?

I'm trying to even the odds. We have Dameon on our side, but I would feel more comfortable if we had Hansen close by. Tell him to double-time it, and when he arrives, conceal himself. Jax is hidden in the tree line facing the cave.

Oh my God!

Don't worry. Jax isn't going to reveal himself anytime soon. He doesn't know I'm here, and I don't think he's going to reveal himself until he knows where I am.

If he hasn't revealed himself, how do you know he's there?

Nathen hesitated, knowing that the answer would upset Authia. *I know because he put an arrow in Dameon's shoulder.*

What!

It's okay. We know he's there, but Jax has concealed himself in the woods, so we can't pinpoint where he is. I think all he wanted to do at this point was to injure Dameon's dominant arm. As far as Jax knows, Dameon is his biggest threat. I also believe that he wanted to hurt Dameon, payback for helping me.

I'll work with Becca, and hopefully we'll find a way to locate the cave. I love you. Please be safe.

Love you, too. Nathen broke his connection with Authia and focused on Mona. *I have another wild card for you. I need you to meld with Joshawa and tell him to focus everything he has on Becca.*

How does that help us?

Please, just do it. I'll explain later.

Mona remained where she stood, between Amy and the cave entrance. Nathen quietly watched as Joshawa shifted his attention toward Mona. He then rested his head against the cave wall and closed his eyes. Help was coming, and Nathen prayed that Hansen would arrive before Jax decided to put an arrow in each and every one of them.

CHAPTER THIRTY-ONE

Becca was curled up on the loveseat, staring into the fire. She hadn't moved since she arrived at the cabin, and to be honest, she just wanted to be left alone. Becca felt so useless because there was nothing she could do to save the man she loved. How ironic, because the man she loved, the man she would do anything to save, had no idea that she loved him. Becca would have given anything to be with him right this minute. To be able to wrap her arms around him and finally reveal to him her true feelings.

Becca was so wrapped up in her thoughts that she didn't notice when her aunt sat next to her. It was only when Authia placed her hand on Becca's arm that the trance was broken.

"You're deep in thought."

Becca remained focused on the fire, and when she replied, her voice was soft, just above a whisper. "All I can think about is Joshawa."

"I'm glad, because we're going to need your help."

Becca turned to face Authia. "How?"

"Any moment now, Joshawa is going to try to reach out to you. We're hoping that the bond between the two of you is strong enough to enable Joshawa to reach out to you and let us know how to find him."

Becca was elated. "I can find him?"

"We hope so. I need you to clear your thoughts and listen for Joshawa."

"Is he going to speak to me?"

"I'm not sure if he'll speak to you or just show you what he

248

sees."

"If he just shows me what he sees, how will that help?"

"I'm not sure, sweetheart. It may help, or it may not, but at this point, I'm willing to try anything."

"And so am I, Aunty."

Tammy walked over to the fire and sat on the floor facing Becca and Authia. She crossed her legs in front of her and placed her hands, palms down, on her knees. "So, Nathen wants Hansen to go to the cave?"

"Yes. He needs all the help he can get."

"It sounds dangerous. Don't get me wrong, I want to find Joshawa as much as you do. But I also don't want to lose my husband in the process."

"Trust me, I understand. I'm not sure how dangerous the circumstances are. Dameon is on our side, but Jax is a loose cannon. I have no idea what he's capable of doing or what his intentions are. That's where Hansen and Becca come in."

Becca put aside the blanket she was using and stood up. "I'll help any way I can. I want to be part of this."

The words no sooner left her lips when she heard a voice resonating from deep within her mind. "Joshawa, is that you?" Becca sat back on the loveseat and closed her eyes. "I see what you see. I can feel what you feel. We want to come and find you. Can you tell me where you are?"

Joshawa was slowly moving his head from side to side. Becca turned to Authia. "He can't tell me where he is. Why can't he? How can we find him if we don't know where he is?"

Authia seemed to be deep in thought, and then suddenly, she was smiling. "He can't meld with you, and his situation won't allow him to speak to you."

"I don't understand."

"He can meld, but since you can't, melding is off the table. However, Joshawa has imprinted on you. There's a possibility that he can speak to you, but it won't be private."

"So what do I do?"

"Just ask him. If he can't speak to you because someone's listening, then have him show you who's in the cave with him."

Becca reached out to Joshawa. "You can't speak to me because someone else may hear." Joshawa slowly nodded his head in agreement. "Okay, your mother wants you to show me who's in the cave with you."

Becca watched as Joshawa started to move his head. She was Joshawa's voice, so as she saw what Joshawa showed her, she shared. "I see a young girl sitting way too close to Joshawa. Billy's there, and the bear. He's huge! Wait, Joshawa's shaking his head. I'm not sure what he's trying to tell me. He's looking at the bear, then the girl, and then back to the bear. Adrian is there. He's sitting with a man by the fire. The man has an arrow in his shoulder, but Joshawa doesn't seem too concerned.

"I'm sorry, Aunty. But all I can see is who and what's inside the cave. Nothing more."

Authia was not about to give up. There had to be a way to get Hansen to the cave. It couldn't be Nathen. Jax didn't know he was there, and according to Mona, it was in their best interest to keep him hidden. Authia rolled her eyes and slowly shook her head. She was so fixated on Nathen that she overlooked the obvious. Mona was her connection to the inside of the cave.

Mona, I need your help.

I don't see how I can help. My only concern is Amy and Billy.

Okay, I get that. But my concern is for everyone inside your cave. Not just Amy and Billy. Nathen's there to help you, but in order to accomplish that, he requires your help.

And what does he require of me?

Stand at the front of the cave where you believe Jax is hidden. Then face inside and tell me what you see.

How will that help? It puts me at risk.

I know, but if we're going to win this battle, I need to know what you see from Jax's point of view.

Mona slowly made her way to the entrance of the cave. Reluctantly, she stood at the entrance, staring in the direction the arrow came from. Mona then turned to face the cave, even though that was the last thing she wanted to do.

I'm facing inside the cave. What do you want to know?

I want to know who you can see and where they are.

I see Joshawa. He's sitting against the wall to my right. Adrian is with him, and the man they call Dameon is at the fire with Amy.

You don't see Billy?

No, not from this angle.

How long has Billy been there?

Most of the day.

Perfect! Then Billy is the one who will help us.

How do you expect Billy to help?

He knows how to find the cave.

You want to use him as bait!

No. If Jax doesn't know he's there, then we could possibly sneak him out of the cave, and he could meet Hansen between the cave and the Jenkins homestead.

That's a lot to ask of him.

Yes. Do you know why he's the perfect person for this venture?

No.

Because he loves you, he loves Amy, and he cares for my son. He will want to do this to save them.

Serena rejoined Casandra and Imani only to find that Authia had also left the meld. *Where is Mistress Authia?*

Imani was about to explain. However, before she could, Authia rejoined the group.

My apologies, ladies. I had to make sure my family was safe.

Serena could feel the fear that enveloped Imani. *I know that Amy and the bear are special to you, Imani, and as soon as we are done here, you can go to them.*

I thank you, Serena, but saving Dava and Joshawa is only part of our responsibility. We also have to save Casandra. Mistress Authia, is my family safe?

Yes, Imani, they are, and trust me, Lord Nathen will do whatever has to be done to save everyone in that cave.

Serena had always been impressed with Mistress Authia's melding abilities, as well as her empathy and the kindness she freely gave, even to those who did not always deserve it. *Mistress Authia, shall we begin?*

Yes, Serena. Please lead the way.

We do not know for certain if Lord Chike will sense that the corridor is opening. So we will assume that he will. Mistress Authia, you and I will start the corridor. Imani, you will follow and protect Cassandra. Cassandra, you will follow directly behind Imani. Once Mistress Authia and I reach Dava, we will form a shield around him. That is when you will remove the spell. Do it quickly. Once the spell is lifted and Dava is out of danger, we will all meet back here.

Nathen heard the meld between Authia and Mona. Authia had come up with an idea on how to show Hansen the way here. However, it involved keeping Jax focused on one section of the cave so Billy could sneak out undetected. Billy was across the cave from Joshawa, so they needed Jax to focus on Joshawa. They didn't have much time. The veil of darkness was close to consuming the forest. They needed to act now.

Mona, do you understand what needs to be done?

Yes, but how are we going to accomplish this?

For starters, you need to meld with Billy and tell him to stay put.

Then, we need Dameon and Adrian to move to the side of the cave that Joshawa is on. Have Dameon call out to Jax. That should keep Jax's attention away from Billy. But to make sure, I need you to stand in such a way that you're blocking the view of the far side of the cave. Then tell Billy to sneak past you. If he crouches down just slightly, Jax shouldn't see him even if he does look your way.

And if this doesn't work?

Then Jax will find out how dangerous it is to try to capture a Bigfoot.

Lord Adeeowale quietly stood as he observed Lord Chike. The answer to the first question should be obvious since Lord Chike had never denied being the Destroyer. The second question was more of a riddle than a question. The question should have been, who *are* the Council of Five, not who *is*. Lord Adeeowale turned to his son and motioned him to sit on the floor. Before he joined him, Lord Adeeowale decided to lay out the rules of this game. Because that was exactly what it was. A game that Lord Chike took great pleasure in.

"Lord Chike, I ask you once again. Since the stakes are high, are we allowed to ask questions before we give you our answer?"

"You bore me with questions I have already answered. But, since I am confident that you will never know the answers, then yes, you may ask three questions."

"And since we are not allowed to leave the room, then the same should apply to you."

"And if I choose to leave the room?"

"Then you forfeit the game. Massai and I will be victorious. Do you agree?"

Lord Chike chuckled as he slowly shook his head. "I'm enjoying your optimism. I agree. I will not leave the room until the game is over."

"One last thing. What guarantee do we have that you will

253

admit that we have correctly answered your questions?"

Lord Chike snickered. "I must say, I am impressed. I have played this game many times, and you are the first to question my honesty, my integrity."

"We both know you have no honesty or integrity. Before we start this game, write the answers on that blank parchment that is sitting on your desk."

Lord Adeeowale stood his ground while he waited for Lord Chike's response. Lord Chike stared at Lord Adeeowale—his facial expression was a combination of annoyance and anger. "Normally, I would be upset with your accusations." Lord Chike leaned back in his chair and placed his arms on the armrests. "However, you are correct. I have no honesty or integrity. I have only hatred and greed and the burning desire to destroy anyone who defiles the Jelani Tribe." Lord Chike leaned forward and picked up his quill. He wrote a few lines and then rolled up the parchment. "I suspect you would not want me to keep the parchment."

"That would defeat the purpose of the parchment."

Lord Chike glanced around the room until his gaze fell on Lord Adeeowale. The smile that graced his lips sent shivers down Lord Adeeowale's spine. "I will place it with one of my tapestries. You will remain where you stand, and once the parchment is secured, I will return to my desk. Does this satisfy your mistrust?"

"Yes." Lord Adeeowale watched as Lord Chike walked over to the tapestry that depicted his near death. "Interesting choice, Lord Chike."

Lord Chike draped the parchment over the top of the tapestry. He turned to face Lord Adeeowale and was about to speak when his face flushed with anger.

"Lord Chike, you appear distressed."

"I will destroy her. I will cause her more pain and suffering than I have caused any vile creature that has crossed my path." Lord Chike turned and headed for the doorway.

"Lord Chike, where are you going?"

Lord Chike slowly turned and glared at Lord Adeeowale. "You knew."

"I am sorry, Lord Chike. What did I know?"

Lord Chike stood, his body rigid, his fists clenched at his side. "Casandra. You knew what she was doing?"

"I am sorry. Who is Casandra, and why has she upset you so?"

One minute, Lord Chike was at the doorway, and the next, he was inches away from Lord Adeeowale's face. Lord Adeeowale had to think fast if he wanted to stay alive. However, it turned out he didn't have to. Massai came to his rescue.

"Lord Chike, I would stand back if I were you."

"Who are you to tell me what to do?"

Massai reached behind his ragged loin cloth and produced a long, curved machete.

Lord Chike frantically checked his belt, and for the second time in his long life, Lord Chike was afraid. "How did you obtain that?"

"It does not matter how, only that I possess it."

Lord Chike was paralyzed with fear. All Massai had to do was end his own life, and that one gesture would also witness the end of Lord Chike's life.

CHAPTER THIRTY-TWO

Authia was working side by side with Serena, to save not only Dava but Joshawa, as well. Serena had come a long way in the twenty years Authia had known her. There was a time when Authia hated everything about Serena. However, in the end, Serena had found her path to redemption. She discovered and suffered the cruelty of not only her enemies but also her family. And then Serena gave the ultimate sacrifice. She gave her life to save Authia's life. Now, she was directly disobeying Lord Chike. If he were to find out, Serena would suffer in ways that only the most deranged mind could imagine.

As planned, Serena and Authia were the first to reach Dava. He was in the priestess's hut with his mother, Tamara. Dava had been placed on his sleeping mat with his hands crossed on top of his chest. His skin was gray, the bones through his entire body were clearly evident, and his breath was barely auditable. Tamara was kneeling at his side. Her left hand covered his, and her right hand tenderly caressed the side of his face. She was softly singing a lullaby, even though Dava showed no signs of awareness.

Tamara's sorrow was etched across her face. Authia's heart went out to her. It was one thing for Authia to know her son was somewhere in a cave suffering from injuries that could kill him. But for Tamara to sit by and watch as her son slowly died while she could do nothing to save him, had to be unbearable. Softly, Authia reached out to Tamara.

Tamara, it's Authia. We've come to save Dava.

Tamara glanced around the small hut. *I hear you, my Mistress, but I cannot see you.*

I'm here as a spirit, though I'm not dead.

I do not understand. I have not the strength to even try.

We'll be your strength. I'm here with Serena. We've made a corridor that reaches from the Land of the Ancestors to Dava. Your mother is close behind. She's here to lift the curse that's killing your son.

My son is cursed? Why? What has he done to deserve this? Tamara was crying uncontrollably. She wrapped her arms around Dava and cradled him against her chest.

Authia had to fight to keep her tears from running down her cheeks. *It's a long story, a story we don't have time to tell. Please lay Dava down so Casandra can heal him.*

Tamara gently laid Dava on his sleeping mat and went to sit at his feet.

Tamara hadn't eaten or drunk anything since Dava took ill. Her head felt heavy, and her body felt as though she didn't belong to it. She watched as a globe of light encircled her son.

Is that you, mother?

Yes, my child.

Why, mother? Why has my son been cursed?

I will heal my grandson, and then we shall talk.

Tamara's mind was weak from a lack of food and water. It was as if her thoughts were all jumbled together. She continued to watch when something in the back of her memories slammed into her thoughts. Tamara gasped, then lurched forward to put herself between Dava and Casandra. She then brought Dava close to her chest and tightly wrapped her arms around her son.

Our highest priestess could not help your grandson. If he has been cursed, then the curse had to come from either Serena or you. Which is it, Mother?

Serena didn't give Casandra a chance to answer. *It was me, Tamara.*

It was you Serena. Then why are you not lifting the curse?

Because Lord Chike made sure that I would not have the power to do so. However, your mother does. We have no time. Please place Dava on his mat and allow your mother to free him of this curse.

Tamara reluctantly placed Dava back on his mat. She watched as the globe encircled her son. *Please, Mother, save him.* Tamara's tears ran freely down her cheeks as she observed the orb spin faster and faster until she could no longer see her son.

Jax had crouched next to a giant redwood as he watched the arrow fly and penetrate Dameon's shoulder. He turned away, resting his back against the tree. Jax chuckled to himself, for it gave him great pleasure to inflict pain on Dameon. Softly, he spoke to himself. "And that's what you get for lying to me." Jax glanced around the tree to get another look at what he was up against. His best plan of attack would be after dark. His night vision goggles would give him the upper hand, and he knew that Dameon hadn't brought his. Jax was elated at the prospect of where his next arrow would go. Again, he softly spoke to himself. "Just wait and see what I'm going to do to you for harboring my Bigfoot."

Joshawa watched as Amy poured water from the bucket into the pot that hung over the fire. She placed three more logs onto the fire, then headed toward the back of the cave. Joshawa then focused his attention on Dameon, who was sitting next to the main firepit. "Don't suppose you know who's out there?"

Dameon turned to face Joshawa and whispered, "Unfortunately, I do. His name is Jax."

"And how do you know him?"

"We're hunters. We've been best friends since childhood."

"Best friends? Wow, I'd hate to see what he'd do if you were mortal enemies."

"You probably won't have to wait long. I'm sure he's waiting until it gets dark to make his next move."

"So what did you do to piss him off?"

"I chose to protect you and your father."

Amy returned from the back of the cave carrying cloth bandages and the healing salve she'd made for Joshawa. She placed the bandages in the pot of water, and then she knelt next to Dameon and examined his wound. "The arrow will have to come out." She was about to break off the arrow tip when Dameon grabbed her hands.

"What are you doing?"

Amy rolled her eyes as she gently shook her head. "Healing you, of course. You're silly." Again, she went to grab the arrowhead, and again, Dameon stopped her.

"You're like twelve years old. How are you going to heal me?"

Joshawa chuckled as he added his two cents. "I think she's older than twelve, and she knows how to heal. She's the reason I'm still alive."

Dameon looked at Amy, completely confused. "You know how to heal?"

"Yes, silly. Can I remove the arrow now?"

"I guess."

Amy broke off the arrowhead, walked around Dameon, and then grabbed the arrow shaft. "This will probably hurt." Before Dameon could say anything, in one swift movement, Amy had removed the arrow from his shoulder.

"Damm, that hurt. Couldn't you give me a one-two-three?"

Amy was puzzled by Dameon's remark. "What's a one-two-three?"

"You're kidding me, right?"

Again, Joshawa added his two cents. "Nope. She isn't. She's lived in this cave pretty much all her life. I'm surprised she knows as much as she does."

Mona scanned the cave as she ambled toward the firepit. She slowly circled the pit until she was behind Adrian and Dameon. At that point, Mona lay on the ground, kept her head up, and focused toward the entrance of the cave. She decided she would take advantage of the fact that everyone else was preoccupied and reach out to Billy.

Billy, please stay where you are and don't move a muscle.

Why? Billy want to sit with Mona.

I know, Billy, but I have something important for you to do.

Mona need Billy's help?

Yes, and not just me. Authia, Amy, Joshawa, we all need your help.

Mona could sense that Billy was getting excited.

Billy can help? Billy want to help.

I know Billy. Now this is very important so you must listen to my directions very carefully.

Billy listen to Mona.

A bad man is hiding in the forest. He wants to hurt everyone in the cave.

He shot the arrow. He hurt Dameon.

Yes, Billy, and this is how you're going to help us. We're going to get the bad man to look only at Joshawa. When that happens, I'm going to stand at the entrance of the cave closer to where you are. When I tell you to go, you need to sneak past me and be as quiet as a mouse. Then you need to head into the forest toward the place where you buried me.

Billy not like that place.

I know Billy. I don't like it either, but you have to go. You know who Hansen is?

Yes. Billy like Hansen.

Good. He's heading toward the homestead. We need you to find him and bring him back to the cave. When you get back, you must stay hidden. Just let me know when you're close. We need you and Hansen to save us. Can you do that for me, Billy?

Billy sounded giddy, like a child who'd been given the best present ever. *Billy save Amelia. Billy save everyone!*

Thank you, Billy. Now remember, don't move until I tell you to.

Mona then reached out to Joshawa. *Your mother has a plan to save us. Your father is going to stay in the shadows until he's needed. Billy's going to sneak out of the cave and meet up with someone called Hansen.*

That's Becca's dad. Why is he coming?

Because we need the upper hand if we're all going to survive this. What we need now is a distraction. We need to keep whoever is in the forest focused on your side of the cave.

For how long?

Just long enough for Billy to leave the cave and get down the path.

I've got this. Amy is almost finished binding Dameon's wound. Ask her to whisper in Dameon's ear that I need to speak to him in private.

Dameon walked over to Joshawa and sat on the ground with his back facing the entrance to the cave. "So, Amy tells me you want to talk with me."

"Yes. Do you need a sling for your arm?"

"No. It would be nice, but I need both my arms if I'm going to defend you from Jax."

"It won't be just you. Adrian can handle a gun. You know my father's here, and you spent time with him. What do you think he'll do if Jax tries to hurt me?"

"Well, let's say I wouldn't want to be Jax." Dameon smiled

as he stared at the back of the cave. When he focused on Josh-awa, he was no longer smiling. "You, your father, and every-one here needs to understand that Jax is fixated on finding your father and you. I know Jax, he'll be well-armed, and he's very dangerous. To him, killing a human being is just part of the hunt. He'll have no issue gunning down everyone in this cave to get what he wants."

"And what he wants is my father and me."

"To him, your father and you are authentic Bigfoots. He wants both of you. And trust me, if he gets a hold of both of you, you will beg for him to kill you."

"Okay, I get it. But that's the reason why we need another person to hide from Jax. To be our wild card. Do you remember meeting Hansen at my cabin?"

"Yeah, I do."

"Well, we're formulating a plan to get him here and even the odds."

"He knows where the cave is?"

"No, but Billy does."

Dameon was about to turn his head toward Billy, but Josh-awa grabbed his leg and squeezed hard.

"What the hell, Joshawa?"

"Jax doesn't know Billy's here. If you turn to look at him, it could mess up our plans."

"All right. So what are these plans."

Joshawa brought his voice down to a whisper. "We need you to stand on my side of the cave and distract Jax. Amy and Joshawa are going to stay at the fire, and Mona is going to block Jax's view so Billy can leave."

Dameon wasn't in too much of a hurry to engage Jax in a conversation. The last thing he wanted was to be shot by an-other arrow. However, Joshawa's plan made sense, and he vowed to do whatever it would take to protect Joshawa and Nathen.

"So when is this all supposed to happen?"

"Whenever you're ready."

Dameon took a deep breath and slowly let it out. "I guess there's no better time than right now."

Dameon stood and walked over to the mouth of the cave. He stopped just inside the cave and stood with his back against the wall. He wanted to make sure that Jax wouldn't have a clear line of sight to shoot him with another arrow. Dameon took another deep breath, then called out to Jax.

"So, Jax, did you intentionally miss, or are you a little rusty with a bow and arrow?"

"I intentionally missed. Unfortunately, I need you to help crate the bear and get Bigfoot and his son back to the cabin."

"We had a deal, Jax. If your Bigfoot turned out to be human, then you couldn't kill him or dissect him."

"Are you kidding me? Look at that thing sitting against the wall. You can actually call him human?"

"Yes, Jax, I can."

"You're putting me in an awkward spot, Dameon."

"You're doing the same to me. You know I'll protect them."

"Yes, I know. And you should know that I'll do anything to capture my Bigfoots."

"Does that include killing me?" There was silence for several minutes. "Are you having second thoughts about killing me?" From Dameon's position, he could see Billy was gone. "Nice talking to you."

Dameon turned to head back into the cave when he heard a whistling sound. Before he could react, the arrow bore into his left thigh. Dameon dropped to the ground in excruciating pain.

Jax yelled out to Dameon, "Does that answer your question? I hope so, because the next arrow will pierce your heart."

CHAPTER THIRTY-THREE

Casandra hovered over her grandson, and the sight of his pale skin and sunken cheekbones caused her great sorrow. How could she have done this to her only grandchild? How could she do this to her own daughter? Casandra cradled Dava and started to chant. She closed her eyes as her words encompassed both of them. The power of her words grew in intensity and swirled around them as if a great storm had engulfed them. Casandra drew Dava close to her chest and continued to chant louder and louder.

Casandra could feel Dava's life force, but it was very weak. He needed to fight to keep himself alive. She opened her eyes, and when she looked at Dava, she found brilliant, green eyes looking back at her.

Dava, you must try harder to survive.

Dava continued to stare at Casandra, and though his lips did not move, he spoke to her. *I do not know you. I do not understand why I am here. I am too weak to care.*

My Lord, you must care.

I am not a Lord.

Yes, you are, and you are so much more.

I do not understand.

My Lord Dava, your destiny is not to die here. You are melding with me. That is a gift bestowed only to the priestesses and Lords of our tribe. Your father is an outsider, so you should not possess this gift, and yet here you are, melding with me.

I am tired. I have no strength.

Your father and your mother are preparing you to be the next

Lord. You have to fight. Fight with me and become who you should be.

Casandra could feel Dava slipping away. If she was going to cure him, Dava had to join the fight for his life. Casandra had to find something she could use to force him to fight in the short time she had left with him. She thought of Lord Chike and how much she hated him for forcing her to kill her own grandson. At that moment, she realized she was focusing on the wrong person.

Lord Dava. You are doing precisely what Lord Chike is expecting you to do. Casandra felt the spark of Dava's lifeforce returning to him.

Who is Lord Chike? What does he expect me to do?

Lord Chike is an evil spirit who wants to purge the tribe of outsiders.

Again, Casandra could feel another spark of his lifeforce. Lord Chike was her instrument to get through to Dava.

Lord Chike wants to murder you and replace your essence with another whom Lord Chike believes he can control. At that point, all you will be is an empty shell. Dava and his essence will cease to exist. Lord Chike will place another's essence into your shell, and when that child becomes Lord, he will kill all outsiders that live in our valley. Then he will kill all those who supported the outsiders.

Dava's life force was now flowing into his body. Casandra was on the right track. *Do you realize what that means?*

I will be forced to kill so many of my people.

No Dava. You will not exist. Only your shell will remain. Another will possess your shell.

And that person will kill my people?

Yes, starting with your parents.

That last comment was all that was needed for Dava to fight for his life.

Lord Adeeowale stood his ground while he observed Lord

Chike. Lord Chike had become pale, and he appeared to be in shock. Lord Chike was focused on Massai and the dagger. Lord Adeeowale studied Lord Chike's face, and as he examined the scar, memories of that fateful day started to engulf his mind. These were memories of the battle that had almost witnessed the death of the Destroyer.

"Lord Chike, we both know the game is off the table. Let us finish what we started three hundred years ago." Lord Adeeowale smiled as he removed his vest and threw it to the ground.

"Lord Adeeowale, you choose to fight me? Your son can end my life by simply cutting his own throat. So why fight me?"

"Because I will finish what I started and save my son in the process. Something I should have done three hundred years ago."

Lord Chike laughed. "He is a shell of who he was. There is nothing to save."

With great difficulty, Massai stood as a warrior would. His stance was erect, his legs firmly planted, and his hand gripped the dagger, ready to defend his Lord. He did not face his father. Instead, he faced the man who had imprisoned him for so long. "You are correct, Lord Chike. I am a shell of who I once was. I can no longer call myself a warrior. I can no longer defend my Lord, my father. However, what I can do is protect him." Massai spoke to his father but remained focused on Lord Chike. "Father, you have the ability to fight, and you are a strong warrior. But there is only one way to win this battle."

Lord Adeeowale quickly turned to face his son. At the same time, he witnessed Lord Chike lunge for Massai. But it was too late. It was too late for Lord Adeeowale to save his son and too late for Lord Chike. Massai slit his throat ear-to-ear, and then he slowly crumbled to the floor. Lord Adeeowale dropped to his knees and cradled his son, holding

Massai's head against his chest. Blood flowed freely from Massai's injury and pooled onto Lord Adeeowale's lap.

Lord Adeeowale cried as he held the lifeless body of his son against his chest. He should have saved his son. He should have protected him against Lord Chike. The memories of that fateful day brought Lord Adeeowale so much pain. He was unable to save his son three hundred years ago, and now he failed again.

Lord Adeeowale turned his attention to Lord Chike. What he saw almost made him vomit. Every injury that Lord Chike received for the past three hundred years now became visible on his body. Lord Adeeowale witnessed Lord Chike's skin as it ripped open. Blood that had once coursed through Lord Chike's veins now created a crimson pool at Lord Chike's feet. His muscle tissue tore in large sections right down to the bone. His face became so distorted and mangled that even Lord Chike wouldn't be able to recognize himself.

Lord Adeeowale glanced down at his son to find his injuries fading. They were being passed on to their true recipient. The fatal injury that Massai had inflicted upon himself appeared on Lord Chike's body and disappeared on Massai's body. But Massai's life was still taken because he was the one who inflicted the injury.

"My son, you forfeited your life so others would be spared. You are a true warrior." Lord Adeeowale laid Massai down and then walked over to Lord Chike's body. He was still alive but just barely. "And your name, Lord Chike, will be banished from all memory. Exactly as you did to me, I shall do to you. Our people will remember that Massai fought a great evil known as the Destroyer and was victorious. They will remember who and what was the Destroyer so that we are not plagued with your kind again."

As Lord Chike took his last breath, the cavern that held the prisoners in darkness now bathed them in light. Lord

Adeeowale walked onto the path and observed all that could be seen. There were thousands upon thousands of cages, and each one appeared to be occupied. He could also see the end of the path and, most importantly, a way out.

Lord Adeeowale refocused on the prisoners and called out, "Who has resided here the longest."

No one answered. The room became eerily quiet. Lord Adeeowale returned to the chamber and unceremoniously grabbed Lord Chike's hair. He dragged Lord Chike's limp body outside and onto the path. At that point, he let go of Lord Chike so that the sound of his head hitting the path would reverberate throughout the cavern.

"Is this the man that you protect? He's dead, and my son gave his life so that others do not fall victim to his cruelty. I promise that your imprisonment will not be as harsh. You will remain imprisoned for your crimes, but I will give you back your dignity, and you will no longer suffer at Lord Chike's hand." Lord Adeeowale peered over the path into the depths of the Realm of Despair. "Does anyone know how deep this cavern is?"

A woman's voice resounded in the cavern. "We are told that it is bottomless."

"Told by who?"

"Lord Chike."

"I take whatever he says as a lie to suit his own purposes." Lord Adeeowale could hear a male voice, though it was somewhat strained.

"I have been here since the creation of this cavern. I was one of many who helped construct this prison."

"Then you should know. Is this cavern bottomless?"

"As far as I know, My Lord, yes, it is."

Lord Adeeowale walked over to Lord Chike and stood at Lord Chike's side. Then, using his foot, Lord Adeeowale pushed Lord Chike over the edge.

Casandra could feel Dava's life force fill his body. But when it reached the point that Dava was out of danger, the life force stopped. It was as if someone had blocked the passageway. No matter how hard Casandra tried, she couldn't get past the block. And if she couldn't break down the block, then everything she had done, everything they had all done, was in vain. Casandra was about to try again when she felt a warm breeze pass through her. It made her shiver but in a good way. She hovered over Dava's mat, still cradling Dava. The warm breeze came again, and for the first time in a very long time, Cassandra felt like herself. It was as if a great weight had been lifted off her shoulders.

And then it came to her. The only possible explanation was that Lord Chike was dead. Casandra didn't think any further than that revelation. She closed her eyes and once again started to chant over and over. Casandra didn't know how long she held Dava or how long she had been chanting. All she knew was that she could feel Dava's life force as it returned to his body. Tears came to Casandra as she laid Dava on his mat. She smiled as she watched Dava sleep.

You will be a remarkable Lord, and I hope you will not judge your grandmother too harshly. I love you, and I will always protect you.

Casandra removed the swirling fog to allow her daughter Tamara access to her son. She watched as her daughter placed her arms under Dava and brought him close to her chest. Casandra continued to watch until Authia broke her concentration.

Are we good, Casandra?

Yes, My Mistress. Dava is himself again. He will suffer no ill effects.

That's so good to hear. Now, I guess we need to deal with Lord Chike.

Actually, we do not. I believe Lord Chike is dead.

Are you sure?

We should return to the surface. We will know for certain then.

Casandra was about to enter the corridor when she heard her daughter's voice. This was a conversation that Casandra dreaded. But she owed it to her daughter to explain what happened to her son. Tamara called out to her mother, and this time she answered.

I am here. Dava is well and safe.

Thank you, Mother, for saving Dava.

You do realize that I was the one who cursed him in the first place?

Yes, Mother, I do. I also know you saved him. And Authia and Imani told me what you went through.

That is no excuse for what I did.

I love you, Mother, and Dava will know the entire story, all you had to endure at the hand of Lord Chike, and to be honest, I do not know if I could have survived it.

I must leave. The corridor is collapsing. I will watch over Dava and the entire village. I love you.

Casandra made it through the corridor and joined Imani on the other side. For the first time in a very long time, she stood on the jungle floor. Casandra was no longer a prisoner in an orb that only brought her pain and suffering. Casandra was free, but as she gazed around at her newfound freedom, she still couldn't believe it. "Imani, is it true? Am I free?"

"It does appear so. Come with me, and we will find out."

Imani led Casandra over to the Gateway and called out to the Gatekeeper. "Gatekeeper, I request passage to the Land of the Spirits."

Casandra was a jumble of nerves but in a good way. Her senses were going wild with the sweet smells of the jungle, the songs of the birds as they chased each other in among the trees, and the sound of the wind as it mischievously played in the canopy of leaves. She closed her eyes as she curled her toes in the grass and moss that made up the jungle floor. She was so preoccupied with the jungle that she didn't realize that the Gatekeeper was present.

"Priestess Casandra. It brings me great pleasure to see you. Do you wish to enter the Land of the Spirits?"

"And it is my pleasure to see you, Gatekeeper. Yes, I would like passage to the Land of the Spirits."

The Gatekeeper stood aside and parted the fog with his spear. Imani stood back and smiled at Casandra. "Here is your proof. Now go and enjoy your life as a spirit."

"You are not coming with me?"

"No. My family is still in peril, and I must return to help them."

"If you need anything, Imani, just ask. I owe you my life."

"You owe no one. Take pleasure with your freedom." Imani turned and headed toward the area of the Realm where Serena called home. The battle to save Dava and kill the Destroyer was done. But now Imani faced another battle — a battle that could end the life of everyone she loved.

CHAPTER THIRTY-FOUR

A drian rushed over to Dameon and helped him to his feet.
Dameon placed his left arm around Adrian's neck, and
together they made their way to the fire pit. When Adrian and
Dameon reached it, they found that Amy had already placed
bandages into the pot hanging over the fire.

Adrian helped Dameon to the ground, which was not an
easy task. Dameon was in so much pain that even the slightest
movement caused him to cry out. Once he was sitting, Adrian
rolled up a few blankets and placed them under Dameon's
injured leg to support it. Adrian then turned his attention to
the entrance of the cave. He needed to find a way to protect
everyone from Jax. At that moment, Adrian noticed Mona as
she ambled toward the fire pit. Mona lay on the ground
lengthwise between the fire pit and the entrance to the cave.
With that one action, Mona proved to Adrian that she was
protecting everyone inside the cave—not just Amy.

The arrow had penetrated Dameon's left thigh five inches
above his knee, and blood was flowing from his wound.
Adrian surmised that the fletching had embedded itself in
Dameon's thigh bone. That was the only explanation he could
think of as to why the arrow hadn't shot right through his
thigh. Adrian was about to ask Amy how he could help, but
when he glanced up, he saw Joshawa trying to make his way
over to the fire pit. Adrian jumped to his feet and went over
to Joshawa. Joshawa had already turned himself so his back
was facing the main fire pit, and he was using his arms to propel himself backward.

"What the hell do you think you're doing?" Adrian placed his hands underneath Joshawa's armpits and turned him around so that his back was facing the cave wall.

"I want to help. Let go of me, Adrian!"

"Not a chance. Your dad will kill me if anything happens to you." Adrian managed to drag Joshawa back to the cave wall. He let go of Joshawa, walked to the front of him, and then knelt on his haunches so he could be at eye level with Joshawa. "Listen, Joshawa, in order for Jax to shoot at you, he would have to leave the safety of the woods and stand close to the entrance to the cave to get a clear shot. That would leave him vulnerable. I think he's too smart to make a mistake like that. Not to mention that your dad is our wild card. If you place yourself in a dangerous position, then your dad will come to your side to protect you, which is exactly what Jax wants."

"You're right. Sorry, I was just trying to help."

Adrian smirked. "If my dad saw the two of us actually working together, keeping each other safe, he'd probably have a heart attack. Don't move from here. I'm going to go help Amy."

Adrian smiled at Joshawa as he stood and started to walk away when Joshawa interrupted him. "Ask Mona to lay behind Dameon to support his back. He'll be a lot more comfortable."

Usually, Adrian wouldn't take Joshawa seriously. He would have considered him bat-shit-crazy. But now, after everything he'd experienced since he arrived at the cave, he didn't give it a second thought.

Adrian glanced around the cave and surmised that the only clear shots Jax had were of Amy, Dameon, and himself. But when Mona lay where she did, Jax no longer had a clear shot without taking the chance of harming Mona, something Adrian was sure he wouldn't want to chance. Mona had to stay where she was, which meant that Dameon was going to have to deal with a little discomfort.

Adrian glanced over to Dameon and sighed. Dameon was experiencing a lot more than just a little discomfort. "How are you doing?"

"How do you think? This friggin hurts. When I get my hands on Jax, I'll kill him myself."

"And I'll help you. But let's get this fixed up first."

"Is the fletching showing?"

Adrian had checked out Dameon's leg when he was moving him. Ninety percent of the arrow was protruding out the front of his thigh, and only a small portion of the fletching was protruding from the rear of his thigh. "Not much."

"Shit. This is really going to hurt."

Adrian shifted his attention to Amy. She was wringing out one of the cloth bandages she'd previously put into the pot.

"Amy, is there anything I can do to help you?"

"Yes. I need you to lift his leg for me so I can get the bandage underneath his leg. I'm going to wrap this bandage above the wound, and hopefully, he won't bleed so much."

"You got it." Adrian placed his right hand on the arrow and was about to break it off when Amy yelled at him.

"What are you doing?"

"Wouldn't he be more comfortable if I broke most of this arrow off? I know I would."

"No, silly! I won't know how much to break off until I know how to fix him."

"Seriously?" Adrian pointed to the long shaft of the arrow. "You want to leave it like this?"

Amy rolled her eyes at Adrian, then held out the bandage. "So are you going to help?"

Adrian sighed as he knelt on the ground next to Dameon's legs. He placed one hand under Dameon's left thigh above the wound and the other just under Dameon's left knee. Adrian glanced over to Dameon. "Sorry. This is really going to hurt."

Dameon screamed in agony as Adrian lifted his leg high enough so that Amy could get the bandage underneath his leg. In the background, over Dameon's screams, they could hear Jax laughing.

Amy placed the rag underneath Dameon's thigh just above the wound. She motioned for Adrian to lower Dameon's leg, and then she tied the bandage as tight as she could. Satisfied with her tourniquet, she moved over and sat cross-legged on the ground in front of Dameon. His face was pale, and even though he tried to smile, his eyes gave away just how much pain he was in.

"Did I hear Jax laughing?"

"Is he the one that shot you?"

"Yes."

"Then yes, he was laughing."

Amy watched as Dameon went from being in pain to being very angry. "Dameon, I have a question?"

"What." Dameon's response dripped with anger.

"Does one-two-three make it less painful?"

Dameon looked at Amy as if she was crazy. "What?"

Amy scrunched up her face and rolled her eyes. "Last time I fixed you, you said I didn't give you a one-two-three."

"How the hell do you think counting's going to make it less painful?"

Amy was confused and a little hurt. She only wanted to cause him as little pain as possible. "I'm sorry. I just wanted to help." Amy stood and went to the back of the cave to get the salve she needed.

Adrian watched Amy, and it wasn't difficult to see that her

feelings were hurt. "So, Dameon, are you just naturally an ass-hole, or do you have to work at it?"

"Yeah, I guess I owe Amy an apology."

"You guess? Amy's only trying to help, and she doesn't understand sarcasm. Tell me about Jax. How concerned should we be?"

"Very concerned. He's an incredible shot. He obviously has his crossbow, and he would have his *Ruger*, as well. That alone makes him lethal. I would guess he brought the *Pax* so he could tranquilize Joshawa and Nathen. And with no backup, he would have also brought the *Barrett*."

Adrian was overwhelmed with the firepower Jax brought with him. "He has a *Barrett*? Are you kidding me? It's a semi-automatic. He could take all of us out with one pass of the cave."

"Trust me, I've thought of that. The thing with that scenario is that if Jax uses it, he could potentially wound or kill Joshawa, Nathen, or the bear. I don't think he'll take that chance. Besides, we also have a *Barrett*, and I'm not afraid to use it. If I know Jax, he brought his night vision goggles. So, he'll probably make his move in the dark. The only part of this scenario that I'm not too sure about is whether he'll attack to-night or wait until Nathen shows up."

"After Amy gets that arrow out of you, we need to put a plan together. And as far as night vision goggles go, both Nathen and Joshawa can see in the dark."

Dameon glanced up at Adrian with an expression of disbe-lief. "They can see at night?"

"Yup, and when it comes to hand-to-hand combat, Nathen's more dangerous than any weapon Jax has."

Serena was observing the interaction between Adrian and Dameon. She also witnessed the injury to Dameon's left thigh.

Serena had passed all her medical knowledge to Amy, and she was doing very well with that knowledge. However, the injury Dameon suffered would entail excising the wound so the fletching could be removed. Amy had the knowledge, but Serena wasn't sure if Amy had the stomach for it. Serena was just about to change into a wisp when Imani joined her. Imani peered over the edge and gasped at what she saw.

"I thought that if we were successful, everything would be fine." Imani pointed to the edge of the Realm. "Everything is not fine. What do we do? How can we help them?"

"We cannot interfere, Imani. We are Ancestors, and as Ancestors, we have to follow the laws of our people. How can we punish our people for breaking these laws if we are as guilty as they are?"

"Was I not interfering when I placed Mona inside the bear?"

"You and I are both guilty of interfering. Why we were not punished, I have no answer. However, when we interfered, there were Ancestors watching us. Perhaps they took pity on us or believed that our actions were honorable. That being said, if we interfere again, I know we will be held accountable, and we will be punished."

"Everyone in the cave is at risk. There has to be something we can do."

Serena thought for a moment, then smiled at Imani. "We cannot kill an outsider or help outsiders to kill each other. However, we can help Billy find Hansen, and we can remind Billy about his animal friends."

Billy ran as fast as he could toward the one place he hated the most. He jumped over fallen trees and ducked to avoid low branches. Billy didn't stop until he reached the place where he had buried Mona. Once there, he sat on the ground, closed his eyes, and listened for Hansen.

Serena had transformed into a wisp and headed toward Amy. Curiosity got the better of her, and she flew to the spot where Jax was hiding. Serena landed on a branch of a redwood tree, and from her vantage point, she discovered what Nathen was up against. Jax's arsenal was more than adequate to kill everyone in the cave. Serena recalled what she had told Imani. As Ancestors, they were not allowed to interfere. Serena's mind was racing as she tried to come up with a scenario that wouldn't be considered as interfering. However, as long as she was an Ancestor, there was nothing she could do. Serena flew off the tree and headed into the cave.

Serena found Amy at the back of the cave standing next to her trunks. She had found the salve she had made for Joshawa and was heading back to Dameon. Serena was thankful that Amy hadn't seen Nathen. As far as Amy was concerned, Nathen was still deep inside the cave. Serena flew close to Amy, and the minute Amy parted her lips, Serena flew in and found the area of Amy's brain that contained the medical knowledge she had previously planted. She rested there and then reached out to Amy.

Amy, do you know what you have to do?

Yes, but I'm scared.

What are you afraid of?

I must open Dameon's leg. I'm not sure I want to do that.

But that is the only way to save him.

Serena could feel Amy's uneasiness. Amy had the knowledge, but she just needed the courage.

Amy, this man has come to the cave to protect you and everyone else in the cave. He cannot protect anyone in his condition. You have to heal him.

Amy listened to that phrase and repeated it over and over. *I have to heal him.* I healed Joshawa. Now I have to heal Dameon.

Yes, Amy. You must heal Dameon just like you healed Joshawa. Will you heal Dameon?

Amy picked up another batch of rags and spoke to the voice in her head. "Of course I'll heal him. You're silly." Amy rolled her eyes at the voice in her head, and with determined strides, she went to Dameon's side.

Amy placed the bandages into the pot of boiling water. She then placed the salve next to Dameon. Amy glanced around the cave and then walked over to Joshawa. She knelt at his side and spoke very softly. "Where's Billy?"

Joshawa also whispered. "He's gone to get help. Don't worry, he'll be fine."

"I'm not worried. She'll take care of him."

Joshawa appeared completely confused, and she giggled at him. "You look silly."

"Who's the *she* that's taking care of Billy?"

"I don't know who she is, only that she'll protect Billy. Can I have your blanket?"

"Sure, take it. Are you going to be able to mend Dameon?"

"Of course I can. You're so silly."

Amy walked over to Dameon and laid the blanket on the ground between him and the fire pit.

Dameon glanced up at Amy. "What are you doing?"

It was clearly evident to Amy how much pain Dameon was in. "I'm healing you."

"How are you going to heal me?"

"I'm going to remove the arrow. How else would I heal you? So many silly people." Amy examined the wound created by the fletching. She had no way of knowing how deep the fletching was. Amy was going to have to probe the wound, which couldn't be accomplished without inflicting severe pain. Amy glanced over to Dameon but said nothing. She was trying to find the right words for what she had to do.

Dameon obviously tried to mask the pain with a smile. "Something tells me that I'm not going to like what you have to do."

Amy chewed at her lower lip while she kept her eyes averted away from Dameon.

My child, why do you hesitate?

I have to cause him a lot of pain, mother. I don't want to do that.

I understand, but sweetheart, you've been given a great gift, and this man is here to protect you. You need to be strong. You have to help him.

Amy turned to face Dameon. "I have to see how much damage there is. That means I have to examine your injury, and it's going to hurt a lot."

"Nothing like sugar coating it." Dameon smiled at Amy. "You do what you have to do."

"I need you on your side so I can see the back of your leg."

Adrian helped Dameon roll onto his side as carefully as he could. Amy put her hands on Dameon's thigh and was about to examine the wound when she looked up at Adrian. "You should hold him down."

Amy placed her index finger into the wound. Dameon screamed out in pain, which caused Amy to freeze.

You have to be strong. He needs you.

Amy took a deep breath and moved her finger ever so slightly in the wound. She discovered that the fletching was wedged between muscle and bone. Amy knew what she had to do, and it made her very sad.

Dameon's leg felt as though it was on fire. Even the slightest movement caused him excruciating pain. He watched as Amy retrieved her filleting knife and placed the blade into the coals. After a few minutes, Amy removed the knife and then used it to remove the steaming hot bandages from the pot over the fire. She then placed the bandages into one of her buckets and moved the bucket so that it was next to Dameon.

Amy placed her left hand on Dameon's hip. "I can fix you, and I can heal you. What I can't do is make the pain go away. I used all that I had on Joshawa."

Dameon looked at Amy. "Can't you make more?"

"Yes. But I don't have what I need to make it."

Adrian moved closer to Amy and Dameon. "Tell me what you need, and I'll go get it."

"It's not that easy. The ingredients are by the river. Soon the sky will be black, and the wolves will come, and they will eat you."

Dameon knew that the arrow had to be removed. Maybe this was his punishment for all the animals he'd killed for sport or for profit. He placed his hand over Amy's. "I trust you. Fix me." Dameon hesitated for a moment. "I don't suppose you have any liquor around?"

"Liquor?"

"I'll take that for a no. How about something to bite down on?"

Adrian stood. "I'll take care of that." Adrian headed to the wood pile and broke off a thick, five-inch-long piece of wood from a tree branch.

Dameon glanced over at the knife Amy had heated up. He pretty much knew what was next but decided to ask anyway. "Amy, what are you going to do?"

"First, Adrian's going to break off most of the arrow." Amy hesitated for just a second. "Then I have to make a bigger hole so that the piece in your leg will come out."

"Can't you take it out from the back of my leg?"

"Only if you want me to make an even bigger hole."

"Small hole works for me."

Adrian broke off the arrow so that only four inches of the shaft was left. Then he sat behind Dameon and wrapped his legs around Dameon's hips. He then placed the piece of wood between Dameon's teeth, then hooked his arms around Dameon's armpits and held him tight.

"Ready when you are, Amy."

Dameon bit down on the wood and waited for the pain to start.

CHAPTER THIRTY-FIVE

Lord Adeeowale walked back into the room that Lord Chike had created for himself. He went over to his son and sat by his side. Lord Adeeowale's memories were colliding with each other. The true memories and the false memories, each fighting to gain control. Lord Adeeowale understood that the only way to fix his memories was through Serena. But first, he had to bury his son with all the honor and decorum that a true warrior deserved.

Lord Adeeowale was about to pick up his son when something inside his head told him to look at the tapestries. He turned and glanced over at them, but nothing was amiss. Lord Adeeowale had nothing but contempt for the tapestries that hung in this room. They depicted many atrocities against the Jelani Tribe. After he buried his son, he would come back here and burn each and every one.

Lord Adeeowale was about to turn away when one particular tapestry caught his eye. It was the one where the Destroyer was almost defeated. As he walked toward it, the tapestry changed right before his eyes. The revised tapestry depicted the death of the Destroyer. It revealed how both Lord Adeeowale and Massai were the victors of this battle.

Lord Adeeowale was confused. These tapestries were a gift to Lord Chike from the Council of Five. Why would they change a tapestry that revealed anything else but his victory? Lord Adeeowale scanned the room and witnessed each tapestry as it changed to reveal the actual events of the battle. His eyes widened in shock as he witnessed the portrayal of the true carnage left behind by the Destroyer. His heart pounded in his chest, his tears ran down his cheeks, and his stomach felt as though he wanted to throw up.

How could the Council of Five permit this? Why would they do this? At that moment, Lord Adeeowale remembered Lord Chike's questions. Who was he? He was the Destroyer. Who is the Council of Five? The answer to everything was in that second question. Lord Chike was the Destroyer, and if the Council of Five was actually a Council of one, was the Destroyer the Council of Five? That would explain why the tapestries were changing. His death meant he had no control over what was revealed in the tapestries.

Lord Adeeowale walked over to his son and lifted him into his arms. "I will take care of you, my son. You will be buried alongside the great warriors of our time. Then I will visit the Council of Five . . . if they truly exist." Lord Adeeowale left the chamber and headed for the entrance to the falls.

Billy had remained sitting cross-legged on the ground in front of Mona's grave. His eyes remained shut so he couldn't see the evil that surrounded him. He hadn't been there very long when he heard a voice within his head. The voice was that of a woman, and it was soft and comforting.

Billy, why do you sit in front of a grave when you should be finding Hansen?

"Hansen, come here. Billy, wait here."

You could find Hansen faster if you let me help. Do you really want to be sitting there in the dark?

"Mona here. Billy sit with Mona."

There is nothing but bones in this grave. Mona is in the cave, and she needs your help. They all need your help. They need you to save them.

Billy opened his eyes and stared at the grave. "Can't find Hansen. Too dark. Billy get lost."

Billy, look up and tell me what you see.

Billy looked up and saw a beautiful blue star. It was on a branch of the redwood that was next to Billy. "Pretty star."

If you follow me, I can find Hansen, and I can be your light back to the cave. But we haven't much time. Will you follow me?

Billy stood up, brushed the dirt from his pants, and then he looked for his blue star. He didn't have to look far. She flew down from the tree and hovered in front of his face. "Billy like star." Billy timidly reached out to the star with his right hand. "Billy touch star?"

I will allow you to hold me after we save our families.

Billy kept his eyes on his blue star. She was fast, and Billy had to run to keep up with her. But he didn't care, because he'd made a new friend. More importantly, he would be able to protect Amy and Mona from the evil that was waiting for them just outside their cave.

Dameon bit down on the piece of wood as hard as he could, but that didn't lessen the excruciating pain. He could feel the knife cutting his flesh to make the wound bigger. He could feel Amy's finger digging into the wound. Dameon always thought of himself as a strong person who could handle anything that was thrown at him. But today, he didn't care if anyone thought less of him. He spit out the piece of wood and screamed in agonizing pain. When the probing was done and the fletching had been removed, Dameon thought he was in the clear. But when Amy removed the knife from the fire and placed the red-hot blade on his wound, Dameon tapped out and fainted.

Jax was sitting on the ground, his back resting against the redwood. He'd organized his arrows and crossbow for easy access in case he needed them quickly. The *Pax* was leaning against the redwood loaded with a tranquilizer that would easily take down the young Bigfoot. More potent tranquilizer darts were at the ready in case he needed to tranquilize the bear or the adult Bigfoot. Judging by the younger Bigfoot, Jax estimated what the adult Bigfoot most likely weighed. Jax also removed his headlamp from his backpack and placed it on his head. He turned it on to make sure it was working, then turned it off. Jax rested against his tree and listened to the cries echoing from the cave.

Jax was enjoying listening to Dameon's screams of agony and was honestly disappointed when they stopped. He figured that Dameon had probably passed out. Jax chuckled to himself because he was having so much fun. At one point, he'd decided that he was going to end Dameon's life quickly, but after listening to him scream, he changed his mind. There was plenty of room in that little cabin for Dameon and Bigfoot Junior.

Jax peered around the tree and watched as the girl worked on the wound. It appeared that she was applying some sort of ointment on it. Jax yelled out to his captive audience, "Hey, Dameon. Having fun yet? Cause I sure am."

Dameon tried to sit up, but the girl stopped him. She placed her hand on his chest and then turned to focus on Jax. "This is not fun. You don't hurt friends."

"Dameon's not my friend. At least not anymore. As of today, I couldn't care less what happens to him. Where's Bigfoot's dad?"

Jax did not receive a response. "Okay, you don't want to give him up. I have enough ammunition here to kill all of you in seconds. But that isn't me. If I'm going to kill any of you, it'll be slow and agonizing. So let's try this again. Where's Bigfoot's dad?"

Adrian had listened to Jax's threats, and according to Dameon, Jax would have no problem making good on them. Adrian turned his attention to Joshawa.

"How are you doing over there?"

"Feeling left out. My fire is out, and I'm cold. Can you help me get closer to Dameon and your firepit?"

Adrian walked over to Joshawa, knelt down in front of him, and rested his hands on his thighs. "You do realize that you're safer here?"

"Yes. But do you realize that Jax wants me, my father, and Mona alive? So whether I sit here or by the fire, the outcome will be the same. Personally, I'd like to be warm."

Adrian smiled, and then he stood and extended his hand to Joshawa. Joshawa looked at Adrian as if he'd grown two heads.

"In case you've forgotten, I only have one good leg?"

"I haven't forgotten. We might have to get mobile real fast, so let's start working on it now."

Joshawa took Adrian's hand, and then Adrian pulled him up so he could stand on his good leg. Judging by the grimacing sounds Joshawa was making, he was obviously in pain, but he never said a word. Adrian put Joshawa's arm around his neck and then helped him move over to the firepit. Amy helped Adrian slowly lower Joshawa to the ground, then sat between Joshawa and Dameon.

Dameon had woken up and was laying quietly on a blanket next to the firepit. The wound had been bandaged, and blankets were rolled up to serve as a pillow for his head. Adrian was awestruck by the skill with which Amy removed the fletching.

Adrian gently placed his right hand on Dameon's forehead. He was checking to see if Dameon had developed a fever. Thankfully, he hadn't. "How are you doing, Dameon?"

"Could use some morphine right now, but other than that,

I'm good."

"So what do we do with Jax?"

"Protect ourselves, prepare for an attack."

"How do we prepare against him? He's hidden, and we're in the open. And we don't have the weapons that he has."

"Sometimes your greatest weapon is your brain."

"Well, my brain's saying we're up shit's creek without a paddle." Both Dameon and Joshawa chuckled at the reference. "I'm serious, guys. What can we do to save us from Jax?"

Dameon leaned forward and rested on his elbows. He stared through the fire in Jax's direction. "The first thing we have to do is to keep him talking. The more talking he does, the less thinking he does. We also have to do something about this fire."

Joshawa glanced over to Dameon. "What do you mean?"

Adrian smiled. "I think I know exactly what you mean. Let me guess. The night vision goggles aren't adapted to bright light. Make the fire bigger, and Jax can't use them."

"Now you're thinking. You and Amy get whatever firewood you can and build an intense fire. If you have enough wood, make the fire pit the width of the cave and as wide as you can. Start with this firepit and work your way out. But remember, it has to last the night."

Amy was looking at all three of her new companions. This was her home, and they were taking it away from her. First they made Billy go away, and now they wanted to burn all her firewood. She would have nothing for the winter.

Sweetheart, did I not teach you anything?

Of course, you did. But this is my home.

And they are here to protect you and your home. However, they do need your help.

If I use all the firewood, I won't last the winter.

If their plan works, you won't need the firewood.

I don't understand.

Child, trust me. Do as they ask.

All right, but I don't have to like it.

Amy was startled when she looked around and found everyone staring at her. "What?"

Adrian was the first to speak up. "Let me guess, you were speaking to Mona."

"Yes. She told me I have to help you."

Adrian offered Amy his hand. "Come on, Amy, let's build a wall of fire."

Billy kept running, not paying any attention to where he was going. Twice, he'd tripped over fallen trees because he couldn't keep his eyes off his beautiful blue star. He'd followed her for only a little while when his blue star stopped and just hovered in front of him. Billy smiled as he again reached out to her. "Billy like star."

Billy, be still and listen.

Billy did as he was told and listened to the sounds of the forest. "Billy like forest."

Shhh, listen for your friend. He is close.

Billy immediately went quiet, and then he heard it. Someone was almost running through the trees. Billy glanced around to pinpoint where the noise was coming from. In the distance, he could see a white light. Billy became excited and ran toward the light.

CHAPTER THIRTY-SIX

Imani sat at the edge of the Realm with her legs tucked close to her chest. She wrapped her arms around her legs, wishing that she could find comfort in the embrace. But that wasn't to be. Sadness consumed her as she stared out into the darkness. Imani couldn't control her sobbing or the fear that was building inside of her. She was afraid for her family, but she could do nothing to help them. Imani desperately wanted to peer over the edge of the Realm and observe them, but why would she?

The man they called Jax intended to hurt her family, and she could do nothing to stop him. Imani knew what Jax was planning. His thoughts came to her so clear, so precise. And even though she knew what lay ahead for her family, she could do nothing because she'd been forbidden to interfere. She didn't possess the strength she needed in order to watch her family die.

Imani decided to return to the Land of the Spirits, where the option to watch her family didn't exist. As she stood, Serena's voice filled her mind.

Billy is with Hansen, and they are on their way to the cave.

They can save my family?

I hope so. I truly do. But I cannot promise you what is beyond my influence.

Imani wiped the tears from her face. She leaned forward just enough to see her family. Anger consumed her as she watched Jax shoot an arrow into the leg of the man they called Dameon.

Serena, I know this man's thoughts, and they are evil. And it is not only my family that is in danger, but Joshawa and Nathen, as well. They are all in danger.

How do you know what his plans are?

His thoughts came to me.

You can meld with him?

No, his thoughts just filled my mind.

How long have you been able to do this?

I do not understand. Can you not do this as well?

No, not with outsiders. Wait for me. I will see that Billy and Hansen make it to the cave, and then I will return to you. We have much to discuss.

Casandra walked among her people, and it brought her great pleasure to do so. She was a priestess, but now all she wanted was to be a tribesman. Her long red hair fell to her waist. Her vivid green eyes sparkled as she took in her surroundings, and her smile portrayed her happiness. She wore an animal skin halter top and a loin cloth that fell to just above her knees.

Casandra made her way toward the Gathering Hut, not that she was entertaining the thought of entering. Granted, she was curious about the Council, but not enough to actually request an audience with them.

Casandra had decided to make her way to the lake and had just passed the Gathering Hut when she saw Lord Adeeowale. He was carrying someone in his arms, and by the expression on Lord Adeeowale's face, it was evident that he was in immense pain. It was not a physical pain—it was an emotional pain. A pain that could only be felt deep inside.

As Casandra drew nearer, she could see the blood that soaked Lord Adeeowale's loin cloth. "Lord Adeeowale, what happened? Are you hurt, my Lord?"

"Lord Chike is dead."

Lord Adeeowale continued to walk toward the village.

Casandra chose not to interfere and walked beside him. "I thought so. I am free from the orb, and I feel no pain. Who is it that you carry?"

Lord Adeeowale stopped and turned to face Casandra. "This is my son, Massai. He gave his life so Lord Chike could die."

"Your son? Then it is not your blood on your loin cloth?"

"No, not mine. The blood belonged to my son. It is a rather lengthy story, but right now, all I want to do is bury my son with all the honors he deserves."

"And that is what we shall do. Come with me to the Priestess's Hut, and we shall prepare him for burial."

Dameon tried to sit up but couldn't find a position that didn't aggravate his pain. He was about to call out to Jax when the most incredible thing happened. Mona had been lying close to the entrance of the cave. Dameon assumed that, in her way, she was protecting the occupants inside. Mona stood and ambled toward Dameon, then lay down behind him and Joshawa. Dameon was a little nervous about resting his back on a grizzly. However, this wasn't an ordinary grizzly. Dameon slowly leaned back onto Mona, and at that angle, his pain was minimal. He shook his head slightly as he smiled at Joshawa.

"Nobody would believe this even if I had proof. I have a hard time believing it myself."

"This is nothing. The last few days have been eye-opening. How are you doing? How's the pain?"

"I'd be lying if I said I wasn't in pain." Dameon glanced over to the entrance of the cave. "I think it's time to get Jax talking." If this confrontation had been only him against Jax, Dameon would have handled this much differently. But it wasn't just him. It wasn't about saving himself. He had to save everyone, no matter what it took.

"Jax, you still there?"

"Of course I am. How's the leg?"

"Pretty good, actually. What's your problem, Jax? We've been friends since we were kids. We made a deal. If this Bigfoot you're chasing was a person, you'd back off."

"Actually, you said you'd protect Bigfoot. We never said anything about me backing off. And even if we did, there's no way that I'm going to walk away from this. You know what my problem is, Dameon?"

"No, but I would sure like to find out."

"You're right, Dameon. We've been friends for a very long time. You can't honestly tell me the hunt still thrills you. I know you. And that's what the problem is. I'm taking the hunt to the next level, and all of a sudden, you grow a conscience."

"I don't hunt people. And I definitely don't want to torture them."

Adrian and Amy made their way to the back of the cave to gather firewood. Adrian couldn't believe what he was hearing. Jax had to be completely insane. And if the truth be known, Adrian was scared to death at the thought of Jax winning this battle. When they got to the firewood, Nathen was waiting for them.

Adrian motioned toward the front of the cave. He spoke softly so that no one at the entrance could hear him. "Did you hear that?"

"Yes, I did. He's got too much at stake. He won't go down easy. How's Dameon doing?"

Adrian glanced over to Amy, and the feeling he felt was that of admiration. "Amy was amazing."

"All I did was fix him."

Adrian chuckled. "And you did a damn good job."

Nathen smiled at Amy. "I know somebody who would love to meet you. In the meantime, what's our plan?"

Adrian continued the conversation. "Dameon wants to keep him talking. Apparently, he can't think and talk at the same time. He has night vision goggles, so we're going to build a pretty big fire, and hopefully, he won't be able to use them. We also sent Billy to meet up with Hansen."

"Yes, I know. They're on their way."

"That's good news. We know Jax has a compound bow. He's used it on Dameon twice. Dameon said Jax will have his *Ruger* with him, as well as a *Pax* rifle and a *Barrett*. On our side, other than the *Barrett*, all we have is my *Ruger*."

"What I'm hoping is that we can deal with Jax without the use of firearms."

"Well, considering Jax has used his compound bow twice without any reason to, I don't think this is going to go very well."

"Is he still blind to one side of the cave?"

"Yes, as far as I know."

"Okay. You two get the firewood. I'm going to make my way to the entrance. We'll see where we go from there."

Joshawa observed Adrian and Amy as they built the fire. There was no denying that Adrian liked Amy. The unfortunate part was that there was no guarantee that any of them would survive this ordeal. Joshawa smiled to himself. If Becca were here, she'd scold him for being a pessimist.

Joshawa really wished he could help, but he was a prisoner to his injuries. The only thing he could contribute was that he could see in the dark. Joshawa sighed, knowing that his ability was of no use if he wasn't mobile. Joshawa glanced over to Dameon to see how he was doing. Dameon was leaning against Mona with his eyes closed and his breathing shallow.

"Dameon, you don't look so good."

Dameon kept his eyes closed and didn't move a muscle. "I don't feel so good. Between my shoulder and my leg, I don't know how much help I'm going to be. Jax is smart. He didn't injure me because he was mad at me. He just wanted to take me out of the equation."

"Didn't think of that." Joshawa glanced around the cave, and all of a sudden, he thought of a way he could be helpful. "You said we should keep Jax talking. How about I talk to Jax? I probably could keep him talking for a fair bit."

Dameon opened his eyes and looked at Joshawa. "And I didn't think of that. You're right. You probably won't be able to shut him up. Go for it, Joshawa."

Finally, he could be helpful. Joshawa focused on the entrance of the cave. "Hey, Jax. I hear you want a piece of me." There was no response, so Joshawa tried again. "You surprise me. I thought you'd want to talk with your Bigfoot. If you don't, that's fine. I could care less."

"Oh, but you should care."

Joshawa glanced over to Dameon, who gave him a thumbs up. "And why should I care?"

"I didn't think my Bigfoot would be able to communicate so well. Have you lived all your life in the forest?"

"Yes, with my parents."

"Your father, he's like you. What about your mother?"

"What about my mother?"

"Is she a Bigfoot, as well?"

"Jax, what did Dameon mean when he said he doesn't torture?"

Jax laughed. "It's not torture. I'm just satisfying my curiosity. I'll tell you what. If you give yourself up, we can leave, and I won't have to hurt your friends."

"You don't want to wait for my father?"

"I won't have to. Your father will come to me."

"Now you're the one who should be afraid. If I go with you, you'd see the wrath of my father."

Again, Jax laughed. "Bring it on. I love a challenge."

Serena led Billy and Hansen to the cave, but she didn't use the path. She had them stay hidden in the forest until they reached the outside of the cave. They would be out of Jax's field of vision and still be only a couple of feet from the entrance. Once again, Serena hovered in front of Billy.

Billy, you must stay here for now. Jax cannot see you from here. Wait for Mona. She will tell you when they need you.

"Billy—"

Serena cut Billy off. *Quiet, Billy! You must be as quiet as a mouse and not move a muscle. Jax is close, and he may hear you.*

Billy hung his head, and Serena could tell he was trying not to cry. *Billy, look at me.* Billy glanced up just far enough so Serena could see his eyes. *I am sorry if I frightened you. But we have to be careful. You are going to be our knight in shining armor. And no matter how this is resolved, we will all be so proud of you.*

Billy held his head high and grinned from ear-to-ear.

I have to leave. Wait here and listen for Mona.

Jax was surprised that his Bigfoot actually showed intelligence. He peered around his tree and watched the young male and the girl extend the fire. Quietly, he thought to himself, *really Dameon. Trying to eliminate night vision is not going to help you. Let me show you why.* Jax removed one of the smaller dosage darts from its case. He placed the dart in his mouth, between his teeth. Jax moved to the side of the tree where he could easily see into the cave. He knelt down on his left knee and then placed his elbow on his right knee to steady his aim. It only took a few seconds. Jax aimed at his target, and before the male dropped to the ground, Jax had already shot the female.

Nathen had reached the entrance to the cave undetected, or at least he hoped he had. He knew Billy and Hansen were just around the corner, which gave Nathen some semblance of hope. He was watching Adrian and Amy build the wall of fire when he heard a strange noise. Nathen watched in horror as Adrian fell backward into the fire. Before Amy hit the ground, Nathen left the security of his hiding place. He ran over to Adrian, grabbed him by his shirt, and pulled him out of the fire. After a quick glance, Nathen was certain that Adrian hadn't sustained any serious injuries. Nathen took Adrian and placed him next to Dameon, then he went to get Amy. Nathen held Amy in his arms and stared in the direction that Jax was hiding. "I'm giving you one warning. Go back to where you came from, and we'll call it a day."

Jax sounded giddy with excitement. "Are you kidding me! I'm having way too much fun to leave. I have to admit, you're so much better than any Bigfoot I ever dreamed of. I might even decide to keep you for myself."

CHAPTER THIRTY-SEVEN

Serena arrived at her section of the Land of the Ancestors, eager to speak with Imani. When Serena entered the clearing, she found Imani sitting at the edge, gazing down at her family. Serena didn't have to see Imani's face to know that she was crying. Serena walked over to the edge of the Realm and sat next to Imani. She then peered over the edge and discovered that Amy and Adrian were lying side by side on the ground. Both were motionless, and Serena feared the worst.

"Can you hear Amy's heartbeat?"

"I feel it as if it were my own."

"Then you know she is alive."

"Yes, but that knowledge does not offer much comfort."

"Imani, what did you mean when you said Jax's thoughts come to you?"

Imani didn't look over to Serena. She just continued to watch over her family. "They come to me. I do not know why or how. They just do."

"Do you receive Adrian's thoughts, as well?"

"No. There is no reason to." Imani glanced over to Serena. "Adrian is helping Amy. There is no reason to know what his intentions are."

"Did you want to learn Jax's intentions?"

"Yes, I did wonder why he was there. But that was all."

"Try wondering what Adrian's intentions are."

Imani looked at Serena, obviously puzzled by her request. "I do not understand. Adrian's intentions are pure."

"If his intentions are pure, as you say, then there should be no harm."

Serena watched Imani peer over the edge of the Realm. A minute later, her focus was back on Serena.

"Can you hear his thoughts?"

"Not yet. He is in a deep sleep. I do not know if his thoughts will come to me."

A few minutes later, Imani paused and crooked her head slightly to the left. To Serena, it was as if Imani was listening to someone. Serena folded her hands on her lap and patiently waited for Imani. Several minutes later, Serena's patience was rewarded.

"His thoughts did come to me. They are somewhat pure."

"Somewhat?"

"He has grown since he started this journey. He has a new respect for Nathen and Joshawa. He likes Amy, maybe a little too much."

Serena chuckled. "Spoken like a true mother. Am I correct in saying that you have no control over how fast you receive the person's thoughts?"

"Yes, but to be honest, I really do not pay much attention to how quickly I receive them."

"What is Jax's plan?"

"He is evil. If you saw what I saw, heard what I heard . . ." Imani closed her eyes, and when she opened them, tears were forming in the corners. "He plans to kill everyone in the cave, with the exception of Nathen and Joshawa. He will put Nathen and Joshawa to sleep like he did to Adrian and Amy. He will take them to a secluded cabin in the woods. Once there, he will sell Nathen and do unspeakable things to Joshawa." Imani could no longer hold back her tears.

Serena watched as Imani's tears ran freely down her cheeks. It saddened Serena to see Imani in such a state. Serena took Imani's hands and smiled as she gently shook her head from side to side. "You are so brave. How you can hear an outsider's thoughts is a mystery to me. But maybe we can use this information not to interfere but to educate."

Imani smiled as she let go of Serena's hands and wiped the tears from her face. "Thank you. So what do we do?"

"We need to communicate with someone in the cave. Not Nathen, he is too emotional."

"Then who? Everyone else is sleeping or hurt." Imani's eyes lit up. "I know someone. Billy."

"Billy has the mind of a child. He would not know what to do with the information we give him."

"Then there is nobody to help my family."

"Not exactly. You forgot one other mind that we can meld with."

Imani appeared puzzled, "Who?"

Serena smiled at Imani. "Your mind is obviously overwhelmed. Otherwise, you would not have asked the question."

Imani returned Serena's smile. "Mona."

Nathen covered Amy and Adrian with blankets to keep them warm and then went to sit between Dameon and Joshawa. Darkness had engulfed the forest, and what little could be seen was from the light given off by the fire. Nathen focused on the entrance of the cave in Jax's direction. "So, Jax, it's just me and you. You had a clear shot of me. Why didn't you take it?"

"Like I said. I'm having way too much fun. Oh, and thank you for the fire. I can see the cave and the pathway quite clearly."

"The fun has to end sometime. When it does, what will be your next move?"

"I'll start with taking the rifle off your hands."

"Why would you want that rifle? Don't you have one of

your own?"

"I'm not new to this game. Just ask Dameon. You're trying to get me to reveal what weapons I have. However, I think you already know. Right, Dameon?"

Nathen glanced over to Dameon and nodded his head.

Dameon continued the conversation. "You know very well I told them everything. Not that it was necessary. You've used your bow and the *Pax*. And I know you also brought the *Barrett*. The only thing you don't have is backup."

"I don't need backup. Two of you are injured, and two are sleeping, which just leaves me and the adult Bigfoot."

Nathen was surprised that Jax hadn't mentioned Mona, nor did he mention Billy. Billy had been in his blind spot, so that could be explained. But not mentioning Mona? Did he not perceive her as a threat? Nathen took over the conversation. "You still haven't answered my question. Why do you want the rifle?"

"Because I'm not stupid. It may be just you and me, but you have far more firepower. I just want to even the odds."

Nathen looked over to Dameon and whispered, "Do I keep him talking?"

Dameon whispered back, "Definitely, yes."

"The only firepower we have is the rifle. So how do you assume that we have more firepower?"

"If you don't know the answer, then I'm sure as hell not going to tell you. You can figure that one out for yourself. Now, bring me the rifle."

"And if I say no?" It took only seconds for an arrow to fly through the air and land in the dirt next to Joshawa.

"You were saying?"

"You hurt my son, and all the firepower in the world won't help you."

"Big talk for . . ." Jax hesitated for a brief second. "What do I label you? Bigfoot, or just some grossly disfigured man?"

Joshawa interrupted with so much anger. "My father is more man than you can ever hope to be."

Nathen glanced over his shoulder at Joshawa. He smiled as he slowly shook his head from side to side. Nathen knew Joshawa understood to be silent, so he turned his attention to Jax. "You can start with my name. It's Nathen. And I'm no different than you."

Jax laughed out loud. "Are you kidding me. Have you looked in the mirror lately? Your boy is pretty spirited. I look forward to satisfying my curiosity when I get him to the cabin. But we are off-topic. Bring me the rifle, or the next arrow will be in your son's chest. And trust me, he won't survive."

Nathen glanced over at Joshawa and then turned to face Dameon.

Dameon's face was riddled with pain, and he was shaking his head gently from side to side. "Nathen, you can't give him the rifle. He's lethal enough without it. Our chances of walking out of this cave are slim with Jax only possessing one rifle. If he has two, then the only ones he'll leave alive will be you and Joshawa."

"I don't plan to give him the rifle. But like he said, we need to even the odds."

Nathen stood and made his way over to the rifle. When he turned, he discovered that Mona was no longer lying behind Dameon and Joshawa. She had moved over to the right side of the cave entrance, which put her in Jax's blind spot.

Mona had been lying behind Joshawa and Dameon to help support their weight. She was listening to the conversation, and when the time was right, she would help Nathen win this battle. As she patiently waited, a familiar voice came to her.

Mona, we need your help in this fight.

Anything, Imani. I want to help protect Amy and the others.

Billy and a man called Hansen are just on the other side of the cave. They are here to help. Jax is prepared to kill everyone in the cave except for Nathen and Joshawa. What he plans for them is unspeakable. We need you to be close to the entrance. Listen to Jax and, if possible, watch him. He intends to tranquilize both Nathen and Joshawa and then kill the rest with a rifle named **Barrett.***"*

"He just asked Nathen to give him ours."

"He cannot. The minute he hands that rifle to Jax, all will be lost. Jax will win."

"I'll speak to Nathen."

"No, Serena said that Nathen is far too emotional to be included in this conversation. Ask Nathen why he is giving the rifle to Jax. And when the time is right, meld with Billy, and they will come."

Mona slowly stood up and carefully made her way to the far-right entrance to the cave. Once there, she reached out to Nathen.

Why are you giving him so much power?

I'm not.

Nathen grabbed the rifle and then walked toward the entrance. "If you want this rifle, walk onto the path."

"Now, why would I do that? How about we meet halfway. Go to the middle of the path, place the rifle on the ground, then back up."

"What are you afraid of?" Nathen started walking toward the middle of the path. "Like you said, it's just the two of us. I'll place this rifle into your hands. Anything other than that, and I'll go back into the cave with the rifle."

Jax's mind was racing, and his body was vibrating with excitement. He could tranq Nathen, but what was the fun in that? He was in a position to have an actual conversation with his Bigfoot. How could he turn his back on that? Jax wasn't sure if he wanted to keep Nathen or sell him. Jax could make a lot of money off him. Or he could take him to the cabin. Jax could shackle Nathen and make him watch while Jax tortured his son. Jax stood, and he knew his excitement and glee were plastered across his face.

"Okay, Nathen, I'll meet you halfway. But you have to hold the rifle by the butt, pointing down. You even flinch, and I'll put a bullet between your eyes. Do you agree?"

"Yes."

"Okay, I'm coming out now." Jax turned off his headlamp and used the fire to guide him to the path.

"Leave your sidearm with the rest of your weapons."

Jax stepped onto the path. He was smiling and not in a good way.

"Not going to happen, Nathen." Jax raised his arms and slightly turned so Nathen could see that his *Ruger* was holstered. "As you can see, my gun is holstered. It's not a threat to you or anyone else unless you try something stupid."

Hansen was listening to every word. From his position, he could see Jax walk out onto the path. This was his opportunity to even the odds. He turned to Billy and whispered, "Stay here, Billy. I'm going to go help Nathen."

Billy kept his voice down as well. "Billy, help, too."

"Do you know how to walk in the woods without making a sound?"

Billy nodded his head.

"Okay, here's the plan. While Jax is talking to Nathen, you and I are going to sneak past Jax and then go steal his weapons."

"Billy like plan."

"Can you meld with Nathen?"

"No. Just Mona."

"Okay, ask Mona to meld with Nathen and tell him to keep Jax talking." Hansen rummaged through his backpack and retrieved a flashlight. He knew he had to be careful using it because the last thing he wanted was to alert Jax of his presence.

Nathen received the message, and as Jax approached him, Nathen could see Hansen and Billy cross the path and then disappear into the forest. Dameon had told Nathen that the way to distract Jax was to stroke his ego, and that was precisely what Nathen intended to do.

Jax held out his hand to Nathen, but unfortunately for Jax, Nathen wasn't overly anxious to hand over the rifle. Nathen watched as Jax's carefree expression turned to one of contempt.

"What are you doing, Nathen? You promised me the rifle."

"Yes. And I intend to hand it over to you. But first, I need some answers."

"This isn't what we agreed to."

Dameon spoke up. "What's the matter, Jax? You don't like it when the rules change?"

Jax turned to face Dameon. "Not smart, Dameon. Piss me off, and you'll beg me to kill you." Jax turned to face Nathen. "The same goes for you. Now pass me the rifle!"

"I thought you wanted a conversation? To speak to Bigfoot. I'm curious. How did you learn about me?"

Jax smiled, glanced over to Dameon, and then focused on Nathen. "I'm surprised Dameon hasn't already told you."

"Dameon's in no condition for bedtime stories."

Jax chuckled. "Really, 'cause usually I can't shut him up. I found a book at the cabin Dameon and I are staying at. It was written by the owner, and he was very prolific."

Hansen followed Billy into the forest. When he was comfortable that Jax wouldn't see the light from the flashlight, he turned it on. It wasn't long before Hansen and Billy located the tree where Jax had hidden his weapons. There was the compound bow, at least a dozen arrows, the *Pax*, and the *Barrett* rifle. Hanson glanced around the tree to confirm that Nathen still had Jax's attention.

Quietly, he slipped back behind the tree and motioned Billy to sit on the ground with him. Then he whispered to Billy, "Do you know how to use any of these weapons?"

Billy slowly shook his head from side to side, indicating that he didn't.

Hansen quickly scanned the weapons that lay on the ground in front of him. If Billy didn't know how to use these weapons, and if there was no guarantee that Hansen could get them to the cave, then maybe stealing them wouldn't be such a good idea.

Hansen believed that Nathen could keep Jax busy for at least five minutes. After that, there was no guarantee that Jax wouldn't return to his arsenal. Hansen decided that disabling the weapons was his best option. He took out his pocketknife and made short work of the compound bow. Then he quickly tore down the *Pax* and the rifle, throwing the pieces into the forest. Then he broke all the arrows in half.

Quietly, he whispered to Billy, "I want you to go back to our hiding place. You have to be really quiet. Do you understand?"

Billy placed his index finger over his lips. "Billy understand."

Hansen stood and was about to get closer to the path when something Billy heard upset him. He dropped to his knees, started shaking his head, and violently rocked back and forth. Hansen knelt in front of Billy and wrapped his arms around him as tightly as he could.

Quietly, he whispered into Billy's ear, "Shhh. Billy, what's wrong? You have to be quiet, or Jax will start shooting." Billy started to calm down, but still, he wouldn't look at Hansen, and he wouldn't stop rocking back and forth. Hansen placed his right hand on the back of Billy's head and held him tenderly against his chest. He rocked with Billy, and as he did, he was able to lessen the severity of the rocking to that of what would soothe a small child. "Tell me what's wrong."

Billy pulled away from the embrace, leaned forward, and whispered into Hansen's ear, "Book evil. Book kills. Not safe. Book not safe."

"Okay, the book's not safe. The book's not here, Billy. It's back at the cabin. You're safe here, with us."

Hansen didn't know for sure where the book was, and he didn't care. He just wanted to calm Billy down. Billy stopped rocking and lowered his head as if he were in trouble and was afraid of reprisal. Hansen scanned the area and was confident that no one had heard Billy's meltdown. He watched Billy as he transformed from a frightened child to a child who was happy and content.

Billy needed to be protected, and Hansen believed that having him close to the cave wouldn't work well for Billy. So he decided that Billy should remain where he was. Hansen had to take Jax down, not only for Nathen's sake but also for Billy's.

Hansen leaned close to Billy and whispered. "I'm going to go and see if Nathen needs help. Can you stay here in case Jax gets past me?"

Billy nodded his head. "What does Billy do?"

Hansen smirked. "I don't know. Knock him out with the flashlight and sit on him until help arrives."

Billy's eyes widened in excitement. "Billy help. Billy sit on bad guy."

Hansen stood and passed the flashlight to Billy. "Don't

turn this on unless you absolutely have to. Do you understand?"

Billy nodded his head, indicating that he did.

"Good Billy." Hansen pointed in the direction of the cave.
"Can you see the cave?"

Again, Billy nodded that he did.

"Good. That's where I'm going. Hide, be quiet, and if Jax
shows up . . ." Hansen didn't get to finish his sentence.

"Billy knock out bad guy. Billy sit on him." It was easy to
tell that Billy was excited. He was proud of the chore he'd
been given. If only he understood how dangerous the task
was. But that wasn't going to happen. Hansen turned to leave
as he whispered to himself, *that's good, Billy. You sit on him.*

CHAPTER THIRTY-EIGHT

Nathen tightly gripped the butt of the rifle as he stared down Jax. He noticed that Jax's gun wasn't secured in its holster — a fact that didn't surprise Nathen. Jax would be prepared for the worst-case scenario, and he definitely wouldn't leave himself exposed. "That book you found. I knew the author."

Jax's eyes went wide, and he looked like someone who just won the lottery. "Seriously? Where is he?"

Nathen smiled at Jax. "Buried six feet under." Jax's expression went from joy to disappointment. "Jax, you do realize that he was deranged? You must have some idea of his insanity."

"How did he die?"

"Why would you want to know?"

Nathen carefully observed Jax's reactions to their conversation. His expression now could only be described as sinister. "Did he die naturally, or did Mother Nature take revenge?"

"Neither. Jax, you read the book. I'm sure the atrocities that he inflicted on his brother are in the book."

"They are. It made for some pretty interesting reading. You're avoiding my question. How did the man die?"

"What does that matter to you?"

"I'm curious."

Nathen hesitated for a moment and then decided to tell Jax a half-truth. "He died by my hand."

"Let me guess, you tore him to shreds."

Nathen was disgusted by Jax's enthusiasm over how Dex was killed. "No. I shot him."

"Well, that's disappointing. I thought it might have been a little more colorful."

"Jax, that man tortured his brother. He did horrific things to him. Do you not have any empathy for the brother?"

"The brother was a half-wit. No harm done there."

Nathen now knew that there wouldn't be a peaceful resolution, and that knowledge frightened him. He had sworn an oath many years ago that he would never release the beast that lived inside of him. Today, he might have to break that oath. "I'll make a deal with you. Leave and never come back."

"Or what?"

"I can be very dangerous, Jax. I would prefer not to, but if you try to hurt anyone here, including the bear, I will kill you."

Jax laughed. "Wow, melodramatic or what. I'm not afraid of you. Now, hand over the rifle."

Nathen noticed Hansen creeping up behind Jax. Nathen needed to keep Jax preoccupied so he wouldn't hear Hansen's approach. "You should be terrified of me, Jax. I've had encounters with Dext. He's the author of the book. In self-defense, I ripped off his arm. Can you imagine what I'm capable of if I lash out in anger?"

Jax held out his left hand while his right hand rested on his revolver. "I could care less. Like it or not, I've already won this battle. Now, hand over the rifle."

Jax's fingers had just touched the butt of the rifle when he felt the barrel of a gun pressed against the back of his head.

"I wouldn't move if I were you. And I'll take the *Ruger*." Hansen removed it from its holster and threw it into the bush.

Jax felt the barrel of a gun pressed tightly against the back of his head. Nathen had help, something he hadn't counted on. Jax kept his focus on Nathen. "Nice move. Must admit, I'm surprised you have a friend that will risk his life to back you up." Jax inched just a little closer to Nathen. "However, your friend doesn't change the outcome."

Nathen stood within arm's reach. He still had the rifle at his side with the barrel facing down. Jax's mind was calculating his next move. Within a blink of an eye, Jax grabbed the rifle, jabbed the butt of the rifle into the stomach of the person standing behind him, then peppered the inside of the cave from one side to the other with bullets.

Nathen felt the rifle being torn from his grip, which caused him to lose his balance. He hit the ground hard, and before he even realized what happened, he could hear the sound of a semi-automatic shooting continually. The reality of what was happening fueled the beast inside of him. Nathen stood, and as Jax started to aim the rifle at him, Nathen grabbed the barrel with his left hand. With his right hand, he slammed his fist into Jax's shoulder, dislocating it in the process.

Jax screamed out in pain as he cradled his right arm. "Round one goes to you." The man who held the gun at his head was getting up from the ground. Jax quickly turned and kicked the man in his chest. As the man went down, Jax grabbed the gun out of his hand and then ran into the forest. He only went as far as the first redwood that he could hide behind. "What's wrong, Nathen? Something tells me you damaged the rifle. Otherwise, I'd be dead. Round two is mine. No more games." Jax turned and faced the large redwood. He took a deep breath and then slammed his dislocated shoulder into the tree. The pain was beyond measure, but Jax didn't say a word.

His shoulder was back in place. However, he knew he'd have a better chance if he kept that information to himself.

Billy hid behind a large redwood so he could watch Jax's tree. He'd be ready to hurt him just as Hansen told him to. Billy was excited, in a good way. He wanted to help. He wanted to protect and save his family. His feeling of anticipation quickly turned to fear as he heard the sound of gunfire. Billy covered his ears, but he couldn't block out the sound that was echoing throughout the forest. And then there was silence.

Slowly, Billy lowered his hands. His breathing was rapid, and his heart felt like it was going to burst from his chest. Billy closed his eyes and thought of Mona and how she could calm him with her soothing voice. He reached out to her, but she didn't respond. Billy's eyes went wide with fear. He knew something was wrong. Billy peered around his tree to see if Jax had returned. Confident that he wasn't around, Billy left the safety of his hiding place and headed for the cave.

Mona stood at the entrance of the cave and observed the interaction between Jax and Nathen. The hair at the back of her neck was raised. She knew something wasn't right. Mona glanced over to where Joshawa and Dameon sat. Then, her gaze went to the rifle. Nathen was still in possession of the rifle, but that fact didn't sit well with Mona. She moved so that she was facing the opposite wall of the cave.

It all happened so fast. One minute, Nathen had the rifle, then within seconds, the rifle was in Jax's hands. He raised it and pointed it into the cave. Without giving it a second thought, Mona propelled herself between the bullets and the people she wanted to protect. She felt the first sting that embedded into her neck. Then the bullets came one after another, with every single bullet burying itself inside of her. And then there was silence. Mona glanced over to Nathen and saw that he now had the rifle, and Jax had disappeared into the forest. It was safe now — her family was safe. Mona took a breath, closed her eyes, and allowed her body to slowly sink to the ground.

Jax carefully made his way back to his nest. He couldn't turn on his headlamp because he wasn't taking any chances that Nathen had more friends. He also didn't want to reveal where his nest was. When he finally reached his destination, he turned his back to the cave and turned on his headlamp. What he discovered was that the only thing waiting for him was a pile of useless weapons. "Well played, Nathen. I guess you now know where my nest is." Jax walked over to his tree and peered around it. He chuckled to himself at the chaos he'd caused his Bigfoot. The creature who gave himself a name.

"Name or no name, Nathen, you're still an animal to me." From where he stood, he couldn't see how many had lost their lives to his attack. But it didn't matter. He was the hunter, and they were his prey. If there was one thing Jax did exceptionally well, it was his ability to take down his prey without the use of weapons. Jax leaned against his tree and slowly sank to the ground. Now, as his prey mourned for their loss, Jax would wait. He'd let fear, sorrow, and defeat manifest inside his prey. And when they least expect it, he'd kill them, one by one.

Nathen dropped the rifle and ran into the cave. He didn't know what to expect, and he feared that his son was a victim of Jax's attack. However, when he reached the fire pit, he realized that every shot Jax made was circumvented by Mona. Dameon and Joshawa had lain flat on the ground in the hope that they wouldn't be shot. Hansen helped both of them sit up, and when they saw Mona, the reality of what had just transpired hit them hard.

Nathen knelt by Mona's head and gently ran his hand along her neck. When he removed his hand, he discovered that it was covered in blood. Nathen glanced over her body, which was riddled with holes. The blood that once nurtured Mona now seeped from every bullet hole. Nathen tried to keep the tears away, but he was unsuccessful. *Why Mona? Why would you do this?*

I had to protect my family.

But Amy was not in danger, and Billy was not in the cave. Your family was safe.

Mona slowly moved her head so that she could look at Nathen. *Why are you here?*

You know why. I came to protect my family.

As did I. Nathen, I consider everyone in this cave as my family, and I'll do anything to keep them safe. If I have to forfeit my life to keep my family safe, then it's a small price to pay.

Nathen wiped his tears away as he looked up at his son.

Joshawa's voice faltered, and at first, Nathen had a hard time understanding what he was asking. "What's happening, Father? Is Mona going to be okay?"

Nathen glanced over at Dameon. Tears ran down Dameon's cheeks, and no matter how often he wiped his tears away, they just kept coming. Nathen knew that Dameon understood what had just transpired. Mona was dying, and there was nothing they could do but watch and wait.

Billy ran to the cave, and when he saw Mona's blood-soaked body laying lifeless on the ground, he simply stood and screamed. Billy wanted to hurt Jax. He wanted Jax dead. As his thoughts grew dark with hatred and anger, a voice resonated in the back of Billy's mind. It was faint, as if it was miles away. *Billy, my love. Calm yourself. It's up to you now to protect our family.*

Billy's screaming stopped, and what followed was uncontrollable sobbing. *Mona?*

Yes, I'm still with you. But I won't be for long. I'm so tired.

Billy went over to Mona and sat on the ground next to her head. He lifted Mona's head onto his lap and carefully ran his hand along her snout and between her ears. *Billy let you sleep. Billy hold you. Billy love you.*

And I love you. Promise me that you won't let your anger rule your actions. You have to be strong for our daughter and for everyone here trapped in this cave.

Billy could feel Mona slipping away, and something deep inside of him knew that he wouldn't get her back a second time. Billy buried his face in Mona's fur and cried till he didn't have any tears left.

Imani watched in horror as each bullet hit Mona. Imani could feel the pain Mona felt as each bullet hit her over and over again. And when the horror stopped, Imani could feel Mona slipping away. She went to step over the edge of the Realm, but Serena held her back.

Imani looked over at the hand that was tightly gripped on her arm. She looked up at Serena, puzzled at what she was doing. "Let go of me."

"I cannot. If you cross over the edge, you will be lost forever."

"If I cross over, then I can join with Mona before she dies."

"With what purpose? You cannot save her."

"I know. I choose to die with her."

Serena couldn't believe what she was hearing. "You want to die?"

315

"Yes. I am ready. You do not understand. Mona is not just an outsider that I saved. She is part of me. If she dies, so must I."

"What about Lord Adeeowale? Will he understand?"

"Yes, he will. My life as an Ancestor should have never been. I should have died long ago. Now, please, Serena, let me choose how I shall die."

Serena let go of Imani and stood back. She smiled at Imani with tenderness and love. "Choose your death, but I ask one favor."

"If I can grant it, I will."

"Allow me to help you join with Mona."

"I do not understand? How do you wish to help me?"

Again, Serena smiled. "You will understand. Please take my hands."

Imani placed her hands with Serena. *You were chosen as an Ancestor for a reason. Your destiny was written a long time ago. Be safe, Imani, join with Mona, and watch your destiny unfold.*

CHAPTER THIRTY-NINE

Hansen surveyed the cave, taking stock of what they had for weapons. There was Dameon's Glock and Adrian's sidearm, but other than that, all they had was Nathen. Hansen glanced over to where Adrian and Amy were still sleeping. Weapons were not the only thing they were short of.

Adrian and Amy were completely out of it. And even if they were awake, Hansen doubted that Amy would be of any help. She appeared too fragile and too young to be involved in whatever was coming at them. Joshawa was injured, and as far as Hansen knew, he'd never fired a gun. Dameon was also injured, and with the amount of pain he was in, there was no telling if he had the strength to fire a gun with any accuracy. Sadly, Mona had given her life so that they could live. That left Nathen and himself.

Hansen sat on the ground next to Dameon and Joshawa. "So, Nathen, was Jax right? Did you destroy the rifle?"

Nathen was standing at the entrance to the cave, glaring in Jax's direction. His arms were folded across his chest, and it appeared as if he were daring Jax to take a shot. "Yes, he's right."

"You do know, Nathen, what happened wasn't your fault."

Nathen walked over to where everyone was sitting. He stood there, but he remained focused on the entrance to the cave. "Yes, it was my fault. I allowed the creature to rise above me."

Hansen looked up at Nathen, and what he witnessed was

pure self-loathing. Hansen wasn't sure how to approach Nathen. He'd never dealt with this side of him before. He was about to suggest that maybe Nathen should meld with Authia when Dameon spoke up.

"I have no idea what this creature is or where it comes from. What I do know is what we're up against. Jax is a sociopath with no empathy for anyone. Nathen, if you have some sort of demon living inside of you, then thank you. Because weapons alone won't stop Jax when he's fixated on you and your son. He won't stop until he has you in his possession or until he's dead. We'll most likely need your creature, and sooner than later."

Nathen turned his attention to Dameon. "You don't understand. I have no control when I let it loose. Whatever or whoever causes my anger, that person will be the focus of my creature."

Hansen wished he had the ability to meld, because right now, Nathen needed Authia. But in the meantime, he'd have to be the voice of reason. "Nathen, I've known you a long time. We went through hell in Africa, and not once did I see this creature. You fought as Nathen. When you thought that Authia was dead, you mourned for her as Nathen, not the creature."

"That was because you'd already killed Obasi."

"I'm not finished. I trust you with my life. And if you need to release this creature, I trust that everyone in this cave will be safe. Don't be so down on yourself. If you hadn't released the creature, we would all probably be dead right now. And Jax wouldn't be nursing a dislocated shoulder. So put on your big boy pants, and let's figure out what our next move will be." Hansen smiled at Nathen, and Nathen smiled back. "There, was that so hard?"

Hansen glanced over to Dameon. "So, even with Nathen, how screwed are we?"

"Completely screwed. We have two guns. He has an arsenal."

Hansen glanced over to the entrance of the cave. "Do you think Jax can hear us?"

"We had to raise our voices to talk to him, so if we keep our voices low, we should be okay."

Hansen slightly lowered his voice. "Getting back to Jax's arsenal. He doesn't have one. Billy and I destroyed all his weapons. So the only weapon he has is my gun."

Dameon smiled. "I would have loved to have been there to see his reaction. What did you do with the case of tranquilizer darts?"

"We left them. Without the rifle, they're not much use to him."

"True. But I wouldn't rule them out."

Hansen glanced over to Adrian. "What happened to Adrian and the girl?"

Nathen spoke up. "Jax shot them both with a tranquilizer dart."

"How long are they going to be out?"

Dameon winced in pain as he tried to find a more comfortable position. "It depends on the dose he used. Adrian and Amy are of no importance to him. I would guess he used the higher dosage to kill them. But, since they're still breathing, hopefully he used the smaller dosage."

Hansen got up and walked over to Adrian. He placed his right hand on Adrian's chest, and he could feel it moving ever so slightly. "So, how do we wake them up?"

"We just leave them and wait for the tranquilizer to wear off. They should be awake in a couple of hours. They're the least of our worries. Right now, we're sitting ducks. Jax could kill any one of us just from the tree line."

Hansen stood up and walked over to the firepit. "Okay, what do you suggest we do?"

"Move everyone out of his line of fire." Dameon looked back over his shoulder and then returned his focus to the group. "We have to move further back into the cave. It'll force Jax to come out in the open to kill us."

Hansen was focused on Nathen. He watched as Nathen glanced to the back of the cave. "What are you thinking, Nathen?"

"I'm thinking that if the mouth of the cave is the only way out, then moving further back just puts us in more danger."

Dameon looked over to Nathen. "Yes, you're right. It's like painting yourself into a corner. The entrance may be our only way out, but it's also Jax's only way in."

Hansen cut in, "So let Jax come to us?"

"Exactly. It's the only chance we have."

Nathen stood and walked over to Joshawa. "Sorry, son. This will probably hurt." Nathen picked up Joshawa as carefully as he could. He looked at his son's face, and he could see his pain even though Joshawa never said a word. "So, Dameon, how far back should we go?"

Dameon looked over his shoulder. "I can't see the fire-wood. How far back does the cave go?"

"I didn't go much further than the firewood. From there, I couldn't see the back of the cave."

"You can see in the dark, right?"

"Yes. Both myself and Joshawa."

"Okay, start walking toward the back of the cave, and I'll tell you when to stop."

Nathen carried Joshawa toward the firewood. However, his mind wasn't focused on Jax or how far back in the cave he had to go. All he could think of was that he had his son back in more ways than one. Dameon's voice brought Nathen back to the present.

"You're good."

Nathen carefully sat Joshawa on the ground close to the cave wall. Then he knelt in front of him. "Are you comfortable?"

"Yes, Father, don't worry about me."

Nathen placed his right hand on the side of Joshawa's face. "I have to. It's my job."

"And you're really good at it."

Nathen smiled at his son, stood, and then returned to help move everyone else. "So Dameon, we'll be just in front of the firewood. However, we do have one issue. It's pitch black back there, and since you can't see in the dark, we'll have to build a fire."

"Well, that's problematic, and to be honest, I didn't think of that. Nathen, go back and start a small fire. When everyone's settled, we'll put out the fire. We'll also have to keep our talking down to a minimum. I don't want to give Jax any help if he decides to venture closer to the cave. Will you and Joshawa be able to keep watch throughout the night?"

"That won't be a problem."

Within fifteen minutes, Nathen and Hansen had moved everyone to their new location. Billy was being difficult. He didn't want to leave Mona. After a lot of persuasion, Nathen managed to convince Billy that it was what Mona would want him to do.

They also brought the buckets of water, all the blankets, and the pot they used to cook in. The only thing left was Mona. Hansen and Nathen stood by her body, not saying anything. However, they were both thinking the same thing. *How do we move a thousand-pound bear, and is it really necessary?*

Nathen broke the silence. "I hate leaving her here. She was more than just a bear." Nathen glanced back to the entrance of the cave and then returned his focus to Mona. "I'm afraid that if we leave Mona here, Jax will use her as a shield."

"Wow, that didn't even cross my mind. But how do we

move her? I know you're strong, Nathen, but are you strong enough to move her? To be honest, I don't think I'm going to be much help."

Nathen was racking his mind, trying to come up with a solution, when he heard Imani speaking to him.

Imani?

Yes, my Lord.

Where are you?

With Mona.

Nathen glanced down at Mona. There was no sign of life, so how was it that Imani was with Mona? *I don't understand. Mona's dead.*

No, she is dying. There is still a spark of life left in her.

Why are you with her?

We are a part of each other, and together, we are whole. My life is entwined with hers.

Does that mean you will die as well?

Yes.

Imani, we need to move Mona so that Jax can't use her as part of his defense. If there is a spark of life within her, can you get her to get up and move to the cave wall?

I will try, but she is very weak.

Nathen glanced over to Hansen, who appeared perplexed. "Nathen, are you melding with someone?"

"Yes. I was melding with Imani."

"Who's Imani? I thought the bear's name was Mona."

"It is, and it's a long story. I'll be happy to tell you once everyone's home and safe."

"Fair enough. So this Imani person. Does she have a way to move Mona?"

The moment Hansen spoke those words, Mona started to struggle to stand. Both Nathen and Hansen stepped back and observed the miracle that was transpiring before them.

Imani, do you need help?

No, my Lord. Where will Mona be safe?

Against the wall of the cave.

Slowly, Mona stood, her body wavering as if she were going to fall at any time. She took one step at a time until her body was against the cave wall. Then her legs gave out, and once again, Mona lay motionless on the ground. Nathen walked over to her, knelt on his haunches, and placed his right hand on her head.

Thank you, Imani.

You are most welcome, my Lord. Please tell Amy that her mother loves her. Now go and save everyone.

Jax pulled his skull cap and headlamp out from inside his backpack. The temperature was dropping rapidly. However, a fire was too much of a risk. Even his headlamp was risky, so he would only use it when he had to. He pulled on his skull cap and then placed his headlamp on top of it. Then Jax removed the sandwiches and fruit he had packed in his backpack.

He'd been hoping to drag out his capture of Nathen and his son. He would've had so much fun watching them and the others suffer. Unfortunately, his injury meant he had to ramp up his plans. He would eat and rest for a couple of hours. Then, using his night vision goggles, he would crawl on his belly to get close enough to kill whoever had survived the barrage of bullets. They would die in their sleep, and nobody would be the wiser.

The next part was a little more challenging. First, he had to deal with the bear. It was a shame to have to kill him. He was worth a lot of money. But money couldn't buy the thrill or the ecstasy that Nathen and Joshawa would give him. He would slit the bear's throat ear-to-ear. It would be dead before it hit the ground. Then he'd have to get close enough to Nathen and his son so he could stab them with a tranquilizer dart.

Jax ate quickly, placed the leftovers in the backpack, and

unfastened his sleeping bag. He would've preferred to sleep on the ground. However, with his shoulder in the condition it was, he decided to stay sitting up. Jax crawled into his sleeping bag, leaned against the tree, and closed his eyes.

Dameon had his back propped up against the cave wall. Sleep eluded him as he stared out into the darkness. After everything Jax had done, one would think that Dameon could care less if he died. But something deep inside of him was not ready for Jax's death. If only the Jax he knew from years ago could surface and prove to Dameon that he could be saved.

In the darkness, he heard Nathen's voice quietly reach out to him. "Can't sleep?"

"No. I keep thinking of Jax. He used to be . . . for the lack of a better word . . . normal."

"What happened?"

"I'm not sure. A few years back when we were in Java, he killed a park ranger. His mind has been twisted ever since."

"He didn't get charged for the murder?"

"No. He fed the ranger to the crocodiles. We were long gone before the ranger was missed. To answer your next question, I don't know why I didn't turn him in. So I guess that makes me as guilty as Jax."

"Guilty or not guilty, that's something you have to deal with on your own. I have demons in my closet. I also bear the burden of my decisions."

Dameon and Nathen sat quietly for several minutes, and then Nathen broke the silence. "What do you think his next move will be?"

"I'm sure he fixed his shoulder by now. But it'll still be painful. He's not going to be able to accomplish an all-out attack. Keep on your toes, Nathen. He'll probably want to finish this sooner rather than later. He'll use the darkness to conceal himself."

Dameon leaned his head against the cave wall and closed his eyes. *A new day will dawn, and hopefully, everyone in the cave will be alive to see it.*

CHAPTER FORTY

Jax felt the vibration of his watch against his wrist. He opened his eyes and checked the time. It was two in the morning and time for Jax to finish what he'd started. There was a small part of him that tried to convince himself that he should keep Dameon alive, that they should just go their separate ways. Jax stared out into the darkness of the woods as he considered his options. Dameon had always protected Jax. They always had each other's backs. However, Jax believed that their arrangement had now changed. After everything that had transpired since the discovery of the journal, Jax decided that Dameon could no longer be trusted. Dameon had accused Jax of changing. It was a bit hypocritical, since Dameon had changed, as well.

Jax rested his head against the redwood and thought back to the first time he'd noticed Dameon's change in character. A few minutes later, Jax sat up straight as if he had an epiphany. It all made sense to him now. Dameon changed at the same time Jax had killed that park ranger and fed him to the crocodiles. Jax smiled to himself as he remembered the crocodile grabbing the ranger and pulling him apart piece by piece. The water surrounding the crocodile turned red with the ranger's blood, and Jax was exhilarated as he witnessed the frenzy. Ever since then, Dameon had made a point of locating their hunts where there would be no chance of human contact. Jax knew now that Dameon had decided back then to protect any human from Jax. This realization made his decision so simple. Dameon had to die.

Nathen had agreed to take the second watch from midnight until the sun rose. He sat in front of the group with his focus on the entrance to the cave. Dameon had suggested that everyone sleep close together. His reasoning was that if Jax did incorporate the use of his night goggles, then hopefully, all he would see would be a large grouping of body heat. Dameon had told Nathen that Jax would have a plan for who he would kill first and how he would get to either Joshawa or Nathen to tranquilize them. If all Jax could see was a large concentration of body heat, then maybe he would have to come closer to carry out his slaughter.

Earlier, the group decided that even though Dameon was in pain, he would still be a better shot than Nathen or Joshawa. With that in mind, Dameon and Hansen slept with their guns close by.

Nathen casually glanced over his shoulder at the people he had to protect. They were all sleeping peacefully, as if they didn't have a care in the world. Nathen returned his focus to the entrance of the cave. Deep down, Nathen wanted this entire ordeal to end without weapons, and especially without waking the creature. But the reality was that to ensure Joshawa's and his survival and the survival of everyone in the cave, Jax had to be hurt and even possibly killed. There were no other options, and Nathen realized that. It was no different than when Obasi had threatened not only his family but also his friends and the Jelani Tribe. *Sometimes, you have to make decisions that go against your morality and who you are as a person.* Nathen wasn't happy about what lay ahead. But the truth of the matter was that he had to protect the occupants of the cave at any cost.

Serena sat at the edge of the Realm, intensely watching what had transpired. It made her sick to think that there was a chance that neither Nathen nor Joshawa could last till morning. And as helpless as Imani had felt, it was now Serena's turn to feel completely useless. As a wisp, she could maneuver herself into Jax's mind and change the outcome of this insane nightmare. But she was not allowed to interfere with outsiders. The last time she had, her penalty was the Realm of Despair, a place she had no desire to return to. Serena closed her eyes and sighed. Once again, she was making decisions about what was best for her at the cost of others.

In the cave was her Lord and her Lord's son. Were their lives not worth a life sentence in the Realm of Despair? If Lord Adeeowale had managed to kill Lord Chike, maybe the Council would be more lenient in their decision.

"You seem conflicted, Serena. Why is that?"

Serena turned to find Lord Adeeowale standing only a few feet away from her. She jumped to her feet, and with hope and promise in her heart, she addressed Lord Adeeowale. "Is he gone?"

Lord Adeeowale approached Serena and took her hands in his. "Yes, Lord Chike is dead." Lord Adeeowale scanned the area and then returned his focus to Serena. "Where is Imani? And why are you so troubled?"

Serena took a deep breath and slowly released it. "Mona is dead." Before Serena could finish what she had to say, Lord Adeeowale let go of her hands and almost ran to the edge of the Realm. "Why is everyone gathered in one spot?"

"They hope to confuse Jax. They believe that he may attack tonight using something they had called night vision goggles. Apparently, those help him to see in the dark, not unlike our own vision. If they are huddled together, then Jax will have to get closer to the group to ensure he does not kill Lord Nathen or Lord Joshawa."

Lord Adeeowale continued to observe the people in the

cave. "Mona is not dead. However, her life force is fragile. She will not last long. Imani is with her. She went to join Mona in death."

"How did you know my Lord?"

Lord Adeeowale looked up and faced Serena. "When Imani saved Mona by transferring Mona's spirit, her essence, into the baby bear, the cost was that if Mona died, so must she."

"I did not know that. Imani left me the impression that it was her decision to die with Mona."

"It was. Imani was asked what she would relinquish to save the life of an outsider. Her decision was easy. According to Imani, her life should have ended long ago. Sacrificing her life so that Mona could live was a small price to pay."

"I thought that the Ancestors had a grander plan for Imani. I told her as much before she left to join with Mona."

"I can say with honesty that there is one Ancestor that is not finished with her."

"Would I be too bold to assume that Ancestor is you?"

Lord Adeeowale smiled at Serena but didn't offer to expand on his comment.

"My Lord, is there anything we can do to save these people? Lord Nathen and his son are in that cave, and they will die if we do not interfere."

"There was a time when I would have walked away and allowed the outsiders to deal with themselves. But that was a simpler time." Lord Adeeowale went back to the edge of the Realm and sat down. "Come sit with me."

Lord Adeeowale waited until Serena was sitting next to him before he spoke. "I am certain that you know the relationship between Imani and myself."

"Yes, my Lord. To be honest, it was not difficult to see the love you two shared. However, you seem unaffected by

Imani's decision to end her life."

"Trust me, her decision affects me greatly. I intend to keep her from dying, just as I am sure that you want to prevent the deaths of the people in the cave."

Serena wasn't sure how she should react. His comment inferred that he was prepared to break the rules to save the woman he loved. "I am not sure I understand what you are saying. Do you plan to ignore our rules and suffer the consequences?"

Lord Adeeowale smiled at Serena. "I have learned many things about the Destroyer and the Council of Five. Trust me when I say that the only higher power that we will have to answer to will be our fellow Ancestors. Besides, what is transpiring in the cave is a result of direct interference from Lord Chike. I believe that since one of our Ancestors interfered, then we have an obligation to make things right."

"What about the Council?"

"All will be explained at another time. I am going to deal with Imani. What is your plan?"

"Will I be allowed to deal directly with the outsider?"

"I cannot answer you. However, you should be cautious."

"So, then no. First, I will give Joshawa back the ability to hear his parents' thoughts and for them to hear his."

"And then?"

"And then I will let Lord Nathen decide how to use me."

Jax climbed out of his sleeping bag and tossed it to one side. Then he reached into his backpack and retrieved his night vision goggles. He placed them on his head, leaving the goggles resting on his forehead. Then he closed his backpack and checked to make sure everything was in place. He had the stretcher on one side of the backpack and various tools on the other. His plan was to sedate the two Bigfoots, strap them on the stretcher, and drag the stretcher to the homestead. He'd also brought extra ropes to make sure the two Bigfoots were secured to the stretcher. Jax placed the goggles over his eyes, and as he made his way to the edge of the forest, he could hear the wolves crying in the distance. At that moment, he knew how he was going to end Dameon's life.

Nathen was feeling the effects of being awake for almost twenty-four hours. He had nothing to tell time by, but if he had to guess, it would be close to three in the morning. Nathen needed his strength if he was going to go up against Jax. Since Jax had been a no-show up until now, Nathen felt comfortable waking Joshawa up so he could grab a few hours of sleep.

Nathen stood and made his way closer to Joshawa so he could wake him without disturbing the others. That was when he spotted her—a blue wisp was hovering over Joshawa.

Serena, is that you? The blue wisp floated closer to Nathen.

Yes, my Lord.

Why are you here? Have you come to help us?"

I have come to undo what I did to Joshawa. When I am finished, you will be able to meld with him. As far as helping you, I am limited in what I can offer.

What do you mean by limited?

Let me fix Joshawa, and then we can discuss my limits.

Serena floated closer to Joshawa, and as soon as he parted his lips, she flew in. It wasn't difficult to find the section of his brain she had tampered with. It was encased in a shimmery blue veil. She was saddened that she had done this to him, hat she hadn't stood up to Lord Chike. But the past was the past, and now it was time to right a great wrong.

Jax walked to the edge of the forest and placed his backpack next to an evergreen. He scanned the cave and discovered that all the heat sources were in a corner of the cave. After Jax had riddled the cave with so many bullets, he wasn't expecting that so many had lived. He had a pretty good idea of how many people were in the cave, so this made absolutely no sense.

Sence or no sense, Jax didn't have the time to figure it out. Quietly, he whispered to himself, "You grouped everybody together so I wouldn't be able to distinguish who was who. Not bad, Dameon, but I'll be able to get close enough that it won't matter."

Jax continued to scan the cave for the bear, but for whatever reason, he couldn't find him. Either the bear was among the people, which was highly unlikely, or it was outside the cave somewhere. Jax moved to the entrance of the cave, turned, and scanned the forest. He didn't detect any significant heat sources, so he assumed the bear was nowhere near the cave. He glanced back inside the cave and decided to hug the cave wall as he made his way closer to his prey.

Nathen watched as Serena flew out of Joshawa's mouth.

Nathen, turn around!

Nathen turned to face the entrance of the cave, and standing at the entrance against the cave wall was Jax. Nathen continued to watch Jax as he melded with Joshawa.

Can you hear me, son?

Yes! Finally. I see Jax.

I know. Wake up Dameon and Hansen. Serena, how can you help us?

I can enter Joshawa and make him believe that he has no injuries. He will be able to fight.

Yes, Father. I want to help you. I want to fight.

Nathen turned to face Joshawa and Serena. *No, enter Dameon's body. He's the one we need.*

Father, I can help.

I won't risk losing you. Besides, this may be over before it starts. Nathen smiled at his son. *Do you think your mother would allow you to fight?*

No, I guess not.

No, she wouldn't, and I don't want to be on the receiving end of her displeasure. Both Nathen and Joshawa softly chuckled. *You can help me by being an extra set of eyes.*

Knowing that Joshawa wasn't going to do anything reckless, Nathen headed in Jax's direction.

Lord Adeeowale stood at the edge of the Realm, knowing what he had to do. Actually, it was more of what he wanted to do. Years ago, when he had helped Imani place Mona's essence into the bear, his love for Imani had clouded his judgment. He didn't want to lose her, so he'd made a decision that was selfish and wrong. He could have given both Imani and Amelia a better life. Now, it was time to correct his mistake. Lord Adeeowale closed his eyes and reached out to Imani.

I see that you are with Mona.

Yes. She is dying, and I have chosen to die with her.

What if I can give you and Mona another option? An option to live.

I do not understand. The bear is dead, and Mona is so close. What possible option can you offer?

I can offer you life as Mona. I can offer you life as a human.

Nathen walked toward Jax, and with every step, he got angrier and angrier. He allowed his emotions to consume him. He was taunting the creature to make an appearance.

When he was ten feet away from Jax, he decided to start a conversation. "I know you can see me, Jax."

"And apparently, you can see me."

"Jax, I don't want to hurt you. Please turn around and leave us."

"Are you crazy? I've waited all my life for you. Now that I have you, I won't be walking away without you and your son."

"I'm sorry to hear that." Nathen continued to walk toward Jax, prepared to do whatever was necessary.

Jax's body was tingling with excitement. He pulled two knives from his vest. He was going to have to hurt Nathen, but at this point, he didn't care. Jax was prepared to bring Nathen to the cusp of death and then watch him suffer as his injuries festered.

Jax held his knives at chest level. "This is going to be fun." He charged Nathen, and when he was within arm's reach, he propelled himself upward, stabbing Nathen with both knives just below each shoulder. Then Jax landed on his feet directly behind Nathen. A sinister smile graced Jax's lips as he watched Nathen's blood drip off his knives and pool on the ground. Jax turned to face Nathen. "That's one for me, Nathen. Do you surrender? If you don't, then I'll take great pleasure in carving you into tiny pieces and feeding you to the wolves."

CHAPTER FORTY-ONE

Joshawa quietly woke up Hansen and Dameon. He turned to check on his father only to witness Jax propel himself over his dad's head and land on his feet behind him. Joshawa couldn't help but notice that Jax held a knife in each hand, and the knives were dripping blood onto the ground. Fear, anger, and dread consumed Joshawa, and without taking his eyes off his father, Joshawa yelled at Dameon, "What the hell, Dameon? Did you see that?"

"It's pitch black. I didn't see anything."

"Jax just jumped over my father, and by the blood on his knives, I'd say he stabbed him, as well. How the hell does he know how to do that?"

Dameon cursed to himself because he knew exactly what happened. "A couple of decades ago, we both took advanced self-defense courses. To be honest, it's been so long since we were in a position to use those skills that I totally forgot."

Hansen chimed in, "You forgot? How the hell do you forget that? This changes everything. How the hell are we going to help Nathen now?"

Without further discussion, Dameon stood and placed his gun in its holster. It took a second before he realized that he was in no pain. Dameon glanced around the cave, though he couldn't see anything. "Why am I in no pain?"

Joshawa answered, "My father said he needed you. I'll explain later, but for now, you can help my father, and you

335

won't feel any pain."

"That's almost too good to be true. As you said, this changes everything. Hansen, start a fire as big as you can. I can't help Nathen if I can't see him. Does anyone have a knife on them?"

Hansen looked in the direction where he was sure Adrian was lying. "Adrian should have one." Hansen felt around for his flashlight. When he found it, he focused the beam of light on Adrian. "If there isn't one on his belt, there will be one in his boot."

Jax yelled out to Dameon. "Hey, Dameon, nice work with the flashlight, though I really don't need it, do I?"

Dameon cursed under his breath. "How about I flash it in your face. Would that help you?" The only response Dameon received was Jax's laughter.

Dameon found the knife and removed it from Adrian's belt. "Shine your flashlight on the knife." When Adrian moved the light to the knife, Dameon was surprised. "This is a serious knife."

"What makes it a big deal? A knife is a knife."

"I'm going to have to educate you on knives. Just not right now. But trust me, this one can cause some serious damage." Dameon removed the one he had in his vest and then stood facing the entrance of the cave. "Get that fire going. We'll need it ASAP." Dameon gripped the handles of the knives and then called out to Jax.

Nathen felt the steel penetrate his chest close to his shoulders. Then he felt the pain as the knives were ripped away from his chest. Nathen slowly turned to face Jax. "That was impressive."

Jax smiled at Nathen. "You haven't seen anything yet."

Once again, Jax charged Nathen, only this time Nathen was

prepared. Just as Jax was within arm's length, Nathen crouched down, then using his long fingernails, he stabbed Jax in the stomach and threw him to the ground.

Jax rolled to one side and then sprang to his feet. "We're both full of surprises. Though I bet I have more up my sleeve than you do."

Jax charged Nathen, and when he was only a couple of feet from Nathen, he slid on his back between Nathen's legs, stabbed each thigh, and then ripped them open as he retrieved his knives."

Nathen dropped to the ground and rolled onto his back. His thighs were burning, as was his chest. He wasn't going to win this battle on his own—he needed the creature.

Jax straddled Nathen's legs and laughed at him. "You disappoint me. I thought you'd last longer. But don't worry, I'm not going to kill you. I'm only going to incapacitate you."

Nathen watched as Jax raised his right hand. The blood that soaked the knife Jax was holding dripped on Nathen's chest. Nathen's anger was building inside of him. He focused everything he had on Jax, but the creature remained dormant. Nathen was just about to raise his arms to shield himself when he heard Dameon call out to Jax. Jax glanced over his shoulder, and as he did, Nathen balled up his fist and punched Jax in his left thigh with enough force to cause Jax to do a faceplant in the dirt.

Dameon took a step toward Jax. "I may not be able to see you, but it sounds like this round goes to Nathen."

"What do you know? You can't see me, and you won't be able to until sunrise. And by that time, everyone will be dead, and I'll be heading down the mountain with my prize."

"You're getting sloppy, Jax. What makes you think that I won't be able to see you." At that moment, Hansen's fire came to life, illuminating the entire cave.

Jax ripped off his night vision goggles and threw them to the ground. He was in the open now and highly vulnerable. He needed to get the upper hand. Nathen was sitting just behind him, and in a matter of what seemed only seconds, Jax was behind Nathen. He'd put his knives back into his vest and removed his gun from its holster. Jax crouched down behind Nathen and placed his left arm across Nathen's neck. Then he pointed the gun at Nathen's temple.

Dameon was standing by the fire with his gun aimed at Jax. He was then joined by another man who also had a gun aimed at Jax. Jax grabbed the back of Nathen's shirt collar.

"Get up."

"You think I'm going to help you?"

Jax wanted to shoot Joshawa, but he was behind Dameon and the other man. So Jax took a chance that the other man was important to Nathen. He aimed and shot the man in his right bicep. As soon as the bullet left the chamber, Jax once again pressed his gun against Nathen's temple. The man he'd shot dropped his gun, but he didn't go down. Jax was shocked when the man picked up the gun and continued to aim it at him.

"Shoot me, and he dies before your bullet even has a chance to reach me." Jax remained focused on Dameon and his friend while he spoke to Nathen. "So, are you ready to help me now? Or should I just keep shooting until I get to your son? Though I must admit, your friend there has a serious set of balls. Maybe next time, I should aim a little lower." Nathen didn't respond, nor did he make an effort to stand. "All right, let's see if your friend can handle this next bullet."

As soon as Jax raised his gun, Nathen started to stand.

"I knew you would see it my way."

Nathen's anger was evident in his reprisal. "This isn't over, Jax. I will kill you."

Jax laughed. "Big words for someone in so much pain. Which reminds me, Dameon, you're looking surprisingly healthy."

"And you're a coward using Nathen as a shield."

"As if you wouldn't."

"Tell you what, Jax. You think highly of yourself. Do you want to make a wager?"

"What kind of wager?"

"You fight me. If I win, I get to choose what to do with you. You win, and you get to choose what to do with me."

"I could care less about you. If I win, I get my Bigfoots with no hassle."

"If you win, I'll not stop you. But I can't speak for the others."

Jax chuckled. "Like I'm concerned about the others. The only person to stand up to me, other than you, is the guy I just put a bullet in. So I don't think he's going to be much of a challenge."

"It's not just him. There's Billy, as well."

"Are you kidding me? Isn't he the half-wit? I can put a knife between his eyes before he even gets close to me."

Billy heard Joshawa waking the others, so he woke up, too. He wanted to help the others. He wanted to save his friends. Billy watched as the mean man hurt Nathen. Billy was getting angry, but Hansen told him to sit still. Billy didn't want to sit still. Billy wanted to hurt the man that killed his Mona. Then Billy watched as the mean man hurt Hansen. He started to get up, but Hansen turned to him and shook his head to say no.

Billy sat cross-legged on the ground with his arms crossed in front of his chest. He was angry at the mean man, but he was also angry at Nathen and Hansen because they wouldn't let him hurt the mean man. Billy heard his name called, so he glanced to his left and saw Joshawa motioning for him to come over. He sat for a moment because he didn't know what to do. He didn't understand what Joshawa wanted, and he didn't have Mona to help him make decisions. In the end, Billy decided that maybe he could help his friend Joshawa, so he crawled over and sat next to him.

Jax was contemplating taking Dameon's challenge. He grabbed a handful of Nathen's hair and pulled his head closer to him. He whispered into Nathen's ear. "What do you think, Nathen? Should I take his wager?"

"I don't give a damn what you do. You're going to die, so you can choose how."

Jax laughed at Nathen. "You're pretty cocky for a person with a gun pressed against his head."

"You're not going to kill me. I'm more valuable to you alive."

"You're right," Jax called out to Dameon. "If I accept your challenge, no one can come to your rescue. Our side arms are tossed to the side, and we keep our knives. It'll be a fight to the death. Just you and me. Agreed?"

Dameon removed his gun from its holster and tossed it aside. "Agreed."

Jax kept holding onto Nathen's hair as he tossed his gun to one side. Then he retrieved one of his knives from his vest. "Okay, but there's just one little thing I have to do."

"And what would that be?"

Jax smiled as he slowly pushed his knife into Nathen's back.

Hansen watched in horror as Nathen dropped to his knees and then fell to the ground. He yelled out to Nathen, but his voice was drowned out by Joshawa's screams.

"No! Father! No, please!" Joshawa was crying uncontrollably, and when Hansen glanced over to Joshawa, he found Billy rocking back and forth, repeating the exact same words. "Nathen good. Man bad. Billy hurt man."

Hansen started to move toward Jax, but Dameon grabbed his good arm and held him back. Hansen was furious. "What the hell, Dameon! Let me go!"

"If you want Nathen to live, then you have to stay here."

Hansen pointed in Nathen's direction. "Does he look like he's going to live?"

"Jax won't kill Nathen. He's too valuable to him. However, Jax has no problem taking him out of the equation. Nathen's hurt, so he'll be of no use to us. But trust me, he *will* live. Now let me take care of Jax."

"In all honesty, do you have a chance to win this?"

"In all honesty, I don't know. But while I have Jax preoccupied, it'll be up to you to figure out how to take him out if I fail to." Dameon didn't wait for a response. He took a deep breath, then walked over to Jax.

Serena had placed herself inside of Dameon's mind. She took away his pain as her Lord requested. Serena was going to leave Dameon's mind, but that was before she witnessed Jax stabbing her Lord. Serena decided there and then that she didn't care what the penalties would be. She was going to save her Lord by helping Dameon win this fight.

Chapter Forty-Two

Jax moved to the middle of the cave. He held his knives down at his side while he waited for Dameon to join him in this battle to the death. Jax had imagined many scenarios of how this day would go. But never in his wildest imagination did he believe he would be fighting hand-to-hand with Dameon. Jax smiled as Dameon walked toward him.

"You have no idea how much this pleases me."

Dameon stood about five feet from Jax. His knives were also at his side. "You're pleased at the possibility of killing me?"

"Yes, I am."

"Wow. I'm not saying that I didn't see this coming. But now that we're here, it's very surreal. I take no pleasure in killing you, Jax. But as I promised, I'll stop you from killing another human being." Dameon raised his knives to waist level. "And so it begins."

Dameon waited for Jax to make the first move. He didn't have to wait long before Jax lunged at him with one knife aimed at his throat and the other at his stomach. With his left arm, Dameon deflected the knife aimed at his throat. With the knife held in his right hand, Dameon positioned his knife between his body and Jax's right arm. Dameon heard Jax curse as he sliced a good six-inch gash in Jax's right arm.

Jax put a little distance between him and Dameon. He paid no attention to his injury because that would have made him look weak. Again, Jax lunged at Dameon, only this time he dropped to the ground, knocked Dameon's feet from underneath him, and used both knives to stab the right side of Dameon's belly.

Jax felt the power as it surged through him because he knew the injury that he inflicted would slow Dameon down. He stood, believing that Dameon would be on the ground nursing his injury. But that was not to be. Dameon stood before Jax. His shirt was torn where the knives slashed at him, but his body bore no visible wound. There were no marks, no blood, no sign at all of an injury.

Jax didn't know how to process what he'd witnessed. He backed up a bit, then pointed to Dameon's stomach with the knife he held in his right hand. "You care to explain?"

Dameon was at a loss to explain what had just happened. Jax had just knocked his feet from underneath him, but he felt no pain. Dameon knew that Jax's knives would have stabbed him, but again, he felt nothing. Dameon examined his shirt and found where it was torn, but there was no sign of a wound.

"I would if I could. All I know is that the pain from my prior injuries is gone. I see where you stabbed me, but I felt nothing. Jax, there have been a lot of strange things going on in this cave. I suspect that my immunity to injuries has been afforded to me by something I can't explain. The bottom line is, maybe we should stop this. You obviously can't hurt me, but I can hurt you. Give up, Jax. This won't end well for you."

Dameon hoped that Jax would see reason, but he didn't. Again, Jax lunged at Dameon, his knives aimed at Dameon's chest. Just before the knives made contact, Dameon stepped to one side and sliced Jax's back from his hip to his waist.

"Ready to give up, Jax?"

"Never!"

This time, Dameon stood still and allowed Jax's knives to penetrate his chest. At the same time, Dameon embedded his knives in both of Jax's shoulder joints. Jax screamed in pain as he dropped to the ground. However, Dameon didn't feel the knives that were embedded in his chest. When he pulled them out from his flesh, he felt no pain. The wounds that the knives had made miraculously healed themselves as Dameon watched.

Dameon couldn't find a logical answer to explain what had just happened. Hansen was already at Nathen's side, and when Dameon glanced over to the others, he discovered that Adrian and Amy were waking up. It was all over, and now Dameon could retire in peace.

Jax lay on the ground with Dameon's knives still embedded in his shoulders. His pain consumed him, but all he could think about was how everything had gone so wrong. Everyone should be dead, and he should be at the cabin with his Bigfoots. Jax mustered up all the strength he could and then pulled Dameon's knives out of his shoulders. The pain was so excruciating that Jax couldn't hide it from Dameon. He felt nauseous, and his mind felt as though it was leaving his body. Jax glanced around to discover that nobody was watching him. He took a deep breath, then he slowly stood up, trying so hard not to let the pain win. Jax glanced over to where he'd left Nathen and found him surrounded by his friends.

Jax wanted revenge. He wanted to win. Jax glanced over to where Joshawa was sitting. He was by himself, with only the half-wit sitting next to him. Jax smiled as he thought *if I can't have you . . .*

He bent down and picked up one of Dameon's knives.

Because of his injuries, Jax knew he wouldn't be able to throw with any strength. But that wasn't a problem. His target was close, and with great satisfaction, he aimed and threw the knife at Joshawa's heart.

Billy was watching all the unrest that surrounded him. However, he was happy because Jax didn't win. Billy turned his attention to where Jax had fallen. But he wasn't on the ground — he was standing. He was looking at Nathen, and then he turned and was looking at Joshawa. Billy saw Jax throw the knife, and without thinking, Billy threw himself in front of Joshawa.

Billy felt the knife as the blade embedded itself into his back. It didn't do much damage, but it did cause considerable pain. Billy was used to pain and was able to bury the pain deep inside of him. Billy stood and glared at Jax. He was aware of the excitement around him, and he could feel someone remove the knife, but he took no notice. Billy started to walk toward Jax. He focused on Jax's eyes, and the anger he felt fueled his desire to hurt the mean man. Jax started to back up, and as Billy approached him, Jax tripped and fell to the ground. Billy said nothing as he grabbed Jax's collar to his jacket and started to drag him out to the path in front of the cave.

When Billy reached the path, he threw Jax on the ground. "You bad. Billy hurt you."

Jax appeared so scared as he pleaded for his life. "Please, let me go, and I'll never come back."

"No. Billy call friends." Billy started howling and smiled when his friends howled back.

"Billy, what are you doing?"

Billy turned to see Adrian standing next to him. He smiled at Adrian as if everything was normal. "Billy wait for friends."

"What friends, Billy?"

"Friends. Teach Jax lesson." Billy smiled as he nodded his head. Several minutes later, his friends showed up. Four large wolves stood only ten feet away from Jax. Billy glanced down at Jax, and he wasn't smiling anymore. "Wolves my friends. You hurt my friends. My friends hurt you."

Billy watched as Jax curled up into a ball and continued to plead for his life. Billy was just about to let his friends deal with Jax when he felt a hand so delicate on his arm. Billy turned to find a woman standing next to him. She was beautiful, with long red hair and green eyes. She smiled at him, and immediately, Billy was happy . . . he was calm.

"Billy, you don't want to do this."

"Bad man hurt friends."

"I know, Billy. But what have I told you about hurting people?"

Billy looked at the woman, squinted his eyes, and leaned just a little closer to her. "Billy know you?"

The woman placed her right hand on the side of Billy's face. "Of course you do. I am Mona. I am the mother of our child."

"You not look like Mona."

"No, Billy, I don't. I look like the person who placed Mona inside of the bear. The bear was Mona, and now I am Mona."

Billy reached up and gently touched the woman's face. His fingers traced her delicate features, and as he placed the palm of his hand on the side of her face, memories started to bombard him. He smiled at Mona. "Billy knows you. Billy fix you."

"Yes, Billy, you fixed me many times."

At that moment, the pretty blue star hovered in front of Billy's face. Billy held his hand out, and his blue star landed on the palm of his hand. A soft, whispering voice spoke to him. *Billy, you do know this woman. You and Amy have been granted a great gift.*

"A gift?"

Yes, Billy. The woman you see is the woman who saved Mona so many years ago. And now she is here in human form. She is Mona, and she loves you and Amy so much.

Tears started to run down Billy's face. He looked over at the woman who stood before him. "Mona is you."

"Yes, Billy. And I want you to free this man. You don't want to become your brother."

Billy shook his head from side to side. "No, Billy not brother."

Billy watched as the blue star floated away. He turned to the woman and nervously asked, "Billy hug you?" The woman wrapped Billy in her arms, and for the first time in a very long time, Billy was at peace.

Adrian was at Nathen's side as he watched Billy, Mona, and Amy reunite. Adrian fought hard to hold back the tears. He glanced over to Jax, who was still lying on the ground only a few feet away from the wolves. "So what do we do with him? And what about the wolves?"

Nathen was lying on the ground while Amy took care of him. He gathered his strength and answered Adrian, "I think we should leave that to Dameon."

Dameon walked over to Jax and knelt down on his haunches. "So, Jax. Where do we go from here?"

"Well, thanks to you, I'll never hunt again."

"Is that all you got from this?"

"What else is there? You and I both live for the hunt. That will never change."

"I'm sorry to hear that. And for the record, I'm done. The only hunting I'll be doing will be to feed myself, and that's it."

Dameon stood and was about to walk away when he

changed his mind. "Adrian, I've decided to take Jax to the authorities and turn him in for the death of the park ranger. Could you lend me a hand?"

"Sure, but won't that implicate you, as well?"

"To be honest, I don't know, and I don't care. I have a responsibility to get Jax locked up. I should have done it a long time ago. With his insane views on hunting, man or beast, he'll never go to trial. They'll put him in a padded room and leave him there."

Adrian glanced down to where Jax had been lying, only to discover that he was no longer there. He was standing a few feet away from Dameon and Adrian. Adrian took a step closer to Jax. "Jax, what are you doing?"

"I'm not going to jail or a loony bin. I'm not leaving this mountain." The words had barely left his lips when he flung himself into the wolves.

The screams were horrific as the wolves tore Jax apart. Adrian removed his gun from its holster, took a couple steps closer, and put a bullet in Jax's head. The screams stopped, and the wolves grabbed the pieces they'd torn free and ran back to their den. The only thing left was the blood and some small pieces that could barely be discernable as human.

CHAPTER FORTY-THREE

Six months later

Joshawa walked out onto the front porch of the family cabin. The snow was receding, and soon the spring flowers would start poking their heads up to the sun. Joshawa zipped up his jacket and then took a deep breath of the refreshing spring air. He walked over to the porch swing, sat down, and gently rocked the swing with his foot. Joshawa's injuries had mended, and with the exception of some arthritic pain in his leg, he was back to his old self.

Becca came out of the cabin carrying two cups of coffee. Since the morning had a chill to it, she wore her jeans and an over-sized sweater. Becca passed Joshawa his coffee mug and then leaned in for a kiss. Since Joshawa had come back, Becca made sure that at least once a day she would say the words *I love you*. She sat down beside Joshawa and curled up next to him. When she wrapped her hands around the coffee mug, her gaze was immediately drawn to her beautiful diamond and ruby engagement ring. Becca loved red, and she loved rubies, which made this ring extra special.

Becca vividly remembered the day Joshawa had finally made it home. He was carried in on a stretcher, and when she saw him, she burst into tears. Becca had run up to Joshawa, hugged him as best she could, and before she could *say I love you*, Joshawa said, "Will you marry me?" Of course she said yes, and they'd been joined at the hip ever since.

Becca placed her head on Joshawa's shoulder. "I love this time of year. Everything smells so good."

Joshawa smiled as he gazed out into the forest. "Then why are you marrying me in the fall?"

"You know why. The minute you were back, you proposed to me. I wanted to make sure you were completely healed."

"You know, Becca, I've never been happier. Sadly, it took my time in the cave to open my eyes. But they're open now, and life is wonderful."

Authia opened the cabin door and stepped out onto the porch. "Okay, you two love birds, breakfast is ready."

Joshawa stood up and offered his hand to Becca. When Becca stood next to Joshawa, she reached up and kissed him on his cheek. "I love you, Joshawa."

Joshawa stared into Becca's beautiful blue eyes. "And I love you."

Authia went back inside the cabin, wearing a huge smile. She had her son back, and like his father, he had found someone to love him. Tammy, Hansen, and Nathen were at the kitchen table waiting for Joshawa and Becca to join them. Authia went into the kitchen and poured herself another cup of coffee. With a coffee cup in hand, Authia turned and leaned against the sink. Her gaze fell on Nathen, and to that day, the fact that she almost lost him weighed heavy on her heart.

Authia's thoughts went back to that morning when Joshawa had melded with her. At first, she was giddy with excitement that not only was her son alive, but she could meld with him again. Her happiness was fleeting when Joshawa told her about Nathen's condition. They required two more stretchers and two men to help carry one of the stretchers. When Nathen arrived, he needed to be transported to Burwood immediately. His medical condition was severe, and at the time, Amy couldn't promise that he would survive the trip.

The first stretcher to enter the yard was Nathen's. Amy had bandaged Hansen's arm, which allowed him to help Billy carry Nathen's stretcher. Two women had also made the trek down the mountain. By the time Nathen arrived, there were already two additional stretchers, and at least a dozen men showed up to help in any way they could. Two of the men relieved Hansen and Billy and almost ran all the way to Burwood with Nathen. The two women had stayed behind, but Authia went with Nathen.

Authia was told that Billy had led four men with the two stretchers back to the cave. Several hours later, Joshawa and Dameon entered the yard, both on stretchers. Unfortunately, when Serena left Dameon, she also removed his ability to feel no pain. Both Joshawa and Dameon were also taken directly to Burwood.

Nathen required twenty stitches on each thigh to close the gaping wounds. Because the knives had been ripped out of Nathen's chest in an upward direction, extra care was needed to close those wounds. They had to be done in layers so that the wound would heal properly. Jax had said he wasn't going to kill Nathen, and he was true to his word. When he stabbed Nathen in the back, he avoided puncturing any vital organs. The wound was deep and also required a lot of stitching, but in the end, Nathen was going to live.

Authia finally had her family back, and for that, she was ever so grateful.

Amy woke to the sounds of birds singing and the sweet smell of spring. Her life was so different now. She slept on a bed and ate at a table. Her mother was now human, and even though they could no longer meld, it was amazing having a mother to hug and do things together as a family should.

Amy, Billy, and Mona all lived with Edward. It was a little cramped, but no one complained. Living in Burwood with so many people made Amy uneasy. All her life, she had lived alone, with only her bear to keep her company. Amy had to learn that people here were good and it was okay to get to know them. Another thing she had to learn was to recognize love when it came knocking on her door. In this case, love came in the form of Adrian.

Amy's medical knowledge fascinated Edward. He took her to the medical building every day to prepare her to take over from him. Amy was a little nervous being expected to take on such a huge responsibility. But after a few months, Amy loved being able to help fix people. She was ready for any role Edward chose to put her in.

Adrian had changed for the better. He had a new understanding of what it meant to get to know someone before making assumptions. All his life, he had hated Nathen and Joshawa because his father did. He'd heard rumors of what actually happened in that blizzard, but he didn't believe them. When Adrian returned to Burwood, he confronted his father. Unfortunately, his father decided to leave Burwood rather than admit the truth. Adrian was sad to see his father go, but deep down, he knew it was for the best.

And that was not the only thing that changed for Adrian. He'd fallen in love with Amy. He went to Billy and Mona and asked permission to court Amy. Adrian chuckled at how Billy reacted. He didn't understand what Adrian was asking. However, Mona was able to explain it to him, and they said yes, as long as it was what Amy wanted. It took a while for Amy to understand how much Adrain loved her and why he loved her. But she came around, and Amy finally discovered that love comes in many shapes and forms. She could love her mother and father, she could love Edward, and she could love Adrain.

Dameon was awestruck when he entered Burwood on a stretcher. The ability to not feel the pain was gone, but only for his original injuries. The injuries Jax inflicted didn't exist. It didn't take long for Dameon to mend. However, it was just enough time to fall in love with Burwood. He was amazed at how they lived without the influence of modern technology. He also became very close friends with Adrian.

Shortly after Dameon healed, Charles sat down with him in the main cabin and offered him a place to stay. It would be his job to teach archery and how to hunt. There was nothing for Dameon outside of Burwood, so his decision was easy. Adrian even offered to share his cabin with him, which Dameon gladly accepted.

Nathen, Dameon, Joshawa, Adrian, and Hansen all went to the old Jenkins homestead, where all the pain and suffering had started. They set up tents on the perimeter of the yard and started to tear down the cabins. Dameon was allowed to re-move anything that directly belonged to him. But Jax's possessions had to remain. They spent three days burning the cabins and their contents until all that was left was ash. After-ward, a group of men from Burwood joined them. They carefully relocated all the kerosene barrels to Burwood.

The homestead was given back to nature so that she could grow her trees, her grasses, and her flowers. The homestead would no longer harbor hatred, anger, and brutality.

Nathen stood at the edge of the property and stared at the emptiness. Could it be that simple? Could the burning of the buildings and their contents rid this place of evil? Evil resided inside of men and women, and it could also find its way inside inanimate objects. Evil wore many faces, and sometimes, it was tough to recognize.

Nathen was about to leave when a familiar voice entered his mind.

You have been busy, my Lord. Have you purged your evil?

Well, Serena, let's just say it's a start. Serena, do you know why I couldn't wake the beast inside of me?

My Lord, there was never a beast. All that lived inside of you was anger and hatred because of who and what you were. When you met Mistress Authia, you found peace. Hatred and anger have not been a part of you for a very long time.

And I always thought it was this horrible beast. Serena, if there was no beast, then how could I be capable of ripping a man's arm off?

Was that your intention?

Of course not.

Your action was to protect yourself as any man would do.

Nathen took a deep breath and slowly released it. His gaze was focused on the remains of the Jenkins homestead.

Thank you, Serena. It's good to put my fear of the beast to bed.

I am glad, my Lord. It pleases me to see that you, as well as Joshawa, have healed.

And how are you, Serena?

I live in the Land of the Spirits now. I am finally at peace.

And Lord Adeeowale?

He lost much in this battle, and for him, it continues.

How? I thought the death of Lord Chike put an end to all the suffering.

Yes, it has. But not for Lord Adeeowale. He proved that the Council of Five has not existed for a very long time. At one time, it did, but the Destroyer turned on the ones that created him. Lord Adeeowale has vowed that he will review every prisoner that resides in the Realm of Despair. He fears that many should not be there.

Nathen smiled as he picked up his backpack. He took one last look at what was once the Jenkins homestead.

Serena, could you do me a favor?

Of course, My Lord.

Please tell Lord Adeeowale that from one Lord to another, he is truly the Lord of His People.

The End

You May Also Enjoy the Following from eXtasy Books Inc

Taming of the Beast
Journey to the Unknown
Discovery of the Lion People
Legacy of the Lion People Part 1

ABOUT THE AUTHOR

Christine Frances was born in the summer of 1958, in Halifax, Nova Scotia, Canada. She was born to a military family, her father being in the Royal Canadian Navy. Christine is passionate about any endeavor she takes on. She has spent most of her life as an accountant helping many businesses to grow and succeed. Christine is the mother to two boys and five grandchildren. Family is incredibly important to her and always comes first.

Top on Christine's bucket list was to finish a story she had started when her boys were still young. Not only was she able to cross that off her list, her passion for writing blossomed and Christine added four more books to her collection. Christine has been a storyteller all her life, and she has many more stories to share.

www.ingramcontent.com/pod-product-compliance
Lightning Source LLC
Chambersburg PA
CBHW061314170626
46817CB00001B/184